From BRISBANE *to* TOKYO *while in* ORLANDO, FLORIDA

This book includes content associated with physical and mental health that might not be suitable for some readers. A list of these elements is included at the back of the book—at the back, instead of the front, so as to not reveal plots and stories for others. If you have any concerns, please check it out before deciding whether to continue to read.

From Brisbane To Tokyo While In Orlando, Florida

ISBN: 978-1-0686519-0-8

English (UK) First Edition

J. J. Tallahay Publishing

Cover design by Julia Horobets

For those who have ever felt alone…

1.

Thank goodness my locker is next to the school toilets. And the showers, too. I try my best to wash the stink off my clothes while still wearing them and then—fortunately with everyone in class—grab my spare set of clothes from my locker, have a quick shower and change.

Class will be over soon. I'm not going anyway. Everybody already stares at me. I don't need them to look at me now, knowing it's probably me that smells of urine. That my head has just had an encounter with the disgusting water in a toilet and was then thrown into a puddle of it on the floor.

I want to get away as quickly as possible. I clean up and decide to go to the senior car park. I'll wait by my sister's car until school ends.

I can't stop thinking about what just happened. I hate it—but hey, at least all my schoolwork was still in my rucksack and didn't come out.

And who is doing this? The school's quarterback, of all people. Jared Steele. And his friends.

Not that long ago, the school-famous quarterback came to me, always in his orange and white sleeved sports jersey, and led me to believe that he could train me with his friends to be on the football team and I could also hang out with him.

I was wrong. I was tricked and hauled into the toilets to be beaten up.

Despite being a junior, he said I had to have a Re-Freshers Week, as they called it, because I didn't have this school's Freshers Week—I only recently moved to Orlando. But when the week was up, and I thought that was it, it turned out I was a bigger fool. There was never any plan to let me join their group. I honestly didn't know what was louder…my heart being crushed or Jared and his friends laughing at me. I actually thought they would let me in. That's what they do in a normal Freshers Week for the freshers, right? The other years stop because you've done the initiation and now accept you as part of the school. However, despite him saying it was a rite of passage as they messed me up, I was stupid and silly enough to believe Jared and the others would do the same and accept me in.

The toilet situation has only happened twice, so I suppose I should be happy that it's not every time they see me. You know, at least they have a reason and not just because they're bored.

This time because I handed in a term paper early—Jared saw me.

Every step I take as I leave the toilets, I just think harder about the bullying. The thoughts make me sick. I just want to lash out. But I don't. Because what good would that do? Bruised knuckles and, if I'm caught, detention. Bruised knuckles sound like I'd actually be able to successfully hit them. I wouldn't—the fact I'm bullied shows I'm not strong.

So, I keep walking. Looking nowhere but at my feet.

"Hayden!"

I stop.

Further down the hallway is Mr Gauran. The school counsellor. Well, that's what he is, but he's so built he could be a sports coach or a professional wrestler who just happens to wear a shirt and a pair of trousers.

"Didn't you hear me the first time?" Mr Gauran asks, approaching me.

"No." *I clearly didn't if I didn't glance up.* My body tenses as he stands before me.

"Why aren't you—why's your hair wet?"

"I've just been swimming," I lie quickly—begging his nostrils are broken because the stench of urine remains on me.

"Shouldn't you still be swimming? Class doesn't finish for another fifteen minutes."

"It's actually a study period, but Coach Rugrosso said it was the only time I could try-out for the swim team."

Wow, even I'm impressed with how quickly I came up with that! However, that doesn't remove this anger in me though. I quickly tell him I didn't make the team. He can't think I now go to swimming practice—he's bound to talk to Coach Rugrosso about it. "But it's fine. I should be heading to my stud—"

"Actually, now would be a good time to have a catch-up. You basically have a free period, so come on, let's head to my office."

I half-heartedly nod.

As we walk into his office, I exhale, wondering how on earth I can make that bell ring now. I reluctantly head to the chairs and put my brown rucksack onto the ground—there's a loud thump.

"Woah, where you trekking to? The Himalayas?"

The guy is toweringly tall, and his arms are huge and brawny. I'm surprised every time he manages to get through the doors; he's that physically big. "Second thoughts, what bank did you rob?"

"I didn't. It's just books." Nearly all my books for the day, in fact, because I don't want Jared to see me by my locker near the toilets. *But that didn't work out, did it?*

"Oh, I forgot you take things literally." Mr Gauran sits down at his desk. Last time, he said I was a one out of five on his humour scale. One being low, of course. "You do realise there are these things called lockers you kids can store them in, right?"

"Yes."

The clock is the same time as it was five minutes ago.

"Good 'cause you should probably start using it," Mr Gauran replies. "Now, tell me, how are things, Hayden? It's been three weeks since you started here at Kingsgate Lee High."

Things are great, Mr Gauran. I sit alone at lunch. Got no friends. People have no problem pushing and bullying me, and I'm currently sitting here praying you can't smell urine on me or that there's still no crap in my hair or my teeth.

"Fine," I say. He asks me if that is all. "Yeah." I fidget in my chair, which I instantly regret because I know he'll take it as a mark of lying.

I glance around the small office. Nothing outlandish. A desk. A couple of large plants. Some wooden chairs with green seats. And a row of metal cabinets situated under the only window in the room. He joked on my first day that the room would have had a three-point-five on EmpireRoomRate if it wasn't for the view.

Out the window are three huge red garbage bins resting by a school building wall that covers any hope of looking beyond.

I guess I like Mr Gauran, even if he tries a lot with his humour. He did on his first day, but I also remember he said that because I was new to this school, this was a time to broaden my horizons and get stuck into new things and aspects here. Just didn't realise it meant getting stuck into a toilet.

"So besides trying out for the swim team—sorry you didn't get in—what about any other extracurricular activities?"

Mr Gauran wants to see if I have friends. It hasn't been easy. I joined in September, when everybody in my year had already got their little groups…and for over two years because we're juniors, not freshmen, it's been even harder.

"I went to a couple—"

"Ooo, I don't like the past tense in that."

Dang it.

"They weren't really for me." Truth is, I tried. I know Spanish, so I thought of the Spanish Club, yet when I went, the room was just filled with students dancing to Hispanic music off a phone, and others were using their mouths for more than just talking. I also checked out the Video Game Club—but one boy instantly shut me down after he learnt I'd never played the latest sci-fi shooting game and told me there wouldn't be any time or patience to show me how to play. Apparently, they were in some major worldwide online tournament against the top school in Japan.

"Maybe I don't need to do any."

"Don't let Principal Shaw hear you say that. She's very strong about all students getting stuck in. *Unity is key*," Mr Gauran says in what I assume was an attempt to impersonate the principal. An abysmal attempt. "And I think it'll be good for you, Hayden. It's a great way to develop skills and adjust to life here. Besides, it'll look pretty good on your application next year when choosing colleges."

"Can't almost anything you do outside of school count as an extracurricular?"

"Well, thank you, Mr Pedantic, for trying to downfall my point." He flails his arms out. "Yeah, but why do something outside when if you do something here, it can also be an easy way to make friends and make school better for you?"

Mr Gauran begins to ask more questions, which I don't like because I don't want to tell him how I am finding it here. And because I'm still furious with Jared and his friends. I lie to the counsellor, but it doesn't seem to work.

"Come on, Hayden. Tell me what you like. Do you like films? Music?"

I vaguely nod. I have nothing against music, but I just don't listen to much. The only times I really hear music is on the radio in a car when my sister or my dad is driving.

I'm not exactly up to date on all the latest stuff. Not just in music but with everything. We were quite restricted with what we could have when I had to be in hospital at the end of the last school year back in Georgia.

"Maybe you should give one of them a try?" Mr Gauran suggests. "Have you tried KingsgateLeeConnect yet?"

"I—"

"Because I've noticed an account hasn't been created under your student login yet."

So the guy's been keeping an eye on me, hey? I realise that's his job, but still. I can't be dealing with a lecture right now on how I should be or what I should do.

"I don't think it's for me," I answer, trying to control my annoyance.

It's basically a school social media programme that only students here can use. We can post anything academic and social-related, and people comment on the posts. Using the platform on their laptops or their phones. It's designed by students for students, Mr Gauran told me when he showed me the programme. The school is invested in allowing students to connect with other students they wouldn't have in person. So invested, huge screens around the school show the most recent posts. It's too daunting for me.

"How do you know if you haven't tried it?"

I meet Mr Gauran's eyes. It doesn't take a genius to know that nobody would be interested in what I had to say or comment on. Why can't he just drop it?

"I see it at lunch on the board."

"Well, looking at chocolate isn't as good as eating it, is it? Watching a roller-coaster isn't as fun as riding it. Seeing people hook up isn't as—actually, I'll leave it there."

"This is ridiculous." I dart my eyes at the clock. Would someone please move the hands quicker already?

"Hayden, how can you expect people to see you if you don't let them look for you?"

I turn back to find him staring at me. I freeze. His words hit me. Catch me by surprise.

"I'm not exactly hiding in the shadows."

"From what I'm getting, you're not exactly going out much and giving things a chance."

"So you want me to wear a T-shirt saying 'look at me' or get a megaphone and call out for attention?"

And just like that, I've admitted I'm alone. I'm too wound up to care. Right now, I just want to be on my own.

"I think turning up in fancy dress may get attention, but no, Hayden, I don't recommend you do that." Mr Gauran then moves closer to his desk. "Sounds like you've decided the world has made up its mind about you. It hasn't. Just be more open to opportunities."

"I'm fine."

I want out. I grab my rucksack and get up from the chair.

"Hayden, the bell hasn't gone yet."

I slam myself back down in the chair.

The bell suddenly goes. I pick myself up and head for the door.

I'm just sick of everything. Jared and his friends picking on me. Unable to do schoolwork without them on me. My sister Robin full-on hating my guts. Having to tread carefully when I speak to my dad or even my brother because I can't let this move to Florida be a mistake. I know I'm partly the reason we moved. And now I have Mr Gauran hammering away at me with what I should be doing at school. *Do you like this? Why not try that? I've noticed you haven't tried the 'oh-so-amazing' KingsgateLeeConnect yet.*

Fine! If it gets him off my back, I'll download it onto my phone. I don't even have to use it; I'll just download it and leave it. Waste of space on my phone—not that I have much, just family contacts and a phone location setting—but if it stops Mr Gauran getting at me, then I'll do it.

By the time I'm in the car, and Robin is singing along to some modern hit that has an Italian chorus in it, KingsgateLeeConnect is downloaded. I shove my phone into my pocket.

"What is that smell?" Robin yells over the radio.

"Oh—someone let off a stink bomb outside History. It got on my clothes, so I had to change," I lie after looking at the rucksack in the backseat.

"Right," Robin replies. "Well, they must've gotten worse because that honestly smells like piss."

I look out the window, hoping she doesn't see my face.

2.

"Fine," is all I give my dad while I stand in the kitchen at home. Somehow, Dad knows to ask the one question I don't want him to ask: *how was school?* Thankfully, a shower and the cooking of salmon have removed the odour of urine on me. I watch carefully at the salmon being fried by Dad as he nods to my answer.

"Don't worry, Hayden, I've been helping him." I glance over to my older brother, Colbey. I always laugh when I remember that my parents wanted to be different from the norm when they were younger—and apparently, adding an extra 'e' in their firstborn's name was the way to do it. If Colbey wasn't so into Sports, I'm sure he'd be a lavish chef in California. "Someone nearly had an accident with spilling oil on his hand and putting it on a heated stove, but we managed to miss that fatality."

I try to push my misery and hardness at school away and force a smile back. I'd much rather force the smile because it stops them talking about school.

Dad turns his head away from the pan, shows Colbey and me his sparkly, white grin again, and nods, but by doing so, he nearly loses his grip and oil slides and sizzles off the side.

How my dad can be bad with his hands at cooking yet is smooth and steady and a perfectionist when it comes to filling people's teeth, looking almost like a mature model too, and call himself a dentist is beyond me.

He takes his job seriously, though. Heck, his dentistry even has a kids club with a blue shark called Sharky as its mascot. I've never understood why a shark, but at least it makes more sense having Sharky the Shark at his practice in Florida than back in Georgia.

I wish the move to Orlando was because of my dad's work. But it wasn't. The reason is partly because of me.

Colbey heads to a cupboard. "I'll set the table, providing you can manage not to destroy the salmon in less than two minutes, Dad."

"Oh *ha ha*," Dad mocks when he notices Colbey looking at him. "I think I can manage."

"I don't know, Dad. You do realise that's salmon, so you can't use a mouth mirror to check when it's done, right?" I joke.

Colbey smirks.

Dad looks unamused. "Really? Anyone else want to take a hit at me?"

"Oh goodness, you've let Dad cook." Robin then enters the room with a pile of schoolbooks. I stare down at the counter.

Dad drops the spatula. "Is my cooking that bad?" Colbey and I look at each other. "Not another word." He points a finger at us.

I laugh when Colbey nods his head.

"Very funny," Dad remarks. When he turns back to the salmon, Colbey gives me a playful wink.

I like Colbey. He may be nine years older than me and have different tastes, but we get along. More than I do with my sister.

"I'm not sure what you're talking about, guys. I did it all myself," Dad says later at the table after everyone finishes eating.

"Understatement of the Year right there," Robin replies. We all know it was all Colbey.

I glance at Robin, forcing myself to crack a grin at her joke.

I've kept to my word since the chat she had with me in the car on the way to our first day of school. How she easily spelt it out to me that the family has only moved states because of what I did, that she doesn't want me near her at school, that I shouldn't annoy anybody, and that I must *do whatever to keep everybody happy. You owe us that.*

And I've stuck to it. What sometimes gets me, though, is how well she is doing at school. Senior year. Popular. She's made being the new kid like a present for her year. I've made it become a nuisance for mine.

"I didn't realise they weren't the same character 'cause of the lack of sleep I had from exams that week," Robin answers.

I've zoned out and I've missed their competition for what has been the Understatement of the Year.

Dad puffs some air out to object. "Yeah, we know. The whole movie theatre heard you snoring." Colbey and Dad start laughing. Robin objects, but Dad continues. "Uh-yeah, you did."

Dad and Robin then seem to go back and forth in repeating their words until Dad suddenly drops his back into his chair and pretends to snore loudly.

"Actually, I think it was when Uncle Chad thought your mom could beat me in an arm wrestle."

Everybody is silent. The realisation appears on Dad's face—him forgetting that Mom left us back in April.

Nobody knew she'd packed her things and left until eleven the next night. Took her twenty-five years to realise that the family life wasn't for her.

"Sorry, I erm…"

Colbey places a hand over Dad's. He looks over at me. "So, Hayden. How's school? Anything new?"

"Yeah. Well—" Colbey's caught me off guard.

There's an urge to say something. Tell him how bad school really is. Today was awful, and I'm still angry and hurting. They could maybe help.

I adjust my mouth with my teeth and tongue as if I'm about to go into battle. "Actually, I've been meaning to say..."

I should just tell them. Dad glances over at me. *Say it, Hayden! Tell Dad you're being bullied. He'll want to know.* Colbey's watching me. So is Robin.

Everything she told me comes back. *Keep everybody happy.*

"I've downloaded something on my phone."

And just like that, whatever little courage I had inside has gone. It's for the best, though; if I tell them, then this move will have been pointless.

"Oh," Dad says. "I hope it wasn't porn."

"Dad!" Robin yells in disgust. Colbey coughs.

"What? No! Oh—it was a social programme." I try to reclaim some dignity as Dad smirks. "The school has a programme for students to message each other. KingsgateLeeConnect. It's so we can message, chat and share stuff in and out of school in a safe place."

Downloading a social media platform without their parent's permission may not seem like a big deal for a boy, but it is if I'm that boy—a boy who has ended up in hospital twice this year. I have our mom leaving us to thank for that.

I was pretty much excluded from everything while I was there, so I wasn't triggered. There are still certain aspects limited to me now.

The main two being parental control on my new laptop and new phone. Social media sites are a no, which is okay. I never had them back in Georgia, and there's no need for them here when I don't have any friends. Even still, it sucks that there's this controlled constraint on me that I have no say in or can't change. However, if I want Mr Gauran off my back, then I need this KingsgateLeeConnect junk.

Dad asks Robin if it's true.

"Yeah, they have screens at school. We can message and help others. Post about work, talk about school activities, share photos and music."

"Yeah, nothing bad, though. The school manages it," I interject, trying to claw back out of the hole I've begun to make. I almost want to laugh because I realise I'm defending something I don't even want. "Only for those at school."

I watch Dad as he works out the pros and cons. "That seems fine to have, I suppose. So long as it's just school-related and safe."

"I don't think the school would allow it or that Mr Gauran told me to get it if it wasn't."

"No, I can't imagine he would." Dad smiles. "You can keep it. Next time, just ask before, though. But thanks for telling me."

I try to push away the guilt by gathering the plates. I put them in the dishwasher and then start to head to my room.

"Aren't you going to watch *Did You Hear That?* with us?" Colbey asks me after Dad and Robin go into the living room.

The TV quiz show, where we even play along, is quite a laugh, but after what just happened, I'm not in the mood.

I stay, standing on the stairs, while he waits at the bottom. "I've got some schoolwork to do." That's not a lie—just none of it is for tomorrow. However, Colbey remains looking at me—I know what he wants to ask. "I'm fine."

"Huh, didn't realise we were playing Understatement of the Year still." I want to smirk at his remark but can't. "I saw you freeze when Dad mentioned Mom."

"I think we all did."

"True. Maybe Dad's starting to be okay to talk about it." I can see where he is going. "Hayden, remember you can talk to me, right?"

He smiles at me. My stomach becomes a tumble dryer of even more guilt and anger from school, spinning around into one at a million miles. I can't tell him. I can't unload my hurt onto everybody else. Robin is right. I must do whatever I can to keep everybody happy.

"I know," but a huge wave of shame hits me.

I launch myself onto the bed and stare at the ceiling.

Something vibrates in my pocket. It's my phone. And that's certainly strange because it can't be a text—the only contacts I have live in this house. And they're downstairs.

I pull my new but restricted phone out.

Welcome to KingsgateLeeConnect, Hayden!

Good grief! My eyes roll at the notification. That's the last thing I want to see.

Remember to add a photo to your profile so everyone can see you.

Urgh, it's like Mr Gauran's everywhere! I drop my phone and stare back at the ceiling. My phone vibrates again. I roll over—it's another notification from KingsgateLeeConnect.

I head to Settings and begin to cancel receiving notifications because I know I'll keep getting them now. I've downloaded it, logged in—that should be fine.

My finger moves towards the Notification Off button. Another notification pops up on my screen. *What? Aw, for crying out*—I've accidentally clicked it.

KingsgateLeeConnect opens.

I'm taken to the main page. I'm about to click back, but my eyes are drawn to the first post.

Annie Merrill
Tomorrow's the Cake Sale! All money raised is
for the Winter Snowdrop Ball. It will only be as
good as what people put in.

It's September! It's not even Halloween yet, but they're on about something for winter? And there's more frustration when that last line reminds me of something Jared would have said during my Re-Freshers Week.

I scroll to the next post.

Angela Branno
Anyone else concerned that the cafeteria
staff aren't wearing hairnets?

Katie Easterlin
OMG! I'm not the only one who's noticed.
Yes! They totally should.

Kyle Savannah
Yeah, I found a yellow strand in my food the other day.
Then I realised it was just my spaghetti :D

I chuckle.

I scroll down to see there are pictures of people's art and discussions about work—the smell of the urine stains my nostrils when there's a comment on a post from one of Jared's boys. I push through and continue looking, seeing the same similar posts—I stop.

There's an image covering my screen. A drawing. There's a boy and a girl standing on either side of a clear, aqua-blue river. The sky looks peaceful and is partly covered by the tall palm trees on either side of the image that lean high over the water. Underneath the drawing, it says Logan Kalo – "Pleasant You're Not Here."

I want to get off KingsgateLeeConnect—but I can't take my eyes off the image.

Something appears in the middle. There's a faded play button. It's a song. I can't explain why, but I grab my headphones and press play.

From the title alone and the sadness on the boy's face, I expect rage or gloat. Maybe screams and violent drumming. But it isn't. The song's soft and natural, like the paradise drawing—but also sad. It's blue, yet at the same time, the tiny electric sounds are pulsing. They totally throw me off. The singer sounds calm. But then, when I put the lyrics and image together, I think I get it. Maybe he's not trying to tell the world he is better off or shove that he's never felt greater in front of the girl he's no longer with—the boy's face of sadness, while the girl is smiling in the image, tells me that. It's reassurance. He's trying to convince himself that he *will* be happy without the person. A plea to himself, almost.

It's probably about a lover, but it's almost how I should feel about my mom. She left my family and me, and although she won't be coming back, I must remember to be happy without her. I just have to live with it. For the best.

And I must remember the parts that I do have in my life. My dad, sister and brother. And I know they love me.

Something inside me feels different. The numbness and fury inside me are smaller, even after thinking about Mom.

I look at my phone to see who posted this, yet my lips scrunch up at the answer.

Tokyo

Is that someone's name? I know some people have geographical names. Brooklyn. Dakota. Sydney. Even met a boy once called Oslo. So maybe, but I haven't heard of that before.

I'm unconvinced. I scroll to the previous post…and then all the way back to Annie Merrill and her stupid cake post. Then it clicks.

There's no surname on Tokyo's. There's no image for the profile photo, either. It's empty. I wonder why. I glance at the writing between their name and the song.

Sometimes, you only have yourself to convince.

I wish it were true, I say to myself, because I honestly feel like whenever I do something, I have to convince everyone. Always.

I click on the name. It takes me to their profile. There's still no image. And none of the posts are about school. No questions about work. No group selfies with friends. Nothing but music.

Wildlicko – "Universe (Somewhere)"

Stolen Nick In Barcelona – "Stay"

The Bandit, Smith And Yang – "When Shocks Become The Standard"

But I just hope that they're as deep and pleasing as the Logan Kalo song. Whether they are sad or upbeat, I hope the songs will be about feelings I have felt and will be weirdly uplifting—because then I will know that I'm not the only person who has felt so down. Because that's how I felt just a second ago with the song.

I put my headphones back on and press play.

And I listen late into the night on my bed. Letting the music take over me.

And at some point, when it's dark all around me, I can't even remember why I was upset and angry to begin with.

3.

It's lunch. I sit at my usual table. Alone. In the corner of the courtyard, tucked near the school building, while everybody else is further out.

On the opposite wall to the cafeteria doors, and three times bigger, there is a large screen outside. The KingsgateLeeConnect board. I don't know how I managed not to stare at it before I downloaded KingsgateLeeConnect—you can't not see the board. Orange background with white boxes and pictures on it, filling most of the screen and split into nine grids, three by three. Each grid shows one post from a student. The posts appear on the left side of the grid, and then on the right side are any comments on the post.

The screen changes—the posts have moved down to the row below to let new posts appear at the top. The bottom posts before disappear. Lunch is the busiest time during the day—due to the school's strict rules on phones during classes.

The posts occasionally move, and replies appear at the side. I glance over at a post and begin to read.

Rafael Gago
Who did people put as the first European to
find North America in Mr Riley's Pop Quiz?

Maiya Barnes
Aw, did someone not revise?

Rafael Gago
Yeah, I did, actually.

Kimberly Jenkins
Leif Erikson.

Maiya Barnes
What? No, it's Christopher Columbus.

Kimberly Jenkins
He wasn't first. Leif Erikson found it 500 years before him.

I look away from the board and see Rafael sitting opposite to me on my table, laughing next to a slightly distraught Maiya, who is muttering *Christopher flippin' Columbus.* Kimberly tries to cheer her up beside me and succeeds when she mentions she's having a Halloween Party. We discuss ideas for fancy dress. Kimberly wants to be Catwoman. Rafael suddenly tells us he has a great idea for who Maiya could go as, to which we all ask who. *Christopher Columbus.* Everyone laughs. Maiya does, too. *Shouldn't that be Christopher flippin' Columbus,* I joke, and they all laugh harder.

The bell rings. A breeze trickles up my sleeve. I glance around the table. There's no one beside me. There never was.

Recently, I've started imagining the conversations from the board as if the people were actually at my table and then playing out what would happen after. Don't get me wrong, it's not everybody on the board I picture I'm with. Jared Steele and his friends, for starters. Or people like Chloe Cassadentini.

Chloe's the It Girl for junior year and posts five times a day, mostly just fancy photos. Girls comment saying she's gorgeous or wishing they had her features, and many boys message that she looks fine. Sorry, *finnnne*, which I find weird when she has a boyfriend—Jared Steele. The classic quarterback and head cheerleader going out scenario. Could it get any more stereotypical?

Chloe Cassadentini seems to be *the life of junior year, if not the whole school*—whereas I'm Hayden Mallard, so I'm guaranteed to know there's no point in my brain trying to picture people like her, her friends or any male equivalent sitting with me.

But I can envision myself with others at lunch, and it genuinely feels real. And it's okay because I don't feel as alone anymore.

I don't even like KingsgateLeeConnect, but the other reason I'm looking at it more is because of Tokyo. I haven't stopped listening to the songs posted by them.

I put my book down and then wait, now staring at my phone. Waiting for another song from Tokyo.

There's a hiss from somewhere. Colbey's straining on the gym machine he's sat on, with his legs pushing out against the foot platform that is connected to some weight plates.

He's come a long way since his injury in his senior year at high school. The partial knee replacement may have ruined a scholarship and his dream of being in the NFL, but he's persevered and not let it hold him back from other things.

"Here, I'll get it." I walk around the gym machine and grab a plate to add on.

"You know I can just flick this and do it myself." Colbey moves a pole to lock the foot platform in place and exaggeratedly moves his legs freely. The plates don't move.

I finish putting the next plate on. "I don't mind helping."

"I know you don't."

He unclicks the pole and pulls his legs into his chest. I head back to another machine, only to use the seat and read a book. Hitting the gym on the first floor in the garage is not really for me. Hitting the gym *anywhere* is not really for me.

"Expecting a text?" Colbey nods at my phone, which, because of how I'm sitting on the machine, is lying on my stomach. "You've been checking it all night."

I have. It's been days since Tokyo last posted anything on KingsgateLeeConnect, and it's taking a toll on me. It's like when a parent has let a kid eat some sweets, and when they say that's enough…all the kid wants is to have that very same sweet again.

After Jared and his friends pay a visit or I think about Mom or the hospital, I just simply listen to one of those songs, and the hurt seems to shrink a little.

I don't know why, but it's like the music has a hold on me. In a good way, I mean.

Tokyo has my curiosity. There's no profile picture, which only supports my theory that Tokyo isn't their real name. And I don't dare write a comment—not when my name is on my profile. And I can't change it.

For now, I've got to wait until Tokyo posts another song.

"You know you, Robin and Dad are my only contacts," I tell Colbey. "I'm just checking the time."

Colbey scrunches his face up, then keeps his legs in. "Hmm. Well, I think that will do for working out. Now, time for some fun."

I look over and tilt my head, confused by his remark.

We've had five races, and it's four-one to me on a cartoon racing game against people online on TV. It's mine and Colbey's go-to game.

Games are another thing the doctors said to be cautious of. Violent games are out of the question.

We only have puzzle games, sports games and this futuristic animated racing game—the latter kind of surprises me.

My eyes stay glued to the screen as I reach out for some chips in a bowl on the coffee table before us. "How you finding work, Mr Assistant Coach and Sports Therapist?"

Colbey's initial dream may have altered, but I'm pleased he's managed to find a path he likes with sports and excels in. And working for a top American university football team is up there. And I know Dad is pleased, too, seeing as he used to be the quarterback when he was at school.

"Really good, Mr Student." Colbey taps a button on his controller frantically. He then overtakes a girl from Brazil after they zoom off the track. "YES! And I am happy with it. But I'd be happier if I saw you going out."

I turn my controller as if it were a steering wheel. "Because I'm beating your butt."

"It isn't that."

"Then what do you mean?" I remain watching the screen. I won't let him stop me from winning—Colbey pauses the game—but that stops me.

He places his controller on the coffee table. I get the sense he's about to say some big, unrehearsed, yet straight-to-the-point speech for me. But it's Colbey, and he's always honest with me, so I turn to listen.

"Maybe Dad's not noticed, or he has and he's happier knowing that you're safe, but you're either at school or here. You're never out. Just because you went to the hospital because you had a bad time doesn't mean you have to stay and lock yourself in these four walls forever."

I'm thrown off. Even for Colbey, that was to the point.

"I don't think that," I quietly object.

"Maybe subconsciously you are."

"I don't—"

"Okay, where are you right now?"

I glance around my surroundings, trying to act bewildered as to where he's teleported us to because unless I'm mistaken…oh no, we're still in the living room.

"Playing games after reading a book while hanging out with your older brother at home on a Friday night."

I get where he's coming from. But it's not like I haven't tried.

Colbey continues to look at me. "You should be at a party, hanging out with friends at a diner, watching the football match at school."

"Football—"

"Isn't your thing, I know, Hayden. But you should be out. This is a new place for us all. It's okay to restart."

I stare at him. "A gaming-related metaphor about me while we're on a game. Nice one, brother," I try and joke because I can't handle how caring Colbey is being. He's being open, and yet I'm sitting opposite him, and I can't even say one honest sentence about how uneasy school is.

"Hayden, part of getting back to being okay is accepting that one moment in the past doesn't define you and that you need to occasionally push yourself to get there and move on. I don't want you to think making an effort for yourself is being a selfish thing."

I couldn't have asked for anything better when I hear the door open and Dad enters—because I honestly felt like I may have told Colbey everything.

"I'm back! Oh, you're playing that? Thought I managed to leave that back in Georgia," Dad says when he sees us on the floor before the TV.

Colbey grabs the controller from the coffee table and presses start. "Nope, we took it out of the trash box after we saw you sneak it in there."

I continue to play, but I'm not giving it my full attention. He doesn't bring up the conversation again, but Colbey's words ring through my head. If there's one person who knows about trying to get up from a terrible place, it's Colbey. I glance over at him, proud of the outcome my brother has made for himself.

Well, Colbey couldn't have picked a worse Friday night for his motivational speech. It rains all weekend—rain in Florida?

By Monday, at school, the rain's clearing up, and despite a wasteful weekend, I can't wipe the smile off my face. There's a new post from Tokyo this morning.

There's some kind of funk that seeps under my skin when I listen to the song.

Suddenly everything around me feels like they are moving slowly, while I'm unrestricted to gently glide down the hallway—and I don't care if it's just me that begins to leisurely sway and fail miserably at dancing, or if all the kids by their lockers gradually start to stare at me or walk by in confusion. I move with elation, yet I am pouring my heart out with the raw sadness of loneliness, but it's okay. It feels good to this beat because I'm forcing the hurt out of me, letting it fly away.

I glance down at my phone when the song finishes. It was all in my head. I've moved not even one step closer to my locker, and yet I feel like I've moved miles inside.

A half-smashed disco ball on the dance floor, with tiny glistening pieces scattered across it, is on my phone. The floor tiles are brightly lit with different colours. Underneath the photo, it tells me Orange Palmer – "You're Just Another Thief Who Took My Soul." I scroll up a little.

Tokyo
They say it's strong for us to hold on. I'd say
it's stronger letting go.

They make it sound so easy—Tokyo—that it could be easy to move on, but it wasn't with Mom. Well, it can't have been if her leaving landed me in the hospital. And I can't expect to quickly forget I had to go to the hospital. That doesn't just go.

But it reminds me I should hope that it does. It tells me I should try.

"Principal Shaw finally spoke some sense into you in doing this class, hey, Palladino?" Coach Rugrosso yells across the gymnasium. I turn, as do all the other non-football team boys in my year, to see a boy walk over. His short brown hair is slightly ruffled. It looks like he's only just changed into his kit.

"Not really. Apparently saying that I'd rather use my time more efficiently ain't valid enough."

Some of the boys and I chuckle—until Coach Rugrosso glares at us.

"Even Ferris Bueller wouldn't be able to get it off," Palladino adds—I have no idea who he is referencing, but it seems none of the others do as well. "Ferris Bueller? As in *Ferris Bueller's Day Off*? Wow, maybe they should have lessons on films here instead."

Coach Rugrosso ignores the remark and then explains what volleyball training he would like us to do. We get into groups—and honestly, I wish I was somewhere else. However, I learn the boy who was called Palladino is named Zeke.

The door opens again. This time, though, it isn't one boy. There's a whole group of them, all wearing football gear and being led by another man in a white shirt and orange shorts. Coach Gard.

"What's the meaning of this, Gard?" Coach Rugrosso asks.

"The pitch is flooded, and if we want it to be fine for Friday's match, we've got to leave it be—so the boys are training in here," Coach Gard says, with his team behind him. "Football overrules any other sport, and you know it. We're taking over."

"You're doing no such thing. If you want your boys in here, they'll have to play volleyball. Otherwise, you can go elsewhere."

"I'd personally not mind giving up this lesson so they can play football."

"Shut it, Palladino," Coach Rugrosso whips at Zeke. Some of us laugh, but I genuinely do second what the boy says.

"Alright then," Coach Gard says. "You heard him, boys. Take off your equipment. We're playing volleyball. It'll be kind of refreshing for my boys to do something different—and still win."

Through some arguing, the coaches settle for a volleyball match. However, as Coach Rugrosso gathers us around, my heart slumps to the ground. Jared and his boys are in the other group.

"Right, boys. I want Van Schie, Mount, Horn, Aslett, Palladino and Mallard."

"Excuse me?" I blurt out.

"You heard me, Mallard. You're not half bad. Well, not half as bad as the rest of these," Coach Rugrosso says. "And don't give me that look, Palladino. Perhaps this will teach you the life lesson that you should always try and put some effort into everything."

"Er, I don't see how. I'm not gonna exactly be forced to play this in the middle of the streets for my life, am I?" Zeke replies. "The only thing this game will do is satisfy the testosterone coming off you two coaches."

"Palladino!" Coach Rugrosso shouts. "One more quip, and it's detention."

My nerves don't calm down—fear hits me again. Jared is on the other team, along with two of his friends. This won't end well.

And it soon becomes clear that the other team are better.

"Hey, oompa, that's what I like!" I hear Jared yell again—something he does every time he wins a point.

"Ooo, I'm gonna oompa my foot in his face, then I'll ask if that's what he likes," Zeke says under his breath as we head back into place. I chuckle and lean into position.

Although the football team won the first set, we're now drawing on the second set.

The ball launches over to our side. Van Schie moves forward—he saves the ball, making it go back into the air. In the middle, Zeke turns—ready to set the ball for the last touch. He hits the ball high. "Hayden!"

I take a run up towards the net. Colbey would say imagine hitting it as you prepare. I try. The ball begins to come down. *You can do it, Hayden! For once, do something good.* I jump. The boy opposite me jumps as well. He's trying to block it. I raise my arms in the air. Search for a space on their side—there!

I pull my left hand back and launch it towards where the ball should go. I hit it. The ball soars down to the opponent's side…

And goes straight into Jared's face.

Shit!

There's a collection of gasps.

Zeke and the boys on my side cheer for joy as the ball bounces off Jared's face and hits the ground. They cheer like we've won the game. I stay frozen.

"Nice shot, Mallard!" Coach Rugrosso yells. Coach Gard and his team crowd around Jared to lift him up. He's got his hand over his nose. There's red all over his face and down his shirt.

The two coaches yell at one another—I stay on the spot while the others laugh around me. However, over their happiness, I hear Jared yell, "I'll get you, Mallard!" Just like something out of a kid's cartoon—but I feel the consequences will be far worse.

Coach Rugrosso walks over to us when the other team have gone. "I'm impressed, guys; it's nice to see some of my teaching has rubbed off on you. We'll leave it there. Go and get changed."

The boys chat amongst themselves as they head out.

"That includes you, Mallard."

"Aren't you going to tell me off?"

"Am I going to—no, I'm not going to tell you off," Coach Rugrosso retaliates. "Do you think I should? There'd be no sport if everyone got into trouble for every little incident or worry."

"I guess so."

I'm still expecting him to spin around and point one of his large, muscular-sausage fingers at me and yell, *you hit their star player! Oh, Jared's gonna have it in for you now, boy, ha ha ha!*

"It's fine, Mallard. Go and get changed."

I want to leave the gymnasium, but what might be waiting for me scares me.

My mind starts to question what Jared will have up his sleeve for me, but, out of nowhere, the lyrics from one of Tokyo's songs slowly begin to play in my head.

With the music following in, it soon takes over my body enough that I'm only thinking about the song.

4.

I head to the sink and wash my hands. My nose automatically scrunches from the constant stench in the school toilets. I look at Tokyo's page on KingsgateLeeConnect on my phone. It's been days since their last post. The only positive thing so far is that Mr Gauran has backed down about KingsgateLeeConnect to me—he told me in the hallway yesterday that he'd seen I had logged in. I apologised to him if I was not my best the last time we spoke. I only feel more ashamed when he accepted the apology and said he understood that I'd just found out about my swimming trials.

There's just an empty circle where Tokyo's profile picture should be. A column of songs with pictures. That's it. Every effort to find the identity, including my last one—pretending to the receptionist that I had a textbook that was signed by the name Tokyo and wanted to return it to their locker—failed. There is nobody with that name here—meaning it's an alias.

But perhaps they may want to stay hidden so they can't be hurt should anyone tease their posts. And it's that last part I kind of get. I may wish to have friends, but with how things are now, all I want to do at school is stay unknown to everyone. So maybe I should leave it—let who Tokyo is go.

There's a loud bang. I jump—the door's been barged open—Jared and his three friends are there.

There's a white strip over Jared's nose. "You're dead, Mallard."

I launch myself forward in the hopes of squeezing through them. But I fail. There's a force and a pain in my shoulder pulling me back; someone's got a hold of my rucksack. I'm yanked back—my head smacks hard down onto the tiled floor.

The lights on the ceiling blind my eyes until there's darkness over them.

Their kicks, pushes and punches force pain across my body and stop me from escaping their huddle.

A tremendous kick to the stomach slams me back down.

Gasping for air, I collapse in defeat.

Something large smacks my ear. Everything suddenly sounds deep.

"Know your place, Mallard," I vaguely hear over the ringing and blurred loudness whilst my body stings immensely. I can't do anything apart from hope it stops soon.

The bell for the last lesson of the day goes.

"There aren't any shortcuts in life," Jared shouts over my wheezing. "Don't get on my wrong side again, Mallard, or you won't have it so easy next time."

I carefully open my eyes—they're heading to the door. When Jared's friends follow him out, I notice there is someone behind them. A fifth person. A Mexican boy in a red hoody and jeans. A new friend who joined mid-way through the attack to have fun with me? He begins to walk after them but then stops.

My body tenses, thinking he might want to get a kick out of his system. I want him to leave me be. He stares down at me—then goes out the door before it closes itself.

I want to shout out the pain—but there's no strength in me to do so. I wish to leave the toilets—yet my body doesn't dare move an inch off the ground. The floor's horrible and sticky, but I take it because the cool surface is the only thing not hurting me.

I remain quiet.

At some point, I eventually get up—not without holding the sink for support. I'm somewhat freaked by my legs shaking, yet my focus is staring at the mirror. My face looks sad, but it's unscratched, except for a small cut near my ear.

I use my free hand to lift my clothes. Large outlines and dark patches are all over my body, already turning purple. I'm no doctor, but even I know they'll be staying for a while. Those guys were smart—only marking where my body is usually covered.

My clothes fall over my stomach when I let go. My face tightens up, ready to cry when I think about how much I hate everything in my life right now. The bullying. The fact my dad felt like I wouldn't be fine back at home and thought he had no option but to take us away. Robin hating me. How much school sucks. How alone I really am.

After a couple of uncontrollable blubs from my mouth, the water stays in my eyes, even though I hate what I see in the mirror.

I pick my rucksack up. The strap rips—everything slips out and goes onto the floor.

I huff.

It's fine. The rucksack's already ruined as it is; the front zip pocket is jammed and hasn't opened since back in Georgia.

Today is the first time that I'm thankful Robin doesn't speak to me in the car. I remain quiet and boil over the day's events.

I run, well, try to run upstairs when we get home. I enter my room, shutting the door behind me, and throw my now unusable rucksack to the side. There's an unexpected deep exhale that comes out of me. I can hear the nervousness in it—it frightens me.

Jared's voice calls out in my head.

Every exhale struggles to last as long as the breath before. My body closes in more and more to my ribs as I pace up and down the room. It's too much. I need a distraction. Reading a book won't cut it. There's some paper on the desk. I grab a piece and try and fold it, but my hands are shaking so much in fright and anger that I give up.

This must stop—I don't want to end up in the hospital again. I must stop overthinking it.

I glance around in desperation. My headphones are dangling out of my rucksack. *Tokyo's songs.*

I pull them out and start playing on my phone the songs that Tokyo posted about. But I need something bigger. Something new.

I click on one of the posts on KingsgateLeeConnect and open the comment section—I stop. If I ask for a recommendation, everybody will see I'm not doing well. It's under my name. They'll judge me. I can't deal with people thinking I'm more of a loser than I already am.

I desperately grip my phone—something pops up on Tokyo's page. A box has appeared.

Name: Tokyo
Year: N/A
Email: TokyoCherryDustZ89@TokyoCherryDustZ89.com

An email address! A line appears out of the pop-up box and finishes beside the middle of three vertical dots next to the profile name. I click the dots—the box disappears. I click it again. The box reappears.

This is good, I try and tell myself. My breathing keeps rapidly changing, but I know what to do now.

I click on the email address. KingsgateLeeConnect on my screen vanishes, and my email opens.

To use our email system, you will need to create an account and assign it to this

Already have an email address?

Thank you—emailing isn't one of the many things prohibited from being on my phone.

I stare at the screen. It's not just the rest of the school that I don't want to know who I am. It's also Tokyo. They'll know my identity if I use my school email address. They've used an alias to cover who they are, and so if they're using a false name, should I not be doing the same? They might think it's lame, but I'm in too much of a state.

Although it's a struggle at first, especially through my pain, I soon have an email address.

Now I can contact them.

But I write nothing.

I breathe in.

Okay, write something.

Anything.

ANYTHING…

Right, okay, just one thing…

…

…*Oh, for crying out loud!*

Calm down.

I let my fingers hover over the phone, and eventually, I write.

"How was school today?" Dad says at some point during the meal. I don't look up because I'm sure they're staring at me. There's some stress and anger still coiled up inside me. I've contacted Tokyo. There's nothing else to do until they reply. I just hope Tokyo's on their phone a lot or that the pain will somehow go. And soon.

I continue looking at my plate. "Fine."

"Just fine?"

"Yes." The tension rises uncontrollably in my voice.

"Are you sure you're fine?"

"Yes."

"Hayden, are you—"

"Look, I'm fine, alright!"

"Hay—"

"No!" I whip my head to Colbey and then stare at them all. "What's bugging me is when people keep asking me if I'm fine, and I've already said I am. So why can't you all back off!"

I slam my knife and fork down. Food splashes off the plate. I push my chair back and storm up to my room.

The bedroom door bangs behind me. My arms wrap around my stomach, wishing desperately that it could absorb the physical and emotional aching.

The door flies open. Robin is standing there.

"What the heck was that?"

"What? Nothing."

"That wasn't nothing. We've let go of a lot to move here. You can't be like that in front of Dad, you can't—" Robin continues, but I don't listen because the sounds of Jared and his friends yelling at me and beating me up take over. Punching and kicking me all over my body.

"—You need to sort yourself out."

No, I need to move. I can't stay. I have to get out.

Something pings. I glance down at my hand. There's a notification on my phone. It's an email…from Tokyo!

I head for the door. I can't read the email here.

"Where are you going, Hayden? I'm trying to—"

I snatch my headphones before leaving my sister in the room. I charge straight downstairs and then quickly put some trainers on.

"Is that you, Hayden?" Dad shouts from the kitchen.

"Hayden, come back," Robin yells from the top of the stairs. I don't bother looking in either direction.

I open the front door. "I'm going for a walk. I've got my phone."

The fresh air hits me when I step out—but I pick up my pace down the street to get away.

My phone vibrates. It's Dad. I reject the call. I quickly send him a text telling him I'm fine. He replies with an *ok*.

I shuffle in my dark maroon hoody to try and feel somewhat comfortable. I go against the urge and wait until I make it to the end of the street before opening the email.

FROM: TokyoCherryDustZ89@TokyoCherryDustZ89.com
TO: BlueC0ast1@bretteodmail.com
DATE: Thu 5th October, 7:46 PM
SUBJECT: Re: Asking For A Friend

Dear Brisbane,

Thanks for contacting me. I'm glad you managed to finally write something, but sorry for the reasons it's for. Unfortunately, I'm not a witch, so I can't wave my wand to vanish the pain.

But music's been helping recently? That's a good thing.

I've learnt there are two different ways music can help remove somebody's anger, depending on what kind of person they are. Some want an extreme song so they can run or smash things to release their anger to it (but be careful, people will think you are crazy if done in the public eye), and yet others want to hear upbeat music, something completely opposite and confident, so they can diminish their anger and calm themselves down. I'm more the second, but it's sometimes good to jump madly around your room when something gets to you.

Here are the song options.

1) Jadario Sundown – Green Limo
2) B-Line-Rocco – Rocco Didn't Know
3) Orange Palmer – Obsessed Redemption

What's this? A third option? Only listen if you're brave and willing to hear a sound even more out there. It's fun, catchy and weird, but listen to the lyrics, and you'll notice how deep it is.

I'm sure someone famous once said music is the best, if not the only, way to express the inexpressible and resolve the unresolvable…or something like that, but it makes sense, right?

I hope at least one of the songs can help you with whatever you're dealing with. I know music does with me.

Oh, and hi does always seem like a good way to start when meeting someone new, so hi. It's good to know somebody's checking the songs out and likes my recommendations.

-Tokyo

P.S. Yes, Tokyo isn't my real name. I hope you chose Brisbane because of the city and that it's got some personal meaning to you, and not just because of something silly like you're jealous it's your family dog's name and not yours.

P.S.S. Now that I think about it, please tell me it's because you have a dog called Brisbane, and you are super jealous.

There are so many things I want to say, so many questions and comments to reply with. I reread the email. My lips slowly turning into a smile.

But the pain is there still—I've got to remove this hatred inside me.

The first option looks appealing, but with how awful I am right now, I put my headphones on and search for option three, then press play.

I walk down the street, not bothering to look ahead or anywhere in particular as people go by so I can be alone with the music.

I begin to wonder how lonely I am. But why does it have to be the loner who must show they are worthy of being acceptable to a group of friends? It's like the only way to join whatever group you desire is if you forcibly craft to whatever they deem acceptable. But I shouldn't have to lose myself just to try and fit into a mould of how you're supposed to be. Can't it be the opposite? That all the groups should hope and desperately want us loners to be with them. A reverse of sorts.

Like they'd all hurry over and beg me to hang out with them because they can't have enough friends—and though I like the decision-making, I decide to just pass by, gliding on with my headphones on and mouthing to the music, because although the choice is mine, I realise I'm content with being by myself no matter what the day brings or no matter who wants to be my friend.

The song finishes. The bruises ache and will take time to go, but somehow, I'm not hurting as much now. I keep listening again, and the song makes me believe that if I just place one foot in front of the other and move forward, then the worries will naturally drift away. The song's good. Really good.

Soon enough, after what's probably the millionth time listening to each song, my lips slowly move to the lyrics. Getting so into them that I almost don't realise when a song suddenly stops. I pull my phone out. Dead. No battery.

I glance around. I'm in a busier part of Orlando now. I should head back home. It will be late.

With the headphones resting around my neck, I've just got the sounds of the area to fill my ears. The cars. The wind through the trees. The thumping music from inside the bars further down the road.

Something wincing in pain.

Something wincing? I turn to my left—it's coming from the other side of the road. From a park. The noise goes again—something's wrong. I run over. Then I see.

I dash down the slope, shouting for whoever is hurting the person by a tree to leave them alone. The towering figure moves up. Panic hits me. They might come towards me.

But the figure suddenly sprints away into the park.

When I reach the person on the ground, they're breathing hastily. There are dark splotches and patches on the grass.

"Here." I bend and help lift the person, ignoring the pain from my own bruises.

"Thanks," the person hisses. It's a guy—but even in the shadows, the voice is familiar.

"Zeke?"

The guy lifts his head up. It is. Zeke Palladino from school. "Hey. Hayden, isn't it?"

I'm still in shock. "Yeah."

He wipes away the blood on his lip and then points at me with that grin he had in the gymnasium. "Knew it." He then immediately tumbles. I grab a better hold of him and lift him back up.

"We need to go to the hospital."

"It's okay. I just need to lie down for a bit. I'll be fine in the morning."

I've heard and even said the word too many times these last few days to know that fine isn't always fine. When he tells me his car is back up the slope, I don't take no for an answer when I offer to assist him up there.

"What are you doing here?"

"I park over here, so I don't have to pay at the diner over there. Walk through all the time, but I'll admit, this is a first." Zeke repositions himself on me as we climb up the slope. "So, do you tend to walk through parks at night alone, or was bashing Jared's nose with a volleyball not heroic enough for you that you must prowl the city to stop crime? Like some sort of real-life Kick-Ass or Peter Parker?"

I don't answer at first because I try not to think about Jared and his friends. And because I don't really know who he is referencing. I hadn't thought of Jared since before listening to Tokyo's music. I want to put one of the songs on again, yet that will be rude to Zeke. And the phone's dead.

"Just walking by." I try and play "Rocco Didn't Know" in my mind.

"Fair enough." Zeke nods. "I never said that day but I'm sure glad something happened to Jared. If I heard one more *hey, oompa, that's what I like* in that lesson then I would have done it myself."

"I thought you wanted to oompa your foot in his face, then ask if that's what he likes?"

"Ha, you remembered?" Zeke grins. "Well, either would have sufficed the aim of what I hoped, but my guess is what you did was the best solution, you know, 'cause it would have looked like an accident and was just into the game. Coaches love it when you say you were just getting into it."

I glance at Zeke. "I didn't aim for him."

"Anybody who saw your face knew you didn't mean to. But it was still nice."

At the top of the slope, Zeke points to a black pickup truck. We go across the road and make our way over to the driver's side until he tugs. "What are you doing?"

"Putting you in the driver's seat."

"Uh, hello?" He nods down and opens the palm of his free hand. I glance below and see he's referring to his injuries. It's true. He isn't in a state to drive. Zeke laughs, but I have to tighten my grip on him when he coughs. "Can you drive me?"

The dryness in my throat stops me from answering. I shake my head.

"Shame. Know any taxi numbers?" My head shakes again. "You don't know much, do you? Have a phone?"

"It's dead."

"Course it is. That guy took mine. And my money—and I bet you've got none? Well, I don't think I can deal with speaking to anyone else either, so we'll have to walk then."

I ignore him, but when he begins to shuffle forward first, I realise he's serious about walking.

With streetlights surrounding us, I get a better look at Zeke. His lip's bleeding, and there's a dark shade over his right eye.

"That bad, hey?" Zeke notices. I tell him it isn't. "I'll be fine. Come on, it's that way. I'll race ya." I whip my head to the side. He must see the stern look on my face because he quickly adds, "Just kidding."

Ideally, I wish I could drive him because I don't want him to make his injuries worse. But I can't drive—or rather, I'm not allowed, not for nine hundred and thirty-nine days. Or, to make it sound more prolonged, two years, six months, and twenty-six days.

This year, on April 11th, my mom left the Mallard family in Georgia. Dad didn't say much; Colbey just somehow accepted it, and then he somehow later managed to calm Robin down and stop her thinking Mom had only left Dad. She soon focused her attention to help Dad.

I thought Mom and I were very close. However, unlike Robin, I never once believed our mom would approach the driveway and ask us to come with her. I knew she had left everybody behind for good. I guess that must be why I found it harder to accept and why it caused me to somehow crack. For a few days after Mom left, so the doctors tell me, I apparently broke—I took Robin's car, drove away and then crashed the car that night into a tree on North Mount Street, a road out of town that goes along the river, a couple of miles from Farm Bridge.

I was asleep in the hospital for two days. Waking up with broken bones, a smashed phone, a destroyed car and no memory of the crash.

But that's not the only thing I can't remember.

They say I left the hospital on May 1st and that was the same day I was given a three-year driving ban. A driving ban before I even had my licence. But I can't argue with it. What I did was reckless. Even if I was upset, it's no excuse. I'm just thankful nobody else was involved or hurt.

A few weeks later, I returned to school. Everything was fine until, and I don't even know how, but I'm told I started to not feel well. About it all. I got so worked up that I had a breakdown. I had to go back to the hospital in mid-June. I don't remember any of that either—except for waking up in the hospital after that breakdown.

I stayed in the hospital that second time until some day in August, when they thought I was finally better.

And I am better.

Just thinking about the talks with doctors, the many tests and procedures I had to do is overwhelming enough. But I've moved on. No, that's not right. I've adjusted. I think. I knew my mom wasn't ever going to return, but the difference after being in the hospital again is that now I've accepted it. Knowing and accepting are different things. And, if I was in a car accident and Dad left answer messages on her phone, and my mom still didn't come back any time I was in the hospital, then it's blatantly obvious that she's gone. It was a wake-up call I apparently needed. I managed to accept it all in the hospital, and I'm okay. I don't like it, but I've accepted she isn't coming back.

It's just whenever I try to remember any of it—my brain starts to hurt, like a migraine but a million times worse, and I feel sick. I only remember before Colbey telling Robin that Mom wasn't coming back and then after waking up the second time in the hospital. The rest in between—me breaking down, taking Robin's car, going to the hospital and breaking down again—is a blur. I've no recollection. I just take everybody's word for what happened to me.

To be honest, though, it's probably a good thing I can't remember those times. I don't think I want to know or feel again how terrible I must have been then.

"Drop me here," Zeke orders later. I place him down on some grass, just a little away from squashing some roses in a flowerbed. We're outside a white house, a large one, with a slight walkway to the front door and a stone fountain on the right. I ask him why we can't head for the door. "No—Billy's parents are having a *civilised* party," saying civilised in a posh accent.

I thought we were off back to his—but I guess he didn't want his parents to see him like this. There are many cars parked here. Who has a party on a Thursday night?

"Leave me here and ask for Billy. We were meant to be meeting up."

I nod, still unsure, and head over nervously before ringing the doorbell and waiting for this Billy guy to answer. I try to smooth my clothes down when quickly remembering there's a civilised party on the other side of the door—but whom am I kidding? I'm wearing a hoody and some jeans.

I double-check it's this house. Zeke gives an enthusiastic thumbs up.

The door opens. A girl with large, dark-orange wavy hair stands there.

"Oh, hi." *Why's my voice shaking?* "I was wondering if Billy was in?"

Compared to her black jeans and denim jacket, there are a few adults in the hallway behind the girl, all dressed in smart shirts and fancy dresses, and all staring at me.

"Yeah?"

"So, is he in?"

"*She* is here."

My body freezes. She is Billy? Oh—she's Billy! I'm so embarrassed for assuming Billy was a guy. I can't work out if I should ignore my mistake or if I should willingly crawl into a ball and let her kick me away.

"Look, if this is another prank Zeke's set up, I won't have it—" The ice-cold shade of her eyes staring at me moves to something beyond me. "Zeke? Get up from there. I told you I don't like you sending random people to my house."

Despite being smaller than me, she barges by me quite strongly and marches towards Zeke. "It wasn't funny the first time, so it isn't funny this—oh my goodness, are you okay?"

She crouches down. There's a genuine look of worry on her face as she checks him out. I almost jump back when the ball of hair spins, and her eyes glare darkly at me. "What did you do?"

"Me?" I ask in a dreadful pitch.

"Billie! Billie! He's the one who saved me."

She stops. I swear if Zeke's words had not managed to get through to her, I'm sure she would have slapped me across the face. I watch, alarmed at Billie, as Zeke explains what happened. However, Billie begins to calm down. She convinces him to get checked so we help Zeke into her car.

"It's fine. You need to get checked. I know my way back," I say to Zeke when he offers me a lift home. I don't. But I don't want to intrude any more than I have.

"Well, thanks," Zeke says. Billie nods from the driver's side and drives away.

The car veers around the corner. And I'm back to being alone.

It's strange how everything happens for a reason, I begin to question. If I hadn't decided to turn back on my walk at that exact moment when my phone died, then I'd have been somewhere else and not heard Zeke needing help. And even if I had turned back at that precise time out of choice, then it's good that my phone ran out of battery, or I wouldn't have heard Zeke over the music I would have still been listening to. And if I didn't let the music control my mind and let my body move by itself, then I may not have ended up on that street.

But then, if I hadn't received that email from Tokyo and also had Robin confront me because of my outburst, then I may not have felt like I couldn't breathe and needed to escape and leave the house. However, if that's the case, then that means if Jared and his friends didn't attack me so badly that it broke me inside because I accidentally hurt him in volleyball, then I wouldn't have reacted how I did at home. Rather horribly beautiful how things plan out, isn't it? I realise.

I put my headphones over my ears and press play for one of Tokyo's songs—nothing happens.

The screen is blank.

I laugh, realising what I've just done.

I head home and start to hum one of Tokyo's song choices instead.

5.

FROM: TokyoCherryDustZ89@TokyoCherryDustZ89.com
TO: BlueC0ast1@bretteodmail.com
DATE: Sat 7th October, 5:16 PM
SUBJECT: Re: Asking For A Friend

Dear Brisbane,

If there's one song you need to get you to be positive, it's Rocco Didn't Know. As for Obsessed Redemption, to me, that tells me I should be ok with myself. And perhaps it will tell you to be as well.

So you *have* been checking the music I post, hey? I thought you might have been pretending. Well, I am honoured you recognised Orange Palmer from a post on my profile. Orange Palmer's somewhere up there on my fave list. They're near the top of my fave Swedish artists, that's for sure. However, for modern duos, I would have to say November Dreams. Please tell me you've heard of some of their songs!

Hang on! I can't believe you didn't take the opportunity to trash your room while listening to Jadario Sundown. Any person would love to do that! But the fact you'd have to tidy the mess up after is enough to stop anybody before it turns carnage. That and the cost of having to replace anything you break. Should point out I've never done anything like that, and I am not some professional. Well, maybe I did listen to Blondie once in my room and smashed a photo frame. But that was just from dancing and swinging my arms excitedly around and accidentally hitting it. Oops!

Yet, on a serious note, Brisbane, I'm glad the songs helped you.

And now, onto a more serious note, I CAN'T BELIEVE YOU DON'T HAVE A DOG NAMED BRISBANE. I mean, what's that all about? Here I was hoping to see a picture of the dog that inspired your name, only to read there isn't one? Oh well, my search for finding a dog named Brisbane continues.

Thanks,

-Tokyo

FROM: BlueC0ast1@bretteodmail.com
TO: TokyoCherryDustZ89@TokyoCherryDustZ89.com
DATE: Sun 8th October, 11:23 AM
SUBJECT: Re: Asking For A Friend

Dear Tokyo,

It sounds like you have a lot of different favourite artist lists. Orange Palmer's also my favourite Swedish artist…but that's probably because they're the only Swedish artist I've listened to. Well, I've heard of ABBA, but that's more my dad's list.

I don't want to admit it, but I've never heard of November Dreams. Music hasn't really been a part of my life. I only hear what's on the radio in the car my sister or my dad has on. So music in the charts or '70s and '80s music.

It never crossed my mind that you were a professional at trashing places—yet what did that photo frame ever do to you? Do I need to get a statement from the photo frame? And yes, I think even if I wanted to completely mess up my room, I wouldn't have enough money to restore it. And my dad would say his son's room already looks like that.

Good luck with your quest to find a dog named Brisbane.

Thanks,
-Brisbane

FROM: TokyoCherryDustZ89@TokyoCherryDustZ89.com
TO: BlueC0ast1@bretteodmail.com
DATE: Mon 9th October, 4:32 PM
SUBJECT: Re: Asking For A Friend

Dear Brisbane,

Glad to know you don't think I'm a professional bedroom wrecker – influenced by the loud assumption of rock/pop music. I was just dancing, yet in my defence though, whenever I was sitting at my desk, that photo frame was always staring right at me. Weird.

A statement? Haha, wow, good luck…you'd have to find the photo frame first.

Wow, just wow. There are so many questions I need to ask about your music limitations. You should be thankful that I won't because if I did, it would take all night to type them up. However, I hope that wasn't a dig at '70s and '80s music—I really do enjoy music from those eras, especially the '80s.

I do have a lot of fave lists because I like music. And I know you do, too. It's just that you haven't been exposed to what's out there. So, you just need to be grateful our paths have crossed, as I'm going to help change that for you, Brisbane. I'm going to right all those musical wrongs and fill all those absent silences in your mind with a broad taste in music.

Seeing as your name is, I'm assuming, in regards to the Australian city and now clearly not a dog, we'll start with November Dreams—an Australian electropop male and female duo. You should check out their music. Doesn't matter if it's while you're jogging, studying or lying on the bed before you go to sleep, have a listen to their albums. There's something beyond this world when you listen to their music—I think it's a great starting point for what will be your epic music adventure. And I won't accept no as an answer.

Good luck,
-Tokyo

P.S. Hang on, if I'm searching for a dog named Brisbane, then you need to find something with my name. A cat named Tokyo? No. A rabbit? A llama? Yes, a llama. I've decided, definitely a llama.

6.

There's been nothing more that I want to do in my free time over these last few days than to listen to November Dreams.

They sound electrifying. Pure. Forward-looking. They send out a vibe, one that makes me strange inside, yet I accept it. I become relieved but hope for more because they make me think that there could be no limitations in my life while still being myself. I hope one time that will be the case.

I think it's due to the fact they're putting their imagination out there in a way that only good things can come from it, and it makes me want to be a part of it. It's weird, but it genuinely makes me like this.

And Tokyo is great, too. They could have just left my email alone. But they didn't. I've gathered Tokyo is a girl—a boy wouldn't call themselves a witch in their email. And I'm cool with not knowing who they really are. There's something rather freeing about the fact that we're both messaging someone we don't know. A reassurance I can be myself because it's anonymous. Sad, I know, but I don't mind.

If I *did* want to search for Tokyo at my school, it would be like a needle in a haystack. A haystack that represents the three and a half thousand students that attend my school. And for all I know, it could be a jock. Well, I'm sure it's a girl.

But that's not the only needle in this haystack. There are two other needles. Zeke and Billie. These are two needles that I want to find, two needles that I actually know what they look like, and I still can't find them. And Zeke wasn't in Sports on Monday either.

There's no rule to say I must speak to them, but I want to know if Zeke is okay. I hardly know the person, yet I care.

By Friday, though, I give up. Classes go by. I eat lunch at the same table alone. I listen to music, and let my mind play out, imagining me talking to people who've recently posted on KingsgateLeeConnect. However, now there's Zeke and Billie here with the three people from a post I've seen.

"And where do you think you're going?"

Robin freezes in the hallway. Dad can't see her from the couch when he called, but it's perhaps for a good reason. She's in a red crop top and very tiny black shorts.

I keep my head down. I was expecting Dad to kick off when I got back from storming out of the house last week, but in all fairness, he was quite calm. He's never one to get angry, but I thought he might. I apologised and explained I was just sick of everybody asking me all the time if I was fine. A partial truth.

Dad simply told me not to do it again and to talk to them. I feel I owe him for being understanding and for me being guilty, so I've tried to spend more time with him. Hence why I'm on the living room floor doing schoolwork while he's watching TV.

"Oh, Dad, hi. Thought you'd gone out." Robin slowly pokes her head into the living room from behind the wall. "I said earlier, I'm off to study."

Colbey shuffles in his chair like he's expecting a film to start. "On a Friday night?"

"Shut it, Colbey," Robin says, hissing at him.

Dad gets up and walks out to Robin before she can hide. "You must think I was born yesterday. You're off to a party, right?"

"Wow, to say you're one of the smartest at school, this clearly doesn't prove it," Colbey replies, smirking at his sister.

Robin whips her head at Colbey as she marches into the room. Her freakishly tall red high-heels click with every step. "Just 'cause you've been able to drink and party legally now for four years doesn't mean you should spoil it for me."

Dad sits back down on the couch. "Oh good, there goes my hope that there won't be any alcohol at this party. Robin, you're not going."

"What? No, I'm not even drinking—please, Dad," Robin says as she moves closer to him. Bending down almost like a beg. "You dragged me here away from my life, away from everything I had. Don't you want me to make new friends?"

"You can do that at school—in the school committee or in the chess club?"

Checkmate.

"Chess club?" Robin looks like she's about to collapse to the ground. "Dad, pleeeease."

Dad readjusts on the couch, purposely making Robin desperately wait as though she's just done a figure-skating dance and is awaiting her score to appear on the screen. It seems it's not so checkmate.

"Alright, you can go." Robin almost jumps for joy and begins repeatedly thanking Dad. "If Colbey goes with you."

Colbey's hand falls to his legs in disbelief. Dad smirks when Robin's mouth drops in horror.

Colbey's eyebrows furrow. "Think it's a little weird if somebody my age goes to a high school house party."

"True," Dad contemplates.

I look back over to Colbey and notice he's staring at me. A single eyebrow raised. I don't like it one bit.

"How about if Hayden goes instead?"

And just like that, Colbey's thrown the shock onto me and given Robin another tonight.

"Me?"

"I like that," Dad says, sharing a grin with my brother.

"You've got to be kidding me!" Robin detests with an absolute callous look of disgust on her face while she marches up and down the room—but she doesn't need to because I agree with her.

"Dad. I'm not bothered. Let Robin go," I say, assuming Dad's already agreed with Colbey.

Robin flails her arms at me. "See, he doesn't even want to go. And Colbey's old—"

"Hey!"

"—Please, Dad."

"That's the rule," Dad confirms.

I stay quiet, confused because I'm sure Dad would always want me here at home if he could.

Robin twists back and forth, desperately wanting to argue, but in the end, she doesn't.

"Fine," she moans. "Please, Hayden." A weird thing begins to happen on Robin's face when she looks at me. Her drooped lips make it seem like she's trying to plead me to go like a cute puppy, yet the harsh rottweiler glare with her sharp raised dark eyebrows tells me it's most definitely an order.

The thought of going to a party, my first party, is scary but not as terrifying as what Robin might do to me later if I say no. "I'll go."

"Yes!" Robin beams with joy.

I gather my stuff to go and get ready, but before I leave the room, Colbey gives me a little wink. Why the—! He's done it on purpose! He's been trying to push me to go out and meet people, and now he's done it.

I'd change my mind if I could, but Robin's excited for the first time here because of me. I can't back out now.

I put my new rucksack I got the other day to the side of my bed—then almost trip over my old, brown ripped rucksack on the floor, the one with the stuck, closed front zip, and I shove that into the wardrobe. I put on some deodorant, change my top and grab my jacket.

Dad gives Robin and me a list of rules to obey—no drinking, no taking drugs, no fights, no smoking, no brownies, no mushrooms, it goes on. Robin reassures him we won't, as she is driving, and leaves. I say thanks to be polite and slowly follow Robin.

"Son." Dad lightly puts his hand on my shoulder. I turn to look at him. "Apart from when you went last week to walk it off, you've not been out since," his voice trails off, but I know what he's referring to. "I mean, just be careful. Don't break any of the rules."

"I won't," I say, trying to smile to show my appreciation. "I'm just going for Robin."

"That's good of you. If you need anything or want to come home early, remember you can contact us."

"Thanks, Dad." He smiles, and in return, I give him a vague nod because I don't think I can handle him being any nicer.

If I thought there were enough rules from Dad, my sister has even more for me in her car—to the point where I have to argue that they might not let me in if I don't walk into the house with her. She eventually obliges to that one.

Robin turns from the mirror to look at me. "Just remember what we did for you."

And poof! The little slice of happiness Robin had with me has gone.

We eventually arrive. I'm having to quickly follow Robin so that I'm not left behind, though I do manage to see the lavish style of the large house, with its cream-walled castle towers at either side, the tall palm trees around the yard and the stone-crafted pirate ship fountain in the centre. There's even water that shoots out of its cannons.

The place looks quite remarkable. It's like one people would expect to be in a rich family reality show, not a house someone at my school lives in.

The music hits us powerfully as soon as Robin opens the large wooden door. It's kind of good as it numbs my nerves because I'm petrified. I never went to parties back in Georgia.

To no surprise, Robin keeps to her word and vanishes. So I stand alone, wondering what to do.

For the first hour, I only move to the kitchen to get some chips, and because I help one person find a drink to mix with vodka, I somehow become the drink finder for everybody. That is until I accidentally bump into somebody's drink!

A girl in a black woolly jumper brushes the patches of drink off her. "Wow, thanks for that."

I look across despite the sarcasm in her voice. She's dressed all in black. However, my eyes are drawn to her bobbed yet electrifying purple hair—but then I notice a difference on her face. Besides the hair, all her other features are dark except her left eyebrow. Her right is black, but her left is light, almost blonde. Must be some fashion statement like her hair.

The purpled-haired girl twists to stare at me when I offer to help. Lips scrunched. "Just leave."

I do. Not just because the girl said, but I shouldn't be near alcohol. I wouldn't have any even if I wanted to—never have—but Dad asked me not to have any. And the doctors back in Georgia would be disappointed.

I venture through the main room and take myself down a hallway away from the heavy bass, stepping over the people who have decided the floor is comfortable to sprawl out on, and then go left.

It's quiet. Practically empty. There are pictures on the wall—I freeze.

There's a photo of Jared Steele. This is his house! Sick churns in my stomach.

Voices come from around the corner—oh damn! It's Jared Steele and his friends.

I run around another corner and fly straight into the first available door. I shut the door, lock it and slam my back against the door. My body slides down against it to the floor.

I'm in a bathroom—which is some silver lining, I suppose, because I think I might throw up at any moment. I cover my mouth as a last attempt to be the quietest I can be.

Oh, flip! They're on the other side. On the upside, if they do catch me and beat me until I bleed, at least the mess will be all on *his* floor. *Not now, Hayden!*

I wait, holding my breath. Their voices begin to get softer.

And then, they're gone. I exhale so loud, yet I'm so hot with nerves. I run over to the sink and splash water on my face.

This is too much. I pull out my phone and click on my contacts.

My thumb hovers over Colbey's name, but I look up at the mirror. I'm so close to calling Colbey. So close. But I don't.

Sometimes, you only have yourself to convince.

That's what Tokyo posted with the first song I saw.

There are loads of people here, I tell myself. Jared and his friends won't hurt me. Not in public.

And what would Dad or Colbey think if I called them to pick me up because I couldn't handle it? Dad said it would be okay, but I don't think it will.

I take a deep breath. I put my phone away. I reline my hair, so it doesn't look like I've been running for my life, and then go to the door.

After a quick trip for a soft drink, I head outside. I try to ignore blushing at the sight of the few guys and girls in their underwear in the swimming pool. Beyond the large rock, where water falls off and into the pool and hot tub, there's nobody I notice across the grass.

I contemplate whether to go over to the people on the deck chairs to my left. My hands feel clammy, but I mean, how else do people socialise and make new friends?

I take a step forward.

Maybe being the drink finder isn't such a bad idea?

"Hey Jas-mine! We're wai-ting for a drink!"

Across the garden, there's a group of girls and guys around a table—with an arm-flailing Chloe Cassadentini, who looks like she's already had some drink.

A blonde-haired girl carries some drinks towards them—having to almost dodge around a beefy guy about to jump into the pool. My body tenses when I see Jared among the people by the table.

There's a loud splash. Water hits my clothes.

Great.

"Didn't anyone tell you it's a guaranteed splash zone if you stand by the pool?"

I spin around to see who it is. "Billie." I try to stay calm but am excited. She's wearing a black dress underneath a denim jacket. Her dark orange hair looks just as wavy, but somehow, it's bigger.

"I never really said, but thanks for helping Zeke," Billie says. "And sorry for going at you."

"It's alright. You were being a good friend."

"I guess." She looks down at the ground.

I can't believe she's here. *I've been looking all over school every day to see you both again.* "How is Zeke?"

"See for yourself." Billie turns on the spot and begins to walk. Nervously, I take that as an invite and follow.

We pass the occupied hot tub, where I'm greeted in amazement by an opening in the large waterfall rock hidden from the pool. A table and a padded booth sit inside the rock. There is one girl and two guys, one of whom looks rather tall, sitting down at the table.

"Hey, guess who I found."

"Billie, please tell me you didn't actually invite the old woman we found rolling watermelons down the aisles at the grocery store?" I hear Zeke's voice ask. Everyone at the table turns to see us. Or rather, they smile towards Billie and then stare at me.

"Hayden!" Zeke launches out of the booth. "My hero! Hold me." I laugh and almost don't catch him when he dramatically collapses into me. Billie rolls her eyes. "Guys, this is the guy I was telling you about."

"Which time? The first time or the nine-hundred thousand and seventy-eighth time?" The other girl says from the table, wearing a slick white and black outfit with a phone in her hand.

"Whatever, Antonia," Zeke says with one eye open at her as he remains leaning back in my hold. His short brown hair grazes my arm when he lifts himself up. He smacks the side of my arm. "Honestly man, you turned up when I needed you the most. Although, I thought I might have to call Jennifer Love Hewitt for advice—like you've been ghosting since. But, anyway, thanks again for helping me."

I try to hide my smile—it sounds like he's been wondering where I've been these last few days too.

"Hey, we're about to play a game of Toniabilzekcre. Want to join us?"

"Toni-bil-what?"

"Sorry, I keep forgetting it's not actually a game that's gone beyond us four," Zeke laughs. "Tonia-bil-zek-ker. A drinking game we made up."

I open my mouth to answer but stop. Zeke must have seen my contemplation. "Unless you've got to go back to other friends?"

There's something warm when Zeke says those words. It's not *other people* or *be somewhere else* or just *friends.* It's *other friends.* I don't even know two of them, but the fact he said it makes me feel already welcomed.

"No, I can. It's just, I'm not drinking," I say quietly and then add, "Tonight." They'll probably think it's lame if they know the truth.

"You can still play without alcohol," Zeke replies as he escorts me to the booth.

"You're not the only one not drinking." Billie shakes her car keys in the air with one hand. "Besides, you won't want to miss out on the fun; the game's just as confusing sober as it is drunk."

With no reason to back out, I agree and sit under the rock in the curved booth—in between Billie and Zeke.

"Now the rules are simple—" Zeke begins. "Actually, where are my manners? Everybody, this is Hayden. Hayden, allow me to introduce you to us. First up, Antonia Lu—which fun fact for you here—"

"Here he goes again," Billie murmurs.

"—Antonia in Latin means 'invaluable' and, in Chinese, Lu means 'musical note' – so really Antonia, your parents named you a pointless sound."

"Autocorrect: it's invaluable as in priceless and being excellent, actually," the girl says. She puts her phone down and offers a hand. I shake it.

"And then, of course, you know Billie and me already." Zeke points to Billie on my other side. "And finally, Dacre here used to be one of the shortest in our year until, like, what? Last year? He came back from summer, and then, poof! Still small."

Billie and Antonia chuckle. I don't—he's sat down, but at a guess, I'd say the guy's easily over six feet tall.

"Yeah, so small we have to be careful where we sit," Antonia comments.

"Oh. Ha. Ha," the other boy says and takes a swig of his beer. I guess it's some in-joke on his height. "I remember you. You smacked a volleyball into Jared Steele's face the other week, right?"

The girls turn to me. "That was you?"

I quickly tell them it was an accident.

"Good on you, I'd say," Billie comments. "Even if this is his party. Brave being here."

I shuffle in my seat.

"Hey, don't sweat it." Zeke pats my back. "The guy's head is so big it was impossible to miss it." And just like that, Zeke cheers me up again.

Zeke, with the help of others, then explains the rules for Toniabilzekcre, and we begin to play.

Basically, we go around in a circle, and each say 'Toniabilzekcre' till it is the group's seventh time—that person then adds a command to do. We then go again, saying Toniabilzekcre and then the person with the eighth turn must do the command—and, if done correctly, they add a new command to follow for the ninth turn. If somebody goes wrong, they drink, and we start again. We keep going till we give up. I won't lie; it's a little confusing to begin with—then gets more as we add more commands.

"There's me, my brother Colbey, my sister Robin, and my dad. Mom's back in Georgia. They split," I lie with the last part.

"Ah, sorry to hear that. Do the others go to our school?" Billie asks.

"Toniabilzekcre." Dacre starts a new round. "Think that'd be effed up if their dad also went to our school."

"Ha. Ha," Billie swats his arm. "That's not what I meant."

"No, my dad's a dentist. It's just me and my sister Robin, who go to our school."

"Thanks for clarifying that your dad doesn't go—wait, Robin Mallard's your sister?" Zeke asks.

"Yeah. Why? Do you know her?"

"Everyone knows who she is. She's like with the popular lot in senior year," Antonia says. "She's got a wicked sense of fashion. Oh, sorry, Toniabilzekcre."

"Wicked? Didn't realise we'd gone back to the nineties," Billie smirks.

It turns out Zeke, Billie and Dacre have been friends since very young. Antonia moved to Orlando in middle school and became friends after being grouped with Zeke and Dacre for a science project—which went horribly wrong. They didn't get a good grade for it, Dacre says, but they got a new friend instead.

They're juniors, which pleases me, except Billie, who is a senior.

Soon, the game has so many commands after the seven Toniabilzekcres. Like the fifteenth turn, you must keep two fingers on your ear so you look like you're the President's security guard speaking to the President—and you can't remove them unless you land on the fifteenth turn again. It's getting too ridiculous, and yet, somehow, we all suddenly focus, sitting on the edge of our seats because we all want to complete the latest round successfully. Billie. Zeke. Dacre. Antonia. And then me. We start to invest in the game.

When Antonia finishes the seventh Toniabilzekcre, I spin a coin on the table for the eighth turn and then slam it down with my hand. Heads is facing up. We cheer. Billie raises a glass to Antonia for the next turn. Ten – Zeke quickly spits out a tongue-twister sentence—but he says it right.

Dacre then takes a sip and reminds us not to laugh last.

"Toniabilzekcre," Antonia says in a Canadian twang. Accent time from now on. Zeke added this command for twelve. Next – everybody rushes to where I point the camera on my phone. Billie dives at the last second and manages to get in the shot; everyone's in, so I sip my soft drink.

Billie leaves the booth to try to herd some people going by as if they were sheep. Antonia laughs so we all copy because number eleven's command was Last One Laughing; should somebody laugh at any point, then we must laugh as well and the last person drinks. Dacre's last.

"Come in, Mr President," Zeke says in an abysmal attempt to sound Australian and then, "Finally!" He removes his two fingers from near his ear.

"Come on—only four to go!" Antonia yells in excitement—in what I assume is Scottish.

Sixteen. Dacre looks around. "Anybody ever had a one-night stand?"

Billie and Zeke raise their hands. Antonia smiles. "Well, well, well."

"Not with each other!" Billie jokes. Zeke throws a finger down his throat. I laugh. Everybody follows. Antonia's last.

Antonia points to herself and Billie, and they swap seats.

"You just had to," Billie tuts when she realises what comes next.

Eighteen. That person, who is me, must pour a drink into the mouth of the person on their right with a straight arm while sat down—which is now Billie. She waits anxiously as I grab her drink, lift it high into the air, and then pour. It spills all down Billie's neck. Zeke laughs—we all join in. Dacre's last. I apologise.

And then finally—it's all on Antonia. She stands up and grabs a piece of candy. She throws it into the air. It lands in her mouth. We all jump and cheer in excitement!

I fall into the hype like the others when we've taken a swig of our drinks and play out a mix of cheering and laughing.

Everyone's ecstatic. So am I.

They might be happy just from completing a game, but my lips can't stop smiling because I'm happy that I'm in on it.

"Think we may have overdone it," Billie says, tapping my arm. I follow her gaze to see nearly everybody who is still outside on this side of the garden is staring at us.

"Ah, who cares," Zeke laughs. We join in—because he couldn't be more right.

7.

FROM: TokyoCherryDustZ89@TokyoCherryDustZ89.com
TO: BlueC0ast1@bretteodmail.com
DATE: Wed 18th October, 8:44 AM
SUBJECT: Re: There's So Much Out There

I'm really pleased you loved Luna Lunalore and that their song Cactus got you pencil-tapping through class.

Do I care a lot about music? Good question, Brisbane.

I love new music. But I love the '80s scene more. Hey, your Dad likes that, too, right? Maybe I should go to an '80s bar with him? ;) Anyway, the fact that there are bands today influenced by the electronic '80s, or disco even, like Luna Lunalore, is a bonus for me.

These guys only have just over 2,000 followers online. That's it. I think it's a shame when there are talented people out there, and they don't have the recognition they deserve.

I mean, out of 3,000 odd people at our school, I bet a twentieth would like to make music or sing or do something music related. Or think of a bar that has different local music acts performing every night. Then you begin to realise that there's more than one school and one bar in Orlando. There's more than one city in Florida, then that Florida isn't the only state in America, and finally that America isn't the only country in the world!

You imagine all the schools and bars and clubs across the globe—meaning there are thousands, if not millions, of individuals who wish or are trying to make a living out of music and perform their own songs—songs they have created from the depths of their souls and experiences. And for what? Only 0.0005%, if even that, to be heard on the radio or seen on TV. Some may get a little buzz where they're from but nowhere else. And when you think of the songs that we hear in the charts, at shopping malls and clubs or that we put on our playlists because it's mainstream and everyone's talking about it, it's just an extremely tiny, fragmented piece of the universe of music that's out there.

And I find it sad. A terrible misfortune that there's so much great music across the world, but hardly anyone knows about them. For artists and bands to come and go without being truly heard.

I just can't help but wonder why more people don't go to discover what's out there. You know? We just stick to what becomes popular or what we're told we should like. And I just wonder why?

Don't get me wrong, I love mainstream music, but I feel everybody should be heard.

Sorry, I'm probably getting too deep about it. But that's why I care. It's not that I know more about music than other people. It's just I'm searching for more and seeing what's out there.

-Tokyo

FROM: BlueC0ast1@bretteodmail.com
TO: TokyoCherryDustZ89@TokyoCherryDustZ89.com
DATE: Wed 18th October, 6:08 PM
SUBJECT: Re: There's So Much Out There

Wow, it's kind of remarkable but scary when you say it like that. I mean, I don't even know where to start. But you are right. I guess people don't think about it like that.

I've never really gone out to find new music; I just let whatever I hear around me come to me like most, I guess.

You don't need to apologise. You really are very passionate about it. Maybe others have noticed your posts at school? I mean, it got my attention. Perhaps other people are discovering new music because of you or just by themselves. Think about how many music blogs like to post about new acts or songs online to their followers. Must be thousands around the world. At least there are others out there who want the same as you. That must count for something.

You don't ever want to go to an '80s bar with my dad. He'd talk about the '80s shows that are no longer on TV, and then he'd be on the karaoke all night singing the Human League and the B-52s. #YouveBeenWarned

-Brisbane

FROM: TokyoCherryDustZ89@TokyoCherryDustZ89.com
TO: BlueC0ast1@bretteodmail.com
DATE: Wed 18th October, 9:56 PM
SUBJECT: Re: There's So Much Out There

Yeah, there are people who create music blogs. Music has gotten broader over the years, so I guess maybe some people are becoming more open to hearing more different genres and styles than just mainstream.

Thanks for trying to make me smile. I was a bit down before I wrote the email, and I guess I vented it through my last email. I went on far too long about my opinions. Don't worry, though. I won't start a rally in the streets. But thanks for trying to see it from my perspective.

You make that sound like it's a bad thing? Because, ooooh, I am so going to go to a bar with your dad now. Someone get the mics ready…Rock Lobster time!

And please tell me you didn't use a hashtag in an email? Maybe I should teach you never to write hashtags as well as show you new music. #SayingItLikeItIs :D

-Tokyo

FROM: BlueC0ast1@bretteodmail.com
TO: TokyoCherryDustZ89@TokyoCherryDustZ89.com
DATE: Wed 18th October, 10:37 PM
SUBJECT: Re: There's So Much Out There

That's okay. Glad you're better. And I'll try and stop the hashtags, so you don't have to teach me. I hardly use them anyway #SoTrue #DontGoToAKaraokeBarWithMyDadAndSingRockLobster #OtherwiseIllStartAStreetRallyProtest

-Brisbane

8.

I walk out of the school cafeteria and am instantly greeted by the brightness of the sun. Georgia's like one state away from Florida, but the weather feels totally different here.

The KingsgateLeeConnect board sits across the yard. The orange screen changes to show three new posts at the top—none are from Tokyo. However, she has been posting more songs recently—which always excites me. I'd like to think she's posted more because we've been emailing, but I don't be cheeky enough to ask.

Over to the side, my usual table waits for me by the walls and a couple of trees. It's empty, as always. But I turn left.

I walk through the maze of tables and students going by. I enter the open area and spot my new table in the distance. One I now share with Zeke, Billie, Dacre and Antonia.

"Hey," Zeke says, waving at me before the others do. They're all there but Dacre. I sit down.

Antonia slams her hands on the table. "Cheese and rice! Have you seen someone's just left a floater in the swimming pool?"

"That's shitty of them," Zeke comments.

Billie scrunches her nose up. "How?"

"Well, I guess somebody went in and used it as a toil—"

"Not that!" Billie snaps, which thankfully stops Antonia. "I mean, how'd we know that when we've been here for the entirety of lunch with you? Of course, you'd know that if you bothered to look away from that."

I follow Billie's eyes to the phone Antonia's holding.

Antonia shrugs. "Well, it's the best thing to get all the latest gossip."

"Nobody cares if it's news like that."

"I beg to differ."

"Oh-kay," Zeke says, twiddling his fingers—he turns to me. "So, how's life after joining our table?"

"Erm, it's good," I say, a little caught off guard.

Zeke launches himself away from taking the sip from his drink. "Just GOOD? Think you'll find this is the best table in the entire school. For firstly and most importantly, you're with us."

He flails his hands out to the table—Billie moans when drops of his drink spill onto her jacket. He makes me chuckle. "We're outside in the sunlight, but if it rains, we're okay 'cause we got this good old tree to cover us. We can see everyone around us."

"Plus the KingsgateLeeConnect board," Antonia adds. Billie rolls her eyes—so Antonia adds, "And Billie can drool over the footballers training on the pitch."

"Urgh," Billie scoffs. "I have a boyfriend, remember? And even if I didn't, I'd much rather watch R2-D2 do a strip tease, thank you very much."

"Well, you're in luck."

I then have to do a double take—Zeke stands up on the bench. He starts making weird robotic noises as he shifts side to side and moves his stretched-out arms, which are down by his sides, closer to his front, topped off by pouting his lips.

Over our laughs and Zeke's noises, I must agree with him. And the view is pretty good here, too. Across the pitch, there is a line of trees; the tops of buildings are poking out from a distance.

"Do I even want to know what he's doing?" Dacre asks as he approaches the table with a puzzled expression.

"R2-D2 strip tease, of course," I say.

"Why, of course," Dacre smiles as he puts his tray down and joins us. He opens his bottle of water. "Hey, did you hear about the floater in the pool? Just seen it on the board."

"Not another word," Billie says, pointing a finger at Antonia, who looks rather smug. She turns to look beside her. "Zeke, get down!"

He's still R2-D2 strip teasing.

Before I get a chance to sit down in his office, Mr Gauran informs me that my scale of humour is still low. He then decides that we'll go outside for a walk instead—what with the weather so nice.

He gets off his seat and walks with me in silence as we go through the school. Some of the other students we pass look over, probably knowing who the guy beside me is and wondering why's that kid walking around with the school counsellor or what's wrong with that kid. Mr Gauran doesn't say anything.

However, as we reach the field outside and head towards the pitch, I cave from the silence and say, "I'm sorry for storming out of your office last time." I only just manage to stop my mouth from nearly telling him the real reason why I left.

"Upset you didn't make the swim team?"

I question if Mr Gauran knows I was lying about the swim try-outs and if he perhaps did speak to Coach Rugrosso about it.

"Well, whatever the reason was, I hope it's okay now."

I nod.

We walk more in silence.

"Aren't you going to ask me questions?"

"Depends. Do you want me to?"

I glance up at him. *Maybe he does know? What trick has he got?* "Isn't that how it normally goes? I answer questions you have, then you tick or cross or write them down and give some results." That's how the doctors at the hospital did it.

"I guess, but where's the book to say we must? I don't think sitting and forcing you to answer my questions is always the best way to go about things. I could ask if you've opened yourself more to the world yet, but I believe you're not that comfortable in talking about it, even though it's something I asked you to look into."

Some students in their track kits run by on the track beside us. My hands remain in my hoody's pocket, shuffling a little.

Mr Gauran stops, resting his arms on a wooden railing beside us. "I may work at this school, but I don't want you to tell me how you are because you must; I want you to say because you want to. I don't care what we talk about in our chats. If you wanna say History sucked because Mr Riley mumbled for the entire lesson, and it sent half the class asleep, tell me. If you wanna say *hey, Mr Gauran, your bald head reminds me of Professor X* then—well, actually, that's kind of rude, but you're scale of humour would go up—but you get the point. I want to hear what's going on in your mind. Sure, I'll ask serious things, but these are times to give you a moment to step away from your life and reflect on it or get whatever you want off your chest. And then for me to see the best solution we can take to move forward."

I bite my bottom lip. I appreciate where Mr Gauran is coming from, but that doesn't mean it's any easier to open up.

"Well…" I try to think, "Mr Riley does mumble." But I quickly add, "But I do like his lessons." The thought of badmouthing one teacher to another scares me.

"And how are you finding the other lessons?" I reply they're okay. "Okay? I've been told you've even handed in some end-of-term assignments already. That's good going, I'd say. And it's good to see missing the last few months of last year hasn't affected your grades."

I don't like that he brought up the end of last school year. But I respect the way he's worded this conversation—making a comment instead of drilling questions at me to see if I think I've improved.

"Thanks."

Mr Gauran pats my shoulder, and we begin to walk—back towards school. "Don't thank me; I didn't do any of it. And it's good to see you're doing well with your classes and assignments." He pauses. "It's a shame about the swimming team, though."

"Yeah, but it's fine," I answer, ignoring the hurt from Jared and his friends and also my shame from lying. "I guess I'm doing okay."

"Good, but how so? What things are you doing?"

Well, I walked into that! Mr Gauran stops to face me. I stop, even though I don't want to.

"Hayden, please don't tell me that that long talk I just gave didn't go in. These meetings are for us to be honest with each other. How can we progress if we aren't truthful?"

I take a moment to think. He's only trying to help.

"I've not posted anything on KingsgateLeeConnect. And, I haven't joined an extracurricular activity, really, but I've found some people to be with."

"I've noticed you've moved places at lunch."

I look up to him.

"But I'm glad." He gives a brief smile and then walks on. I stare bewildered at him. The man always seems to know more than he lets on. "But you still need to try and push yourself out there more. And what else?"

I move and pick up my pace till I fall in line beside him.

"Well, I, I," I stumble on what to say. "I do like that we're outside, especially when the weather's good."

Mr Gauran nods.

"And I suppose for you, too, it beats your office view."

"Was that a joke?" Mr Gauran looks at me—nerves hit me—I've pushed it. Then a smirk appears on the man's face. I smile back. "Funny—you're onto a two out of five now."

9.

FROM: TokyoCherryDustZ89@TokyoCherryDustZ89.com
TO: BlueC0ast1@bretteodmail.com
DATE: Sat 21st October, 9:42 PM
SUBJECT: Re: Caldera Boulevard

Come on, Brisbane! You're going to have to be more elaborate about the song if you want me to open up more about the name Tokyo. The point of your music adventure is so you can be exposed to the world of music, to the beat of it, to the lyrics of it, to the emotion of it. You need to go further in and try and understand why you feel a connection with the song. A sentence simply won't do.

-Tokyo

P.S. I, too, have had no luck in finding a dog named Brisbane in Florida. I thought about buying a cuddly toy dog and naming it Brisbane, but I don't think that counts.

FROM: BlueC0ast1@bretteodmail.com
TO: TokyoCherryDustZ89@TokyoCherryDustZ89.com
DATE: Sat 21st October, 10:46 PM
SUBJECT: Re: Caldera Boulevard

Ok. Ok. I get it. This is just new to me…trying to be open.

I guess the lyrics are of the singer being in love and would do anything the person wants because they love them. It sounds quite summery. But it's titled Paradise Migraine, so maybe it's not as perfect as it sounds. And I now think the singer's basically saying they're under that person's spell—and yet would still do anything for them. And it gives the song a new level of depth—a haunting one to this upbeat rhythm. I don't know if that's the singer's intention, but that's what it makes me think.

And when I put myself in their shoes, I think of someone I loved. My mom.

I looked up to her. Somebody who was always there for me. Well, that's what I thought. A parent abandoning and walking out of their family to never return is a cruel thing. Hurt me…more than anybody could imagine. I had to face some hard-hitting moments for it to sink in so I could try and move on.

And I guess hearing Paradise Migraine reminds me that I once thought everything was perfect. That I'd have done anything for someone I trusted. And it hurts when a sudden truth came and hit my family.

You might think that's pathetic or sad, but I don't know, I'm just trying to say how it makes me feel.

-Brisbane

FROM: TokyoCherryDustZ89@TokyoCherryDustZ89.com
TO: BlueC0ast1@bretteodmail.com
DATE: Sat 21st October, 11:27 PM
SUBJECT: Re: Caldera Boulevard

Brisbane, I'm sorry to hear that happened. I've had my own share of family issues, but I can't imagine what it would have been like to have a parent willingly leave like that. I'm sorry. But I'm pleased that you've somewhat been able to move on from it.

I think that's the beauty of music. It can evoke so many emotions for us. Thanks for sharing.

I suppose I best be open, too, then. I chose Tokyo because, obviously, I want to go and see it, but there are two main reasons. First, I guess the way to word it is that I feel like the city, and yet, at the same time, I also don't. What I mean is Tokyo has many diverse aspects—more than people realise—and I feel I, too, have many different attributes. Some people know and want to see, and some I don't dare share. Some I know my friends wouldn't get.

I've been with my friends since kindergarten or middle school. And I guess they've grown to have their set ways. Ways I've realised recently I don't admire or want to follow anymore. So it's an awful big leap…to change or show them I have different tastes. And not simply music. I mean with much more. It might be considered vain or petty to think that—that I'm scared my friends may no longer want to be my friend if I change or am not like them—but truth be told, it's a leap I don't think I can take yet.

-Tokyo

FROM: BlueC0ast1@bretteodmail.com
TO: TokyoCherryDustZ89@TokyoCherryDustZ89.com
DATE: Sat 21st October, 11:59 PM
SUBJECT: Re: Caldera Boulevard

Thanks. I've not spoken to anybody else at school about my mom.

I don't think anybody should ever have to hide their passions or interests. If you knew who I am and what I'm like, you'd probably think I'm a bit condescending saying that—but I still say it because I understand that it takes time. To share yourself with others. I still am trying. But I guess if you're not able to express your emotions, and in this case, follow your passions, then you're not really being you. And from what they say, it's hard to keep denying who you are.

I sound like a fortune cookie or something a palm reader might say. I'm still learning myself, to be open, that is—and I've just got to remember that and learn to be able to do that. Maybe the people you're scared to be more yourself around with won't judge you as much as you think.

-Brisbane

P.S. You said relating yourself to Tokyo is the first reason. What's the other?

FROM: TokyoCherryDustZ89@TokyoCherryDustZ89.com
TO: BlueC0ast1@bretteodmail.com
DATE: Sun 22nd October, 12:24 AM
SUBJECT: Re: Caldera Boulevard

You do sound like a fortune cookie—well, maybe not fortune, an advice cookie? I wish I could do as you say, but it's not that simple.

Ah, yes, the other reason for Tokyo. My father. Japan is known for its cherry blossom trees. The Ueno Onshi Park in Tokyo is one of the best places to see cherry blossoms. Apparently, 1,000 trees.

My father said that the uniqueness and speciality of cherry blossoms are that they only peak for about one week before they begin to wither. May not seem much, but thousands of people go to Japan just to see them—see them at their most beautiful. They even have festivals to celebrate it. I have photos on my bedroom wall, and the trees do look wonderful.

My father used to call me Cherry Blossom when I was younger—which isn't shorter than my actual name, but he loved calling me it. He even gave me the photos of them. And he'd keep reminding me that when I was little, I apparently asked him once if he called me Cherry Blossom every day because he thought I only bloomed to my peak only once a year. But he said, 'On the contrary, it's to remind myself that you don't peak only once a year. But every day.'

-Tokyo

10.

As I pay for my food in the school cafeteria and head to go outside, I realise that I really like talking to Tokyo, and I seem to be more open to her. Maybe it's because there's a screen that keeps our identities hidden, but still, it's quite nice and more honest. I'm surprised I spoke about my mom to her, but I'm pleased I did. I even tell her why I chose Brisbane.

I used to love the regular family road trips up the Eastern Coast so much, seeing the animals and the coastlines, that I want to go to the Great Barrier Reef and the Gold Coast in Australia. A place so diverse with species and sea life and has a different lifestyle than here. And signing the emails as them or GBR for short doesn't flow as nice as the city of Brisbane, which is near the latter. I'm fascinated so much that I want to study Marine Biology or Marine Science at college. But I didn't tell Tokyo that bit in case she tries to figure out who I am and—

The door to outside abruptly bumps into me!

I keep a firm hold of the tray—but there's green covering the other side of the door.

"Oh no!" A girl yelps. The green pieces of paper soar in the air and scatter across the ground. There are lots of them.

I walk through to outside, place my tray down and begin helping the girl collect them. "I'm sorry."

The girl is on her knees, gathering them up. "It's okay."

When we have all of them, I get up and hand her the pieces of paper.

"Thanks." She lifts her head up, moving her blonde hair out of her view.

I think I've seen her before, but I can't place where.

I grab my food tray, then ask to be polite, "What are they for?"

Her eyes flick down and then back up to me. "The posters? I'm looking for a Spanish tutor. I sort of need help."

"Spanish? I know Spanish."

The girl stares at me—her eyes open. "Yes, you're in my Spanish class, right?"

I can't recall if we are or not, but I nod. Maybe that's where I've seen her before.

"You're pretty good. Right?"

I blush. "I'm okay, I guess." I cough to give myself time to brush my act up—and to hopefully sound more confident the next time I speak. "Well, my aunt and cousins are Spanish."

The girl's face turns into a smile. "You'd be perfect. Do you think you could teach me?"

"What? Me? No—I—"

"Please, I really could do with the help."

"I—" I pause. The back of my neck feels like it's starting to sweat—I rub my hand against it. I don't know how I've got myself into this position—I wasn't implying I could teach—but how can I tell her no?

My eyes catch onto something in the background. Mr Gauran is talking to some kids at a table.

Just be more open to opportunities.

His words linger in mind, but then so does Tokyo's. *Sometimes, you only have yourself to convince.*

I look back at the girl. She's staring right back at me—clinging to whatever comes out of my mouth next. Something on her face tells me she really means it. *She must be if she's printed all these posters.*

"I guess I could do it—"

"Really? Oh, thank you! That's great. Thank you." She looks down at the pieces of paper, nearly chuckling to herself. "Wish I'd found you before I started putting these up."

I grin and say, "Perhaps best keep them should you decide I'm not a good teacher. You know, you could have just asked people on the board." I point to the KingsgateLeeConnect board across the courtyard.

"Oh, I don't use that," the girl replies. She turns to the board. "Oh great."

I look over.

Chloe Cassadentini
OMG, where are you, Jasmine? Get over here now!

Angela Branno
Yes, Jasmine Olivia-Claire Keery – we must go over our Halloween plans

With Chloe's post is a selfie of her on a table outside with some girls behind, one I assume is Angela, as well as some boys—which includes Jared Steele.

She was the girl I saw at Jared's party, taking drinks to a drunk Chloe on the table.

"I guess you're Jasmine, then?"

The girl nods. "And you must be Hayden?"

I pause. Jasmine points to the board.

Zeke Palladino
OMG, where are you, Hayden? Get over here now!

Dacre Ronsan
Yes, Hayden Whatever-Your-Middle-Name-Sorry-We-Haven't-Asked-Yet-Is Mallard – we must go over our Halloween plans

I look over to the usual table—Dacre, Billie and Antonia are waving me over. Zeke, however, waves frantically. I shake my head in embarrassment. "Yes."

"Well, looks like we best go to them," Jasmine says. "Is after school today okay with you?"

I nod, trying to ignore the hands waving at me from the side.

"Great, meet you at the school entrance."

A blue car pulls up to the school entrance. The window goes down to reveal Jasmine in the driving seat. "Hey, do you mind if we study somewhere else?"

I say it's fine and hop in. I messaged Robin earlier that I no longer needed a lift. All I got back was *fine*.

Jasmine explains on the way that she prefers to be away from the pressures of what school is meant to do for you—where she can learn freely and calmly. And I sort of get it. The idea of me being at the hospital was to get better, but that didn't mean it was any easier when doctors and nurses constantly surrounded me.

She arrives at our studying spot. A big red neon sign shines above the white-walled building before us. *The Cerise Wave Diner.* I smile—I'd already planned to meet Zeke and the others here later tonight.

We head inside the '50s-styled diner, find a table, order drinks and get down to work. Jasmine wants to be better at everything, but with a one-to-one speaking test a week on Monday, she wants to brush up on that first.

"*Bueno,* but it's *hacen.* Not *hacer,*" I correct Jasmine after I do a mock test.

"*Claro.*" Jasmine then playfully taps her hand on her head. "Because it's *they.*" I tell her she's correct. "I'm going to need a miracle to pass."

She looks over at me. Rosy in the cheeks. "Sorry—I didn't mean because of your teaching, I meant I just—"

"No, I know what you meant."

"Thanks. I mean, *es frustrante porque es difícil.*"

"We've got time. And hey, that Spanish was pretty *bueno,*" I say while giving her an okay sign.

She glances down, probably to hide the look of awkwardness or to think what a creep this boy is sitting opposite her. My light-hearted joke has fallen flat.

But when she lifts her head back up, there's a smile. "Maybe I should find something to get angry at before I walk into the exam?"

We laugh.

The table vibrates. It's Jasmine's phone. It's been vibrating quite a bit. Probably from 'the Populars' group—that's what Zeke and the others call the popular kids in our year. However, Jasmine's not once checked her phone.

"You can take it if you want."

"No, it's fine," Jasmine replies, looking at me. "Probably a group chat that's manifested into a constant stream of messages. Won't be anything important."

Soon enough, the lesson finishes, and Jasmine has to go. I stay sat in the booth as Jasmine packs her bag. "Thanks, Hayden, *muchas gracias.*"

"*De nada.*"

"How much do you want?" Jasmine asks. I stare, perplexed. "For the tutoring."

I immediately object—I seriously wasn't expecting money. What surprises me more is my nervousness didn't scare her off through the tutoring because she thanks me for not charging and then arranges another lesson with me before saying goodbye. And that makes me happy.

However, when I view the menu later after everybody arrives, I see I do need money. Since Tokyo's suggestions, I've been buying the songs and albums she's been recommending. And doing the chores at home isn't bringing enough in.

"None of the Populars would have missed a little spec from their wad of cash," Billie jokes—I had to confess money is low when they noticed I'd gone for just a small dish as a main.

"I don't think Jasmine's like that," I say. And I don't. And taking money from Jasmine didn't feel right.

"Well, what you need, I think, is a job," Zeke states. "A part-time or weekend job."

Some of the others around nod.

"A job?" I ask him—because honestly, although it may be a good idea, I have no clue what job I could do with the little skills I have.

"Yeah." The others smile, and before anybody can give suggestions, Zeke then says, "And I know just the place."

Zeke turns into a car park by the International Drive. I come in awe at the view in front of me—so much so that I don't take my eyes away as we get out of the car.

Through glimpses in between and poking above the wall of lush-green palm trees, there appears to be ancient white ruins and a huge man-made mountain towering before us. A family cheers. As we walk towards the entrance gateway that's guarded by two large Greek merman soldier statues, I see the crazy golf course holes nestled on and around the mountain and meandering through the ruins on the ground.

My eyes latch onto the source of the biggest noise—a huge waterfall cascading down the side of the mountain and vanishing behind the trees.

"Welcome to working in paradise. A.K.A. My aunt's crazy golf. Or, to be precise, Mt. Okesea!"

"Well, she still has to give me the job first."

And somehow, my dad agreed I could have a job—I think he spoke to Colbey last night after I asked, for not long after my brother got in, Dad came to my room and said I could apply—but *one weeknight and one weekend day shift a week max*, he made clear to me, *and if I see it's too much, or your grades drop, I'm ending it.* I hugged him to show my thankfulness to him.

Zeke leads the way to the office and then introduces me to his aunt.

I expected a full-blown interview from a smartly dressed woman, yet before me sits a woman in black leather motorbike clothing, with a white T-shirt that has printed on it the words *Mrs Efron.*

"So long as you're better than me—" Zeke begins.

"Anybody's better than you," Aunt Sandra says, holding a hotdog in her hand, then faces me. "You're hired."

We shake hands and I leave with a job just like that. I never knew interviews were so easy.

Zeke first takes me around the course, giving me tips and tricks on each hole. The course begins outside by the stoned temple ruins, the numerous mermen and mermaid sculptures and the little streams of water. Then it goes in and up the mountain—with holes poking in and out of the sides—before coming back down and finishing off near the entrance.

"Now, this is probably the true test of whether you have skill or not," Zeke says at the last hole.

I question his statement because it's a simple hole, just a long incline that goes up to a hole at the bottom of a plinth. On top is a large, white-stoned letter *O*, which at the bottom inside has the carving of a mountain and the initials *Mt.* within that—the company's logo. However, I soon see the hole isn't easy. The incline is jagged, with no barriers, and with a width no more than the size of a hand.

"It's a hole in one or nothing," Zeke says. He points to other holes at the bottom of either side of the incline. "Where the losing balls go. To a compartment in the plinth." I realise that's why the green is all enclosed by a metal cage—so nobody can cheat.

Zeke walks around and shows me the compartment. He takes something out. A bold pink ball.

"Best part is if you get the ball in that hole at the plinth, then you make the mountain come alive."

"Alive?"

"Yep, Mt. Okesea comes alive, kind of, and water blasts out the top. It's really cool."

"Okay," I say sceptically—this feels like one of his jokes. "And the reason you've got that ball is to show me this finale?"

"Oh no, not at all, Mr Mallard," Zeke grins. He goes around and places the pink ball down at the start. "If you want to see the magnificence of this mountain, then you must make the hole-in-one yourself—or maybe see someone else do it on your shift. It's like losing your virginity. When that cherry's popped, it's popped. You know, right?"

My cheeks blush. I don't.

"And if I show you now like this, cheating the hole almost, then you ain't gonna get that fine euphoric feeling you should be getting."

I flick between the ball and Zeke—still unsure. "Right."

Zeke shoves a club into my chest. "Let's see if your moment is now."

I get into position. Then swing. The pink ball rolls under the metal caged wall. It begins the incline, hops over the first jagged drop—but the ball slows down and then suddenly rolls back to the bottom of the stage. It hits the wall, slides off—and then disappears into a losing hole in the ground.

"Ah well," Zeke shrugs. "Just ain't your time yet. You'll learn eventually how to run this place, for here, I am your Mr. Miyagi, young LaRusso."

I stare blankly at him.

"Really? *Karate Kid*? Wow, this is worse than I thought."

He takes me back near the entrance to the small hut where people pay to play golf. It's where we will mainly work. It's painted white and blue and styled like the gateway entrance. A wooden sign is above saying *Mt. Okesea Crazy Golf*. When we get there, there's somebody inside.

Zeke whistles. "Hey Kamala, say hello to our newest recruit."

Bent over, and with her back turned to us, we wait as the girl gets up from behind the counter inside.

"How many times do I have to tell you to put the clubs back on the club rack? Put them to the side, and they'll topple over—"

I hold my breath. The purple hair is immediately recognisable.

"You." And she definitely remembers me—me who knocked her drink onto her at Jared's party.

"You know each other?" Zeke asks, flicking his finger between us.

I scrunch my lips. Kamala doesn't say anything. One of her eyebrows is still light tinted yet it's now also raised at me.

"I'm sure you'll get along now that you'll be working at the same place."

Kamala's mouth drops to Zeke. "What?"

Before Kamala can make it any clearer that she hates me, we hear a family wanting to play golf approach the hut.

"I'll show you how to use the till another time," Zeke says as we walk away from the hut, leaving Kamala to deal with the family. "I mean, if looks could kill…that was nearly it. I don't get why, but Kamala's got the wrath of an Indian goddess."

We head through some trees. He's going to show me the restaurant, which is next to the other side of the mountain. We won't be working on it, but he says it's good to see it anyway.

"If we had superpowers, that would be hers." Zeke turns to point at his eyes and then at mine, as if shooting lasers out of them. "But don't sweat it. Kamala acts annoyed with everybody. And hey, she's probably angrier with me with the amount of silly stuff I've done. But it is who she is."

I try to take in Zeke's words, but it's still hard not to let go of the fact that somebody dislikes me when they hardly know me. It's not on the scale of Jared and his boys, but it's still irritating. But I just need to forget about it and try not to let it ruin the excitement—that I now have a job!

11.

FROM: BlueC0ast1@bretteodmail.com
TO: TokyoCherryDustZ89@TokyoCherryDustZ89.com
DATE: Fri 27th October, 12:36 PM
SUBJECT: Re: Seasons

Wow, Tokyo, you've gone beyond with this next choice. I gave Alliss a listen this morning and reached their Jacob album now at lunch—I think I should have waited until I got home. In my room and on my bed, just so I'm alone and can shove my face into a pillow so nobody can see how much their song Is Searching For Happiness Too Big Of A Journey? really hit me. Especially with knowing the backstory to it—to cancel their tour and take time out after their bandmate died in an accident, but then write new music because they knew their friend wouldn't want them to stop. I've just watched online the first TV performance they did since the accident—and I could really see their sorrow for him as they played. Their music is so hard and raw. I don't know how I'm going to focus on my lessons this afternoon after this.

And, sidenote, you watch the same film for each season every year? So you're a season geek? No, a season lover? A season-aholic? A fussy seasoner?

I don't really do that with my family. We have the regular TV shows we watch together, but not anything seasonal.

I'm guessing Christmas is your favourite season?

-Brisbane

FROM: TokyoCherryDustZ89@TokyoCherryDustZ89.com
TO: BlueC0ast1@bretteodmail.com
DATE: Fri 27th October, 4:48 PM
SUBJECT: Re: Seasons

Oh goodness, did you make it through the afternoon, ok?

I agree. Listening to that specific song at lunch was not the wisest of decisions. It made me cry when I first listened.

Really? We're going there with the season nicknames? Just you wait.

Yes, I take the seasons so seriously that me and my sister have a must-watch film each season. This weekend we'll be watching *Hocus Pocus* for Halloween. Christmas – *Home Alone*. New Year's Eve – *Some Like It Hot*. That isn't a film about NYE, but we used to watch it with our grandparents every year around then. And Tony Curtis and Jack Lemmon are great as the two best friends. And for Valentine's Day, it's *Ghost*.

Personally, I'd see myself as a season enthusiast. But I don't wear a Christmas jumper every day in December. Let's make that clear.

I love the happiness seasons give people and the closeness they bring everybody together, but Halloween is my fave…because it's not all jolly. Hear me out!

All the other celebrations are all about making and having things perfect in life—when sometimes they aren't. Halloween is the only occasion that actually rejoices in all things not perfect. To admire that some things aren't so sweet and loving. Again, should point out I'm not a girl who dresses in cloaks and swoops down the school corridors threatening to suck the blood of other students or run away from garlic, but it's my favourite season. A time for the fun and mischief.

That's sad you don't do that with your family. You should try this weekend with *Hocus Pocus*, or if it's too soon, you should watch *The Nightmare Before Christmas* as your first Christmas film—I'd say somewhere around Thanksgiving (you know, Halloween just gone, Christmas soon arriving), give it a try.

-Tokyo

FROM: BlueC0ast1@bretteodmail.com
TO: TokyoCherryDustZ89@TokyoCherryDustZ89.com
DATE: Fri 27th October, 5:32 PM
SUBJECT: Re: Seasons

All I can say is I just about managed to get through the lessons.

A season enthusiast? Hmm…more like a season-maniac from the sounds of it.

I've never looked at it like that. I suppose Halloween is special in its own right. Makes you wonder why there aren't more Halloween songs. There's Monster Mash by Bobby "Boris" Pickett & The Crypt-Kickers and Rocky Horror's Time Warp—nowhere near as many as Christmas.

You know my dad loves to remind my family every year that the Monster Mash is about monsters doing a dance called The Mash to a mash…and yet we're never told what the moves to the mash are or what the song they are listening to even sounds like—because the Monster Mash is about them listening to it and isn't the actual mash they hear.

I'm guessing if you're a Halloween person, you'll be out this weekend either haunting locals or partying?

-Brisbane

FROM: TokyoCherryDustZ89@TokyoCherryDustZ89.com
TO: BlueC0ast1@bretteodmail.com
DATE: Fri 27th October, 7:34 PM
SUBJECT: Re: Seasons

I most certainly will be out going to a party after trick-or-treating with my sister. I'll be dressed up, of course. You can't turn up to a Halloween party without a costume. What are your plans?

I'll ignore the maniac remark, Brisbane, and stick with enthusiast. Maybe it's not that I'm too into the seasons. Maybe others aren't into them enough? *cough* Brisbane *cough*

And maybe there should be more spooky-themed songs for this time of year. I think Rockwell's Somebody's Watching Me or Michael Jackson's Thriller must be the obvious choices.

That's insane! I wanna know what The Mash is! Hang on, is that music knowledge you've brought yourself to this adventure that I didn't know about? I think it is, Brisbane. You should have a drink this weekend to celebrate if you're at a party. I will in your honour.

-Tokyo

FROM: BlueC0ast1@bretteodmail.com
TO: TokyoCherryDustZ89@TokyoCherryDustZ89.com
DATE: Fri 27th October, 7:57 PM

SUBJECT: Re: Seasons

Fine, we'll stick with season-enthusiast. For now.
I won't be trick-or-treating, but I will be attending a party. I'm presuming you mean a high school party and not a family gathering. What are the chances we'll be at the same one?

-Brisbane

FROM: TokyoCherryDustZ89@TokyoCherryDustZ89.com
TO: BlueC0ast1@bretteodmail.com
DATE: Fri 27th October, 8:39 PM
SUBJECT: Re: Seasons

Thank you for finally appreciating and acknowledging my official role as titled season-enthusiast. I don't like that 'for now' part, though.
And yes, it's a high school party—a classic plot of somebody's parents aren't there so they've decided to throw a party. It's probably best we don't say whose house in case we actually are at the same one.

-Tokyo—Season Enthusiast

P.S. But it's true, we could be at the same house and not even realise it. And I admit, that's exciting.

12.

Every year, Dad finds a way to stop kids from getting sweets from our house on Halloween. Last year, he pretended to be a dead corpse hanging upside down from the tree on our front lawn so he could scare the kids into dropping their bags and running away—because, as a dentist, he's set on kids not overeating sweets.

I ask him while Colbey is giving him another cooking lesson what his plan is for tonight, concerned that I will return home later with either rotten egg stains on the front wall of the house or toilet paper thrown all over.

I shake my head when he tells me he's making them go apple bobbing for sweets in a barrel, but all the wrapped sweets are sugar-free mints!

"So toilet paper over our house it is," I joke. At least it's not raining tonight. Otherwise, it will be horrendous to remove.

Colbey smirks as he guides Dad on how to cut the peppers properly, like teaching a baby to walk, then looks over at me. "You don't look really Halloweeny."

I'm in my normal clothes. "My friends have it. A group outfit."

"Dad, watch—"

"My hands! Alright." Dad looks down, not before giving Colbey an aggressively forced smile.

The pair do make me laugh.

And, out of nowhere, it makes me think of how well Dad is doing after Mom leaving.

I forget that it must have been hard on him, too. Maybe still is. They were high school sweethearts. Yet I'm pleased he looks like he's doing well.

There's a car beep from outside. It will be Dacre.

"No drinking," Dad shouts as I leave the kitchen.

"I won't!"

"Wait—you never said how your first day at work was!"

To be honest, I'm surprised I didn't see Dad there sneakily hiding behind a tree, watching Zeke and I work. Or when I was cycling back from Mt. Okesea.

"It was good," I answer as I put my shoes on and then go to leave out the front door. "Have fun with the toilet paper!"

"Oh, brother," Billie murmurs from behind as she, Dacre and I exit the car a little further from Rafael Gago's house.

Zeke is stood on the sidewalk in normal clothes—but I double-glance in surprise when I notice Antonia. She's dressed up. All in pink and, more strikingly, wearing a blonde wig.

"Why's Antonia dressed like *Legally Blonde*?" Dacre asks.

"Oh, you've noticed?" Zeke says, arms crossed. Even without the irritation in his voice, I can tell he isn't pleased. "Well, somebody's decided to be a complete party pooper and ruin our plan."

"I never agreed to your idea," Antonia says back. She turns to Dacre. "And I'm not Elle from *Legally Blonde*. I'm Regina George from *Mean Girls*."

She then flicks the end of the blonde wig back as if that gives us a clue to know who.

"It's fine," Billie reassures Antonia. She turns to Zeke. "We can still do our plan."

Dacre walks around the car. We all follow and watch as he opens the trunk. We stare down at the costumes.

"So then," Zeke begins. "Ready for some fun, guys…or should that be…ready for some fun, *ya dirty kangaroos*."

I can't tell if it's brilliant or completely insane—but we're dressed as characters from Billie's favourite retro arcade game. Dacre tried to explain on the way that it's an anime-styled fighting game that focuses on a music band formed up of four red kangaroos, who must travel and fight through various lands to retrieve their music that was stolen from a rival band—a duo of a Humboldt penguin and a dolphin. Although it sounds like a kid's game, it apparently has a big adult following. We're dressed as the two bands. Billie's boyfriend, Andrew, is inside and will join our group outfit. There would have been all four kangaroos, but because Antonia's pulled out, it's just the three kangaroos and the villains.

"Shouldn't we have gone to the house first and *then* wrapped these cords around our legs?" Billie asks, almost out of breath, as we each bounce down the road to the party—I glance down at my own legs. They're stuck together from the bungee cord that's tied tightly around them. I'm having to jump and hop down the street. We all have them around our own legs. Zeke asked or rather forced us to do it so we can also move like the characters as well. I admire the detail, but we're not at the party, and I'm already exhausted.

"Yep," Zeke confidently quips near the front. "But we're almost there."

Antonia walks by with her free legs. "I'm glad I decided to be Regina."

"Don't you be going ahead of us—aah!"

Zeke trips over.

If the rumours are true, then I don't know how Rafael Gago decorated this place if his parents only left a few hours ago. The house is like a horror house. Creepy paintings on the walls. Fake glistening cobwebs in the corners, with spider's eyes shooting purple lights across the filled dancefloor. There's a thin layer of fake smoke hovering along the ground and bold green shining from lights around the room.

I'm excited. Not just for the party—but because Tokyo could be here. I may not know if she is here, but the thought that she could be does make my stomach flutter. Because the truth is, I think I could be falling for her.

It's stupid—falling for someone you've never met, but at the same time, maybe it isn't. Well, at least I think I am falling for her. I've never felt this way about somebody before.

I'm not going to find her, but I hope she is here because I know she'd have loved to have seen this place.

The group walks by a hallway guarded by huge medieval knights—*wonder which fool's going to try and put that on later?*—and we head outside. The pool is black, like oil or a dark potion witches brew, and there's a fake graveyard on the lawn, with tombstones sticking out of the ground, each etched with a silly pun name. They're not real, but out of respect, I try and walk between them.

We take seats on the few bales positioned at the back. It's been made to look like a farmyard. Carved pumpkins are spread out before a huge centrepiece scarecrow that has a large pumpkin head with a menacing look carved in it.

"Boo!"

I jump in fright—holding onto the bale I'm on so I don't topple backwards from the ghost that has come out from behind the trees. None of the others seem to have noticed, totally oblivious to the addition of the ghost while they continue chatting to themselves around me.

The ghost pulls off the white sheet, revealing a tall, slim and good-looking guy underneath.

"Sorry, didn't realise I'd scare you that much. I'm Andrew. Billie's boyfriend. You must be Hayden?"

He slides his hand through his sharp pushed-back black hair and then puts it out before me. I nod and shake his hand.

"Nice to meet you, Hayden. I go to a different school. Heard a lot of nice things about you."

"There you are," Billie smiles as he sits down between us.

We begin to chat, and I learn Andrew Kwong's planning on teaching kids in kindergarten. "It's very rewarding when you help broaden their minds." He even went to Africa on a volunteering programme this summer to teach children in a village and is returning next summer.

It's awesome…but also amusing—Billie tells her parents she doesn't want to follow in their footsteps and become a teacher, and yet she's going out with someone who does.

My stomach rumbles in anger, wanting to be fed. I decide to get food, yet it's a mistake—I end up becoming a delivery service and take orders from everybody.

The fake smoke looks like it's now covering the entire room. Cloud-green with the occasional splash of purple dots. I brave it and carefully bounce in.

In the kitchen, Robin is at a table, dressed as the girl from *The Hunger Games*, chatting to some people. To my surprise, Chloe Cassadentini is with the group—dressed in a silky nightgown. She looks stunning, even with the fake blood smothered over her outfit. Somebody near comments she's dressed as Amy Dunne from *Gone Girl.*

Antonia would be gawping in fascination at the outfit.

With the pizza boxes and candy in hand, I hop outside.

But there's somebody outside by the door. Their head slightly crouched over.

I decide to go over. They look like they're alone. Upset maybe. And I've learnt with the emails to Tokyo that it's nice to have somebody there.

"Oh, hey, Hayden." Her voice is familiar, as are her features. I remember her eyes—but they look a little watery.

"Jasmine?"

The girl nods—her blonde hair is brown! She is in some desert outfit.

"Wow. I nearly didn't recognise you. Rey from *Star Wars*, right?"

I have Dad being a big *Star Wars* fan to thank for me knowing that.

I'm still shocked by Jasmine's commitment to the outfit—we never talked about this once in our tutor sessions.

Jasmine nods again. Zeke will love it—he loves films. I ask her if she is fine. "It's just so smoky in there. It's playing on my eyes and hurting." Jasmine wipes a finger under each eye.

Now that I think about it, mine are a little itchy after being in there. "Yeah, same. Do you wanna join me? Unless you think your friends will be out soon?"

Jasmine looks over to the house and then back at me. "They probably haven't even noticed I've gone—because it's so hard to see in there, I mean. But yeah, that would be nice."

I smile and then lead the way. She glances down at my legs. The bungee cords.

"Nice touch." Zeke will be glad to hear that because, honestly, my legs don't agree. "So, Mak, I'm assuming you've not come alone, and certainly not without the rest of your band?"

I glance up and down to try and look at my outfit—each kangaroo has a different hat. Mine has an extremely tall and wide-brimmed ranger hat—Mak must be its name in the game. "Yep. They're here."

Now, under better light, I see that Jasmine has even gone and styled her hair like in the films.

"Hey guys, food's here," I say when we arrive at the bales.

Everybody welcomes Jasmine in as they grab the food I brought. Antonia, meanwhile, looks like she's been hit with a pan to the face. Shocked. "Jasmine, Jasmine Keery."

"Because that ain't creepy, saying somebody's name in full." Ham and mushroom pizza almost soars out of Dacre's mouth when Antonia whacks his stomach from embarrassment. The kangaroo's head above his head slams into the pizza box on his lap.

"Hi, Antonia. Antonia Lu," Jasmine smiles. I chuckle a little—Antonia is about to collapse and go to heaven. "So, why are you lot dressed as the best band in gaming history?"

"Good question—but I've got a few minutes before it's top of the hour," Billie says, now in the blue dolphin outfit, which wears a red baseball cap and holds an inflatable orange guitar. She gets up and then leaves.

Apart from making us hop like the characters in the arcade game, I explain to Jasmine that Zeke's also got us playing a game around the party. Every hour, we swap outfits, and whoever is the rival duo—the penguin and dolphin—must hide before it reaches the top of the next hour. When it does, the others, dressed as kangaroos, leave the bales and have ten minutes to find and catch the villains. Whoever catches one of them receives five points, but if the villains aren't caught, then they get ten points. And it's a lot harder when we can only hop!

Jasmine finishes her slice of pizza. "Wow, that's next level."

"Yeah. Except it's hard when everybody keeps stepping on your tail." Zeke then flails his kangaroo's tail with a loud whack onto his lap.

"The only rules are you can't leave the house grounds, and you can't use the locks on the doors," I tell her.

"Currently, Zeke and Hayden are in the lead—"

"I'd like to point out that's only because when Dacre was Abrielle the penguin, we all forgot the time until Hayden walked over and said he caught Abrielle," Zeke interrupts Dacre.

I give a little helpless shrug. Jasmine giggles, and before I know it, Jasmine is joining in. Andrew happily sits this round out, after eating too much, and gives her his turn to be the penguin.

"I wanna play too."

We all turn to Antonia.

"You said earlier this was silly, and the outfits were stupid," Zeke remarks.

Despite this, Antonia's keen to join and so gets in the unused fourth kangaroo outfit—this one has a cowboy hat on.

Jasmine bounces away to hide as Abrielle the penguin. The rest of us wait. Eagerly waiting for Andrew to tell us when we can start. "GO!"

Dacre, Zeke, me and Antonia, who still decides to wear her blonde wig, leap up and begin to bounce. Billie and Jasmine are bound to be in the house. The others must think the same because they're following. Antonia's far behind. She isn't adjusted to the new way of moving as we are.

There's a cry—Dacre's tripped over a fake tombstone.

My eyes can only just see through the heavy smoke when Zeke and I get inside the house. Somehow, squinting makes it better to see.

Zeke's kangaroo with a top hat costume hops towards the hallway near the kitchen. Billie's hopping madly down it, going by a drunkenly moving knight. I focus my attention now on Jasmine.

There are all sorts of characters and creatures on the dancefloor. She won't be in there; she said the smoke hurt her eyes—and that's where the smoke seems to be the heaviest.

I look up. Smoke hasn't reached the landing. I hurriedly go upstairs, which is way harder than it looks.

She's there!

Jasmine squeaks in shock at the sight of me upstairs and jumps away into a room. *I have her now.*

When I enter, Jasmine's standing behind a green couch. I want to laugh at the view of Jasmine frantically waddling about as the penguin's head bobs about—but I continue to focus. I begin to race around but end up where I started as she goes back and forth. She stops.

"I don't think you have much time left," she teases.

My eyes glance down at the green couch. Nothing but an object between us.

Jasmine's face drops when she sees what I'm thinking. "You wouldn't?"

I beam back a grin. "You sure?"

I jump onto the couch—and then leap over. I grab Jasmine's arm—we topple over.

My elbow bashes hard onto the floor. A bit of air gets knocked out of me, too. It's nothing serious, though.

I roll over. "I'm so sorry. Are you okay?"

I watch—but she laughs. I start to panic that she's hit her head.

"Yes," she says through her giggles. Hair poking out of the head hole of her costume and resting over her face. "It's just—I didn't think you would, but you did!"

I find my stomach move, and I begin to chuckle as well.

"A well-deserved five points." She turns to faces me. Some of her hair drops down, grazing my shoulder. She smiles. I return it.

"We best head back."

I manage to get up, still bungee-corded on my legs, then try my best to pull Jasmine up. She begins to laugh again when we struggle. It's so loveable and cute. It's almost contagious and makes me join in.

"Everything alright?"

The joy inside suddenly evaporates. Jared Steele's standing at the doorway. I immediately let go of Jasmine's hands and look down, scared to face him. A horrible mist plagues me.

"Yes, just playing a game," Jasmine answers.

"Is that what that's all about downstairs?" Disappointment oozing through his voice.

I carefully look up. He swaps hands to hold the small red board. He's dressed as a lifeguard. *Dressed* is a stretch because he only has lifeguard red shorts, some trainers, the board and, rather peculiarly, also a knight's metal hand on his left hand. His built stomach is on display.

The mist brewing inside me gets bigger. I don't want to be here. I need to be down with my friends, where he can't do anything.

"Yeah, it's quite fun," Jasmine says, still beside me.

Jared scoffs. "I'll take your word for it."

I tightly hold the ends of my costume, feeling almost sick.

"Come on, the others will be wondering if I was caught."

I don't waste another second and follow Jasmine out, not without having to brush by Jared and receive a strong whiff of the mix of deodorant and aftershave he's swamped himself in.

We hop downstairs, with Jared probably watching as we leave, and make our way outside. I move—but really, I'm just trying to forget seeing him.

Something touches my arm. It's warm. I assume Jasmine's holding on for support as we bounce along. But she stops me.

"You look like you've seen a ghost." My mind is so foggy, I don't listen to her. "It's alright."

Her hand moves up my arm to my shoulder.

Something inside me changes. I smile back. "Thanks."

The sickness slowly diminishes—the mist moving away—and I get back to being in the moment of the party. Feeling calm from Jasmine's kindness.

However, the feeling later evolves into embarrassment when she tells the group how I caught her.

"You leapt over the couch?" Antonia says, shocked. I nod.

"Wow, that's taking it serious, man," Dacre comments. The others agree. My cheeks go red.

"I can't believe we're allowing that," Zeke says, dumbfounded, as his kangaroo's head whips side to side. "And you're disallowing mine—those guys held the study door shut for me to get Billie."

"Technically it's not breaking the rules," Dacre explains. "We said doors couldn't be locked. Not blocked."

As she cuddles next to Andrew, Billie grins. "They were so drunk I told them I'd buy them a beer each after if they did it. The fools—just went to the kitchen and got two beers from the fridge."

Zeke tries to object, but the verdict stays the same.

With this news, it means I'm in the lead, which is kind of exciting.

"I'll get you next time," Zeke says to Billie, who replies by sticking her tongue out at him. He turns to me. "Oh, it's on, Mallard." I think he's being serious, but then a jokey smirk appears on his face—so I decide to play along.

"Ha, I've not even started yet." There are a few sounds of pretend tension around the group—it only encourages me to continue. "Tell you what, Zeke—it's thirsty work, all this winning."

As the group laughs, I take a sip from my cup—only to taste nothing but air.

I roll my eyes, hoping nobody noticed it's empty. But when I look over, there's a line of grinning faces at me, along with a wave of empty red cups being held up in the air.

13.

The Halloween weekend was fun, but the following week gets better as it's our Homecoming. Traditionally held earlier in Fall for other schools, Kingsgate Lee High coincides their Homecoming Week to be on the same week of when the school was founded—November 1st.

Part of the entertainment is that everybody dresses up to a different theme each day—and Zeke's made sure we're heavily involved.

Day of the Week – Theme – Organised By:

Monday – Movie Monday – Angela Branno

Tuesday – My '80s Horror Nightmare – Chloe Cassadentini

Wednesday – Rock 'N' Pop, Don't Forget Hip Hop – Enrique Lorigzo

Thursday – Tourists, Tourists, Tourists – Sam Brazell

Friday – Subjects – Robin Mallard

I'm a little sad when it's Friday because of how quick the week's gone by. I've tried to get stuck in with it all. On Movie Monday, we all dressed up as *The Goonies*, but Wednesday was better because, despite the tension, a Pussycat Doll Robin was silent from shock on the way back from school in the car because I was sat in the passenger seat dressed as part of Kiss. Zeke, Dacre, Antonia and I went as the famous rock band. I think Antonia agreed to this because of how she was with the Halloween party costumes. However, it's Billie who won everybody over, with more praise than Chloe Cassadentini's "Hips Don't Lie" Shakira. Billie went as Madonna from the "Hung Up" video. I didn't think that would be her thing, but it's brilliant.

It doesn't surprise me that Robin is involved in Homecoming Week—but Subjects? It's an interesting theme. Each year has a different subject to dress up as. Juniors have Languages.

Jasmine chuckles at me from in her car at the end of the day. "I know we're trying to improve our Spanish, but don't you think dressing up for the tutoring might be going a little bit too far?"

I laugh mockingly—for I'm dressed still as if I'm going to take part in the Spanish Running of the Bulls Festival—the event where everybody runs away from bulls chasing them through the Spanish town.

I take the collar off when I get in her car and explain it was Zeke's idea—and that I forgot to bring spare clothes for the tutoring.

"Please tell me somebody was dressed as a bull."

We did. It was Zeke. He wore black, made some horns and even had a fake ring dangling under his nose. But he didn't stop there. He would charge at any of us if we had red on us.

"But isn't Dacre's rucksack red?"

"Yep." He had to leave it in his locker and carry his books for the day.

Zeke was so adamant in his role that he charged through Mrs Duboy's Art class when Antonia picked up a red pencil. And Zeke went stir-crazy when he entered the cafeteria and saw everybody holding a red tray.

Some people through the day made comments that Zeke looked ridiculous and an idiot, but he didn't seem to care. I admire that words don't get to him.

"What is he like," Jasmine laughs after I tell her that Zeke ended up with a detention for his antics.

Still embarrassed in my outfit now we've left school, I ask if we can go via my house to get changed, but Jasmine turns with a huge grin on her face. It worries me.

"No, no, no, Señor Mallard, you should have remembered to bring some."

I try to argue; I even joke she isn't paying me, so time shouldn't matter, but she isn't having it.

So here I am, at a park with Jasmine, wearing white jeans and a white T-shirt. Jasmine can't stop smiling at the view.

I begin to lean into her car to grab my rucksack so we can use the books.

"Don't bother." Jasmine lifts her trunk door open. "I've got a better plan."

The trunk slams shut. Next to her are two pedal scooters resting against her car.

I get out of the car, shut the door and stare at her in disbelief. "I thought I was meant to be the tutor."

Jasmine finishes setting one up and steps on the scooter. "It's now the weekend—and it's the Homecoming game tonight. We can have some fun as we do it!"

Before I reply, she locks the car and pedals away—I have no choice but to follow.

We pedal gently along the path that goes in between the trees and soon start to talk in Spanish. First, we point at things, and the other says what they are in Spanish, and then we soon begin talking in more of a conversation in the language. I get a few looks in my outfit, but I pedal on.

We discover she and my family watch the same action series. I explain my dad's dentistry tips. Jasmine tells me her dad used to dress up as an evil elf for Christmas. Her family would have to try and persuade him why Christmas was important so they could have their presents. Kind of traumatising—but clever, I guess.

The sun is soon lowering in level with the trees, and the sky has become an orangey pink. We lay our scooters down on a small grass slope and sit beside them, looking out at the lake before us. There are some people still about in the distance, but it's quiet.

The air rushes by and causes my hair to blow gently about. I like the feeling. It's something I never thought I'd say I'd appreciate, but I do.

Most of the time I was in the hospital, I was stuck inside, and when I could go out, it was only in the courtyard, which was in the centre of the hospital. So the views weren't particularly great, and there was no breeze. No fresh air making its way through to play on my skin. Just the sky, and then maybe the sun or rain. I've missed this—the touch of a breeze.

"I don't know when I last came to this park." Jasmine breaks the silence, brushing her hands down her white buttoned top. I feel myself gaze at her eyes as she stares out at the lake. Her large, brown eyes. And I swear they're glistening, twinkling from the reflection of the sun's shine on the lake.

I suddenly turn away, hoping she doesn't notice.

The wind slowly causes little ripples across the water of the lake, making the ducks bob gently up and down.

"I don't know when I last went on a scooter," I reply. "Probably back in Georgia."

"Do you miss it?"

I look over at Jasmine. She's laid back with her elbows on the ground to keep her up, hair dangling down underneath her.

"Being on a scooter? Yeah, sure."

Her lips partially crack to reveal her teeth, but I know what she is really asking.

Everybody has always asked how I'm finding Florida. I've been asked so many times, and think why I should like it, that I've never stopped and considered if I miss Georgia. Nobody's asked until now.

"There's places, I suppose, or times at those places."

I don't miss where I spent the last few months in Georgia. Would anybody? But I do feel sad that there are places there that I probably won't see again. The local library. The park. The bowling alley. And sure, my old home, the place I've only ever lived in before we moved.

"But I guess I knew they'd become memories at some point." Like when I would leave for college or for a job. "Maybe just sooner than I thought, though."

My finger slowly wraps around a piece of grass. I refrain from telling Jasmine that the only person I do occasionally miss from there is my mom. Sometimes, I wish I could hear her voice…just once.

I don't even have her number on my new phone—the one I got after the car accident—to call and hear her voicemail.

Doesn't matter, though—Robin said on the day we moved to Florida that Mom's number was no longer available.

The ducks are now waddling out of the lake and towards the trees as I remain thinking about Mom. I've not told anybody in Florida about her…except Tokyo.

"But I guess I don't miss it."

She nods, taking it in.

I wonder if that's not the answer she was expecting, but when I feel like I might stare at her eyes again for longer than I should, I decide to return to the lake.

The ducks have disappeared beyond the trees now.

"Thank you."

I ask Jasmine for what yet remain watching the lake.

"For the tutoring."

I face towards her and tell her it's nothing.

"No, it means a lot, Hayden. Not many people would be kind to offer or take as much time out to help. And to be honest to me. So, thank you."

There's a sudden warmth on the back of my hand. My eyes look down at it on the ground. Jasmine's hand is on top.

She's looking back at me. My throat becomes slightly dry, and I'm unsure what to say or do. My lips instinctively curl to give a small smile back.

I swallow the nerves down, and eventually my voice returns—but the back of my hand feels lonely—Jasmine is getting up off the grass.

"Come on, we best head back. The game will start soon, and Chloe wants me to see her Homecoming cheerleading performance." Jasmine wipes her hands on her jean shorts and then picks up her scooter. "*Vamos.*"

She may tell me to go, yet I find myself on the ground. Trying to make sense of why I feel strange. Then I suddenly realise.

I understand why my insides are the same now as they were after I caught Jasmine as Abrielle the penguin at the Halloween party.

Tied-up and yet free all in one.

Not only have I been falling for Tokyo, but I really like Jasmine too.

14.

FROM: TokyoCherryDustZ89@TokyoCherryDustZ89.com
TO: BlueC0ast1@bretteodmail.com
DATE: Sat 4th November, 8:26 PM
SUBJECT: Time To Return The Favour

Brisbane,
I realise you've not replied to my last email yet, but something has happened. I don't want to go into it, not yet. Don't even want to think about it. I once helped you a few weeks back when you were down and felt like there was nobody to go to. And I now need to ask for you to do the same for me.
I need you to cheer me up. Try and take me away from how I'm suddenly feeling. I'm sorry to sound desperate. I'm feeling low and didn't know who to turn to.

-Tokyo

FROM: BlueC0ast1@bretteodmail.com
TO: TokyoCherryDustZ89@TokyoCherryDustZ89.com
DATE: Sat 4th November, 8:48 PM
SUBJECT: Knock Knock

Right. No worries, Brisbane's here. I've been told by someone I've only recently been in contact with that music's a great way to let out your emotions. I've attached a list of recommendations. Yes, that's right, Brisbane's been searching music for himself. However, sometimes you must do something completely different to be distracted and calm down. Something to get away from what you normally do to distract you. So, if you think you're brave enough to step away from the pillow that is music, then please agree before I tell you. I'll wait for your reply.

-Brisbane

P.S. It's not illegal. Should clarify that now. All you need is paper. Probably best you have a lot.

FROM: TokyoCherryDustZ89@TokyoCherryDustZ89.com
TO: BlueC0ast1@bretteodmail.com
DATE: Sat 4th November, 9:30 PM
SUBJECT: Who's There?

Uh oh. Now I am concerned. I've just bought a pack of paper. Coloured even. Now what?

FROM: BlueC0ast1@bretteodmail.com
TO: TokyoCherryDustZ89@TokyoCherryDustZ89.com
DATE: Sat 4th November, 9:34 PM
SUBJECT: Spell

Coloured paper's probably better. For now, Tokyo, I need you to make an origami parrot.

I know, you're probably thinking, why are you getting me to do this? But just search online how to make an origami parrot and follow the instructions.

Trust me.

-Brisbane

FROM: TokyoCherryDustZ89@TokyoCherryDustZ89.com
TO: BlueC0ast1@bretteodmail.com
DATE: Sat 4th November, 9:57 PM
SUBJECT: Spell Who?

If it wasn't weird enough going into a shop and buying a pack of paper late at night, then it is now. I'm currently sitting outside on my car hood with scrunched-up pieces of paper around me, with people walking by and staring at me, all because I'm trying to make this parrot. I've been at it for twenty minutes, and I'm getting nowhere.

What's the point of this? Because I tell you, Brisbane, it's something I'd currently consider not fun. You should be lucky there's a screen keeping me from being able to origami you. This is ridiculous.

-Tokyo

FROM: BlueC0ast1@bretteodmail.com
TO: TokyoCherryDustZ89@TokyoCherryDustZ89.com
DATE: Sat 4th November, 10:14 PM
SUBJECT: Fine, W-H-O

That's because you're not focusing. You've got to be silent, concentrated and coordinated. Focus on where you're folding while making sure everything before is still correct. And to do that, you can't battle with whatever has caused you to be angry. You've got to let your mind flow down whatever river it must.

It's used as art therapy, not just for patients who need help to build their hand muscles or regain control of their movement, but also for those with low self-esteem, anxiety, autism and other conditions. Even prisoners have classes on it to help calm them. There have been reports that people who are feeling low believe that origami gives them hope. So that's what I want you to do: make an origami parrot so that at the end, you will feel you have hope in overcoming whatever it is that's getting you down.

And the parrot? Let's consider that as an additional challenge. It's a difficult piece, but if done right, the parrot should balance on your finger with just its claw. But if one wing is slightly longer or shorter than the other, then it won't stay. Only when it's perfect is it right.

Just keep at it. I know you're not the giving-up type. Otherwise, you'd never have tried to help me.

-Brisbane

P.S. Also, how could you 'origami' me if you can't do the parrot? ;)

FROM: TokyoCherryDustZ89@TokyoCherryDustZ89.com
TO: BlueC0ast1@bretteodmail.com
DATE: Sat 4th November, 11:04 PM

SUBJECT: Oh, Brother! That's Terrible

I did it! I actually did it, Brisbane! I've even attached a photo to prove it. One that sits perfectly on my finger.

I was ready to quit, but somehow, after pausing and reading what you said, I achieved it. And it did relax me. It made me think about why I was upset and that maybe I shouldn't have gotten so worked up.

Thanks for your words.

-Tokyo

P.S. I don't know, but I'd have found a way, ha.

FROM: BlueC0ast1@bretteodmail.com
TO: TokyoCherryDustZ89@TokyoCherryDustZ89.com
DATE: Sat 4th November, 11:26 PM
SUBJECT: No, It Wasn't

That's a pretty good parrot, Tokyo. Maybe better than any I've ever made.

I'm glad it's given you some comfort. Because that's what it's all about. Because, sometimes, we must remember to take a moment to breathe when it feels like everything is on top of us. And once we're able to do that, then we can focus and make the perfect piece of origami.

You're most likely wondering why I asked for you to send me music to help me relax if I had this technique?

Sometimes, methods can lose their value when we use them regularly. Become accustomed to it that it becomes a normality, something that can then be easily taken over. I don't want to say it's weakened it. I guess what I'm trying to say is that my body, or my anger, to be exact, must have worked a way to override the aim of the origami.

I do origami from time to time now, yet when I first emailed you, I was in a terrible place, heading closer to a place I've been before. And I don't ever want to go back there. And doing origami wasn't working. But hearing the music you posted and then emailed me made me feel better. Trying something different that also felt difficult to do—to relate to others yet feel and think for myself—helped. It gave me a new way to get that extra breath.

And besides, aren't the best things in life difficult?

-Brisbane

FROM: TokyoCherryDustZ89@TokyoCherryDustZ89.com
TO: BlueC0ast1@bretteodmail.com
DATE: Sat 4th November, 11:45 PM
SUBJECT: Yes, Yes It Was

Thank you, Brisbane. I know that won't have been easy to do. And thanks for saying I helped you, too. I don't think I've ever heard anybody say that before.

But you were right about the origami for me. Furious at first—have had a few strangers gawp at me as they went by—but it gave me time to think about what I was angry at and try and listen to why I felt angry about it and how those on the other side of my anger may have felt.

I'm not exactly there with my 'inner peace' but it was enough of a step to help.

These emails have been an extra breath for me, too—I thought posting songs out to people on KingsgateLeeConnect was something like it, but this is an extra breath I didn't know I needed until it happened.

So thanks. I hope you like the file I've attached for you.

-Tokyo

I see in the email that the attached file is a music file. It's titled "Do You Remember." I've heard that somewhere—then it clicks. It's that song in the charts that Robin always sings in the car to and from school. By Kaiya Prior ft. Dante Buffon. The song features an Italian verse in it. Everybody seems to be mad about it—so why has Tokyo sent it to me?

When my headphones are synced to my phone, I click on the file.

I expect to hear the fun but robotic bass of the song I've heard a few times begin, but instead, I hear what I think is a flute. A bamboo flute. The hairs on my arms slowly rise. The loop of some drums comes in, followed by a short guitar riff. I'm confused. This isn't "Do You

Remember"—then the vocals begin. It's Kaiya Prior. This isn't the original song, though—it's a remix!

The more I listen, feeling the sounds of synthesisers, the more I realise that it's been produced to become some '80s mid-tempo ballad.

I've heard the original perhaps a hundred times, but I've never felt the lyrics hit me so hard. And the chorus…it makes me think of those memories I have of when I was younger with my dad, Colbey, Robin…and my mom. I've never felt a rhythm make me want to confess my own heartbreaks in life before. To own up to say that I know how this singer is feeling when I probably never have. Even Dante's Italian rap has been made into something that sounds like a hopeless fool's slow poetry letter of love confessions.

And suddenly, a saxophone comes in. A saxophone solo that isn't even in the original. The solo gives a new bursting wave of emotion that hits me—makes me feel more for the singer. That I want to get up and dance, sway, or just move in unison.

But the song eventually begins to end, with an electric guitar solo continuing to lower into a bliss—yet my body remains still tingling from the ecstasy it's given me. So much so that I click the file again.

FROM: BlueC0ast1@bretteodmail.com
TO: TokyoCherryDustZ89@TokyoCherryDustZ89.com
DATE: Sun 5th November, 12:19 AM
SUBJECT: Woooow

I'm pleased these emails are just as valuable to you as they are to me. Because they do. They really do mean a lot.

Now that remix is…wow, it's incredible. I've heard the actual song so many times before, and sure, it's good (probably more than good, seeing as it's been in the charts for weeks now), but that remix just gives it a new life. One I feel I understand. I actually prefer it to the original.

Where did you find it?

-Brisbane

FROM: TokyoCherryDustZ89@TokyoCherryDustZ89.com

TO: BlueC0ast1@bretteodmail.com
DATE: Sun 5th November, 12:28 AM
SUBJECT: Re: Woooow

It's so pleasing to read that you enjoyed it, Brisbane. That means a lot. But what makes you think I found it? Do you not think that I could have made it? ;)

-Tokyo

FROM: BlueC0ast1@bretteodmail.com
TO: TokyoCherryDustZ89@TokyoCherryDustZ89.com
DATE: Sun 5th November, 12:38 AM
SUBJECT: Your Own Mixes?

You did the remix?

That's amazing! I don't want to be biased because I know you, well kind of, but it is. And it sounds like an actual recording. I wouldn't even know where to begin to try and make that. You've completely transformed it. No, enhanced it. I love the '80s feel of it, and now that I write that out, of course you created the mix! You love that decade. But why? If it isn't too personal.

-Brisbane

FROM: TokyoCherryDustZ89@TokyoCherryDustZ89.com
TO: BlueC0ast1@bretteodmail.com
DATE: Sun 5th November, 9:29 AM
SUBJECT: Re: Your Own Mixes?

Yes, I did it. I've done a few, actually.

Sorry for the late response—when you asked why I did the remix, I wasn't sure if I could explain. But you've been open to me about things, and it's made me realise that I can be open to you.

When I was younger, my mom used to work weekends, so it was my dad who had to take care of me. He used to take me out, do all sorts, but sometimes we'd just drive, just so we were out of the house. He always had the radio on in the car. He'd start singing and shouting along. And I'd join in. Every time we were in the car, we'd sing like it was the only thing we knew.

I felt the happiest then, so much so that as soon as it was Monday and I was at school, I desperately wanted it to be the weekend, so I was back in the car with my dad. He'd tell me that the 1980s were the best. He was a teenager then. A time when he felt there were no rules. No restrictions. No responsibilities as such. I should point out that he loved his family, his job, and his life, but I think he missed that care-free spirit that must have disappeared overtime when he became an adult because he once said *it was an age I took for granted and didn't realise how much I loved them till they were gone.*

I never understood what he meant at the time. Not until a few years ago, not till after he passed away.

I don't think I took those times with my dad for granted, but I get what he means about the last part. You don't know how much you truly love something or somebody till they've gone.

-Tokyo

FROM: BlueC0ast1@bretteodmail.com
TO: TokyoCherryDustZ89@TokyoCherryDustZ89.com
DATE: Sun 5th November, 10:00 AM
SUBJECT: Re: Your Own Mixes?

I'm sorry to hear about your dad. I can't begin to know what that must have been like. It sounds like you have great memories of him. And I guess doing those remixes reminds you of him?

-Brisbane

FROM: TokyoCherryDustZ89@TokyoCherryDustZ89.com
TO: BlueC0ast1@bretteodmail.com
DATE: Sun 5th November, 12:10 PM
SUBJECT: Re: Your Own Mixes?

Thank you, Brisbane. And I do.

My mom doesn't really speak about my dad much. I don't think she's ever dealt with it—she's moved on with her life but never dealt with

Dad going. How could you? How do you deal with a loved one dying?

My mom doesn't ever talk about him. Not even to tell a story or a memory that's suddenly come back to her. The only time is on his birthday when the family visits his grave to pay our respects. Maybe it's too hard for her to say. I understand that, but it's just as hard for me not to talk about it. Just because it might be the easiest thing for her doesn't mean it is for me.

And last night, we argued about Dad. That's why I needed you to calm me. I was so angry with her.

But if there's one thing about my family, it's that we keep our emotions in, not out. We never talk about anything sad or too personal. We celebrate the highs but never talk about the lows. It's that kind of family. Well, on my mom's side—I don't see anybody from my dad's side anymore.

Just because I've been taught that, though, doesn't mean I want to just leave things. But I guess I do it. I guess because I'm used to it—brought up by it. Maybe that's why I've kept quiet about my different tastes to my friends. Why I let everybody else seem to plan everything for me and keep hush.

I suppose that's why I do the remixes. Not just to remember my time with my dad, but I guess doing this is the closest way I can be with him. Taking music from my time and making them into his. I've never told anybody or shared the remixes, not because I'm just scared of what others think, but because it's also the only place and way that I can let my guard down and be me. A place to shove all my concerns in and let my emotions out.

It makes me feel like I'm not so alone.

-Tokyo

15.

I stare across at Mr Gauran. This time, he's decided for us to stay in the office—he's sat not behind his desk but on the other green chair across the coffee table.

We talk about my new job. He's pleased my grades are still high and that I'm hanging out with new people at school. I let him know about some of the things I do with my friends. The trips to Bailey & Lone's Drive-In Movie Theatre. The hangouts at The Cerise Wave Diner. What we did for fancy dress at Halloween—he wishes to use that idea at a future fancy-dress party. And I tell him I'm teaching Spanish.

It gets me thinking about how much has changed recently. A lot.

There's a cold sense against my body—like I've just dived into a pile of snow, bare-naked. And it isn't pleasant.

"What's wrong?"

My eyes instinctively glance up at Mr Gauran and then back down to my legs. "It's just…" I try to think of the best way to explain, but the longer I pause, the more he'll think something's up. "What if something happens?"

Mr Gauran slowly leans back. "Everything's good now, though, right?"

"Yeah."

There's silence. I'm scared to admit what I'm thinking. "It's the most friends I've ever had before. I feel close to them, and I'm doing some stuff I haven't done before, and I like it, and I guess I'm…"

"You're scared if it alters." He says more as a statement than a question.

"Yeah. If something happens—and I can't change it. And I can't cope, and I end up like before."

"That's understandable." Mr Gauran then looks around the room. He suddenly grabs something from on top of the cabinets behind him and turns around. "Okay, I'm gonna put this ball here." I watch as Mr Gauran leans forward and places the ball down on the coffee table near his side. "And say, at some point, I'm gonna hit that ball at the wall right there."

He points one of his beefy fingers right at me. I turn around to stare at the blank wall behind me.

"But I'm here."

He shrugs. That's all he does. Shrugs as if it doesn't matter—but the ball will hit my face, and quite powerfully with how built Mr Gauran is.

He begins to talk, but all I can think of is the ball. Nervously waiting, waiting for him to suddenly pounce for the ball.

"Tell me, what would you do if a rhinoceros bursts in through that door?"

I'm perplexed by such an odd question. "I guess I'd hope you'd be able to stop him while I jump out the window."

"Three now," Mr Gauran says. I briefly look at him; he means my scale of humour. "Point is, Hayden, if something happens, your instinct will kick in. To do something or not." He moves the pen in his hand to the other. "Tell me a time when instinct has kicked in for you."

I think it over for a moment. "I helped someone the other day."

"Really?"

I was thinking of Tokyo being upset—and now I realise I've walked into a boobytrap trail of Be-Careful-What-You-Say. "They were down and angry about something, so I helped them calm down."

"So you chose to help?"

"Of course." He asks me how it felt, and I say good, yet it wasn't really about me. It was about the other person. "I told them to do origami. It was something Dr Oace got me to do when I was in hospital to help me relax."

I think Dr Oace (pronounced O-ace, not O-ac) at the hospital back in Georgia would have been pleased to learn his origami advice helped someone other than me. It was something he got me and some other kids to do when I was in the hospital the second time. I found it infuriating at first. In time, it did help me calm down, though.

"And do you find yourself still doing origami since you've come out of hospital?"

Ah flip. I walked right into that.

"I did at first. Because there wasn't much to do except read before I started school," I carefully yet still truthfully answer. "But I find listening to music is quite refreshing now. Able to hear others have felt the same. Happy, I mean."

"Music is a powerful thing," Mr Gauran comments. "And so is instinct. It seems you can already weigh what to do when problems arise. Perhaps you're more capable of dealing with unexpected crossroads than you believe."

Maybe, I wonder. I helped Zeke when he was beaten up. I went from being alone to having friends. Got a job when I needed money. Checked on Jasmine at Halloween when I thought she was upset.

The school bell goes.

"Seems your next crossroad is whether to be on time for your next class or be late," Mr Gauran jokes.

I smile and reach for my rucksack. "Maybe best be on time."

I give my thanks and head out. I stop at the doorway and turn back. He's still sitting in the chair towards me at the coffee table, with one leg across the other.

"You never hit the ball at the wall."

A smile, so bold it would be hard to miss, appears on Mr Gauran's face. With a quick flick from his crossed leg, the football on the table suddenly soars into the wall beside me, bounces back, and he catches it. I stand in silence, impressed by the scene.

"Exactly."

It doesn't take long to arrive at another crossroad. All week, my mind has been battling between Tokyo and Jasmine.

I like hanging out with Jasmine in our lessons, but there's always a rush of excitement as I wait till lunch or back at home to see what Tokyo's written to me.

Sometimes, when I'm writing to Tokyo, it's Jasmine I picture at the end, waiting for my emails. And when I read Tokyo's emails, it's Jasmine who's lying on her bed on her phone and writing and saying it back to me. It's insane! And all confusing. Things would certainly be easier if Jasmine were Tokyo.

And there's things I can match them together with—such as they each have a sister—but also things that can't. Tokyo feels she's separating from her friends—yet when I see Jasmine with Chloe and the other Populars, she doesn't look distant; she looks in her element.

Come Friday, I'm none the wiser, yet I desperately would like Jasmine to be Tokyo. And I'm excited, for tonight I'm hanging out with her. Just us. And there's no tutoring. She aced her Spanish test—and as a thanks, she offered to take me out. My hopes flooded with excitement until she said *to say thanks for the tutoring. You've been a great friend, and as you won't let me pay you, this is the least I can do.* It sucks she meant as friends, but I'm just glad she said that before I asked her if she meant a date...that would have been awkward.

After school, I head to Mt. Okesea, quickly visit the office to check my rota and then walk up to the gateway.

Under the light of the fire, torches lit on either side, Jasmine is there waiting. Her blonde hair cascading over and down the back of her denim jacket.

"Hey."

She turns around. And then I see the pure perfection of her. Her large, dark eyes reflecting the light as she stands in a short-skirted, dark blue dress. *It's not a date, Hayden. She may have chosen the restaurant here, but that doesn't mean it's a date.*

But, right here, I so wish she is Tokyo. *Stop it.*

"Oh, hey. Wow, check you out. If I'd known you could have looked like this, then I'd have said wear a shirt instead of your hoodies ages ago." Her eyes widen, now holding a strange glare of scaredness. "That was really insensitive—I didn't mean it like that. I'm sorry—"

I tell her it's fine.

"—I just meant you don't see what you look like under your hoodies." Jasmine abruptly stops herself. She closes her eyes and breathes out. A smile appears on my face—and perhaps my cheeks change pink, too. It's nice to see I'm not the only person who fumbles over what they say.

"It's fine. And you look amazing." In my head, I sound calm and smooth, but I probably don't. The smile that appears on her face, though, seems to hold my nerves off for a short while.

"Thank you."

Before I wish she were Tokyo any longer, we make our way to the restaurant.

After meandering through some trees, we are greeted by a stoned courtyard filled with people sitting by tables. It's what I expect a small Greek mountain village to be—there are white walls and sea blue-tile roof buildings surrounding the courtyard, except to the left, where there's the crazy golf mountain. A small waterfall—smaller than the one for the crazy golf—pours down into a stoned pool of water.

We're shown our table—near the centre of the yard, which is great as we can hear the music, see the waterfall, feel the warm night air and be dazzled by the hanging lights above us. Just perfect for a date—*A MEAL! AS FRIENDS*, I shout at myself, although who can help but think it if we're sat in a romantic setting such as this—*STOP IT!*

"Hayden, what are you doing here? We literally just went over the shifts. You're not on tonight."

Aunt Sandra walks by us—I tell her I'm here for a meal. She nods. I turn around only to see Jasmine with a mask of embarrassment on her face.

"You work here?"

"Yeah."

Jasmine shoves her hands into her face. I'm puzzled, but then I understand—she didn't know.

She then pulls her hands away. "I asked you to eat out at the place you work."

"I thought you knew—but hey." I take her hand. "I don't mind. It's a great place. And besides, I'll probably be able to get us a discount." Her lips curl ever so slightly. It pleases me—yet that only makes it harder to push down my real thoughts about her. "Not to mention, now when people ask me at the golf hut how the food is here, I can actually say it is good without pretending to know. Well, assuming it is good, of course."

Jasmine giggles.

"It is good." Aunt Sandra walks back by.

My hand lets go of Jasmine's as I clench my teeth in awkwardness towards her and not my boss. But it makes her laugh more.

"Well," she says. "I suppose we better help stop you from lying then."

Before the night has even begun, Jasmine and I have had our food and are heading back through the trees to the entrance.

"I've really had a good time," Jasmine says beside me. Her denim jacket now just hanging off from her shoulders.

I nod. "I enjoyed tonight, too. But I really didn't mind paying for mine."

I feel her push the side of my shoulder gently with hers, feeling that warmth—and wishing it would stay there. *Friends, Hayden.*

"No, Hayden, I said it's to say thank you for the help."

I stare down at my feet as we walk because I'm not sure what I will think if I catch sight of her brown eyes looking at me. But they're so mesmerising, though. "I know."

There's another warmth, this time lower on my arm, stopping me from walking on. Jasmine is holding onto me.

"I mean it, Hayden. Thank you."

Her appreciation brings out a smile from me. We're standing close. I can smell the lime scent fragrance she has on. It's nice.

"And now we know I'm not lying when people ask about the food here."

"No, I guess not. A double win for you." She returns the smile. It's really cute.

A weird yet fantastic feeling inside suddenly rises. I continue staring across into her eyes. If this was some movie or even just another guy at our school, this is where they'd say something cool to impress the girl—because they'd want to kiss her. Like I do right now.

Despite all the parts of my head saying this is just friends, something is wanting me to move closer—or to say anything to indicate I like her.

But nothing happens.

"Is that you, Jasmine?"

I spin around to follow Jasmine's gaze. Further ahead, beyond the gateway, is a woman standing and looking down at us.

"That's my mom," she says.

Coldness spreads across my arm—she goes around me and up to her mom. The moment that could have been has gone. I slowly trail behind. Deflated. The rush inside me changes to sadness.

Beside her mom, Jasmine then hugs a man with glasses who comes into view.

"Hi, sis! Come on, Dad, I wanna Bubba Watson you all and win! Let's go!" The young girl beside the man says as she pulls his arm to move him after Jasmine stops hugging him.

I stop. The man is their dad. My sadness plummets—because I know what that means. I have my answer with Jasmine and Tokyo. I wish to grab my bike and leave, but I awkwardly stand, having to hear Jasmine's mom explain her family came to play crazy golf with her.

"When do we ever do stuff like this as a family?" Jasmine asks.

"Jasmine, not in front of your friend," Jasmine's father says. I then see all eyes suddenly stare at me.

Jasmine begins to introduce me, saying I'm the person who has been tutoring her Spanish—but I just smile nervously through my teeth for the whole time.

After a few words, a handshake with her father, and hearing her younger sister Amber desperately wanting to play, they set off to the crazy golf.

Jasmine steps in. "Thanks again. I'll see you at school."

And then she hugs me. Warm. Soft. The lime scent rises to my nose—it's not as pleasurable as I thought earlier.

When I'm finally alone, I want to collapse. However, I head over to the bike rack to unlock my bike. How can the night have changed so suddenly? From being so great and now…to this?

I pull the bike out and jump on.

I felt something between us. But, I guess, just like I used to do at lunch when I pictured the conversations I could have with people on the KingsgateLeeConnect board, it must have been all in my head. The sooner I can get home and pretend I never thought Jasmine was Tokyo, the better. *How could this night get any worse?*

I put my foot down on the pedal and begin to ride. I glance down. The front tyre's flat.

Great.

I try later to think of a silver lining about tonight's events as I push my bike along the side of the road—but can't. And I can't exactly message Tokyo about feeling upset about Jasmine because, well, obviously, I'm upset she isn't Tokyo.

How did I think Jasmine was Tokyo?

Because she's just as wonderful. And kind. But then maybe it's because something is missing about Tokyo. Normally, you'd see a person before you speak to them—Tokyo and I have done the reverse. There's an empty chair behind a screen, and I've been trying to fill it with somebody.

Perhaps my mind has been trying to fill the part that's missing about Tokyo—the part that would appear in any normal new connection—a face. Maybe Jasmine was that person because she is popular, beautiful and has been kind to me. Somebody I've recently known and grown fond of quickly.

But Jasmine isn't Tokyo—it's upsetting to say that, yet I've somehow got to come to terms with this.

"I think you're meant to sit and ride on that. Not push."

I jump. I look to the side for the unfamiliar voice. It's one of Jared's friends. The boy who stayed at the end and watched me lying on the toilet floor after they had beaten me up because I injured Jared in volleyball.

I'm already distraught—I could easily run off, but I don't.

"Whatever plan you, Jared and the others have for me, I don't wanna know. I don't care." I move over from him, yet my sick brain suddenly decides to question then if getting beat up might actually help the aching of Jasmine stop. *Really, Hayden?*

I begin to push my bike and move.

"It's only me here. I just saw you and wanted to check."

I scoff.

"To tell you the truth, I've been trying to find a way, and the right moment, to say I'm sorry."

I immediately glance over at him. There might be sorrow etched on his face, but I don't buy it.

"No trick. What they did—what we did, was wrong. Horrible. I shouldn't have joined them."

He takes a step closer but then stops when he sees my harsh look. "We never should have hurt you. I only play in the football team with them now, and that's it. I don't expect you to forgive me. I wouldn't. But I thought—"

"I just needed to know," I finish for him.

"Something like that," he comments. "I've been trying to amend it. I mean, have they hurt you since then? Noticed they haven't been playing any wicked games on you since?"

I stop. I push some air out of my lungs, trying to think. And after a moment, I can't. Sure, there's been stares, but nobody has physically hurt me since that time in the toilets after volleyball. I just assumed they had backed off because I then started hanging out with Zeke, Billie, Antonia and Dacre. That I was no longer alone. It never crossed my mind to consider if somebody had actually gone and told them to stop.

"Why?" I ask him curiously, still unsure. "Why the change of heart?"

"Human nature, I guess."

I nod, trying to understand—but to be honest, I don't fully. But maybe he did have a change of heart. Maybe he needed to see the mess I was in to realise it wasn't right. And people do change. *My mom did.* Not the best example. But it's what I want with myself. To change. I wasn't in a great place a few months ago, but I want to be better. To have changed.

"If this is some sort of redemption, some passage you feel you gotta do to feel good about yourself, it's fine. I forgive you."

The boy shakes his head. "I don't think I could ever make up for what I was involved in. I just saw you now and thought I'd check on you."

I watch—but now not as hesitant as before.

"Well, to answer your question—I would use the bike, but—" I then push down on the handlebars. There's a quick hiss sound as the rubber underneath the wheel flattens and spreads out. "So unless you got a pump hidden in that hoody somewhere, I'm pushing it."

The boy smiles. "Ha. Unfortunately, not. But I'll be sure to carry one for next time."

I glance over as we walk along together.

"I'm Cassio Socorro."

I nod. "Hayden."

"I know."

16.

FROM: TokyoCherryDustZ89@TokyoCherryDustZ89.com
TO: BlueC0ast1@bretteodmail.com
DATE: Fri 10th November, 10:55 PM
SUBJECT: Re: Dads In Cars

My dad was like your dad in the car, but instead of acting like the DJ on the radio was a friend in a bar, he would pretend to be the DJ. When a song was finishing, he'd turn the volume down and start speaking like the presenter, saying what the song was and making some comment about something we'd see outside the car, '…and it's warm this evening, warm enough to go for a jog, but remember folks, please wear the appropriate attire and not shorts that are way too small for you, just like that guy passing Bill's Super Looper Burgers on the left right now. We've already got a moon. We don't need another. And now it's time for…' but he'd have to turn the volume up a little because he didn't know if a new song had started or if it was advertisements.

But I get what you mean about memories—I'd like to remember similar things. The nights in with my sister, where we're watching movies and filling our mouths with ice cream so quickly that we'd forget that we'd get a brain freeze. The big school events that have happened and are yet to come. The trips out I had with my dad.

And the emails I've been sending and receiving from an unknown fellow high schooler.

-Tokyo

P.S. Hope you like the new mix.

FROM: BlueC0ast1@bretteodmail.com
TO: TokyoCherryDustZ89@TokyoCherryDustZ89.com
DATE: Fri 10th November, 11:19 PM

SUBJECT: Re: Dads In Cars

I can't believe you did an '80s version of Luna Lunalore's Cactus. I didn't think it would even be possible. Tokyo, that mix is amazing. Where do you even begin to make something like that?

I'm sure you've thought about it before, but have you considered posting these on KingsgateLeeConnect? Or have you put these online somewhere for people to hear?

Hilarious—I think I would cringe if my dad did that. But your dad sounds like he was really fun to be with.

The good thing about memories, though, is that you can not only hear them play out in your head, remembering the sounds around and the voices of people there, but you can also visualise how everything was. You can resee it. Like, with a scene at lunch at school, you can picture where your friends were sitting and how, what they were wearing, and even remember the smell of the food on their trays. But I guess the main thing to remember is that it can just take a tiny thing, like a certain smell or hearing a specific word, to bring those memories back.

And yes, I also like to remember these emails I've been receiving recently, too.

-Brisbane

FROM: TokyoCherryDustZ89@TokyoCherryDustZ89.com
TO: BlueC0ast1@bretteodmail.com
DATE: Fri 10th November, 11:54 PM
SUBJECT: Re: Dads In Cars

Yeah, my dad was. He was the type of dad that, although slightly embarrassing in front of your friends, they all loved him and thought he was the coolest parent to ever meet.

I love remixing an old song, but I kind of feel that it's more powerful, more beautiful, if you can take a song from now and send it back into the past.

Well, I listen to the original. Listen to each sound, every instrument and part of the song, as well as the lyrics, and sort of imagine it in my head as an '80s song and then try and play it. I begin with the bass to give me a starting point. Then, drop in some synth cords—everybody knows the synths are the blessing of the '80s—and then I put the beat in, too.

Next, I add the instrumental solos—so I might either play the guitar myself, or if it's an instrument I can't play, like the sax, I'll use a music programme to make one. Then, finally, I add the vocals (sometimes, I have to slightly alter them to fit the mix) and put it all together.

I haven't posted these mixes anywhere. Maybe some things are best kept to themselves.

Yes, Brisbane, the tiniest of things can bring memories back to you, but sometimes it's hard when you can't live in the moment.

Sometimes, I feel like everybody and everything around me has everything sorted. Like every person and thing is their own unique sound. And when you listen, their sounds are flowing peacefully together like a song, joyful and in sync. But then I'm there with my friends or family, and my sound is off. I don't have the right parts in me to play or know the tune to follow. I try to ignore it, but I can't.

And when I think I fit into part of their song, it still isn't right. It's like I'm off. Like I belong to another song, because here I'm just an unnecessary and invaluable note.

-Tokyo

17.

I stare down at my phone on my desk, gawping in disbelief. It's like someone's shoved a pufferfish against my back. I know who Tokyo is.

She let her identity slip. She feels out of tune or not playing the correct song. Playing a note out of time. Or a note that wasn't needed. A note, as she said herself, invaluable.

My mind fixates back on my first party here. At Jared Steele's house. The night where I became friends with a group of people—the night when Zeke introduced me to a girl there, where he explained the translation of her name was exactly that, an invaluable note.

Antonia Lu. She is Tokyo?

I try to let it sink in. Antonia did correct Zeke and said her name meant invaluable as in precious—but that doesn't mean she can't feel like the opposite at times.

All week, I try to pace my mind and think it through. However, in Algebra, I almost choke on the end of my pen when I wonder how Tokyo feels about her friends. I'm disheartened.

If Antonia is Tokyo, then that would mean she believes she doesn't fit in with Zeke, Billie, Dacre and me. She's been their friend for a long time. But she's the only person who's obsessed with fashion, the Populars and even KingsgateLeeConnect. But she must know we don't think differently of her? None of us are the same, but everybody respects each other. I hope she knows that.

After a few days—when I try to be as normal as I can around her at school—I realise I can't assume Antonia is Tokyo. There's some reason to think it could be, but I need to be sure. I did that with Jasmine—let my heart control my brain and muddle my feelings. And it hurt when I found out Jasmine wasn't her.

This time, I need to be certain. I need guaranteed proof.

I wonder about Tokyo's family. I know Antonia lives with her mom and has a little sister—but she's never mentioned her father—he could live with them, or her parents could be separated.

The truth behind her dad could probably be a key clue to it all, yet I quickly skip that observation because I find it morally wrong to wander down that rabbit hole.

There must be some other way, though.

I jump out of Esteban, Billie's car, with the others and stare up ahead. A futuristic-styled building that holds a yellow neon light outline of an armadillo with a purple circle and left slash flashing over it. Underneath is the writing *No Armadillos Allowed*.

It's an arcade—a favourite place for Billie, seeing as she wants to be a game designer. It's a bizarre name. But apparently, not in the gaming world. An armadillo is what gamers call a person who plays too slow. So, I guess I won't be finding Robin there anytime soon.

Andrew has joined us tonight. The six of us head through the large purple doors, and I immediately think this is the closest thing I'm ever going to feel what it would have been like to be standing in the '80s. It's darkly painted with large, thick coloured lines zooming up, down and across the walls, with only the different colourful neon lights and a vast number of screens from the games to brighten up the place.

There are white swirls and circular planets on the deep blue carpet, and I can see what it must be like for God to look down on us with the mirrored tiles across the entire ceiling.

Music's playing from speakers somewhere, but the room is filled with the sheer volume of whizzes, plunks, gunshots and engine sounds going on around us.

Zeke turns around to face us. "Right. There's six of us, so tonight's a team battle." Some of the group make sounds of excitement. "We split into twos, and whoever gets the most tickets by eight wins. Are you ready? Grab a partner, and let's get gaming!"

Before I know what's happening, Zeke grabs Andrew—before Billie can get him. And because of that, Billie glances at us and drags a shocked Dacre away. And I'm alone. With Antonia.

I look around for something to talk about. Out of everybody in the group, I probably talk least to Antonia. Not on purpose—just not much in common to discuss. But if she is Tokyo, then maybe we do.

Antonia takes the lead, and I follow her. She tells me she knows where we should go if we want loads of tickets. The Carnival Section. There are images of tigers, clowns, fishes, bears and ringmasters beside each physical funfair game.

We head to the nearest game and are given a minute to knock as many teeth as possible down from a large cut-out of an alligator wearing a large sombrero with some colourful bean bags.

After we finish, the machine makes a scratch noise. Tickets begin to pour out.

"I thought you weren't much of a gamer," I say to Antonia, who looks delighted with our score.

"I'm not, but if you're friends with Billie, you kind of have to know the basics." Antonia grabs the tickets and then suggests we try the next game. "You weren't exactly a beginner either."

I smirk. I wouldn't say I was great at that game, but I think Coach Rugrosso would be pleased with some of my shots. Better than how I was with my throwing in dodgeball yesterday.

I put some money into the next machine. There's an elephant named Frank on the board. We must throw as many rings as we can onto the elephant's tusks—but it doesn't help when Frank's trunk suddenly begins to flail about and knocks our rings from hitting our targets.

As we start, I can't help but question how I can see if Antonia is Tokyo. How can I work out if she is her?

"Oh, watermelons!" Antonia says one of her Suitable Replacement words when her ring misses the tusk. These are words she says when she doesn't want to use a more explicit word.

We begin to talk about school, and then Antonia speaks of Billie.

"Billie's my best friend. She's so much fun, clever, and doesn't care what others think. She's confident. I'd love to be that."

You'd love to be confident because you're Tokyo and you're concerned about what others think if you share your remixes? My mind instantly wonders. But then I realise what she is saying.

"I think you're pretty confident." I throw a ring. It just misses Frank the Elephant's trunk and spins around and down onto the tusk. I quickly lean over to grab some more.

"Me? No way." She's a little taken aback by my comment. "I couldn't dare bring myself to wear a kangaroo costume at Halloween until everyone saw you guys in them at the party."

I'm certain *you guys* just means Jasmine—but I keep hush on that.

"But you stand for what you believe in. Look at the other day. You wouldn't let that senior go until he picked up his bottle and put it in the recycling bin. I wouldn't dream of doing that." I then notice the multicoloured woollen cropped jumper and white tennis-like skirt she has on. "Besides, Halloween was fancy dress. Look at what you wear every day. Really cool stuff. You know what you like, you create your own style, and whenever I see you, you look like you own it and aren't afraid. You're like the most fashionably confident person I know."

The sound of an elephant toots from the machine—it's the end of the game. We score twenty-two tickets.

Antonia pulls the bottom of her jumper down slightly. "You think so?"

Well done, the ringmaster's voice on the machine says.

I turn to Antonia. "Yes." And it's true. I do. Antonia glances, and her folded lips smile.

What do you think of that, Frank?

"Thanks."

There's another loud toot. In the corner of my eye, the elephant's trunk rises, and something begins to shoot out.

"Look out!" I grab Antonia's shoulder and push her back—a huge squirt of water splashes into my cheek.

"Oh, Hayden." Antonia's words were for concern, but her voice doesn't sound it. I'm not pleased I'm wet, but it makes me happy when I hear her laughing.

"D'you mind if we play another game? One where you don't get wet?" I ask, wiping my face.

Antonia smirks and takes me to another game, and from then on, we seem to begin to talk more. After telling me stories of her, Billie, Zeke and Dacre, Antonia then begins to talk about fashion—not that I have much knowledge on the subject. I mostly wear hoodies because they're comfy, which she says is fine because wearing something that is comfortable to you gives you positive energy.

However, most interestingly of all, I learn, after smacking a clown on its head with a hammer, that Antonia wants to be a doctor.

"Wanted to since I was little. My mom's one, and I've always been fascinated to help injured people."

I think it's cool she wants to follow in her mom's footsteps. Robin's doing the same with Dad. And it is great how Antonia wants a career in that profession. However, it's thrown me off—I never knew she wanted to be a doctor. I guess I assumed she was going to go for some job associated with fashion because she always talks about that industry.

Later on, we join Billie and Dacre and begin playing air hockey.

As we play, my mind realises that my attempts to check if Antonia is Tokyo tonight have, in fact, been pointless.

If Tokyo's scared to be honest about herself in real life, to her own friends, then Antonia clearly isn't going to open up to me right now. To her friend. And never will in person.

There's a loud ping. I bring my eyes back to the game. Something orange soars straight to my forehead. I blink and smack my hand immediately onto my head. It was the puck.

Billie comes rushing over. "I'm so sorry!"

Antonia holds my shoulders and twists me to face her. I tell her I'm fine.

"You've got a cut. And it's bleeding," she objects. Billie orders Dacre to go to the till and ask for a First Aid kit or something.

"No, it's fine. I can sort it—" But Dacre's already left.

"It doesn't matter. He won't come back for ages," Billie says.

"How serious is it?" I ask when Antonia opens her gold-chained purse. I tap where it stings on my head, just on the top of my left eyebrow. There's the tiniest dab of red on my finger. "It's nothing."

"I'll decide on that."

Before I can object, she pushes me to lean back against the air hockey table. After a little rummage, she pulls something out of her purse. A plaster.

"Really?"

Antonia nods at me as she opens it up.

"I guess it's good I've learnt you want to be a doctor tonight, hey? Don't think I'd trust anyone else to put a plaster on me," I joke. But then she gently presses the plaster on my head. Her soft fingers touching my skin.

There's a trace of lush raspberry coming from her hair.

"I suppose it is," Antonia replies. She taps the plaster again. "All good." She then squints as if to mock. "I think you'll be fine."

I laugh. She's funnier than what I made her out to be.

The only concrete way to find out if Antonia, or anybody, is Tokyo, I understand now, is if she tells me herself or I find more hard, physical, concrete facts. But now's not the time.

"Hang on." I turn to Billie, remembering what she said. "Why won't Dacre come back for ages?"

"Oh, he's been going over a few times trying to persuade the guy at the till to lend us some tickets," Billie answers—her eyes wide open. "I wasn't meant to tell you that."

There's no surprise that Billie and Dacre win the Team Battle—and that's without actually being able to borrow any tickets from the arcade till guy. And to say Dacre spent most of the night at the till, I'm just glad the air hockey injury to my eyebrow wasn't that serious.

On Thursday night, I work at Mt. Okesea, thankfully with Zeke and not Kamala. Once again, nobody makes the ball go in one on the last hole. Some guys ask Zeke if we can put a ball in to see the mountain come alive, but Zeke stands by his rule—that it would ruin my first time seeing it if it wasn't done properly. He does let me have another go at putting it, but the ball gets to the second incline block before it rolls off the side.

Our school football team plays on Friday—and we cheer on Dacre when he plays. We yell and jokingly shout he's doing rubbish or that he needs to watch out for the ball because he's so small when he's actually doing well. We have fun but have to stop laughing when the hotdog sausage Zeke flings misses Dacre—and hits Coach Gard instead.

When we leave the stand, after our school wins, I hear my name being called out. I know right away who it is. I turn around and see Jasmine approaching me. The others continue walking as I wait. However, we're not alone—in her short orange cheerleading uniform is Chloe Cassadentini.

My cheeks turn red when I approach Jasmine. We haven't really spoken since the meal at Mt. Okesea. Since I discovered she isn't Tokyo. Not on purpose. We've both been busy.

"Hi."

"Hayden, this is Chloe. Chloe, Hayden. You know, who's been helping me with my Spanish," Jasmine explains.

Chloe makes some vague acknowledgement without looking up from the phone in her hands. She then begins to walk away. "I'm off to the car. Don't be long. The film's going to start soon."

"Bye," I say to be polite despite Chloe being rude. Jasmine apologises for her behaviour. "It's fine. What film are you off to see?"

"*Field of Dreams* at Bailey & Lone's Drive-In."

"No way? So am I. Billie's request. I didn't know you were into them."

"What? Films? I think everybody likes films," Jasmine teases, like nothing is different. Well, it isn't. Not for her. Maybe I'm just overthinking things; why should things be different? I liked her before I started wishing she was Tokyo; it can go back to before for me, surely? Just friends. "To be honest, it's Chloe's idea to go. I better head off."

We say our goodbyes, and she heads by me, but she stops.

"Actually, the reason why I called—I wondered if you could continue tutoring me? We've only covered speaking—and reading and writing are totally different things."

Part of me questions whether it's a good idea as it was only the other week when I was imagining her as Tokyo. It's taken a while to stop thinking that. But she's a friend, I remind myself.

"Sure."

The huge, delightful smile that beams on her face almost wipes me off my feet because it's so cute. I feel nearly guilty for thinking that.

Jasmine thanks me a few times happily, and after we say our goodbyes, she finally does leave—yet I can't help but be a little wretched inside. She isn't Tokyo.

I manage to push that feeling aside as I watch *Field of Dreams* with the others. But now, with her just sat beside me, I can't stop worrying about Antonia—sad that if she is Tokyo, then she believes that she doesn't belong with her real friends. Us.

When the film finishes, and we head to The Cerise Wave Diner, I learn Antonia's mom is taking her sister to a dance competition in Miami next weekend. The group knows what that means. Another party.

I grin more, though. A party. At Antonia's house—it's the best chance to get an answer if Antonia is Tokyo.

18.

FROM: TokyoCherryDustZ89@TokyoCherryDustZ89.com
TO: BlueC0ast1@bretteodmail.com
DATE: Tue 21st November, 12:34 PM
SUBJECT: Everybody's Got Something Holding Them

I can't believe what you're telling me! Douglas Lovina's The Best Night is apparently a song about a girl finding her prince, but then wishing she was dancing with a better prince? How have I never known this before? I feel…I don't know how I feel…vile? Oh goodness. I'm just thinking of all those birthday parties I went to as a child, and they got us to do the dance moves to that song. I don't know if I can ever dance to that again!

I've given some thought to posting my '80s remixes on KingsgateLeeConnect, but I don't think I can. It's just I'm not certain if I can face what others will think. I haven't even posted any online. I've only emailed them to you.

-Tokyo

FROM: BlueC0ast1@bretteodmail.com
TO: TokyoCherryDustZ89@TokyoCherryDustZ89.com
DATE: Tue 21st November, 4:44 PM
SUBJECT: Re: Everybody's Got Something Holding Them

Yep, that's exactly what I'm saying. It's totally traumatised my childhood school dances. Then imagine being at a wedding reception and seeing the bride and groom dancing to that…eek!

I understand the worry about putting your music out there. But like somebody told me once when I wasn't sure about telling them something—well, something along these lines—how will you know if you don't try?

Isn't that the same for every artist when they release new material?

Is it scary? Probably. But don't sell yourself short, Tokyo. You've shown me the strong, fun, and determined person you are in these emails. They're good, Tokyo. Those mixes are really good.

-Brisbane

FROM: TokyoCherryDustZ89@TokyoCherryDustZ89.com
TO: BlueC0ast1@bretteodmail.com
DATE: Tue 21st November, 6:23 PM
SUBJECT: Re: Everybody's Got Something Holding Them

That poor couple. But if we're going for the worst songs for brides and grooms to dance to, I can top it. I was at a wedding two years ago, and the couple's first dance was to Thoughtless Journeys. Great song, don't get me wrong, a masterpiece. But I'm sure it's about a girl in a relationship and her regret about cheating with the one she really loves.

You raise an interesting point. And thanks for the support. But I just can't. I'm sorry. I don't dare risk letting others hear the remixes. Maybe some things are too big of a risk. And I don't know if I'll ever have the courage to find out.

-Tokyo

FROM: BlueC0ast1@bretteodmail.com
TO: TokyoCherryDustZ89@TokyoCherryDustZ89.com
DATE: Tue 21st November, 7:50 PM
SUBJECT: Let The Battle Of Who's Heard The Worst Song At A Wedding Commence…

Ah, so we're having a battle of who's heard the most inappropriate song played at a wedding? Well, I'll give you that song in the First Song edition, but overall, at my cousin's wedding, the DJ played Rex & The Readingfield Brothers – I'm Always Looking For The Perfect Ending I'll Never Find. Picture dancing closely and holding your loved one in your arms and mouthing those words. Awkward.

It's fine, Tokyo. I understand. There are still things I'm scared to do, and I seriously doubt I'll ever overcome them. And you don't ever have to apologise. But just know, you have a fan here.

-Brisbane

FROM: TokyoCherryDustZ89@TokyoCherryDustZ89.com
TO: BlueC0ast1@bretteodmail.com
DATE: Wed 22nd November, 8:12 AM
SUBJECT: Re: Let The Battle Of Who's Heard The Worst Song At A Wedding Commence…

I open my hands and bow down to you, sir. I believe you have won this round. All I had left up my sleeves was The Girl Likes Money by Daniel Wattorby—the irony was that it was at my mom's friend's wedding, her second time to say 'I Do' after her first marriage mysteriously ended with a divorce just a few weeks after it had been announced her rich husband's business went bust.

But anyway, I congratulate you on your win. I hope it takes you far with your other achievements.

-Tokyo

P.S. Thank you

FROM: BlueC0ast1@bretteodmail.com
TO: TokyoCherryDustZ89@TokyoCherryDustZ89.com
DATE: Wed 22nd November, 8:24 AM
SUBJECT: Re: Let The Battle Of Who's Heard The Worst Song At A Wedding Commence…

Really? Wow, that must have been the easiest win in history. And I didn't even play my best card. But I'll take the win. I'm expecting to be given my dream job just for holding this win—not because of my grades or my hobbies—just this.

-Brisbane

P.S. Have you heard about Antonia Lu's party this Friday? Are you going? I'm not asking so we can meet. It might be too soon. I just quite like the thought that we'll be under the same roof, seeing the same things and listening to the same music.

FROM: TokyoCherryDustZ89@TokyoCherryDustZ89.com
TO: BlueC0ast1@bretteodmail.com
DATE: Wed 22nd November, 8:33 AM
SUBJECT: Re: Let The Battle Of Who's Heard The Worst Song At A Wedding Commence…

You had something better for hearing the most inappropriate song at a wedding? Let me guess. Was it The Kallidge's Love's Overrated?

-Tokyo

FROM: TokyoCherryDustZ89@TokyoCherryDustZ89.com
TO: BlueC0ast1@bretteodmail.com
DATE: Wed 22nd November, 8:35 AM
SUBJECT: No, Is The Song This?

No. Moose Metro & The Green Garage's I'll Get Through This?

FROM: TokyoCherryDustZ89@TokyoCherryDustZ89.com
TO: BlueC0ast1@bretteodmail.com
DATE: Wed 22nd November, 8:39 AM
SUBJECT: ANY OF THESE!

There Was A Murder At My Wedding by Melvin Jonert?
My Exes Never Get Over Me by Olivia Curves? Because the bride really did have ex-partners wanting her back before the wedding day?
Rainn Plutio's Forever Is Too Long? Warren Wertlay's I'm A Cheat? Potion Sivor's We Could Have Done Better?

-Tokyo

P.S. And yes, I did hear about the party this Friday. But you do realise we go to the same school and are already under the same roof? But yes, I will most likely be there.

FROM: BlueC0ast1@bretteodmail.com
TO: TokyoCherryDustZ89@TokyoCherryDustZ89.com
DATE: Wed 22nd November, 8:57 AM
SUBJECT: Re: ANY OF THESE!

Claro Harve Claro – She Was Just A Back Up.

19.

Thankfully, when Dad places the turkey down on the table, it seems to have been cooked to perfection. Not by Dad—no way, he did the vegetables. But by Colbey and Aunt Maria.

Uncle Chad and his family, who are from my dad's side, came from Dallas yesterday to share Thanksgiving with us like they usually do. Even though being here will probably be more chaotic than relaxing, I'm quite pleased to see them because it brings a bit of normality back to the household, even if we're in a different house compared to last year.

I thought the weirdest part about Mom not being here on Thanksgiving Day would be that she wasn't here to prepare the food. It's usually her and Aunt Maria's thing. However, it's when we all sit down at the table, and we all know that we're one person short, that makes me feel most uncomfortable.

I hadn't expected anybody to mention Mom—during the entire week or even just today—but somebody does. Dad.

"It's been a tough year. For various reasons. Like Mom leaving."

There's a second of absolute silence. Even my cousins, Rico and Isabella, freeze when hearing the words.

"We've even moved to a new place. But I'm thankful for us here. For being together. And seeing my children adapt. For Colbey, starting a new and great job at the university. For Robin, already making a mark at school so quickly, still hitting top scores. Because soon she'll be flying the nest to college next year." There are a few laughs from around the table at Dad's bird puns. Uncle Chad even flaps his hands and makes a birdcall. It's more of a crow than a robin, in my opinion, but still funny. "But I'm still expecting you to migrate back here for Thanksgiving Break every year." Then he turns to me—nerves swamp me up. "And for Hayden. It hasn't been easy for you, son. There's nobody to blame for what's happened this year, but I'm proud of how you are now. How you've managed to get back out. Not just with grades but in life. I thank you, my children, for making me proud."

There's a lump in my throat as everybody makes the sound of

agreement—thankfully Uncle Chad starts to say his thanks.

I look over at Dad.

I wasn't expecting that. I mean, he said my brother and then my sister, so I knew he was going to say something about me. Maybe to say, thankful for the good grades I'm getting. Nothing like what he actually said, though. And it touches me that he cares so much.

When it's my turn, I'm thankful for my family and the friends I've made here. I think of Zeke, Billie, Antonia, Dacre and even Andrew. But mostly, I think of Tokyo when I say friends.

Robin twists in her chair ever so slightly—it reminds me of her being taken away from her old life to come here. I want to say thank you to her—for being able to cope when it was my fault we moved from home. But I don't. She'd think I was putting her on the spot in front of everybody—forced to accept my gratitude when she clearly doesn't agree.

"And I'm thankful for you all being patient with me," I say instead. And leave it as that. There's a bit of awkward silence. Fortunately, Isabella doesn't notice and begins her thanks. And I'm thankful she does.

We dig into the food after everybody has said their thanks. We watch the football game on TV and end the night playing the board game Uncle Chad has brought.

After Robin wins nearly all the games, we call it a night. When I'm in bed, I open my laptop and do what I said I would do for Tokyo. I put on *The Nightmare Before Christmas*. I think it's too early, but I do it anyway. As the opening credits begin, it makes me feel like this is our thing. Mine and Tokyo's. And although she isn't here with me watching, I feel like she is.

On Friday evening, the emotions are a whirlwind. I'm watching the football game. But this time with Colbey, plus his coach from university. And at halftime, the team's losing.

I couldn't exactly tell Dacre why I couldn't help Antonia and the others set up for her party, but I did message him earlier to do well in tonight's game. Colbey would kill me if he knew I let slip that they were here scouting.

I don't really pay attention to the halftime cheerleading performance as I try to listen into Colbey and his coach discussing players—but when my phone vibrates to inform me that I've received an email from Tokyo, my lips curl in glee and I'm glued to the phone instead.

Somehow, despite losing at halftime, Dacre and the team manage to pull it back and win.

"This is better. For us, I mean," Colbey's coach says to me as everybody leaves the stand. "There's nothing more powerful than a clawback. Shows us that despite being down, despite everything going against them, they don't let the black hole of defeat and the long challenge ahead suck them up and let it be over with. The players can either be swallowed up or face it head-on. These guys dug somewhere deep and bare within to find that grit and rise to the challenge and got out."

The passion in the coach's eyes gleams brightly. I nod, though my eyes stay cautious of him; it's the most emotion I've seen in him all evening. But I get what he's saying—they want players who can not only make winning easy but can also overcome any pressure or fears in their heads and act.

The coach strongly shakes my hand to say goodbye, then leaves with Colbey to talk to Coach Gard—but I suddenly get an idea. I know how to show my thankfulness to Tokyo than by just saying it in an email. I just need to go back to mine with Dacre before going to help the others at Antonia's party.

The stand's now empty. I wait outside the locker rooms for Dacre.

The door bursts open. I almost dive around the corner when Jared Steele storms out, kicking anything in his way. To say they won the match, he looks furious.

Seconds later, more of the team leave. They look pleased, as I'd expect winners to be. However, there's no Dacre.

I wait alone, with my rucksack full of clothes for the party, wondering what's happened.

Eventually, the door opens again. It's Dacre. There's this huge cheesy grin on his face, and I've never seen anything like it on him.

"What?" I ask, on guard.

He pulls me under his arm and ruffles my hair. "Coming to spend time with Colbey, my ass! Antonia was furious you were coming here instead of helping the others—you came because you knew your brother was scouting, didn't you? That's why you texted today telling me to make sure I played well today."

"Yes," I grittily say as he begins to move us. "But he told me not to say. I didn't mean to lie."

"Hey." Dacre stops rubbing my head and slips his arm back so it's just dangling across my shoulders. "I'm not angry. I'm thrilled."

Turns out my brother and the coach wanted to talk to him after they'd spoken to some of the seniors. He was the only non-senior told to wait back. They were impressed with him. That much, they want him to head down to the university for a talk. Like an interview and discuss options for the future after high school.

I'm so thrilled for him. The brightness on his face makes me happy, too. I'm pleased—we're so caught in the moment that I nearly forget to ask to divert to mine before we go to Antonia's.

He's so elated with what's happened that he says yes before I even have to make up an excuse for needing to go there.

"You're not even dressed yet?" Antonia shrieks when Dacre and I arrive. Her house is filled with disco balls—but what can you expect for a retro-themed party? Before we can explain, or I can admire her outfit—white and blue check leggings and a loose blue shirt tied in a knot before her—she quickly scurries us to the downstairs bathroom.

I take off my hoody and then my shirt and grab the plain white T-shirt I'm wearing for tonight.

Dacre takes his top off—but even with his height and his sort of slenderness considered, I'm a little taken aback by how muscular and developed his upper arms are and even his chest. Pecks with abs below, as in not a six but an eight pack, and very toned. His stomach is a washboard; the ridges are easily visible. The guy has it all. He's been crafted by the Greek gods, like a statue at Mt. Okesea.

"Hayden, are you checking me out?"

My eyes flick up—Dacre's staring at me, in nothing but his black boxers. "No, I—I wasn't. I'm just—you're like that," I stumble over my words. "And I'm—" I look lower down to my bare stomach, "—this."

I'm not built or even partially built on my chest or my arms, but I'm not flabby either. My stomach's just sort of flat—though, at times, the belly looks a little stuck out.

"You're in good shape." I puff some air out at Dacre's response. "I mean it. I play football, train all the time, have a strict diet and constantly have checks."

I kind of get what he means. I saw how much Colbey used to do when I was younger. He was relentlessly training his body. He doesn't do anywhere near as much now since his accident and is on the coaching side of things, but he still works out as much as he physically can. And he's still in pretty good shape, too.

"I know. But still—"

There are no fine tones of muscle or cuts of ribs. And when I see Dacre like that, it makes me wonder what Tokyo would think. She won't exactly be going, *woah, he's handsome.*

We've admitted we like each other's company, but what if she discovers who I am and wants nothing to do with me because it's me? This scrawny average boy. And if it is Antonia, will she still want to talk because I'm Brisbane?

"What if I'm not attractive enough?"

Dacre stares at me. I panic if he asks why I'm bringing this up. And guys don't talk about this. I can't imagine they do this in the locker room before they go out to play. I'm embarrassed—I don't even know why I said it.

I'm about to apologise, but Dacre steps forward.

"You know it's not all about your appearance, right? People who find true happiness with someone have it because they're attracted to who that person is inside. What is it they say? Looks fade, but personality always stays. And you aren't the person who's vain in wanting to be attractive just so they can have anybody. The right one will come. They'll see how attractive you are—inside and out."

He's standing before me. He's right. I know he's right. Personality is what we truly fall for. And I think deep down somewhere, I've been aware of that since I realised I liked Tokyo. And maybe the right person is Tokyo.

Dacre's still looking at me but now via the mirror beside us. I try to smile back—but it's somewhat forced.

"Besides, I think you're too innocent to know this, but you're quite easy on the eyes." Dacre then ruffles my hair. "And, you know, I think the Floridan sun has lightened your hair. And girls like light-haired guys."

He turns away and continues getting ready. I look back in the mirror. I think he's right; my hair has got lighter.

The party is in full swing. Everybody looks great. Some people have gone for the silly stereotypical retro decade clothes like the famous *Saturday Night Fever* white suits, the colourful flower dresses with pink-tinted glasses and flowery headbands, and some are rocking the plaid shirt and high-waist trousers look.

Dacre's rocking an old neon ski jumpsuit—the ones parents wear in their old ski holiday videos—it's a bold aqua blue but with purple and black sleeves. I'm just glad I'm not wearing that because I'd be sweating in it. I've gone for a simple denim-on-denim look with a white T-shirt.

"Well, the kids in *Sister Act 2* just rang—they want their clothes back," Zeke says over to Billie while sitting on the headrest of one of the couches. The others around make some noise and stare at Billie in her denim dungarees, with the straps dangling at either side, and a black cap that is facing backwards and squishing her hair down. "Look if Depp can wear it in *Nightmare* and Winter does in *Excellent Adventure,* then I sure as heck can rock a crop top."

Zeke flails his arms out to display his grey crop top jumper. It's a bit rugged at the bottom, almost like somebody's cut a normal jumper from just above the belly button with a pair of scissors. A blunt pair at that.

I pull my phone out after remembering I've been too busy to reply to Tokyo. I email her to be in the room where everybody is dancing to the DJ at ten. I explain not to worry and that I'm not trying to do something to catch her out. It's just a surprise I think she'll like.

Everybody's ecstatic with Dacre's football news—well, Antonia's half celebrating, half running around and being paranoid about things breaking. And when everybody becomes slightly irritated because she constantly pauses whatever game we're playing, I offer to go and check instead.

I offer to be kind, but I have my own reason.

I try to run through the things Tokyo has said about herself. Something from her emails that I can use and search for around the house and lead me to an answer if Antonia is Tokyo.

I search the ground floor—saving a small bonsai tree in a plant pot in the process from a drunk guy who's singing into it like a microphone—but end up finding nothing.

Looking back, perhaps it would have been easier to get this confirmation if I had come here earlier to help set up than gone to the game. But I needed to be there.

Now, with a plant to store somewhere safe, I search for some cupboard or closet for me to hide the plant in, but there's nothing.

My eyes catch the stairs. There's some rope across to stop people going up. That's where I can take it. I walk over—only to stop. Against the flashing lights, there are slightly faded outlines of where photos are normally hung on the walls—taken down for safety.

I pause to look down at what's in my hands—the tree—then back to the empty photo spaces. I gasp.

Tokyo said she has photos of cherry blossoms on her bedroom wall.

Antonia's room is upstairs. That's how I'll get my proof.

I dart over to the stairs, duck under the rope at the bottom, all while feeling excited and nervous at the same time.

"Move it, Mallard."

My bodes tenses. I turn around—my eyes meet Jared Steele's. A wave of panic comes over me. He's dressed in a black tank top and a pair of short green shorts.

"It's out of bounds," I try to say. Jared's eyebrows furrow. His eyes somehow seem to go darker. "I'm house checking for Antonia."

He scoffs. "I won't tell you again, Mallard. I know your brother was that assistant coach tonight at the game. He and that coach did wrong in not wanting to speak to me."

Now it makes sense why Jared was furious after the game. But I don't move.

"Look, just because your new friend asked us not to mess you around doesn't mean I won't take my word back. I can easily start it again."

He means Cassio.

My free hand grabs the railing beside me—queasy at the memories of their abuse. The agony brewing inside—yet now I want to lash out. Show Jared he doesn't have a hold on me. I stare back—but I don't give.

He leans forward. I close my eyes in fright.

"If I heard it from over there, then you did too."

I open one eye. Andrew Kwong's standing behind Jared, with his arms crossed. The music is loud, but for a second, I swear it suddenly disappears, and there's only us.

Jared twists his head at me. I hold my stance. His upper lip pricks up to the side. "Fine."

He turns around, after giving another horrid stare at me, and ventures into the pool of people. A load of air suddenly exhales quickly out of me. I push my hand through my own hair, trying to reclaim some control and then step off the bottom step.

"That guy seems like a jerk," Andrew says. He unfolds his arms, revealing his huge-oversized black and dark green Anaheim Ducks top, and pats my shoulder. Black pushed-back hair bounces as he puts an arm around my shoulders.

I say thanks, and when he suggests we go to the others, I tell him I'll be there soon after I take the bonsai upstairs.

Andrew nods and leaves me to get back to my plan.

Call it invading privacy. I don't think it is. I'm helping Antonia to check that everything and everybody is fine…and if I happen to stumble into Antonia's room on House Check, then so be it. Besides, this poor plant needs to find a safe home.

Excitement begins to rush inside me—I step onto the landing. Crap! An array of random objects from downstairs clutter every inch of the landing—brought up here for safety yet blocking and guarding each of the five doors.

My cheeks puff out the slight frustration in me. I place the bonsai down next to a dining chair and begin moving stuff about.

After a few minutes, I reach the first door. I tut—Antonia's sister's room.

I try the second room after blocking the first with the correct objects like before, only to find it's not her room either. I eventually reach the third room.

There's nothing but white paint on the first wall—and then Antonia's schoolbag on the floor. This is it. I take a deep breath—are there photos with cherry blossoms on them?

My eyes follow the room. The bed. A desk. A window. A built-in wardrobe with large mirrors standing from ceiling to floor.

My heart sinks—nothing.

I step into the room, defeated. I catch myself seeing the discouraged person that is me in the mirrors—my eyes flicker to the surface of the mirrors. There are things on them. Photos.

I quickly examine them all. There could still be a chance—

None. No cherry blossoms.

I become disheartened again—the realisation that Antonia isn't Tokyo.

I'd been so sure she was. I was shocked at first by the possibility, unable to believe it might be one of my friends. I tried to adjust and be cautious and not overthink or get quickly attached to the thought she was Tokyo without proof. But I guess I somewhat have. Because I'm a little sad.

My eyes advert back to the photos stuck onto the mirrors. A young Antonia coming down a slide with a young Billie, still with large, wavy hair, waiting at the top. There's Antonia, Zeke, Billie, Dacre and Andrew on an inflatable raft at a water park, all screaming, except Zeke, who's pulling a weird face directly at the camera.

And there's a collection of photos taken from parties. Then I see me.

There's Billie, Zeke and Dacre with me squished together. We're outside somewhere but not posing. It's slightly blurry. It's from my first party—when we played that game. Running madly to get into Antonia's shot in time so we didn't have to drink.

I'm sad I didn't find what I was looking for, but I've found something else. I was concerned Antonia didn't feel she could trust us if she were Tokyo, but when I look at these photos, I see that Antonia *does* feel comfortable.

I leave the room and block the doors again with objects so nobody can get in, and then head back down to the party, not feeling as dismayed as before.

As the music swamps my ears, my phone vibrates. It's an email from Tokyo.

She's asking questions about why I've asked her to be in the main room at ten. I don't reply; she will object and try to stop it if I do. True, that might be a chance to see who she is, but that's not why I'm doing what I've got planned.

I check the time. There's not long left. I make my way over to the DJ set. The guy, some senior, is chatting to a girl at the side. He's facing away from his laptop. *Now's my best chance.* I pull out the USB that I got from home before I came. I quickly place it on his laptop, right way up, and hurriedly back away in case he turns. Soon, he'll notice the USB and read the note attached to it. A message which I've pretended is from Antonia—the host.

I head back to my friends—not without having to squeeze through dancers, which includes a very drunk Chloe Cassadentini, who is wearing a revealing tight, orange, sleeveless jumpsuit. The zip has only made it as far as just under her belly button, showing her bare skin all the way up the middle. Jasmine grabs Chloe before she trips over and continues to dance elsewhere. She's definitely drank a lot.

I escape and find myself in an open room that looks out to the garden. There's a loud jumble of cries and laughter. People are sprawled out on the floor in the centre after playing some game.

However, my eyes are caught by the people sitting on couches. Well, the couch that's occupied by two people sprawled over and making out. I notice the bright neon suit. It's Dacre. Hands are rubbing on his bare chest between his unzipped ski jumpsuit as another mouth is locked onto his. He's with another guy.

Zeke and Antonia rush over to the door to look out at Dacre in the other room after I tell them what I saw. "No way!"

"Actually, I think it's the guy on the till at No Armadillos," I say, realising who the boy Dacre is with might be.

"Now that makes sense why he kept going over to get us tickets and sucked every time," Billie comments back on a couch.

Zeke twists back from peeking out of the door. "Sucked being the correct word."

"Zeke!"

"On the lips! On the lips, I meant! But honestly, if they go anymore, they'll be going off-piste."

Andrew walks over to sit next to Billie. "Leave them be."

"I think it's cute. He deserves a good guy," Antonia says.

It's the first time I've seen her since discovering she isn't Tokyo, and to be truthful, it hasn't bothered me as much as I thought it would.

Zeke moves away. "I wouldn't say them doing their own ski ploughing in a room filled with people is cute. But good for him."

"It's too early to be from drunk courage," Billie says. "It's not even halfway through the night."

From Billie's words, my body almost jerks in panic. I get my phone out—it's nearly ten. I ask if people want to head to the main room. I expect everybody to say no. But, thankfully, they say yes.

We grab our drinks and head through to the dancefloor. We have to practically drag Antonia away from happily watching Dacre and the No Armadillos guy on the couch.

People are dancing in front of the DJ as lights flash everywhere, and more people are standing around towards the back and to the kitchen. Kamala and her fellow doppelgangers dressed in leather biker outfits—besides the purple hair and her one light eyebrow—are drinking on the couches.

The room's very warm. So is my skin—especially wearing this denim jacket, but my breath feels cold. Cold with nerves. I'm in the same house as Tokyo. A trickle of worry hits me—I consider whether to stop what I've planned. But I don't move.

The current song ends naturally, with the music and lyrics fading out—then I hear it.

The sound of the bamboo flute alone catches people off guard. So much that the people on the dancefloor aren't moving. I start to panic if they hate it. But it's too late.

The drums come in, and then the guitar riff. Some people around are tapping their feet and bopping their heads. I don't feel as nervous, but

I'm still frightened. Nobody's dancing yet. But then her voice comes out to the room. Faces turn to recognition when they hear Kaiya Prior's voice, and more follow when they realise they've heard the lyrics before. The looks around me soon turn to intrigue when they don't know the sound. They don't know it because this is Tokyo's remix. Playing from the USB that I got from home and put on the DJ's laptop.

I knew Tokyo wouldn't have gone beyond her laptop, not without a little push.

Zeke asks me if the song is "Do You Remember." I nod.

The synthesisers kick in—and the vocals are in their element. My body remembers how to breathe again—people are starting to dance. Andrew walks by with Billie's hand in his and leads her to the dancefloor. Antonia and Zeke follow—but manage to pull me with them.

Soon, everybody's smiling and singing along to the lyrics of this popular hit, but their moves are different. Fresh. Freeing. They beam and dance wonderfully and passionately thanks to the new mid-tempo ballad style it's been given.

I see Robin and her friends dancing along, and I can make out Chloe and her friends are also moving to the track. Everybody's loving it.

I did it for her, though. Not me. To show how incredible she is.

I may not know who Tokyo is yet, but I hope she, wherever she is in here, knows now how special she is to me.

20.

FROM: TokyoCherryDustZ89@TokyoCherryDustZ89.com
TO: BlueC0ast1@bretteodmail.com
DATE: Fri 24th November, 11:59 PM
SUBJECT: Is That My Music?

I can't believe you did that! You took my mix, my creation, and went behind my back to play it out to the party in front of everybody!

And I just want to say…thank you. I was shocked when I heard the first notes of Do You Remember? because I knew instantly what it was. Even though you told me you had a surprise ready, and I was in the room waiting, I wasn't expecting that.

Smart move, Brisbane. Leaving a USB with instructions and pretending it was from the party host.

I may have asked the DJ where he got it from, but don't bother questioning him who asked if you're trying to discover who I am. Loads of people have asked him where he got the mix from. Fortunately, he had the decency to not claim it as his own.

I wanted to find you so I could strangle you. Maybe even origami you. But then I saw people weren't complaining or ordering the DJ to change the song. They were dancing, and the place became alive, and it warmed me inside. To see people be delighted with something I helped create. It gave me joy.

Things have been difficult recently for me, and they knocked my confidence. To a point where I didn't feel like I was myself. And still kind of don't at times. But certainly to a point where I'd never have the courage to put my stuff out there, for it to be heard and be judged.

So I understand why you did it. So, thank you, Brisbane. For giving me that step I needed but never knew how I could take. I hope I can do the same for you, too.

Love,
Tokyo

21.

"How did you feel when you were told your mom had gone?" Mr Gauran questions me on Tuesday.

"Confused. Angry. I think." My head is already slowly starting to hurt—doing what it always does when I try to remember. Mr Gauran asks why. "Because whether the parents split or not, they should still support their kids—be there for them. And she just went."

I reposition myself on the small brick wall we're sitting on outside near the car park. "I suppose. It was hard."

He jots some notes down on his clipboard. "Because you were close to her?"

My nose instinctively twitches. "Yeah. Maybe more with her than my dad. I think I was her favourite. But I read somewhere the youngest always are."

"Possibly. I was an only child, so my parents had no choice but to accept me as their favourite." Mr Gauran flashes a quick smile at me.

"Or their worst," I try to joke back.

"Three point five." My scale of humour. Mr Gauran studies me. "So the few days after your mom left. How were you?"

The pain begins to grow when I think about it. I get nothing, though. "I had a breakdown."

"That's a fact. Not a feeling. Did you get angrier the more you thought about her leaving? Did you speak to anybody at school about it? A close friend, maybe?"

"I don't think I had many friends back in Georgia." Not even one. The kids back in Georgia used to bully me, too. They didn't do anything as harsh as Jared and the others here, but it was still tough. The bullying there stopped at some point—I try to recall how, but a sharp pain in my brain forces me to quit. Mr Gauran asks if I'm okay when he sees me rub my head. I tell him I am. "I just remember Colbey trying to tell Robin Mom wasn't coming back, and then the next thing is waking up for the doctors to tell me I had had a breakdown again in the garden at home."

Mr Gauran turns to me.

"You mean you don't remember anything between some point before you had the crash in Robin's car in April and when you woke up at the hospital in June? The second time you went to the hospital?"

I glance down at my trainers. My legs dangling freely off the edge. "Yeah, well, I recall Colbey and Robin arguing over Mom days before I crashed Robin's car. I think that's the last thing I remember, before it all changed. Everything else is just what the doctors or my family have told me. I got upset or lost it. Took her car. Went to the hospital after the crash. Went to court and was banned from driving. I returned to school, and then one day in June in the garden at home, I cracked and broke down. Dad was there to take me to the hospital. I don't remember anything or how I felt during that whole time."

"And it happened because you weren't over your mom going?"

"Must be."

"Nothing else?"

I shake my head.

"And nothing has come back to you from that time?"

"No."

There's some yelling. A group of students are getting out of a car. Laughing and pushing each other about. All in a whirl of fun while I'm here with my head whirling in pain about my past.

"I remember everything after that, though. Being at the hospital again. The tests the doctors did on me. Me having to say over and over to them what I could remember, which was nothing. Guess it was to see if I'd snap again."

"Did you mind being there?"

"Their job was to make me better, so, no. They gave me exercises to use to keep calm."

"Like the origami? And now the music?"

I nod. "But I listen to music all the time because I want to, not because I need to—maybe that's why I haven't felt bad in a while."

"That's good you feel like that. And how do you feel about your mom and what happened now? Looking back."

I think about it for a moment. "Fine. Well, as can be." Mr Gauran nods some more. "But don't you think that's weird, though?"

"What?"

"That I'm not upset or still angry she left. I was so nervous about Thanksgiving because we've always had the five of us together for it, and yet, on the day, I was fine. If I was so upset over her going that I flipped out and took Robin's car to get away, and then I had breakdowns and was sent to the hospital, then surely I should still feel emotional over her being gone? Some rage or hurt when I think of it now or something instead of this nothingness?"

Mr Gauran waits—he then puts the clipboard down. "You don't miss her?"

"I miss the times I had with her. Some things remind me of the memories I have with her. But that's not what I mean," I try to explain—pushing through the pain that still stings in my head. "I'm saying I'm not sure I feel hurt or upset that she isn't around. Not as much as everybody says I was during that time I can't remember. Isn't that weird? Or, I don't know, messed up?"

Mr Gauran places the pen in his hand behind his ear.

"Perhaps it is weird. Or maybe you've not realised that inside you've been able to move on. To forgive. Maybe you should acknowledge that there's more to things than getting angry or saddened. Sounds like you're ready to put that behind you."

The emails from Tokyo always put a smile on my face. More than before. Since she put *Love, Tokyo* at the end after Antonia's party, both our emails have been ending with that. I know that there's something between us. Something special, worth holding on to.

And I smile more when Antonia gallingly says she's just had the millionth person ask for a copy of the remix when she arrives at our table at lunch.

"Well, it was pretty good," Billie says, opening her drink.

"Yeah, but I had nothing to do with it. Anyway, that's not even the big news—" Antonia almost smacks into me as she abruptly slams her tray down. Somehow, none of her food leaves the tray or spills. "—Jared Steele and Chloe Cassadentini are over. As in broken up!"

The others give an unconcerned look—nowhere near as fascinated as Antonia is.

"I thought you were gonna talk about the Winter Week," Dacre comments. Some of the others nod—there are blue posters about the week stuck everywhere in the school. It's held on the last week of school before Christmas, where lots of activities and events happen. Antonia's on the committee for it, as is Robin.

"No. This is bigger. Chloed is finished. And it was at my party!"

I guess that makes sense why Jared was angry on Friday night—it was more than just about the football. And why Chloe…had had a few drinks.

Zeke tilts his head to her. "I always thought Jarloe sounded better." He bites into his apple. "Jar-low? Jar-oe? Jar-e-oe?"

"I wonder what caused the split?" Antonia questions as she sits down.

"Don't think it's really any of our business," Billie interrupts.

"Think most of the school would disagree." Antonia throws her head to the side.

There, on the KingsgateLeeConnect board, people are posting about Chloe and Jared's relationship. Some show their sadness, but it's the others that will cause a stir. Comments from girls showing their excitement there's a new bachelor available at Kingsgate Lee High. Guys tagging Chloe and starting with some note of endearment but then ending it with some indication of having some action and fun.

"That's disgusting," Billie says.

"Surely the school won't accept it," I say.

And it seems they don't because, suddenly, the posts begin to vanish. And when new posts appear, they're quickly gone.

"Seems not," Billie replies. "But, what should be our business is somebody hooking up with a certain arcade guy." She creepily spins her head around with a grin and stares at a now slightly blushed Dacre.

Zeke claps his hands together. "Oh, yes! That's much more fun."

"I'm not saying anything," Dacre mumbles, trying to take his tray away as an excuse to leave—Zeke and I pull him back down.

"How did the arcade guy even know to come to the party? He doesn't go to this school," Antonia points out.

Dacre glances down at his food. "I may have invited him—"

"I knew it!" Antonia smiles at Dacre.

As we laugh, my ears prick up. I hear something in the distance. It's music. I glance around but can't see where it's coming from.

"That's the mix from the party," Billie says, confirming my thoughts. It's Tokyo's "Do You Remember?" remix.

I dart my eyes around more seriously this time. I can't see where it's coming from—but I can tell it's being played off a phone.

It won't be Tokyo, but my heart's racing as to why it's being played.

People who I recognise from the party give a sound of excitement or cheer and begin to merrily dance in their seats when they hear the song—which pleases me to see.

"Guys, look," Antonia says, pointing to the big screen.

Tokyo

I'm glad you enjoyed this on Friday.

So much that I thought it was only right
to share it.

She's posted the mix on KingsgateLeeConnect! Underneath the text, there is an image of Kaiya Prior and Dante Buffon standing together in front of a plain white background. Underneath them on the image is the song title, but in a scratched purple kind of font, it also says *'80s Mix*. I see the faded play button over the image—the person's played it off that.

My eyes stay fixed on the screen—comments soon start appearing by the post.

Angela Branno
Searching all week for this. Who knew I needed the
'80s so much in my life?

Chris Nerrioll
Never thought I'd like a Kaiya Prior song, and when I
hear this, I still don't…I LOVE a Kaiya Prior song!

Sam Brazell
Amazing! The edit on that Dante Buffon rap,
smoooooth!

I'm excited for Tokyo—more comments keep coming in.

"Tokyo? Does anybody actually call their kid Tokyo?" Zeke asks back at the table.

"It's an alias," I answer before forcing myself to not say anymore.

Soon, the group begins to discuss who is the person behind the remix—it seems they're not the only ones, though.

Jade Edivan
Work of genius. Please tell me you're a girl! I wanna
personally say how awesome this is.

Kylo Savannah
The '80s are back. I need to know who this is! You're
not Benny the science lab cleaner, are you?

The comments all praise the remix and Tokyo. Most assume it's a girl;

some think it is a guy. All the speculation just keeps me grinning inside during the week because I'm the only person who knows Tokyo. Well, more than anybody else does.

Even Jasmine comments about the song in our Spanish tutoring after school, saying that she likes it. I try to ignore that I once thought she was Tokyo, and when she asks what I think, I'm honest with her and tell her that when I first heard it, it really took me away.

To be polite, I ask her how Chloe is coping.

Apparently, she's doing okay, but she was a little upset. With the breakup and then the comments.

I think it is awful people got involved—and Jasmine agrees.

"Even though comments have been taken down, it's still been out there and seen," she says. "Principal Shaw's been strict with those who have posted anything."

By Friday night, there are more posts appearing on the KingsgateLeeConnect board next to the football pitch about Tokyo than about the game itself. She's not replied to any, though, and she hasn't posted anything else.

The school cheers as our team scores, and we yell even more when Dacre has the ball. Each waving a paper flag of our school's team mascot for support.

Just before it's halftime, Andrew offers to get us food and drinks. Nobody objects.

"Dacre is on form tonight," Zeke yells later as the cheerleaders continue their routine. Chloe isn't on the pitch performing—I can't blame her, although it is the first she's missed all year.

"Imagine if your brother and that coach were here tonight," Billie says. I'd imagine they'd want to sign him up immediately.

"Imagine," Zeke replies. "Hey, where's your BF, Billie? My stomach's aching for that Kinga Kingsgate hotdog."

"Yeah, halftime's almost over," Antonia says. The place where we can get food and drinks is behind the stand, so there's no chance of seeing how long the queue is.

"I'll go and check," I offer. Nobody objects.

I go to the food hut alone—Andrew isn't in the queue. He's not in the scatter of people around here, either. It's not that busy. I wonder if I've missed him—no, I'd have seen him. There's only one walkway. I decide to check the toilets.

The toilets are in a small building, a little away from everything else. I get close—but I hear something to my side.

I glance over. Nothing—except the side of the building and some trees beyond it. I walk over cautiously. The sound is a person. I'm certain. People, actually. Coming from around the corner.

I go over, then turn at the end.

I stand and watch in disgust.

"Andrew?"

He spins his head around. His black hair is partially flopped over his face—and looking back like a deer staring at headlights—and so does the girl who's still wrapped in his arms I've just watched him make out with.

And it isn't Billie.

22.

I spin back around and storm away. I'm shocked. Disgusted. Furious.

"Hayden." I hear behind me. I don't stop.

There's a sudden tightness on my shoulder that twists me around—it almost topples me over to the side from the strength, but I manage to hold myself up.

Andrew is standing right before me. "Hayden, let me—"

"Explain? What were you thinking? I watched for nearly a minute of you two together, and in case you need a reminder, you have a girlfriend."

He doesn't speak. He knows he's been caught. He can't climb out of this hole. I'm just seriously pissed at him for betraying Billie. I begin to leave.

"Hayden, where you going?"

"Back to the stand. To Billie."

"Don't you dare tell her!"

I suddenly stop to glare back at Andrew. In the distance, I hear the game has begun again.

"You're cheating on her. It's unforgivable." In the corner of my eye, I see a figure walk by. It's the girl he was making out with. I don't recognise her.

He's made a commitment to be with Billie and broken it—Billie deserves to know. "I'm telling her."

"Wait. Can't it be—you know…" Andrew then flicks his index fingers back and forth at him and me. I stare, wondering what he's suggesting, and then it clicks.

"You're unbelievable," I hiss in disgust. Who even is this guy? This is nothing like the kind person I've known these last few weeks.

I spin back—but my body's suddenly hit by something. I wince—yet I'm immediately pushed to the side. My back is forced to slam hard against something. It's uneven. A tree.

I flinch from the sting, but a hand on my shoulder keeps me pinned. Andrew's standing against me. His breathing coming down at me. His face close with his hair split over it. His eyes glaring at me. Deep and menacing. Possessed almost. And it scares me.

"You ain't gonna tell Billie! If you do, I'll hurt you. I'll make you wish you never came here, Hayden," Andrew spits. I feel his scowl hit me hard. My body aches from the tightness he has me pinned. I begin to worry; he means every word. "Or better yet, you tell her, and I'll kill you."

He shoves me to the ground. I land horribly, and my head smacks against the trunk. I hiss from the pain.

"Grow up, Hayden, and do what's best. Keep hush."

Footsteps fade away, and there are roars and cheers from further away, but my body trembles as I remain on the ground, curling into itself. Terrified and alone.

The last time I was like this was on the toilet floor in school after Jared and the others beat me up. Andrew didn't hit me like they did, but I feel worse.

At some point, I make myself get up. I walk towards school—arms folded, head down—and go straight by the back of the stand. Andrew will be there already pretending nothing has happened, probably saying he never saw me. I decide to go home.

My phone vibrates as I head through the main car park. A text from Zeke. There's also a missed call earlier from him. I open the text. He's asking where I am. Seems Andrew's gone for the 'I haven't seen him' answer then.

I reply that I'm not feeling well and had to go home. I shove my phone back in my pocket and press on. The sooner I can get home and lie on my bed, the better.

But I'm not calling Dad or Colbey to pick me up—I won't be able to manage sitting in a car with either of them. So I walk.

"Hayden." I don't bother to turn around to whoever said my name. I hear my name being called out again. It's nearer this time. I look up and see the person has somehow walked around to stand in front of me. It's Cassio. "Hey, did you not hear me? Where's your head at, man?"

"No, I gotta go."

"In the middle of the game? Nobody leaves a game halfway through," Cassio says, his voice fading.

I continue to walk on.

"Pretty sure your team will win."

I don't hear Cassio reply or hear footsteps coming after me. I squeeze and shuffle in between two cars. I'm nearly at the end of the car park at the school entrance.

"Hey, are you okay?"

I glance over. Cassio's now standing on the other side of one of the cars.

"I'm fine." There's a snap in my voice. I'm not in the mood to try and justify my actions and have somebody quiz me or tell me I am not okay.

I reach the end of the school grounds and head down the main road, passing the large block sign mounted in the grass side that says *Kingsgate Lee High*.

"You—"

"Look! I don't need you trying to make me feel better, alright? Just leave me be."

My thoughts rush crazily around my head as I walk off. It stings. Like an impulse, I pull my phone out. I need to listen to music. Tokyo's music will help me—help me fly out of my aching body and be somewhere else.

But I don't have my headphones. The memory of what's just happened appears fresh in my head again. My breath quivers. I notice my hands trembling—and immediately shove them into my pockets.

"Hay—"

I swirl to the side aggressively.

"Would you stop it? Leave me alone!" I flail my arms in the air in fury at Cassio. A rush of heat bursts around my body. My lips tremor—I don't know if I'm about to crumble or lash out.

"That's not how it works."

I glare at Cassio. But there's pity and concern etched on his face—it makes me feel stupid. I bite hard into my bottom lip. Eyes ready to let their dams break. Like back when Jared and the others used to bully me. And that group included the guy stood right before me.

"I know something's up."

"Yeah, maybe there is. But that doesn't mean I have to tell you," I blurt at him. I want to run, yet I don't move.

"No, you don't. But that doesn't mean I'm gonna let you walk off alone like this."

"We're not even close! You don't care. I don't give a damn about you."

He doesn't shift. Instead, he holds his lock with his eyes on mine. "Doesn't matter."

The street's occupied with houses on either side, with cars parked along the road, yet the entire place is empty. There's just us. He'll easily catch up if I run; he's on the football team.

I can't work out the guy's angle. But my body aches in defeat—I can't deal with this now. Not after Andrew. "Whatever. But I'm not talking."

I make a move down the road so he doesn't have the chance to reply.

Fortunately, he stays quiet.

Desperately, I try to override Andrew by playing Tokyo's mixes in my head. Thinking of the beats and the tempos, the synths and their solos, and then the lyrics, but they jumble with Andrew's words, and I get nowhere.

At some point, I turn to Cassio. He's in a red hoody and jeans. Something doesn't seem right. "Shouldn't you be on the pitch?"

A slight dread hits me. I hope he is not missing the game because of me.

No. He can't have changed at half-time from the kit and into casual clothes for only the break. So, did he even play in tonight's game? Come to think of it, I don't recall seeing him on the pitch an—

"Injured the other week," Cassio answers as if he could read my mind. He lifts his left arm up slightly. But there's no sling or cast, though. "Only a sprain. But Coach said I couldn't risk it."

"Oh," I mumble, and then add, "Hope it gets better soon."

"Thanks. Football season's over soon, so probably won't get to play again."

"That sucks."

"Yeah. It's just annoying—that I've already had my last high school game."

He's a senior then. That'll be why I've never seen him in my classes.

"Kind of just wished I'd have known before my last game that it was going to be my last game at high school. You know?" Cassio says, walking beside me. "Guess sometimes you never know when something's your last thing till it is."

My mind instantly thinks of Colbey—him being oblivious that when he went out onto the school pitch to play, with his NFL career set in his mind, it would be his last game ever.

And then I'm reminded of us moving to Florida. My family may have planned the decision, but I was only informed not long before we were leaving. Never got to visit the local park again. Or the movies. Or the mall. To say goodbye to it all in Georgia.

Then I think of Mom. Try to, at least—I can't exactly remember the last time I saw her. Maybe the day she left. We all ate together or watched something on TV before I went to bed—either seem logical. Whether it's because my brain won't let me or I'm just muddling my memories to something before, I don't know, but I can't recall.

And then, when I think of that time, I feel like something's missing. Well, my memories, obviously, but just something seems off. Why did I suddenly decide to grab Robin's car keys and drive off days after Mom left? Why was I on North Mount Street, heading away from Farm Bridge? Maybe there's no reason for it all. Maybe I was just so built up with anger I drove wherever.

But it bugs me at times. It's like I can be my own worst enemy, or maybe it's because of—

Cassio coughs.

I look up to take note of where we are—we're walking through a park.

"I know you won't talk to me about what's wrong," Cassio says, staring at me. "But I hope there's someone you can speak to." I stare down at my feet. "And for what it's worth, even if it sometimes doesn't feel it, you should know there will always be someone who will care about you."

Cassio may not be referring to himself, and he will presume I'm thinking of someone in my family or a friend—but when I turn to see Cassio, I feel nothing but ashamed. A guy I don't know, who did wrong to begin with, is trying to make me feel better, and yet I've only been mean to him tonight. Maybe he feels like he must be here with me. He doesn't have to be. And yet, perhaps I'm glad he is.

"Thanks," I eventually say. He asks for what. "Just being here."

23.

FROM: TokyoCherryDustZ89@TokyoCherryDustZ89.com
TO: BlueC0ast1@bretteodmail.com
DATE: Sat 2nd December, 10:20 PM
SUBJECT: Home

My mom has just told me we're moving.

Not to a new country or state before you panic. We're still going to be in Orlando. It's just another suburb, so I'll still be going to Kingsgate Lee High. Mom said the house is bigger, and there's a pool, and there's all this new stuff…but I don't care.

It really threw me off. It's so out of the blue.

I've never moved before. My home is where I grew up. It reminds me of my dad. We don't have much of his belongings or even the car we used to sing in. This house is the last physical thing I have of him.

The deal for the new house has been done. We're moving in after Christmas. So, if I hadn't seen the architectural designs of a house on the kitchen table before my mom walked in, then when on earth was she going to tell me?

What's most upsetting, though, is that she didn't ask. She didn't sit me down and tell me she was thinking about moving. I probably still would have been mad, but at least she would have included me in it.

My head's all over the place, so I need you to help me make sense of it or make me smile. Do something to ease me. Because I know you can.

Love,
Tokyo

FROM: BlueC0ast1@bretteodmail.com
TO: TokyoCherryDustZ89@TokyoCherryDustZ89.com
DATE: Sat 2nd December, 10:43 PM
SUBJECT: Re: Home

That is big, Tokyo.

I was going to say it doesn't matter how far away you are, you'll still be able to chat with me on here…but that probably doesn't sound as sweet if you're only moving suburb. So, my attempt at being charming has failed. And this is about you, not me.

Well, I've noticed that I'm always reminded of you even though I don't know who you are. I was watching a music quiz show with my family, and for every question, I was like, Tokyo would know that. (Quick diversion: I love the last band you gave me to listen to.)

Or, if that's too obvious, how about graffiti?

Someone the other day was sitting outside the shops with loads of spray cans. He had many bowls, bits of newspaper and other random objects to use as he was spraying onto a large piece of card. It was mostly tourists watching, but I was curious too, and when he finished, it was this beautiful landscape painting.

There were pyramids, a waterfall with a grand castle beside the pool of water, and there were stars and planets in the sky. Honestly, Tokyo, it was beautiful.

People clapped when he showed it, and the painting made me think of you. Because I know you'd love how creative it was—from the painting itself to how the guy did it from scratch with a few items—and because of how beautiful you are, too.

Redemption of my last attempt at being charming: redeemed.

Heck, even the school bell made me think of you. Not because you'll hear it as well, but my mind instantly thought you'd somehow be able to use that sound in some '80s mix. Too much of a stretch? I know, but it did.

Whether this is helping or not, I don't know. It's been a strange time for me, too, but the thoughts of you and seeing you in my world helps. So I hope I, or at least these emails, do the same for you now.

Love,
Brisbane

FROM: TokyoCherryDustZ89@TokyoCherryDustZ89.com
TO: BlueC0ast1@bretteodmail.com
DATE: Sat 2nd December, 11:14 PM
SUBJECT: Re: Home

Wow. That's very sweet. However, just a bone to pick, everything is only *now* making you think of me? Shouldn't that have happened when we first began emailing? ;)

That spray paint sounds incredible. I would have loved to have seen that. And yes, the charm has certainly been redeemed.

I get you. I was in the shop with my little sister, and I saw a cuddly toy fish and it made me think of you and wonder if you'd seen a fish like it on your trips to the beach with the family. Or when I drove by billboards promoting a zoo, and there were different animals on each of them. Like bears. Elephants. Zebras. Lions. Flamingos. They got me thinking if you're able to make an origami version of them.

(Quick diversion: I made another origami parrot while I waited for your email, and even I must admit I'm impressed with this one. See the image for yourself.)

(Quick quick diversion: Can you do an origami of a llama? And if so, that doesn't count with our quest if you make one and name it Tokyo. Don't think I've forgotten about that quest, as well as your music adventure.)

But yes, to sum it up, even though you didn't ask, everywhere I go, I seem to be reminded of you. Not that I'm complaining.

I'm sorry it's been a weird one for you. Wanna share problems together? I've heard I've been good to chat to by a boy that goes online by the name of Brisbane.

Love,
Tokyo

FROM: BlueC0ast1@bretteodmail.com
TO: TokyoCherryDustZ89@TokyoCherryDustZ89.com
DATE: Sat 2nd December, 11:38 PM
SUBJECT: Re: Home

To be honest, Tokyo, it did happen when I first began emailing you. Not as deeply as now, but I did think of you a lot. Just thought it might sound a bit creepy if I admitted it.

Phew *wipes forehead* glad it's been redeemed.

There seems to be a theme of animals that makes you think of me. Should I be concerned? I'm not some elegant flamingo, heroic lion or a big grizzly bear.

(Quick diversion: That's really good. Probably the best origami parrot I've ever seen.)

(Quick quick diversion: Shoot, I thought an origami llama would be accepted. I haven't tried yet to make one. And I haven't found a real llama named Tokyo yet. I'm guessing you've had no luck with a dog named Brisbane?)

And thanks for the offer to help, but it's ok. I'll manage.

I've moved to a new house before and didn't get much of a say either. I understood why we were moving, but I still didn't like it.

The thought of leaving everything behind…is difficult. Because of the memories there. But you've got to remember memories don't stay in that one place. They go wherever you go. Locked in your heart. Forever. And if some don't stay with you, that's ok, too. Something else will trigger you to remember them.

My last moment at my home was leaving in sadness—I found out we were moving very soon before we left. Not long at all. But you know when you're leaving. You have time. So make it memorable, and leave it with goodness for yourself and your family. Because sometimes you don't realise when it's your last time until the moment has gone. And you do know.

I can't say I know why your mom wants to move, and maybe that's my point. Maybe you should hear her out so you at least know why and can leave with some closure.

A home isn't the thing that has four walls and a roof; it's wherever your family is.

Love,
Brisbane

FROM: TokyoCherryDustZ89@TokyoCherryDustZ89.com
TO: BlueC0ast1@bretteodmail.com
DATE: Sun 3rd December, 10:26 AM
SUBJECT: Re: Home

Haha, that's not creepy at all. *Slowly leans over to get the phone while pretending to write and stare at my laptop*

(Quick quick diversion: I'm also in the same predicament with my Brisbane dog. It seems some things are impossible.)

I'm so sorry that happened. There must have been some BIG reason for you to have hardly any time to adjust to the news, pack and then move.

I hope it's all good now, though—realise it probably happened years ago, but still.

And what you say does help. I managed to sleep last night and let myself calm down and think about it. It didn't help Mom continued talking about the move first thing this morning, but I know what you're saying is right. I need to try and emotionally accept it.

I should be clear: there are non-animal things that make me think of you. Haha, I hope for my sake you aren't a big grizzly bear. Then there'd definitely be no way I'd meet you. There'd be claw marks on my back if we hugged, or there'd be drool on my lips.

Well, in my eyes, you're a heroic lion.

Your emails have saved me from going crazy. You know how to cheer me up or make me feel better about myself when I don't think it's possible. You help me see things differently. You are the person I feel most open to.

Something I haven't had for a long time.

Puts phone carefully back, slightly at ease the police have been contacted

Love,
Tokyo

FROM: BlueC0ast1@bretteodmail.com
TO: TokyoCherryDustZ89@TokyoCherryDustZ89.com
DATE: Sun 3rd December, 12:29 PM
SUBJECT: Re: Home

Yes, I think I've managed to settle to the move now.

Well, I hope you managed to cope with the idea of the move. And I wonder if you will be moving closer or further from me? (Not that it matters online.)

Rushes over to the window—but smacks foot into the edge of the desk on the way and yelps, holding it as I continue—looks outside and down the street to see no for sale or just sold signs beside the houses Shame.

Thank you. I don't think I am a heroic guy, but it's nice for somebody to tell me I mean something to somebody.

Hears a car pull up and looks outside—the police?

No, that wouldn't be ideal if I was a bear. I can't imagine a lion would be any easier to hug, though.

Hang on, why would there be drool on your lips…?

Oh.

OOOHHHH.

…Ohh.

24.

Tokyo thinks I'm a heroic lion. And yet, really, I'm more like a cowardly possum.

I'm terrified on Monday when my friends are at the table. I automatically feel like they've somehow discovered about Andrew's cheating and my knowledge of it, and so they'll kick me out of the group.

But they don't know anything…they welcome me like any other day. It just makes me feel worse.

I don't say anything through the week, either. I just become guilty every day when I see Billie—and I think of every excuse I can when they want to meet up. Just in case Andrew is there.

I've been listening to Tokyo's music to block the thoughts of Andrew out and sink into her mixes. By the end of each day, though, there are origami parrots on the side of my desk.

"It would be nice if you could. You could meet Dean," Dacre says on Thursday when I say I can't go to No Armadillos tonight. Dean is the guy from the till at the arcade.

I place my tray on the rack after putting the rubbish in the recycling bin. "And that's important for you? For me to meet him?"

"Well, yeah," Dacre almost scoffs. "Because you're my friend."

"Really?" I feel the need to ask as I follow Dacre.

"Why else would we be hanging out with you all these weeks if we didn't think so?" Dacre answers back with a grin. I glance at our table in the distance. Zeke's trying to dangle an eaten apple over Antonia, who looks completely disgusted and horrified in one. Billie, on the other hand, is laughing.

It feels like a wave from a wave pool has smacked me in my back. It's the first time someone's said to me *you're my friend.* Nobody ever really tells people—they just go by connecting with people and assume. It's nice hearing Dacre say it. And yet, now I've finally heard those words, I don't think I deserve it.

"You're a good friend," Dacre repeats. A second wave comes at me, this time though it's guilt.

"I want to apologise," I blurt out.

He stops—almost chuckling. "For what? Being busy? You can't help that."

"Not that. It's that—" My body's urging me to say I saw Andrew cheating. Dacre's here and being so nice, I'm ready to almost tell him—Andrew appears in my mind.

I cave. I let the lie suck me back into defeat.

"It was me who let slip to the others that you were with Dean at Antonia's."

Dacre's face moulds into a cheeky smile. "Let slip? We were making out at a party. I'm just glad you saw me first—and not the whole group. I wouldn't worry about it."

I try to smile back.

"And it doesn't bother you?" Dacre asks. I have to ask him what he means. "That I'm gay."

"No. Why would it?"

I remain silent as Dacre looks at me. He taps his hand on my arm and points to follow him. I cautiously leave the hustle of the crowd around us until Dacre sits on the grass verge that slopes down to the field. I take a seat beside him.

"You know, the dilemma I had with being gay was not about being gay, like questioning if I was or wasn't. I knew I liked guys as soon as I saw Ryan Gosling in *Crazy, Stupid, Love.* The difficulty was about coming out, that paranoia of how people I've known my whole life would react. Would they think differently of me?" Dacre explains. He rolls a stone between his finger and thumb. "But I took the plunge and told people last year. My family, well, some are okay, and some needed time to adjust. And most of the school was surprised. My friends were fine and happy for me. My teammates, too. There were some of last year's seniors who didn't like it. Thought I might check them out during the showers or try and grab more than I should in the game; I didn't like hearing that and being judged like that. It was tough. But surprisingly, the rest of the team told those few guys where to go. They stuck up for me when I never asked. But they did. Especially Jared."

I go cold when I hear Jared's name, but then what Dacre says sinks in. Jared Steele—the guy that used to bully me and is still rude—is nice?

"He was quite supportive. It felt nice to see people were not just fine with it but were also sticking up for me. My friends have as well," Dacre pauses. "I didn't open up because I needed people's approval. It was so I could be myself around others without feeling bad about myself. And hearing you ask why it would matter to you if I were gay, well, it's darn sweet to hear. So thanks."

My lips close in on themselves. The emotions inside hit. Dacre is being open, and I find even more respect and care for this guy. I want to tell him there is no need—but then he hugs me.

Hugs are meant to be special and supportive for someone. To make people feel nice and good. I know this, and I can sense that, and yet it's because of that reason that the hug makes me feel more horrible about myself.

Dacre's trying to be thankful to me, being pleased and happy, yet I feel awful because of the Andrew situation.

I bite my lip. It's terrible. I feel like I'm betraying them.

Despite our chat, I keep to the decision of not going to No Armadillos. I lie that there's a family thing tomorrow night and so I must swap shifts at Mt. Okesea and work tonight. Fortunately, when I ring Aunt Sandra, I'm able to live up to the lie and swap a shift and work this evening.

I may have dodged a bullet for another day, but when I arrive at Mt. Okesea, there's another fired up and ready in the small hut—Kamala. But I'd rather face her than my friends, whether they are with Andrew or not.

Kamala holds the usual displeased look. "You know where the mop is."

Before she can complain about whatever, I do as she says. I clean the toilets. The pavements. The balls. And the clubs.

I put all my effort into my work, just so it washes the Andrew situation out of my brain. But I must have put too much in as no sooner have I started, I've finished and I'm back at the hut with Kamala.

The silence becomes too much—and I desperately try to strike up a conversation. It's a silence my brain will fill with Andrew and the lies if I don't.

"So, what made you dye your hair purple?"

Kamala turns. "Must there be a reason?"

"No," I quickly answer. "It's cool, though." I notice her blonde eyebrow while the other is black. "As is your eyebrow. How did you manage to dye it? I'd be afraid to try that."

"I didn't. It was born blonde."

"Oh—sorry, I didn't know." And just like that, I've messed up any chance of being on good terms with Kamala.

Thankfully, we get a huge rush of visitors arrive to kill the awkwardness. Kamala collects payments, and I get the equipment ready for them. When the rush finishes, I check my phone quickly to see if there's an email from Tokyo. She hasn't emailed all night yet. I then check to see if she has posted a new song on KingsgateLeeConnect.

"Fan of that, hey?"

I glance over to Kamala while putting my phone away. "I don't use it much."

"Yeah, surrrre. Nearly everybody at school does."

"Do you?"

"A creator never indulges in their creation. They just create it."

"You created KingsgateLeeConnect?"

"Yeah. Well, a group of us. For a school competition. Principal Shaw liked it so much they developed it." Kamala grabs the two clubs on the counter and reaches over near me to put them with the other clubs. "But they've hired some tech business in Utah to control it now."

"That's pretty cool."

Kamala turns back to look at me, sternly, with no attempt whatsoever to hide that she's deliberating if I'm being sarcastic. I'm not.

"I guess. It does the purpose of connecting people. Got its flaws, too, though. No doubt there'll have been a spike in activity this week because the students at our school are too sad and vain that they must gossip about Chloe Cassadentini and Jared Steele's break up. And I also suppose that mix from that Tokyo."

My ears catch onto Kamala's last words—then I register the entire conversation we're having.

Kamala helped create KingsgateLeeConnect. What Tokyo uses!

I wanted to wait to find out who Tokyo is when the time is right for both of us—but a thought itches at me, it's a chance to shrink the number of possible girls that could be her. It's too tempting.

"Do you think there's any way someone can have more than one account?"

Kamala's eyebrow rises. "What do you have planned?"

I tell her I'm just curious.

Kamala stares at me. She does it for so long in silence that I begin to wish another family would arrive just so we can be distracted and this can end.

She rests her elbows on the counter. "You have to use your student ID number to create and sign into an account, so I doubt it."

I suddenly feel a skip in my heartbeat. That means the girls who are already on it, where their names are on the posts, can't be Tokyo. It's somebody else.

"But it wouldn't take much to find a loophole. Hardly protected, so you could easily create another. Or use another student's ID, or ex-student's—or be given another ID for whatever reason."

And just like that—the breakthrough has gone.

"Hey, Hayden."

My heart sinks by the new voice in our conversation. I look out the hut—panic slams into me. My skin itches in fright.

There I see him. It's Andrew. And smiling at me.

My eyes force themselves to blink harshly, hoping I'm just imagining him there and he'll disappear. But he doesn't. He's there. My body clams up.

"Just one?" Kamala asks dully beside me.

"Actually, just came to have a word with Hayden. Just be a minute." He flicks his eyes to me. He's not pleased with something.

Before I can give some excuse, Kamala mundanely answers for me. "Fine. Don't be long."

Despite my head and my heart saying no, I slowly move out of the small hut. Andrew walks back under the gateway and goes a little to the side out of the entrance.

I have to almost step back when he spins around once we're out of view and in the car park.

"What do you think you're playing at?"

"What?" I ask.

"Don't act dumb. You're avoiding the others, and you're avoiding me out of school."

Crap! Was I that obvious?

"Well, sorry if I don't feel like being best buddies with you right now."

Immediately, I regret it. Andrew's head bobs a little. Just a little. But it's enough to unnerve me.

"Yeah, well, either do or be gone 'cause they think something's up with you." Andrew's piercing eyes force me to look away. "Hayden, you gotta help me out?"

"Help you out? You're cheating on your girlfriend and threatening me to keep quiet."

Andrew doesn't budge.

Out of nowhere, I recall the chat with Dacre. Maybe if his words nearly helped me, maybe I could help Andrew? And maybe then this could be over with. "Why don't you tell Billie the truth? If you're honest and sorry, then she'll see how much she means to you."

He scoffs.

"Alright, *oh wise one*," Andrews laughs momentarily but instantly returns to his serious tone. "She won't forgive me. Not with her track record of guys cheating on her."

So why do it? Why risk something you have? "She might."

"No, she won't." Andrew moves quickly to me—pressing his hand on me. "And you're not going to say anything…otherwise I'll make sure you wish you never left Georgia." *Well, I'm already starting to wish that, so there's no need there.* "Who they gonna believe? Someone they've known all their life, or you? A loner that's walked in five minutes ago."

He's so close to me that I'm squished against the fence wall.

If he really felt Billie and the others wouldn't believe me, then why not let me say? *Because he doesn't believe it himself. He's scared Billie may believe me. It's just words.*

The angry spark when he mentions how little I've known my friends in me should be brightening, but instead, it diminishes; if he's scared, then his threats are real. The hand that is against my chest and so close to my neck right now suddenly feels a lot more terrifying to me.

"What I want is for this to blow over and pretend you saw nothing, but with the others getting concerned, you need to sort your head out. Either get over it and be yourself so you can hang out with them still or cut the cord with them entirely."

He's giving me an ultimatum over my friends.

"I don't care which, Hayden, just stop floating around and alarming them. Am I clear?"

He shoves his spare hand against the metal fence. I automatically flinch from the sound—and then again when his other hand grabs my neck.

My throat closes in from the tightness. It's hard to breathe.

"I said, am I clear?" He repeats as the metal fence rings. His face is against my cheek, whispering the words intimidatingly to me.

The grip is so tight—I'm straining desperately to breathe.

My eyes close. Everything is faint, except the grip.

Somehow, I manage to nod.

"Good." He squeezes my neck—I screech—then he releases. My back pushes into the fence—I collapse down against it, wheezing. "And remember that or else."

When I slowly open my eyes, with fear rushing all over me, Andrew is walking away to his car. I briefly hear smirking until my own breath trembles over it.

A car pulls out and drives away. I stay staring at the now empty space. The guy has a hold on me. A hold that I can't seem to get out of.

A family cheers behind the trees. Kamala won't be pleased with how long I've been gone.

I slowly brush my work shirt down, still shaken, and try to compose some level of normality from the mess I feel right now and head back to the gateway.

Kamala's in the small hut tending to a group who've just finished playing. She moves her mouth, but I can't hear what she's saying. I make my way under the gateway and down the path and attempt some deep breaths. But they don't work. It's like the strain of the grip is still there.

"Hayden."

"Cassio?" I say when I turn around to the entrance. He walks over to me. "Why are you here?"

"Thought anybody could come and play?" He smiles, but I don't find it amusing. Now's not the time for jokes. Cassio must understand and adds, "I wanted to check you were okay. Haven't been able to see you at school since Friday, so thought I'd check if you were here."

I watch as Cassio sits down on the knee-high rock wall that follows the path on either side and separates it from the trees. Midway between the small hut and the gateway. I sit down beside him.

"And have you forgotten to go home and get changed, or do you always wear that same hoody?" It's the red hoody again and jeans.

He smirks—though I meant it more as a jibe. "It's my lucky hoody."

There's a mock laugh going off inside my head because I know that's something I need at this moment. I'd probably take the hoody off him if it were guaranteed to hold the power of luck. I'm *that* desperate.

"I saw you now with that guy outside. Is something wrong?"

"That obvious?" I ask, fed up. Do I have worry etched all over my face? I notice the group Kamala dealt with is walking by us. They each stare at me with perplexed looks and confused glares. *Apparently so.*

"I'm betting that guy's got something to do with you being upset Friday night," Cassio says. I glance down, which is stupid because he takes it as a yes. "Don't let him see he gets to you."

"I tried standing up to him on Friday, and it made it worse."

"There's a difference between standing up and not letting someone get to you. Maybe the same ballpark, but it's a different base."

I turn. "And things get to you?"

"Doesn't something to everybody?" He replies. I guess so, but I don't say. "My family ain't exactly the perfect family everybody wishes they had. They're kind of rough. And, when I was a freshman, my dad was stupid enough to think he and some mates could actually pull off a bank robbery."

My eyes widen. *Do people actually do that?*

"I know—thought it only happens in westerns or only stores get robbed in real life. Not banks. But he did. And they got caught. Didn't even make it to the vaults. *El gran tonto*. He went to prison, and when news broke out, everyone at school treated me differently. They disowned me. Cast me out. Even the teachers were scared. The only time others talked to me was to make remarks about my family being poor, thick low lives." In his eyes, I see he is reliving those times in his mind. Deep. Distant. Desolate. "It worked me up; I hadn't changed, but they all treated me like I had, like they seemed to think I was some rebellious thug just because of my father. Some point, though, it got me. I reacted, lashed out, whenever anybody said anything. So much that I ended up being suspended."

I glance down.

"And when I was off, away from it all, I realised I had changed. Not because of my dad's arrest, though, but from the way people treated me. I'd become this angry person—one I didn't like. And I needed to return to who I was. But I knew I'd always have people despise me; your dad being a criminal isn't something easy to hide. It's something that will never go away."

"So what did you do?"

"Nothing. I stopped."

I stare blankly at Cassio. I've no idea how doing nothing can do something.

"The remarks continued, but I didn't let it get to me. I chose to ignore them. The less you react, I think, the better. I stuck with the friends that saw me as me, and now I don't respond to anybody trying to get to me."

"Then what happened when you decided to join in and bully me?"

He sighs. "I was only there once. And I never hit you; I was just there."

"Just as bad."

Cassio hangs his head. "I slipped." I assume it's something to do with his dad, but I don't ask.

"It wasn't right," he continues. "What I did to you. But what I'm saying is. Don't go on that merry-go-round; don't let people push you onto it because all it does is spin you out of control. You have the choice to walk away from it. Don't let anything get to you. Otherwise, it already has a hold on you."

"Fore!"

A purple golf ball bounces across the path before us—followed by a man chasing after it. Further back, at the last hole, a young girl in a pink dress swings her club around, smirking at her achievement.

The big rush of players will soon be on the home stretch. Kamala certainly won't be pleased if I'm not there to help. More than she probably is now.

"See you around, Hayden."

I turn to see Cassio is now back up and near the gateway. I feel ashamed. This guy's come here to check how I am, even tried to give advice, and I've pretty much said nothing in return.

"Thank you. I'll think about what you said," I say. He nods—but I continue. "And for what it's worth, I don't think you're bad."

Slowly, a smile appears on Cassio's face. A beat of silence occurs. And I smile back.

I spin around and jog back to the small hut. And I'm right. Kamala isn't happy—leaning on the counter, with her face mushed into the palm of her hand.

"Took your time."

"Sorry," I apologise as I get into the hut.

"So, do you do that often?" I glance over at her. "Talk." I think she's being silly, but she twists her head and looks out to the gateway.

Cassio's gone. But then I get it. She means that I left the hut with Andrew and then saw me come back chatting to a completely different guy.

"Oh, sorry, it won't happen again." I hope.

Soon, we find ourselves in the long, busy rush of people finishing their games. We're stuck in the hut for over an hour, just retrieving clubs.

"Five to ten," Kamala tells me when the last group hand in their clubs. "Might as well begin closing. You get the balls, and I'll sort the clubs out."

With no complaint, I go out with a basket and retrieve the balls from the compartment in the last hole. It's almost full of a blend of different coloured balls. I begin to scoop them out, but my mind drifts about Andrew's threat.

I try to tell myself that even though all this Andrew stuff seems to be the only thing my mind focuses on, there are good things in my life. Good things do happen to me. I think of meeting Zeke, Billie and the others, going out with them, the tutors with Jasmine, watching shows with my family and even enjoy watching the football games at school.

I shut the compartment door when I've got all the balls and head back.

No matter which option I take from Andrew's ultimatum, either go back and continue seeing my friends like I used to, or I go and abandon them, I will always have to keep hush. And when I think about what Cassio said to me tonight, I know I might not be able to stand up to Andrew, but I can show that he isn't getting to me. He has a hold, but he doesn't have to ruin everything.

And I like my friends. I've seen first-hand they like me for me. So I know what I need to do. I'm going to get back out there and continue seeing my friends. It isn't just because I want to but because I need to. I'd rather be facing this dilemma alone yet surrounded by friends than facing it alone and being by myself. I'll just have to somehow suck it up, for the thought of going back to having no friends again is unbearable.

The small hut door bursts open. A yelp comes out of me when it hits my hands wrapped around the basket and I'm pushed back.

Balls suddenly soar into the air. Zooming in all directions. I fall back onto the floor. Hundreds of pings go off—the balls bouncing loudly on the concrete around me. Some even hit me. And they hurt!

"Oh shit. Are you okay?"

I open my eyes. Kamala's leaning over and looking down at me. Her purple hair dangling down and partially over her view.

"Yeah," I wince. I see her hand is out—I grab it, and she helps me up.

There's a slight ache in my back. We tread carefully—trying not to stand and slip on the balls.

"I'm so gonna get a copy of that."

"What?" I ask her.

Kamala points up.

A little red light flashes every few seconds near the top of the gateway structure. It's a security camera. I feel even more embarrassed.

"Great," I grumble.

"That's not all."

I follow her gaze from the balls scattered around us on the path to the little blue line beside us. The stream that goes around the course. My eyes follow the flow of the water. It meanders in and around the holes and ruins—then we see them.

Lying at the bottom of the large pool of water that sits against the mountain, with a statue fountain in the centre, are newly added coloured dots.

I look over to Kamala—she's staring back at me.

I roll up my jeans; I know already she won't budge.

25.

FROM: TokyoCherryDustZ89@TokyoCherryDustZ89.com
TO: BlueC0ast1@bretteodmail.com
DATE: Fri 8th December, 7:56 PM
SUBJECT: Home Sweet Home Again

In just less than a week of me knowing, my mom decided to take the family to our new home. And I'll be honest, I kicked off—not at first, but later on. I didn't mean to. It just sort of happened.

The place itself is nice. Real nice. But I got angry. I told myself on the way there to go with an open mind. To remember what a home really means. And I was doing fine until I didn't. To stand inside and view the rooms, hear the others plan out how everything will look—I realised I'd no longer be driving back my usual route from school or walking through the same door and retreating to my room like I have done my whole life. I couldn't stand it.

But then my mom came and spoke to me by the pool. And I knew she was going to come in armoured and ready to battle.

But she didn't.

She spoke calmly and kind of considerately. And so I took a note out of your book. I listened—I heard her out and then told her about my concerns. I put my emotions and feelings out there. I explained it felt like we were getting rid of Dad and that nobody seemed to care.

She told me she did and questioned how I could think she didn't. I replied saying that she never talks about him. Ever.

So she did talk. About my dad. To me. It was the first time in what felt like forever.

She finds it hard. Because every day, she thinks of Dad, and it upsets her. And speaking about him makes her feel sad. I understand that. I get it. I just never knew how raw it was for her.

We talked for most of the evening about Dad, and when I said remembering people and grieving isn't meant to be done alone in our heads, she agreed and then thought that sounded like a lyric from a song Dad would have listened to. That pleased me.

The reason for the move isn't because everything reminds her of him and needs to escape. But because it feels like the right time. It's not letting him go or moving on from him, she said, because he's always going to be with us; it's just time. My little sister doesn't remember much of Dad, other parts of our family have already changed, and not too long in the future, I'll be at college. So it's just time.

And weirdly enough, despite how much is going on inside my head, I get it. I can see where my mom is coming from. It's something she has to do, and I shouldn't be the person to stop her if it's something that will make her better.

I'm saying all this to you, Brisbane, to say thanks because, yes, your thoughts did play a part in this, but also because I feel talking about these kinds of things is fine with you. No judgement. Just encouragement or helpfulness. You're the person I want to tell things to. The guy I want to go to when something happens or changes in my life.

And I realised from the chat with my mom that it's time I make a change for myself. I've been so concerned about trying to be perfect for everybody that it's become exhausting. And I need to start doing what's right for me. Not in a selfish way. But in a better way. I need to do what's right for me and for others. Because it's time.

Love,
Tokyo

FROM: BlueC0ast1@bretteodmail.com
TO: TokyoCherryDustZ89@TokyoCherryDustZ89.com
DATE: Fri 8th December, 8:24 PM
SUBJECT: Re: Home Sweet Home Again

Tokyo, I'm so pleased you managed to talk and make some progress with your mom. It's wonderful news! I know it can't have been easy for you. You're on the same page, though, and that's a good thing to be grateful about.

And I feel the same about you, too.

And you're ready to change? That's good. But what does that mean? Ready to speak to your friends? To be more yourself around others? To let people know who Tokyo is? To tell me who you are?

Love,
Brisbane

FROM: TokyoCherryDustZ89@TokyoCherryDustZ89.com
TO: BlueC0ast1@bretteodmail.com
DATE: Fri 8th December, 9:54 PM
SUBJECT: Re: Home Sweet Home Again

Thank you. There's still a long way to go with my mom, but a bridge has started to be built between us.

I'm pleased.

Steady on. I love the thought of us finally telling each other who we are. And finally meeting. I want it badly. But I can't rush it. I've only just understood I need to do things because they're right. And there's quite a bit to do. Not with you—I honestly mean it when I say I do feel a connection between us—it's just with other parts of my life. And they will take time. I've got to sort things on my end—parts of my life I need to take control of first before this leap. I hope you understand.

But to show how I feel…how I see everything when I speak to you, please listen to the new song I've uploaded on KingsgateLeeConnect. The song is called Our Beam, and it's from a band called Star Dirt Lagoon. They're an Aussie band, so I know you'll already be intrigued by them. In fact, you should listen to all of their music, but please listen to this song. To the lyrics. And you'll know.

Love,
Tokyo

FROM: BlueC0ast1@bretteodmail.com
TO: TokyoCherryDustZ89@TokyoCherryDustZ89.com
DATE: Fri 8th December, 10:46 PM
SUBJECT: Re: Home Sweet Home Again

Sorry if I sounded pushy when I asked those questions, Tokyo. I was just excited by what you could mean. The thought that we're approaching a point where we could meet does make me happy. But I understand. And I agree.

And Star Dirt Lagoon? I totally love them. I just love the energy they give out.

And their song Our Beam. I love how it changes me as I listen. The jazziness and smoothness at the beginning and then the song turning into this celebration of life with a collaboration of sounds of what I can only think of as modern disco. And the electric droops and the deep synth sounds—are they synths? I just love it! And all while this is happening, the singer is saying they're transitioning. Feeling out of place and unsure of where they are at the beginning, to then be awoken by something. Or rather someone. And he knows that person is changing, too. And they both feel ecstatic.

I know why you picked that song. I think it perfectly sums up this moment between us. I couldn't agree anymore. You've awoken something in me, too. Something I'm deeply fond of.

Love,
Brisbane

26.

"Absolutely not!" Zeke protests, slamming the scissors down in front of Dacre, Antonia and me in one of the classrooms. We've been helping Antonia and the committee with preparations for the Winter Week. With it only being next week, everybody's offered to get the decorations sorted. I'm not sure why we've volunteered all week, though, because we've been given the hardest task—making paper snowflake chains. Billie isn't here yet.

"Please, Zeke, I've got enough girls, but I need more guys to be part of the raffle," Antonia practically begs. "And you, Hayden."

"I don't think I even know what the Snow Date Raffle is," I remark, sitting beside Zeke. There's Santa's Xtreme Talent Show, this Date Raffle and then the Winter Snowdrop Ball—but I'm not sure what they actually are.

"A chance for people to throw themselves up for show like meat on a plate and let other people buy a ticket to be in that raffle to win a date with them," Zeke explains while overdramatically flailing his arms about.

"Basically, there's a raffle for each person—so you can choose who you go for," Dacre adds, more calmly than Zeke did.

I immediately shake my head and give as much hate to the idea. The thought of putting myself out there like that makes my legs turn to jelly.

"It's for charity!" Antonia states. "And the dates get to go bowling and have a meal for free."

Zeke clasps his hands together and then bats his eyelashes. "Wow, so romantic." He suddenly and exaggeratedly pretends to throw up—then grabs his scissors and begins cutting again. "I thought this would be right up Jared's street. Get him."

"He's already one of the five guys."

Everybody whips their head to Antonia.

"That didn't take long," Dacre comments. I agree. The guy's only just broken up with Chloe Cassadentini, which, with so many rumours flying around, nobody knows how or why it ended.

"He came over and asked me last week. Said there was no point wasting time, and it's just for fun and nothing serious."

I still can't believe it, and from the looks of the others, neither can they.

"Pfft, I bet Chloe isn't gonna be happy when she finds out," Zeke remarks, lowering his voice—Chloe's only on the other side of the room, working on some other project.

Antonia looks back at us and whispers, "She wasn't. I had to update everybody in the last committee meeting, and she's helping organise the talent show. She was angry."

We've never been close, but I imagine it was hard for Chloe to hear that after her breakup with Jared. And it won't have been great after all the things people put on KingsgateLeeConnect. Thinking she had cheated. Been around the football team. And the cheerleaders.

"Come on guys, you're two fine strapping men," Dacre says. Zeke holds his unamused glare at them. "You're a funny guy, Zeke. Girls know that, and they love that in a person. And I'm sure there's some girls intrigued by the new guy in our year from Georgia." He raises his eyebrow up and down, playfully teasing, but I don't laugh.

"Ooo yes, the fun joker guy and then the mysterious newcomer wild card. Love it! Come on, guys, pleeeease," Antonia squeaks.

Antonia shows us her big button eyes—blinking as if they were twinkling stars in the sky.

Part of me wants to help her. It's for a good cause, after all. However, a huge part doesn't. Because I don't want much attention on me—what with Andrew. And, also, because of Tokyo. How I feel towards her.

"I don't think I can," I mumble. "I'm sorry, Antonia."

The desperate glee on her face fades a little, but she gives a nod of understanding, which I appreciate.

"Well, if he isn't, I'm not."

"Aw, come on, Zeke. Please," Antonia says with her hands clasped around her phone, begging in his direction.

"I've just been telling Hayden how it's another display of popularity and—"

"I'll do anything. I'll help you with your schoolwork. I'll let you plan and choose where we go on our next five outings."

"Don't recall you asked our permission for that," Dacre notes from Antonia's offers.

Zeke's back broadens—his lips beaming with delight. "Really?"

She nods.

He scratches the bottom of his chin, milking the power he momentarily has. "Fiiiine."

Antonia claps with joy. She leaps over and hugs him. A lot of times. "Thank you, thank you!" She pulls away. "Thanks, Zeke. Oh, and today's the last day to get these snowflake chains cut, so make sure we've made enough to hang and fill all the hallways."

"ALL THE HALLWAYS?" Zeke repeats at Antonia before letting his body go forward and his head slam onto the table. He then mumbles underneath, "Really?"

"Yep," Antonia answers, smiling, and then walks away to leave us, dumbfounded, with the pile of paper snowflakes on the table.

Dacre laughs. "Come on, guys, we've got nothing better to do."

"Except live our lives," Zeke protests, now with his head back up. "We've come in this early every day this week—and we're not even getting paid! And I don't think I can do more—we've been cutting the same thing so much I've started to wake up at night and find myself doing this." He lifts his hand and begins madly clipping his index and middle finger together like a pair of scissors.

We laugh. It's moments like this that I'm pleased I chose not to abandon the group after Andrew's threatening ultimatum.

Even if I still feel awful with myself.

There's a vibration in my pocket when I put the chain in the centre. I pull my phone out, eagerly hoping it's an email from Tokyo. It's a text from Jasmine—asking if we can skip the tutoring after school tonight—she has some work to do. I quickly reply, telling her that's fine.

I pick up some paper and start cutting.

"Hey guys, how's it going?" The three of us look up. I'm worried Antonia's seen my last abysmal attempt at a snowflake chain and caught me putting it into the completed pile. But it's Chloe Cassadentini.

"Erm, hi," Zeke says. I tag along with a hey. Dacre's the only one who sounds normal about her approaching us, but I'm just pleased I'm not the only person confused by her appearance.

"It's going okay," Zeke answers. His eyes overly flick between her and us with pure bewilderment. "How's it—going with you?"

Still holding the clipboard against her chest with one hand, she flicks her hair back with the other. "Oh yes, all good. I'm sure it will be great next week; we certainly want to print our mark on the school history of Winter Weeks. Or should that be snow print our mark." Chloe then gives a tittering laugh at her own joke.

Dacre smiles back. I remain quiet, but when I face Zeke, I almost laugh, and not because of Chloe's joke; it's because of the wide-eyed what-the-heck-is-happening-look he glances at me.

"Haha, yeah," Dacre answers. I try and smile as if I had laughed at Chloe's joke to be kind.

"Well, just thought I'd come over and check you're okay. Loving the work you're doing, and I really appreciate the help you are giving to this."

Somebody in the room calls Chloe's name. She glances to see where it came from. It's my sister. I look down and focus on my snowflake chain. "I best go over and help. Keep up the great work guys. That's coming on nicely, Hayden. See ya."

With a dashing smile printed on her face, Chloe gives a little bye-bye wave with her free hand. She spins around, letting her lime-green, short skirt twirl, and walks away. I try to nod a thanks to her, but I'm thrown off.

"What in the Old Georgie from *Cloud Atlas* was that about?" Zeke asks—eyes still in shock. He then stares at me. "Any clues Zachry?"

I shake my head—to his question, and the film references.

"She's just being nice. Excited for next week," Dacre acknowledges. I'm not too sure. I'm with Zeke. That was odd.

"Chloe's never happy without reason," Zeke says. "She does realise that only a senior can be Snow King and Queen at the Winter Snowdrop Ball, right?"

Another oh-so-popular popularity contest, Zeke would call it.

"Yeah, I think she learnt that after trying last year to be the first sophomore to win it."

"I hope so—'cause it's giving me some serious Ernesto de la Cruz vibes," Zeke comments. I turn to Dacre—he mouths to me, *Coco*. "Oh hey, I forgot to say man, congrats on how it went the other day at the university interview."

I join in with Zeke and congratulate as well. Dacre went to my brother's university, and they really want him to join after high school, providing he passes all his exams in senior year.

"Thanks, guys. I can't wait, I just—what the—Billie!"

I turn to Dacre's gaze. Gone has the big, curly orange hair, and now Billie enters with her hair straight, smooth, and put in a slick ponytail—a river of orange, but now with a new thin, black stream striking through it.

Zeke and I make a comment of surprise as she sits down. It's completely different to her usual look, and yet it looks more like Billie than ever before.

"You guys like it?"

"Yeah," everybody agrees. Billie bows her head a little and toys the end of her ponytail with her fingers.

"Wait till Antonia sees," Dacre jokes. "Did you change it for the Winter Snowdrop Ball?"

Billie blushes a little. "Well, it's my last year and, well…" Billie's voice trails off.

"It's nice, but honestly, I think that thing could do some damage." Zeke takes hold of her ponytail, and before she can protest, he moves it around and puts on what can only be described as an attempt of a female voice. "Take that, you fool."

He flicks the ponytail, almost a whip. The end taps the table.

"Get off." Billie tries not to laugh while she shoves his hands away, and everybody else chuckles.

My eyes catch two guys by the door in the hallway. At first, I think they're laughing along, but the mocking smirks towards Zeke make me disagree.

"What a clown," I hear one of them say as they walk away. I look over, hoping Zeke didn't hear, but I see him turn back from them and to the table. He begins to talk, joking about the snowflake chains. I smile when the others laugh, proud that Zeke doesn't step on the merry-go-round, as Cassio calls it. Something I wish I could do with Andrew.

I really wish Jasmine didn't cancel our tutoring tonight. I've tried to hang out with my friends, and yet right now, I'm squished between Zeke and Dacre pushing each other about and a couple drunkenly making out on the couch at a house party—and with no option but to witness Andrew cosying up to Billie opposite me. Arm around her. Her leg resting over his. Him making her laugh. Then kissing her.

I try to stop the thoughts of what Andrew has done and is doing to me—the cheating, the threatening, the lying—and focus on whatever game the rest are playing. I know not to get onto that merry-go-round in my head, but it's so hard to maintain the anger when he's there. Deeper. Darker. Deadlier.

And he's frequently been looking my way, too.

I can't take it—I squeeze myself out and begin to head off.

"Ah, ah, ah, Hayden. Where do you think you're going? It's your turn to answer the honesty questions next," Antonia says, perched next to Andrew and Billie. They both turn to face me.

I tell them the toilet. None of them buy it.

"Yeah, come on. Or are you scared?"

My eyes avert over. Even Andrew's now getting involved. Sitting there, looking like he's part of this group and loyal to them, like besties, all while Billie lays against his side. Toying with his hair with one hand.

He's acting all loved up, making poor Billie feel like she's the one. A show, for who knows what reason why. Scared to be alone?

It infuriates me to see this sham before my eyes.

"No," I answer—yet despite knowing I shouldn't be on this flippin' merry-go-round, I take a step on—for a second. "But maybe you lot won't like my answers."

There's a collection of gasps, laughs and whoops around, but there's a brief strip of pleasure in me when I see the alarm in Andrew's eyes—the thought that he's unable to do anything. But as soon as the fear is there, it disappears, and he's back to his usual self—and my hatred and worry return. Stronger now—knowing I should have stayed off the merry-go-round.

I leave the room before anyone can actually stop me. I need to be alone. The toilet isn't a bad decision, so I head that way—but a hand gets my shoulder. I flinch.

"Woah. It's just me." Billie. I turn around, but not before I try and gather any energy to fake a smile. "Hey, are you okay?"

Was it that obvious I wasn't?

I nod. "Just a bit squished on that couch."

Billie chuckles. Her ponytail flicks as she moves. The new style suits her. "I know I apologised for how I was that night we first met when I saw Zeke injured, but I don't think I've ever said how grateful I am you've come into our lives."

I face Billie, surprised by her words, along with the softness in her voice and the honesty in her eyes. "You're grateful?"

She gives me a gentle shove. "Yes. You're always supportive. You see things differently and can make us feel better. You're extremely kind. Heck, you're even giving Jasmine Keery Spanish lessons for free."

"But I'm just being myself."

"And what? That doesn't mean it's special to someone else? I thought you were smarter than that, Hayden Mallard."

I bite my lip—it's the first time we've been alone since Andrew confronted me. Despite the warmth of Billie beside me, my body instantly turns cold.

Billie then holds my hand. "I know you've been busy recently and couldn't meet up, but I want you to know if there's anything up, you can chat with us. Or just one of us if you prefer."

Everything inside me becomes poisoned with guilt as she speaks. She's noticed I've been distant—that's how Andrew knew.

And here my friend is, opening up to let me know that they are there for me. And I know that. I've seen them in action. When Billie saw Zeke was injured. When Dacre opened to me. Even I tried with Antonia at No Armadillos. They are a strong unit—because they trust each other. Yet I'm holding this secret. This secret which is to do with Billie.

"Thank you, but yeah, you're right—it was just busy with family and schoolwork. That sort of stuff."

I'm terrible.

"That's okay then." She moves closer and, without asking, leans against my side. "Because although it's been a short time, I care about you. We all do. We're all important to each other."

And just like that, I feel like the worst friend in the world.

I take a moment in the bathroom to gather my thoughts and calm down. It's too loud! I rip off some toilet paper and focus on folding a piece, remembering Dr Oace's words over and over as I attempt to make an origami animal—an origami parrot because it reminds me of Tokyo. I force myself to recall the happiness I have with her and all the times making origami helped me in the hospital.

The toilet paper rips. I throw it down the toilet in fury and grab another. I keep trying, but I continue to mess up. I start to become sadder as I go along—upset, lonely, hurting—but then also angrier with myself.

There are loud knocks at the door. I flush away the remains of the unsuccessful origami parrots and leave in defeat.

The hurt is still there. I can't face the others—yet Zeke's my ride home. I head to the kitchen to give myself some more time alone and get a soft drink.

I find Kamala there, beside a black tray with some beer bottles and then loads of tiny glasses with some sort of clear liquid in them. There's a brief smile when she realises it's me.

"They're not all for me," Kamala says, grabbing some more cups from the side. "But I wouldn't say no." Her voice sounds a little more enthusiastic than normal, well, more for Kamala, that is. I guess she's tipsy or just happy from a little drink.

"What are they?" I point to the small glasses.

Before I can reject, she pushes one into my hand. I look down. I know it's alcoholic. I contemplate what my dad and the doctors in Georgia would say. But all I can think of is Andrew and the mess I'm in. It infuriates me.

I do my best to ignore the stickiness of the glass on my fingers and down the drink—but I cough uncontrollably, almost choking because my throat's being scorched alive. It tastes horrid.

"Woah there."

"What—was—that?" I manage to ask, feeling like I have swallowed fire from a dragon.

Kamala laughs. "Tequila. Best to have two more to ease it, I find."

I quickly grab two glasses on the tray and drink them down. I cough more. My throat can't feel anything—but my head's becoming a little lighter.

Kamala stands—mouth open. The first time I've seen her look so alive with expression other than hate. "Wow, I was just joking. But you took that better than I thought. Here." She pulls a bottle of beer from a blue bucket that's filled with ice and various bottles poking out from the top, twists the cap off and hands it over. I look at her dubiously. "This *will* ease the wrath of the tequila."

I've already drunk and gone against my dad's rules, but this doesn't mean I will drink at every party now. Tonight can be the *I tried it once, and I won't do it again* sort of situation.

I take a swig—but immediately spit it out, almost spraying it like one of the fountains at Mt. Okesea into the sink. Kamala laughs.

"That tastes like urine from an elephant," I say, flicking my tongue around from the taste.

"Oh, so you've had that before, have you?" Kamala jokes. I laugh. "It's got rid of the sting, though, right?"

To be fair, it kind of has, but that doesn't mean I like this taste any better. I keep a hold of the bottle, though, because it would be rude to reject the rest in front of Kamala.

We chat a little, mostly about working at Mt. Okesea. I take a few sips here and there in order to try and quickly lower the amount of beer left in my bottle.

But soon, things become a little lighter, along with a warm and cosy feeling tingling around inside me. And I like it. Everything seems to become more exciting. The conversation, the people around me—it all suddenly looks more inviting. And fun.

We somehow go on about how nothing feels more important in the world right now than how annoying it is when people return the golf clubs and not the short pencils we give them to write their scores down on the scorecards. And. It. Is.

"Yeah, it's extremely annoying," I tell Kamala. *Do people think we have an endless supply of pencils in that hut? Nooooooope.*

A noise from the side catches my eyes to turn, but when I whip my head back to Kamala, things are a little weird. Off almost, disorientated. Everybody seems to be floating around me or moving slower than usual, which is odd because people can't do that. Right? As Kamala talks, I try to feel my fingertips. I can't sense anything. Not even my tongue. It's weird. Wee-eerd. Dee-lay. Is there a—

Kamala's no longer beside me. But then I hear Kamala's voice say goodbye. I glare around with just my eyes, completely puzzled. I wave with confusion, but I don't know who to.

Everybody's suddenly incredibly loud. I leave the kitchen, which takes like forever, bringing my bottle with me, pressing it near my chest because it's my new best friend. Is this house a boat because everything and everybody is slightly swaying, or do my legs have no bones to hold me up?

"Hey, are you okay?"

I blink—and as if I've never used my eyes before, I focus real hard on where the voice came from. It's Zeke. "You—" Zeke stops and holds my shoulders, looking right at me. "Wait, are you drunk?"

I smile. And lift the bottle in my hand.

"Wow. That's a first." Zeke slaps a hand on my shoulder—my shoulder dips from the light impact. "I thought you prefer not to drink—never mind, come on, let's get you some fresh air."

"How? You got a canister? You can't catch air, you know?"

"Oh man, I wish the others were here for this," I hear Zeke comment. He begins to help me move, not that I really need it—but my legs smack into a table. I hiss. Okay, maybe I do need help.

We reach the front of the house and rest outside, a little off from the front door. The fresh air does feel kind of soothing, but my head says otherwise. It's spinning more than before.

"So, what made you have the drink?"

"Just thought I should try it."

"Even when you said you already had?"

I eagerly nod to Zeke—ignoring the old lie that I told them I had. He asks me how it's going.

"My head stings—if that's what you mean?" I retry my answer. But I can't. I'm suddenly reminded of my reasons why. Andrew. Maybe I should spill now—I can't. Even drunk me can't. "Probably because of the tequila from Kamala."

"Tequila? No way!" Zeke grins. I try to smile back, but I don't feel as good as I did just moments ago back in the kitchen.

I cross my legs. Zeke's eyes are on me. But I also think I'm sitting on a bouncy castle, so who knows? I look over to him. "You know, I think Coach Rugrosso's Whiplashin' you."

Zeke raises an eyebrow—I hiccup loudly.

"You know, like in the film *Whiplash*—we watched the other week, where the teacher pushes the student so hard to the brink of breaking because he sees the potential the kid has. Whiplashin'."

The bottle slips out of my hand. I chuckle when it rolls away.

Zeke's mouth drops open. "Is that—that's your first movie reference! Why is there nobody else here to see this?" He glances around. "Finally! The hours of hammering people with film stuff is paying off—well, I'd say film treasure—but ah! I'm so proud!"

He enthusiastically wraps his arms around me for a hug. He pats me on my back—I throw up.

We stay in the hug. There's a horrid stench of tequila mixed in with beer—it's all down Zeke's back.

"Urgh, should have seen that coming."

"Sorry," I mumble to him, with my stomach really aching now.

He lets go and leans back. "It's okay. Oh—think you're gonna have it a lot worse, though."

"Why?"

Zeke continues to stare beyond me. "Becau—"

"Hayden?"

I turn my head around. Extremely slowly—to see who said my name. Standing outside the front door is Robin. And unless my mind's playing on me, she looks mad. I don't take much notice—I vomit again.

27.

The entire inside of the school is covered in white and blue decorations. A zillion paper and card snowflakes dangle across the ceilings in all the hallways and the cafeteria, with blue ribbons on the walls and around every doorframe. Fake snowmen are guarding the hallways with their top hats and their carrot noses. It's really got everybody in the Christmas mood. And normally, I would be, too.

But I feel terrible and fed up inside—which isn't ideal as I sit across the table from Mr Gauran in his office.

"So, it's our last meeting before the Christmas break," he begins.

I shuffle a little in my chair, yet I play it off like I'm getting comfortable. My eyes stay down—I'm struggling to fight against my own thoughts and worries inside myself.

He notices that I am quiet and comments on this.

"Aren't observations just a loose way of asking the questions you want to ask?" I reply—I instantly regret it, though.

"And saying nothing at all gives off more than what the person intends."

Well, I walked into that, didn't I?

"Hayden. These sessions aren't for silence. Nothing gets resolved like that. And they aren't for me to go all Jessica Fletcher on you and find the truth or for me to Jedi mind trick you into telling me."

I keep my lips shut.

He tries a new approach—he states that my friends and I helped decorate the school. I nod, only to give him some satisfaction I've contributed to the meeting. "Rather impressive, even if a snowflake chain outside the staff room clotheslined me." He goes on to sound excited about the activities coming up this week and insists I must be at least excited for the Winter Snowdrop Ball.

I shuffle in my seat again. "I doubt I'm going. I'm grounded."

Dad wasn't pleased with me drinking—he made it clear the day after the party. Grounded me until he decides—and he's banned me from my phone and laptop. And that sucks—I can't stay in touch with Tokyo. I managed to send a quick email to her before Dad took my phone, informing her I'll be out of reach for a little while—I'm just glad there were no drunk emails in my sent box.

I'm a bit upset, but I know I deserve the grounding. I broke Dad's rule. The rule from the doctors. My own rule.

But I realise being around my friends and Andrew isn't working like I wish it would. *I suppose I have a valid excuse now why I can't be with my friends after school if it gets too much.*

Wow, I hate my brain sometimes.

I stare down at my feet when Mr Gauran asks why I'm grounded. "I got drunk at a party."

I don't recall much apart from Robin being seriously angry, and then I had my head out of the window of her car, and then I was sprawled out on my bed, aching. I think Cassio must have been at the party and helped Robin take me back because I'm sure I saw him standing by my bedroom door before my dad and Robin left the room.

"From what I've been told, you spewed most of it back up as well."

My eyebrows furrow in confusion—then I realise. Dad told him. Angry is nowhere near the word I'd use right now with how furious I am with Dad.

"I just wanted to see what the deal was about drinking."

But it doesn't take a brainiac to see straightaway he doesn't buy it.

"When you know how drinking could affect you after how much you've progressed since you left the hospital and are here? Don't make out you're that dumb."

"Everybody at school tries a drink. There doesn't have to be a reason for everything I do. Maybe I wanted to?"

I try my best not to get riled up before it becomes an interrogation. However, it's like I can feel Andrew here, standing close to me, ready to hurt if I let out about him. It infuriates me more, but I battle so hard to keep it together.

"Why now, then?"

My eyes give a rapid set of blinks as I stare at him, confused. "What?"

"If it genuinely was to just try alcohol, why now? Because I'm calling bull on that. You've been to parties before and been fine." He pauses. "I've noticed a change in you these last few times we've met."

I stay sat in silence. I have no clue what to do except remain still.

"Man, I'm having to now talk more than you to get you to talk in these meetings. And I'm sure the reason is what made you want to have a drink." He leans close towards me. I'm ready to snap. "So I'm calling bull on you, Hayden. So don't sit there and lie to me because otherwise you're throwing away everything we've done so far—everything you've put into feeling better. And you don't deserve that."

My fury freezes. My anger to shout halts. Something he says hits me, blocks me from unleashing this wrath—his last words.

"Don't," I object—my voice so quiet because I don't want the walls I've tried to keep up to break.

"What? You don't deserve that? It's true. You don't."

I stare at my hands. They're repeatedly trying to cup each other. The walls are starting to crack.

"I do," I tell him. He asks why. My eyes fixate on my hands—too weak to see how he's looking at me. "Because it's hard. All of it. To abide by everything. To please everybody. I've even got to accept there's a part of my life that changed everything, yet I've got no memory of it—and I just have to believe what everyone says?"

I force my hands to stop trembling and close them together tightly on my lap.

"Why do you think you have to please everyone?"

I breathe in, pushing myself to keep it together—but when I breathe back out, there's a cold quiver that cuts the flow.

"I know we moved here because of me." I don't know how long I take to continue. "I'm the sole reason we moved—not Mom. She left us to go who knows where—so we could have stayed in Georgia. Mom might be the reason why I'm the reason we moved—but the move is on me." I feel sick when I think about how life would be the same for Dad, Robin and Colbey if we had stayed. "They've done so much for me that I can't let them down."

"So you think there's this pressure?"

"Yeah," I stumble. "Yeah, to do right. Robin loves to remind me how much they've given up for me. And it's difficult."

"How so?"

I don't want to go on—but Mr Gauran says I need to.

"Well—" I stop, hoping to pause the mad thoughts spinning in my mind. I can hear Andrew threatening me. I instantly try to turn that off. This isn't about him.

Mr Gauran gives a short smile, one that tries to reassure me that it is okay. I return to my hands because I don't think it is.

"My mom used to teach us to surf when we'd go to the beach. I was terrible. She'd say that when there's an oncoming wave, you've got to dip below it with your board and swim under to get further out. Otherwise, you won't get anywhere. And I just feel like I'm there now.

Trying to stay on that board, with wave after wave of things coming at me, things that I've got to simply accept and let it override me to maybe get somewhere."

I think of all these waves repeatedly coming at me. My life, my past, my family…Andrew.

"But it's not just a wave or a series of waves—it's an ocean. Mom said the further out you go and get through those waves, the more fun you'll have on the way back. But when is that?" My voice cracks from the dryness of my throat, but I don't seem to stop, even with how much emotion is seeping out. "I just wanna ride the wave and head back already or get across the ocean so I'm somewhere else 'cause I've no idea where this ends." I quickly sniff to regain some control of my body before it caves in and I cry. But I fail. My eyes water. "And if I slip, I'll have let them down. And I can't. I can't do that to them."

My vision becomes blurry. The few tears that have escaped slowly fall down my cheeks—I don't bother wiping them away.

Mr Gauran repositions himself in his chair. "I can't tell you where the end is hiding. Only you can find that out. But pressure. That's a terrible thing. Because it gets us worked up—why? 'Cause it means we've got something we care about. Too strongly that we don't want to mess it up. But we weren't born perfect—to deal with every situation perfectly and get the best outcome. Yet we weren't created to keep it all in, either. That's not possible. Because whatever fears or irritations you've got bottled up will build until there's no room—then it all floods out. You've got to let some of that go, Hayden. I'm telling you, it's okay to let people know that you aren't dealing with things in life."

I glance over—then quickly look away because the reassurance he wants to give me is becoming too much.

My lips scrunch up as I cry—it's the only thing I think I can do right now. My body shuffles a little, but moving makes me want to give in more.

"Are you ashamed of your past? With what's happened, I mean."

My body suddenly forces me to sob—and there's no holding back.

"Yes," I say through my sobs. I've thought of it long ago but never truly knew how much until hearing it aloud. "Why wouldn't I be? 'Cause who'd want to be friends with the boy who had to go to the hospital twice? There wasn't anybody I had back home, and now I have people here who like me, *me*, without knowing these constraints and my history. But it's like I'm lying. This guilt on me. But I can't say."

"You should," Mr Gauran tells me. I look up, questioning why.

"Because it's swallowing you up. You know that."

I want to shake my head. Desperately wanting to disagree. But it is. More than I cared to consider or think I could admit. How it's all putting more pressure on myself than what is already there.

My voice breaks—I want to let everything out. How every little thing has a hold on me. And I think I could tell him—except about Andrew. His wrath still wraps tightly around my neck like his hand did that night. The heat of it scorches me inside.

No, I can tell Mr Gauran everything, everything but that.

And with that, I cry even harder. Dismayed and terrible that, once again, I've caved into Andrew having a grip over me.

Mr Gauran waits, letting me cry before he says, "Nobody ever said you can't tell your friends. And don't say you can't—because you've just taken that first step here with me."

Hearing those words only makes me worse.

I try to gather myself up.

Mr Gauran looks right into my eyes with such assurance and determination that his next words must reach me. "You need to know, Hayden, you shouldn't ever have to feel ashamed of yourself."

I'm such a mess, so upset and reeling that all I do is nod to him through my tears. Because he's right. I know he is—I shouldn't feel ashamed, and yet I do.

I'm so upset and so extremely quiet that Mr Gauran rings my dad to collect me. I don't argue—I don't even speak.

I begin to realise that I took the drink to stop constantly thinking of Andrew and what he's doing to me. To have a moment away from myself.

I'm sure that's how my first breakdown started after Mom left—why I flipped suddenly and drove off in Robin's car—why I needed to get away. Because I must have always been thinking about her, always questioning why she would leave—repetitively overthinking the ordeal to the point where I broke. I mean, what else could've made me want to escape and take the car? And how else could I have had another breakdown later if it wasn't for suddenly becoming overwhelmed again with her going and all that I had done?

I drank because I didn't want my mind to follow that same pattern of persistently overthinking so much that I crack—because that's what I'm doing, only this time with Andrew.

School will finish soon, yet there's two weeks of holiday—I can't deal with being with my friends for that long. Hanging out with them while keeping this secret and threat isn't a great combo, especially if Andrew is to be there. *Maybe Dad will ground me for the entire Christmas break?* So I can clear my mind. That might work.

I'm so in my thoughts, though, that I don't realise Dad pulls over and parks the car outside a park. He grabs something from the back and then gets out. He perches himself against the hood and pats at the space beside him with a smile on his face. A smile he's holding on purpose, I reckon, to make me feel better. It just makes me feel awkward, but I reluctantly go around and join him.

"Mr Gauran told me you had a rough time in your meeting just now," he begins.

I immediately look away when he faces me—it will break my heart if he's upset. But, nevertheless, I admit that I did. "Yeah. Did he tell you what I said?"

"No. You don't have to tell me, but please remember, I am here for you."

I cave and glance to face him. His amazing white teeth are hidden from the whimsical smile on his lips. I open my mouth to speak—nothing comes out. I let my fingers begin to stroke my palm. I look down and watch. To calm myself, to prepare myself. And then I tell him.

I explain about how I've been—with the move, the pressure to not let him and Robin and Colbey down, and the fact that the rules, which are to prevent me from having another breakdown, actually add more pressure. I attempt to reassure him that I understand why I'm not so free to do things, and yet that doesn't mean I like being constrained with no say.

There's a part of me that wants to say I was bullied when we arrived, but when I see his face is now bleak, my kindness tells me not to, and so I don't.

Dad pushes himself off the hood. He's got a hand over his mouth—I don't know what to say. He paces a little, which unnerves me. I can't tell if he's seriously mad or disappointed with me. I haven't seen him this quiet since the day Mom left.

"Why have you never said anything?" He then asks, looking over to me.

"Because you guys would think all you've given up would have been a waste. I'd have been a let-down."

My dad put his hands to his face. I watch even more concerned when he pushes them up against his face as if trying to scrub this news off like it was dirt. When the hands come off, though, there's water forming in his eyes.

"I'm sorry," I feel the need to say.

He whips his head around to me. "Hey, hey, look at me."

When I turn, he walks over to me and stands against the front of the car. He puts his large yet dentistry-smooth hands on my cheeks. He gently lifts my head so I must face him. He is seriously crying.

"You can never be a let-down to me, son. And you've got nothing to be sorry about, okay, kid? Nothing. I'm the one who should be. You were never meant to feel like this was all on you. I failed you."

He lets go of my face.

"No, Dad, you haven't—"

"I've tried so hard to make sure everything is okay for you that I didn't really check to notice if you were. And I am sorry I didn't." He then puts his hands on my shoulders. "I want you always to remember that you are awesome, Hayden. And that I love you. It hasn't been easy this year but know I will always be here for you. No matter what."

"I know." And I do. I really do. This year might not have been simple for me, but I know it's been just as hard for Dad if not more. There's not just having to deal with me. He's had to deal with the love of his life—his childhood sweetheart—suddenly leaving him, to be left alone to look after the family and restart in another state.

I watch him cry. Like, seriously cry. He tries to rub the water away, but when I see how much this means to him for me to hear this, it makes me want to cry, too, because of the love he is giving to me. For the love I have for him.

"Shit, Dad. You're making this like some soppy drama. You've watched too much TV."

Dad briefly laughs through his sniffling. "I think so. And hey—" he then points at me. "No swearing. You can be honest to me but not explicitly."

I chuckle. He leans over and then holds me while I'm still perched on the hood. I feel him grip me tightly. But I like it. So I accept it and fold my arms around him.

Dad wipes more tears away after we eventually separate. He really is a big softy.

He leans back against the hood next to me.

"Why did you bring us here?" I'm sure he, too, would have preferred the crying session to have happened behind closed doors.

"You used to go somewhere like here with your mom whenever you weren't feeling great and needed cheering up."

"You knew?" I ask, unable to hide the surprise from my face. He nods. "You know we used to have—"

"Popcorn?" He asks. Dad leans down to the side of the car and comes back up with two bags in his hands. "Salted, right?"

I nod. He passes me the popcorn bag. I carefully open it, letting the salty contents inside escape and waft under my nose.

Dad has already started eating his. There's a temptation to make some dentist dad joke that I'm surprised he's letting me have it, even after all these years he knew that Mom and I did. But, instead, I smile and just say, "Thanks."

28.

Mr Gauran gave my dad some suggestions for therapists for me to go to. I don't really want to go, but if it's to make me feel not so hard on myself, then maybe I should.

As I sit around with my friends at lunch the next day, I realise there's a long way to go, but there's one thing I can do. Be open about my past with my friends.

Mr Gauran thinks that I'm not giving them much credit, and I guess he's right. Telling them may make it easier staying around them.

"Hey Zeke, turn around. I think Hayden might be sick again." Billie pretends to panic and grabs Zeke.

Instead of twisting around, he leans forward—some mush of sandwich seeps out of his mouth and slowly slops onto his tray. Everybody groans at the scene.

Antonia pushes her tray away. "That's me done."

With some force, I pretend to laugh with the others. I want to tell them everything, but right now at school isn't the right place. It must be done somewhere alone—which doesn't help when I'm grounded.

Zeke begins to run off a list of films that I must watch over Christmas as we both head to his locker so he can dump his books in before Santa's Xtreme Talent Show starts. The others have already headed over.

Straightaway, my mind thinks Tokyo will love that he's doing this to me—he's obsessed with films during seasons, too. I'm sure that when we finally meet, Tokyo and Zeke will get on well. In fact, she'll be great with everybody in the group.

I desperately want to email her, but it's hard when I don't have my phone. I miss her.

We walk by a table in the hallway. There are posters with students displayed on them—including Zeke! Underneath, in white, are the words, Snow Date Raffle. There are posters of all the ten available dates stuck down the hallway—with raffle tickets now available to buy. Antonia's really pushed the boat out for this to work.

"Has that started today?" I ask Zeke.

He stops his film talk momentarily to look back while we continue walking.

"Yeah—not exactly screaming my lungs Rachel Green style about being peer pressured into it by Antonia, but I should try and be open to dating. I need to be more Will *Hitch* Smith and not Will *I Am Legend* Smith. Maybe I need this—but don't tell them I said that." Zeke points at me, pretending to be serious, yet the curved smile gives it away.

I stand and lean against the other lockers as he continues with his Christmas film list. His head vanishes into his locker to dump his books away.

"Hey Jared, you seen this?"

A little prickle works its way up inside me. I turn my head slightly to look. Jared and some friends are further down our side of the hallway. I keep my head low.

"Who's this guy?" A boy asks, pointing to something on the wall. Some of the girls wolf whistle while the guys howl.

"Okay, knock it off," Jared says when he sees his poster for the Snow Date Raffle.

"Woah, check this out. Zeke Palladino's in the Snow Date Raffle too," the first boy says.

"That doofus clown?" A guy I recognise as being one of Jared's bully chums asks. My body tenses from his words. He rips the poster of Zeke off the wall.

"Does he actually think anybody's gonna want to pay for the chance to win a date with him?" Another guy, who has short spikey black hair, adds. He was one of the guys laughing at Zeke when we were doing the decorations.

"Ew, no," a ginger-haired girl answers as she scrunches her nose up.

"He's so silly and such a loser. Why would any girl wanna date him?" A shorter girl with black hair says.

"I wouldn't even go on a date with him if it was free," the last girl adds.

"I wouldn't even if you paid me."

The group laughs. I feel awful. Horrible they're picking on Zeke so cruelly and personally like that.

"Hey guys, it's fine."

Jared steps forward. I'm in shock. Is he actually stopping them from making fun of Zeke? I watch intensely as they all stare back in silence at him. Maybe Dacre was right—Jared is kind?

"He should do it. It means I'll get more tickets sold." The group laugh out loud. "Besides, it is for charity."

This makes their laughter roar. Jared closes his locker, and they begin to walk away.

I whip my head back around to the open locker beside me. "Zeke?"

He slowly comes out of the locker and shuts it. "It's fine."

I try to move closer because he isn't.

He picks up his bag immediately before I can speak and begins to walk away. "It's fine, really. I just wanna be left alone."

Something inside me obeys. I stand and watch him go down the hallway until he's lost among the crowd of students.

Why do I have to be grounded? I can't message the others with no phone. Santa's Xtreme Talent Show will be almost starting now—but I push that aside, as well as Zeke's words, and I go after him. On my own.

I search the toilets first on either side of the school—Zeke wanted to be alone—that's where I sometimes went after Jared hurt me. But they're unoccupied. I travel down the quiet hallways, now with everybody in the auditorium. I glance through each window on the classroom doors in case he's in one. I don't see him.

I used to think it would be cool to walk through the school empty and silent, and it is, but it's also kind of freaky.

Zeke isn't at our usual table outside, either. I'm almost ready to give up when my eyes fixate on a small dot in the football stand—I squint to look better. It's Zeke.

"Didn't realise there was a game going on?" I joke and point out to the pitch when I arrive and take a seat beside him. It's empty. Zeke doesn't react. He just stays sat with his feet on his seat and his arms wrapped around his legs. "Who's winning?" Zeke doesn't react to that terrible joke, either.

I turn to look at him directly, deciding to approach the reason we're here. "You should ignore them."

Zeke merely nods, but he's not looking back at me. That lovable smile that's always on his lips is nowhere to be seen.

"I wasn't always this fun guy to be with. I was kinda reserved when I was younger."

I tilt my head. Zeke Palladino being quiet? To see him be, well, like me? "But you always know how to have a laugh."

"I do now. But when I was a kid, nobody wanted to know me. My parents sent me to a summer camp one year, nobody cared to approach me. Not until I acted like, alive and kicking and always—I don't know—onboard with it. Until I forced myself to be." Zeke sniffs, wiping his nose even though there's nothing there.

I stay quiet for him to continue.

"So when I returned to school, I kept being that kind of person. Somebody always willing to do stuff for fun—no matter how silly. Because if it made people laugh, and it made them want to know me, then it made me happy."

I nod, acknowledging how imperative it sometimes feels to be liked.

"I ain't saying that I don't enjoy being like this—it's made me more comfortable with finding who I am and what I like—but it's exhausting. And I try and brush off the shots at me—but—"

"There's only so much you can take," I finish his sentence.

He turns to face me. "Yeah. And when I hear things like earlier and with this stupid date raffle, I wonder what girl would like me. There may not be a girl who's into things I like, but that back then just made me think that maybe I shouldn't be worried that there isn't the right girl out there for me—maybe I should be concerned that I'm not the type of person any girl would like. Because all they see me as is some clown. And it hurts to think that might be all anybody sees me as."

The grip Zeke has around his legs is tighter.

"Yeah, I can get that," I say. "You've got a lot more than that, though. More than just one thing. You're supportive. Charming. Loyal. You even let me use your back as a bucket to throw up on—"

Zeke chuckles. "Don't think I had much choice on that."

"—and if others can't see those other great points, then that's because they're too stupid to be able to look further. Not just at you. But with me. With anybody," I continue. "You're more to me than some comical guy. You were my first friend here, Zeke. You saw me when I wasn't onboard, and you took the chance to get to know me without any judgement. Not because you were playing some part and thought you had to, but because of who you really are."

The KingsgateLeeConnect board by the pitch changes—I notice the school itself is uploading the talent show acts. I ignore it and I place a hand on Zeke's shoulder. He shifts over to me. He's trying to keep fine with it all. "And hey, if it's too much and you feel tired from it, remember you can always be switched off around me."

Zeke's lips crack apart—that huge grin that I've become so accustomed to appears on his face. "Switched off?"

"Yeah." I scratch my head, laughing with him. "That sounded better in my head."

Zeke smiles. "I bet. But I get what you mean. Thanks." He lets go of his legs and grips lightly on my shoulder. "You're a good guy."

I smile back to show my appreciation—but it's also there to camouflage the sudden stab I feel hit me inside. I'm ready to tell them about my past, but it's the fact that I can't talk about Andrew that really twists the knife in deeper.

When Zeke and me head to the auditorium, everybody is roaring with applause after some boy dressed up as Pikachu finishes playing a guitar solo. We see the others—with spare seats they've saved for us—and join them. Zeke brushes off where we've been with some excuse.

The crowd takes a while to simmer down. As some students dressed in black move equipment about on the stage, Chloe Cassadentini comes on. The stage light follows her.

"Thank you for that, Chris," Chloe begins, speaking into the microphone in her hand. "And now it's time for the last act of the show before the judges vote on who will win this year's Santa's Xtreme Talent Show!"

People cheer—we join in. With all the harsh comments that were posted on KingsgateLeeConnect when she and Jared split, I do admire Chloe's courage to go up and stand before everybody.

"So please, everybody, a round of applause for…the final act!"

Chloe leaves the stage as everybody claps. But when it finishes, nobody's replaced her presence.

The speakers abruptly come alive. It's a song. It's something lively and upbeat. Despite the confusion, people in the audience stand up and start to clap.

A light beams down—at the entrance of the auditorium. People's heads spin around. A girl is standing at the beginning of the other aisle. I can't see who.

Heads abruptly whip back around like a wave; the girl's running down the aisle. I manage to see her leap forward and slide onto the stage. People cheer. She gets up and begins swaying around to the music. She's wearing an electro-blue leotard. She spins to face the audience, her purple hair twists with the motion—I almost have to sit down.

"Is that?"

"Kamala," I answer Zeke. I watch in amazement because when the music picks up to the chorus, Kamala begins to throw more moves in and dances around the stage. But then she struts and jumps, and flips, and rolls, and she even somersaults. All I can do is watch in astonishment that the person doing this is Kamala. The girl who's always moody and strongly opinionated at everybody.

However, everybody is still up and clapping to her.

A drum kit on a moving platform slides onto the stage at the side. Kamala runs over, and when the song breaks, she grabs some drumsticks and starts drumming madly. Purple flicks frantically about. The drumming's loud, and it's crazy, but it all works. And I can see on her face that she loves it.

Out of nowhere, she throws a drumstick across the stage. It smacks into a large gong—I've got no clue when that appeared. The song kicks back on out of the speakers. Kamala leaves the drum kit—she starts gliding almost across the stage in a straight line by continuing to spin perfectly around. We cheer as she leaps into the air. She finishes the jump by landing the splits. The music ends. The entire room erupts!

Everybody claps immensely. The floor shakes as people stamp their feet. I join in.

"Well, I know who should win," Zeke says to us over the noise. "Kamala Bay, that's who!"

I smile in agreement with Zeke, not only because I see he looks better than before we came here but also because he couldn't be any more correct.

Zeke then adds to me. "You know what to do now if I'm ever down. Dance that ass off."

The others agree. I laugh as everybody continues to applaud. "Sure." But really, the thought sounds terrifying.

I want to congratulate Kamala for winning the talent show when I get to Mt. Okesea for work later that night. However, when I arrive, I'm working with neither her nor Zeke this Tuesday night. It's Aunt Sandra.

Work is busy as there are loads of families here in Orlando over Christmas. But I don't mind the busyness—because I have my phone back. Well, not for the long term. Dad has allowed me to have it tonight in case of emergencies—as I'm still cycling to and from work.

When I write to Tokyo in the staff toilet, I realise that I've missed this. The contact with her. It's only been a few days, but we've been messaging so much it's become almost not normal to not be receiving word from her.

I explain I'm able to email a little tonight because I have my phone at work—I decide to tell her I'm grounded so she doesn't think I'm no longer interested or care for her. Because I do. I immensely do.

I head back to the small hut when I'm done, but I'm surprised to see Jasmine there. And she's with her family.

She calls me—and with no alternative, I go over. Her sister, mom and dad head through the trees to the restaurant.

"Woah, you guys must really love crazy golf," I joke to Jasmine.

"Haha, no, we're just going to the restaurant tonight. They wanted to eat out somewhere this week before we leave for the Christmas holidays. And this is my sister's fave."

"You're not staying?"

"No. My mom's half Swedish and some of the family lives there, so we spend Christmas and New Year there every year. Celebrate six hours earlier than you lot here."

"That's nice. Definitely more winter festive looking than here."

"I know. I can't wait to just jump right into the snow on Saturday."

"Saturday? Does that mean you're missing the Winter Snowdrop Ball?" I ask, although I have no idea why—I probably won't be attending if I'm grounded.

"Yeah, unfortunately. Chloe and the others aren't too pleased about it. She really wanted all the girls to go with her since she was meant to be going with Jared. But I'm seeing them on Thursday night and helping her with last minute preparations for the ball to make up," Jasmine explains.

There's a slight hesitation when she finishes, but I'm more focused on not reacting to hearing Jared's name for my own reasons.

I ask her if that means there won't be any more Spanish tutoring until January.

She smirks. "I love them, Hayden, but doing them on a video call during Christmas might be too much dedication. That's what I was calling you over for, actually, to say I won't be able to do any now till I am back."

"That's okay."

Now I really need to hope Dad grounds me for all of Christmas break if I only have my friends to see…and Andrew.

"And, it's pretty remote where we're staying, so phone signal's very temperamental," she comments.

"Jasmine, do you want to eat or not?"

I glance beyond Jasmine. Her mom's standing on the path near the trees.

"Coming." She spins back to me and says her goodbyes. "Thanks again."

"No worries." I watch as she walks away, but for some reason, I decide to call after her. "It's probably a good thing you won't have phone signal." She turns around—there's a little confused expression on her face. "Because then you won't get a happy New Year message at six in the morning from me." I watch her trying to work out my joke—I instantly regret it. I look like an idiot. "You know because you'll be in Sweden, six hours ahead of here. You'll have already had New Year."

The clockwork inside Jasmine's head clicks until it strikes correctly. She smiles. More out of kindness than humour, I think.

"Ah, funny," she comments. There's no laughing—I feel like a fool. "I better head off." A complete fool is what I am. "And I'll make sure I don't message six hours earlier for you."

I look up, just managing to catch the cute smirk she leaves on her face before she heads away to the restaurant.

A thrill rushes inside me…only to slowly disappear—it feels ages since I thought she was Tokyo.

Despite Jasmine finishing with a little remark about my joke, I still feel stupid with mine. I mean, *What an idiot!*

"If it's any consolation, I got it right away." I turn to the side to find Aunt Sandra looking at me as she rests on the counter in the small hut beside me.

Yep, an idiot.

I take my time slowly around the course when I'm litter-picking and bin-checking. It's not the most glamorous part of the job, but I offered so I can keep checking for emails from Tokyo and reply to her.

There are lots of families playing, but it's the few couples that get to me. Fooling around as they play, teasing with one another, laughing. It's nice—for them.

When I return to the small hut, I'm surprised to see Zeke, Billie, Antonia and Dacre there.

"What are you guys doing here?"

"Er, to play golf," Zeke answers with a little pretend snap to his voice. "Or aren't we allowed?"

"Really? I just asked, and you said you'd come to see Hayden," Aunt Sandra says, poking out of the small hut.

Zeke rolls his eyes. "I know."

My body relaxes—Andrew isn't here. I ask them why they want to see me.

"It's the only way we can see you outside of school," Billie says. "You know, with you being silly enough to get drunk and get grounded."

"And well, we miss you," Antonia says. Dacre smiles in agreement.

A sudden surge of warmness grows inside me.

"Thanks, guys," I manage to say, smiling.

Before it can get any soppier—they're Aunt Sandra's words—she lets me have my break. I tell the guys to follow me. I know what I need to do.

I lead them around the small hut, by the office and through a staff door that opens into the mountain. The others stare at the fish that are swimming happily in the large tank walls as I open the door beside it. I tell them to go up the staircase. It spirals up, coiling around a large brown pipe. There are no windows, but the tight yet tall room is brightly lit.

"Are we in the centre?" Dacre asks. We are. Large clanks and clinks are going off above us.

I listen closely to hear water gushing up the large pipe we are walking up around.

"This pipe pumps the water up to the waterfalls and for the eruption," I say, although, despite the many shifts I've been on, I'm still yet to discover if the last part is true.

We keep climbing until, eventually, we reach the top. Zeke has to push the ceiling door open so we can get out. After a couple of attempts, it opens, and he continues up the steps that lead to where I plan to take them.

"Welcome to the top of the mountain," I say. "Or the break room, as some of us call it."

Billie, Antonia and Dacre gawp around in amazement. The walls surrounding us are all rocky-brown and jagged like the rest of the inside of the mountain. However, instead of a crazy golf course, there's an open space holding a home for a red couch, a TV, a vending machine, a coffee machine, a soccer table and even a ping pong table. But it's not these items that catch their eyes, nor is it the pipe that continues up through the ceiling. It's the large open gap to the side that looks out to the waterfall seeping down before us. Through the breaks of the descending water, the International Drive goes off into the distance to one side, with a small skyline of hotels dotted about, all while the moon shines high in the starry night sky.

"How are you?" I quietly ask Zeke as the others look around.

"Better. Thanks for earlier," he says. I smile, pleased.

"You've had this all this time—the entire time!—And you never told us?" Billie says, staring at Zeke.

"Thought we were friends, man," Dacre says as he lets his hand slide across the soccer table.

Zeke laughs it off and explains it's meant to be just for employees. We joke a little about the place until Billie asks the ultimate question; why I brought them up here.

"Yeah, Billie was ready for another round of watching parents get angry at their own golfing," Zeke comments.

I take a deep breath. The warm air travels into my lungs. This is it. To tell them about me in Georgia.

"I wanted to just be with you guys alone. Because—because I wanted to be honest with you. I'm not allowed to drink—"

"Because you're underage? Hey, we all are," Zeke jokes.

"Sssh," Antonia hisses and smacks his arm. He winces. I try to smile it off, but inside, everything's knotting up inside me. Trying anything to stop. Anything to stop me. Because once it's out, it's out. But that's what I need, I tell myself, to stop putting pressure on myself.

"Well, yeah, but I'm not supposed to, more than you guys, I mean. And I can't drive, even if I could or if I had a car, because, well—" I stumble over my words, and I can feel all my friends watching me, who are no doubt wondering what on earth is happening to this kid before them.

"Hey, it's okay. You can tell us." Billie's big eyes look at me. Sincere. Worry. And yet also reassuring.

My head nods with Billie, but it doesn't feel like it's me. A few seconds go by, breathing slowly, as I focus on collecting myself.

"I said my mom is back in Georgia, but the truth is I've no idea where she actually is. Like no clue. None of us do." I pause, wondering how I can explain. "She's quite a free-spirited kind of person. Always dreamed of travelling—I saw glimpses of her feeling free and wild. But life intervened, I guess because she and my dad became parents with jobs at a young age. And I guess a free spirit can never stay in one place because, earlier this year, she left us. My dad and me and my brother and my sister. No real explanation."

My head stays down as I hear them take it in.

"How come you told us your parents had just split and she was still in Georgia?" Antonia asks.

I briefly glance over at her but turn away when it starts to get too much.

"Because it was easier. Easier than saying out loud me and my family weren't good enough for her to stay—than admitting the truth of what happened after she went."

Hands close in together, just like they did during the talk with Mr Gauran.

I try to push on.

"I guess I didn't handle it well. I had a—a—a breakdown, and I took Robin's car and drove off. I crashed it into a tree and was taken to the hospital." One of them gasps. My eyes stay down on the ground because I'm not ready to see how they're looking at me. "I was fine, physically. And nobody was hurt. Nobody else was there, thankfully. I was let out of the hospital—banned from driving—but then a few weeks later, I broke down again and went back in."

I glance up briefly. They're all silent. All we can hear is the waterfall outside.

"I'd tell you how it happened, but I've no memory from some point before I took the car until I woke up in the hospital after the second breakdown. Nothing. There were a lot of tests, lots of treatments, before I could come out again, and when I did, my dad decided we should move. And that's why I'm here. And that's why there are things I'm not so inclined to do," I continue. "It never crossed my mind, to be honest, to tell people because—well, I was too scared of what they might think. What you might think. I never had close friends back home, and I really, like, really wanted things to be different here. So I thought keeping quiet would make life simpler. But it hasn't. Because it feels like I'm constantly lying. To people. To you. To myself. And I hate the thought of losing you guys, but I can't keep it up. To pretend like I have all the choices in the world. When I don't. Except this. To tell people I'm not all okay. And I'm sorry—you guys mean so much to me and—"

I don't know what comes over me. The quivering as I speak becomes a huge, complete sob on the last part—so much I can't finish speaking. The pain takes it all out of me, and I just sink onto the couch behind me. I want to stop crying, but my body doesn't let me. They're so watery I can't even open my eyes.

But something gently has a hold of me. I don't flinch or push away the warmth that comes with it and wraps itself around me. And as I continue to sob, feeling terrible the more I cry, I hear movement—then feel more warmth close in and surround me. Through the tears, I manage to open my eyes. Everything's dark, but there are four pairs of shoes next to mine on the floor.

My body forces me to keep weeping. I try to push through because I want to tell them about Andrew. I do. I so desperately do! Billie needs to know. She deserves to know.

"And Andr— Andr—"

I open my mouth to speak—yet something holds me down from saying anything. The hold Andrew has on me. It tightens in my chest.

And soon, my sobs become worse. I hear them muffled under the comfort of my friends hugging around me, changing now from sadness to guilt.

29.

FROM: BlueC0ast1@bretteodmail.com
TO: TokyoCherryDustZ89@TokyoCherryDustZ89.com
DATE: Thu 21st December, 6:53 PM
SUBJECT: Re: Making Waves

Yes, this isn't my ideal turn of events either, but I'm glad somebody dropped out of work tonight so I could work again this week. It means I can have my phone again and chat to you. Hopefully being grounded won't last long, and I can chat with you all the time again.

It's felt weird not being able to just get my phone out and contact you. It's kind of felt like part of me is missing.

Love,
Brisbane

FROM: TokyoCherryDustZ89@TokyoCherryDustZ89.com
TO: BlueC0ast1@bretteodmail.com
DATE: Thu 21st December, 7:21 PM
SUBJECT: Re: Making Waves

No worries. You've decided to go rogue, and now you're facing the consequences. We've got to spend this time wisely. Especially if there's no end date in sight. It does make me question, though, should I really be emailing somebody who's such a rebel? Somebody who could have a bad influence on me?

But yeah, I can't help but feel the same…it's been strange not having you there beside me…well, via email—you know what I mean.

Love,
Tokyo

FROM: BlueC0ast1@bretteodmail.com
TO: TokyoCherryDustZ89@TokyoCherryDustZ89.com
DATE: Thu 21st December, 7:40 PM
SUBJECT: Re: Making Waves

Hang on, if anybody's the bad influence, it's definitely you. Hands down. I seem to recall a certain somebody who got away with hurting a poor, defenceless photo frame—example of bad influence or what?

Sorry that I've restricted that freedom to message. And for making that sound like we're chatting in a prison during visiting hours. But you must have found other things to distract you while I've been offline? It's the Winter Week at school, after all. There was the talent show the other day, and then tomorrow it's Friday—the results of the Snow Date Raffle and then the big Winter Snowdrop Ball.

There may not be an end date of me being grounded yet, but you should know that my dad's given me the all-clear to go to the ball.

Love,
Brisbane

FROM: TokyoCherryDustZ89@TokyoCherryDustZ89.com
TO: BlueC0ast1@bretteodmail.com
DATE: Thu 21st December, 7:48 PM
SUBJECT: Re: Making Waves

Hears the bell in prison for visiting to be finished but fortunately for the prisoner I stay sitting

For the record, Mr Brisbane, the photo frame was staring weirdly at me, or did you purposely not remember that part? Although saying that, I did offer a song for you to listen to so you could release any anger and trash your room.

Oh no. Maybe I am the bad influencer?

Yeah, the fact it's been the Winter Week when you've gone rogue has helped a little. The talent show was awesome. I'm excited to see the results of the Snow Date Raffle, as well as to see how much money was raised. And yes, I think everybody will be looking forward to the Winter Snowdrop Ball to finish it all off.

Has he now? So you're allowed to leave the house for a few hours to attend the ball? Are you sure you're not Cinderella?

Love,
Tokyo

FROM: BlueC0ast1@bretteodmail.com
TO: TokyoCherryDustZ89@TokyoCherryDustZ89.com
DATE: Thu 21st December, 8:09 PM
SUBJECT: Re: Making Waves

Called it! You ARE the bad influencer between us. Luckily, I was just wise enough not to choose that song and follow your path. But hey, I won't hold it against you, Miss Bad Influence.

Or should that be Tokyo The Mysterious? Tokyo The Unpunished? Or Off The Hook Tokyo, you know, because you got away with that photo frame ;)

It's nice that school's been different this week and not so overflowing with schoolwork. Hope we don't get much to do over the break. The talent show was fun. I definitely think the right person won.

Oh really? Did you happen to buy a ticket for the Snow Date Raffle?

Haha, if you could see my cleaning skills then you'd know I'm no Cinderella.

Love,
Brisbane

FROM: TokyoCherryDustZ89@TokyoCherryDustZ89.com
TO: BlueC0ast1@bretteodmail.com
DATE: Thu 21st December, 8:19 PM
SUBJECT: Re: Making Waves

Tokyo The Unpunished? Now that is cheeky. I like Off The Hook Tokyo, but that makes me sound a little crazy. I mean, I may have one time, as a dare, shook a new fizzy bottle and tried to drink it straightaway—only for it to burst back out my mouth and out my nose, but I'm not crazzzzzzzzzyyy. I'm not. I'm telling you, I'm not! :D

I do like Tokyo The Mysterious, though. Is that how you see me?

Kamala so deserved to win. I agree.

And I didn't buy a ticket, no. Unfortunately, the guy that I've been falling for wasn't on the list. That I know of, at least. There wasn't any clue in their bios that could lead me to an Australian city.

Why? Did you?

Love,
Tokyo

FROM: BlueC0ast1@bretteodmail.com
TO: TokyoCherryDustZ89@TokyoCherryDustZ89.com
DATE: Thu 21st December, 8:40 PM
SUBJECT: Re: Making Waves

No, I didn't get a ticket either. And I'm not one of the guys available on the raffle. I didn't look at the bios for the girls, but I don't think any info could make me see there was a Tokyo in the midst. Or was there? *Begins to sprint to school to find the posters*

But even though it's for charity, I do hope something comes from some of the dates. I've always thought I'd have to search across the world to find someone for me, like in Brisbane or Tokyo. Or I'd find it later in life when I'm working or long into a career. Because how often do you find the one in the same town or the next town from you? But somehow, I don't think I have to search. Somehow, I understand those who find it nearby. Because joking aside, I don't think I need to enter the raffle. I think you've already won me over.

And, because I think that, I want to ask you something. I feel like I know you, even though there's just one thing left for us to each know—I guess that's why I thought Tokyo The Mysterious—and I feel like it's the right time. I think we should finally meet. I think we should see each other at the Winter Snowdrop Ball.

Love,
Brisbane

FROM: TokyoCherryDustZ89@TokyoCherryDustZ89.com
TO: BlueC0ast1@bretteodmail.com
DATE: Thu 21st December, 9:05 PM
SUBJECT: Re: Making Waves

I've thought the same. You've won me over too. You have for a long while. I also feel like I know you without physically knowing you. But I can't meet you.

I am interested in you—deeply fallen for you. You're all I think about. This may have started as me helping you and then helping you broaden your mind to the endless supply of music out there, but this has become so much more. We've become so much more.

I've sorted some things out in my life where I am better. There's still more to do, though. But you must realise it won't be fair for either of us to meet tomorrow? Because we'll then have to spend weeks apart with little chance of seeing each other over the Christmas break, right? I'm sure you'll have things you've got to do with your family, and I will with mine. But that doesn't mean I don't want to. Because I so do. But it wouldn't be fair. And I need a little bit more time.

I hope you can respect my decision because I think when we come back to school in the new year, that's when we should finally meet.

And to show you how much I care about you, about us, and what can be in store, I want to share this with you. Call it an early Christmas present.

Tokyo – From Brisbane To Tokyo While In Orlando, Florida

Love,
Tokyo

When I finish reading the email, I find myself collapsing back onto the couch in the break room at Mt. Okesea. I try to take the information in. A little sad, a little glad, a little understanding and also a little confused. I don't know how to respond.

She's shown me other people's music. She's shared her '80s mixes of famous hits of today. I helped her overcome that barrier of fear of not sharing her work with everybody—I've shown her people like her stuff—to believe that she is good and have faith in herself. And now she's shared her own song. About us!

I take my headphones out of my bag beside me and press play.

FROM: BlueC0ast1@bretteodmail.com
TO: TokyoCherryDustZ89@TokyoCherryDustZ89.com
DATE: Thu 21st December, 9:32 PM
SUBJECT: Re: Making Waves

I don't know where to begin! As soon as the song started, with the choir of voices, the hairs on my arms all prickled up. It felt like paradise.

And when the music kicks in—it's so upbeat and harmonious!

I love the lyrics. Love them!

All of it just makes me happier, and it makes me excited about us. It's incredible. I can't believe you produced this yourself. I mean, I can because you're talented, but still…

Just hold me, heading down to the beach,
I'll swim that ocean, even if you're out of reach

And

They say heaven ain't really here,
Yet I'd question that to you,
So don't try and prove me wrong,
Because it's pretty sweet, you know,
And I found it,
From Brisbane to Tokyo

I've never received anything like this before. It really got to me. Tokyo, I love it. Thank you.

I've got to ask, though, is that you singing? Where did you get the choir vocals from?

I can't say I'm not sad about not meeting you tomorrow. However, I understand how it wouldn't be reasonable—to go back to emails or texting or some virtual way of connecting with you after briefly meeting. I get it—because I'd just want to be with you in person all break. So I respect your wish. I can wait because I know this is worth waiting for. And that I seriously think I love you.

Love,
Brisbane

FROM: TokyoCherryDustZ89@TokyoCherryDustZ89.com
TO: BlueC0ast1@bretteodmail.com
DATE: Thu 21st December, 10:01 PM
SUBJECT: Re: Making Waves

I'm so pleased you enjoyed it. I was more scared for you to hear this than when everybody heard my mixes. Because you mean that much to me. I'm so pleased you do love it.

Yeah, I had to get a beach reference in there for you somehow, didn't I? And I realise it was me that wrote this song to you, to us, but "From Brisbane to Tokyo…" sounded better than the other way.

I thought you might ask questions like that. Well, unfortunately for you, the female singer isn't me. I got my cousin to do them. She's got an amazing voice. And before you try and work it out, she doesn't live in Orlando. The choir was a local group I paid to do those parts.

Thanks. For understanding and willing to wait till we come back to school in the new year for us to meet.

Me too. I seriously think I love you, too.

Love,
Tokyo

30.

The last few days have been difficult for me at school. Really difficult. After the talk at Mt. Okesea on Tuesday night, my friends don't treat me any differently. They don't run away or give me looks of pity as if they're unsure what to do or wish I wasn't hanging around. They're exactly the same as before. The only difference is they spend more time with me during school hours. That's more than what I hoped for—but it makes me feel worse. It shouldn't, but it does.

I feel like there's not less but actually more weighing down on me—not in terms of quantity of how many different things have got me but in the heaviness of the *one* thing. Andrew. I've tried too many times to somehow tell them, or at least tell Billie, but I can never run through the finish line and say it. I'm genuinely worse than before this week began, before I spoke to them about my past, before I opened up to Dad, and before I spoke to Mr Gauran. And that's not how this is meant to go.

My emails with Tokyo are the only thing going for me right now. I've not mentioned to her what Andrew did or ask how to deal with his cheating—the emails are the single place I don't focus on all the stress and pressure I'm getting from that.

It's Friday—the last day before the break—and all everybody's talking about at lunch is the Winter Snowdrop Ball—it's tonight! Even the teachers have all somehow mentioned it in their classes.

Dad made it clear yesterday that despite being grounded, I am to attend. *We've bought that suit, so you're going to have to get your money's worth.* Colbey will pick me up and drop me off.

I'm disheartened even more because Tokyo won't meet me there—I thought it would be rather romantic to finally reveal our identities there. Something to excite me and get me through this mess. She was going to be the main reason for me to be okay with going to the ball. But I agree with her reasons for us not meeting yet.

But now I must manage to deal with spending an evening with being with my friends and, because the school allows students from other schools to be a plus one, also Andrew.

Tokyo didn't reply to my last email yesterday, but I didn't send it till late—just giving more appreciation about her song and then agreeing again that I understand her reasons for not wanting to meet. Unfortunately, I had to return my phone to Dad when I got home after finishing work—so I don't know if she ever replied or not.

I'm brought to my surroundings though when I catch Zeke powerwalking up and down in front of me in the yard outside the cafeteria. They're about to draw the winners of the Snow Date Raffle.

"What if the girl doesn't like me? What if she only entered to do some *She's All That* bet on me? Or what if it's *Drive Me Crazy* and she only wants a date to make her real crush jealous?"

"Quit it with the film scenarios." Billie grabs his shoulders and stops him moving.

"Hello, everybody!"

We look to the side. Antonia's standing on the stage they've built outside. There's a huge cheer from the crowd before her.

"You'll be great," I say to Zeke. Dacre nods.

"It's time for the reveal of the Snow Date Raffle!" Another cheer erupts. "Let's bring on the dates."

As some of the committee start pushing the dates to the stage, we quickly wish him the best and hurry around to the front.

My eyes skip when the first boy to come up is Jared Steele. However, my attention focuses quickly on the next boy because Billie and Dacre scream beside me. It's Zeke.

The five boys line side by side on one side next to Antonia, and the five girls stand in line on the other, each with a podium and a covered bowl in front of them. I assume with their sold tickets inside.

Zeke catches us and gives a timid and kind of nervous smile, along with a steady thumbs up. He's scared. He's got what happened the other day with Jared and the others in the back of his mind. Nerves start to arrive and play on my skin. Surely somebody's bought a ticket to go on a date with him?

Antonia explains the prize is that each winner from the raffle will get to go on a date bowling and then eat at a fabulous five-star restaurant with their winning date. The crowd roars—and even more when Antonia announces that as an additional prize this year, each date will get their own limousine ride to and from the Winter Snowdrop Ball tonight, courtesy of Chloe Cassadentini's uncle's limousine and entertainment business.

"Bet she wished they could retract the rides when Jared became a date," Billie mutters beside Dacre as Chloe exits the stage after smiling and waving, almost like a beauty pageant.

The crowd claps when Antonia reveals how much money has been raised. "And now for the reveals."

She begins with the boys. Billie hooks her arm around mine in excitement because Zeke will be up. I accept the grab yet have a little taste of shame in my mouth.

We wait as Antonia announces which girls are lucky with the first three boys. Soon, she moves along the line and reaches Zeke. Billie tightens her grip on my arm—Antonia walks straight by Zeke.

Nerves hit me. He looks just as confused. I hear the others say my thoughts—all puzzled.

Did nobody buy a ticket for him? Somebody must have, I tell myself. And Antonia's hosting it—she wouldn't let her friend come up on stage and be humiliated like that, right?

Antonia continues as if nothing's wrong and announces the next date up is Jared Steele. There's probably the loudest set of screams from the girls watching.

Jared steps forward and gives a sly wave to the audience, looking all cool and jock-like in his school jersey. Antonia picks a piece of paper out of the covered bowl before him to reveal the *lucky* winner is Alexandria Selva—a senior netballer.

She goes up on stage, and we're forced to watch Jared give her a hug and then a kiss on the cheek.

"And finally, with the boys, we have Zeke Palladino!" Antonia turns around on the spot.

Oh goodness, he didn't get a ticket; they're gonna bid on him now. Like an auction. And no one's gonna go.

"Our most popular date out of the males! That's right, forty per cent of the tickets sold was for Zeke!"

He looks shocked. I'm surprised. Dacre's stunned. And Billie looks the same next to me—until she starts whooping with the crowd, cheering and repeatedly smacking my arm.

Zeke beams. I'm so happy for him. Jared, meanwhile, grunts displeased from the side, but I ignore it. I let out a few cries of joy in Zeke's honour.

"Yes, yes," Antonia smiles. "And now, to reveal the lucky lady who's got a date with the most popular guy." We all wait in silence as she puts her hand in the covered bowl and pulls a piece of paper out. "It's…Kamala Bay."

Everybody around us claps. However, I turn to my left. Billie turns to her left. Dacre turns to his left. In the distance with her own group of friends, Kamala stands there, slightly fluttered.

She walks up to the stage—with a smile on her face. The surprise in me then turns into excitement. I glance back at the stage. Zeke also looks amazed, but then, as Kamala walks over to him, his face changes. He's pleased. My heart melts a little.

They exchange some words as Antonia rounds up the results of the boys on the microphone to the crowd. They seem glad. Kamala's smiling. And Zeke looks just as nervously happy.

When Antonia moves onto the girls standing on the stage, the boys and their dates come off.

There are a few words exchanged between Zeke and Kamala before she leaves and we approach him.

"Well, that was…" Dacre begins. "Surprising."

"Yeah," Zeke replies—his eyes wide open. He bounces a little on the balls of his feet. "But it's good, right? You don't think she just entered as a friend? Like, out of pity in case I didn't get a ticket from anybody."

"No way, she must genuinely like you. You work together, and you've been hanging more outside recently," Billie says.

"True." Dacre nods.

I join in and nod—but the truth is I wasn't aware of how much more time they'd been spending together.

"And Antonia wouldn't allow it, especially if she knew who had the most tickets sold, Mr Most Desirable Kingsgate Lee High Bachelor," Dacre jokes. Zeke grins, not before shoving him for the jest.

"I guess. You're right." He puffs out air like a deflating balloon. "I need to eat."

"But we've already had lunch," I remark as he heads towards the cafeteria doors.

"And you're all meant to get a photo after the girls get their dates," Billie adds.

"Yeah, and I'll come back—but I need to eat something to push these nerves down."

Dacre shrugs. He and Billie follow, but I tell them I'll wait—and get them if they want the photos with all the dates before they return. And to support Antonia. The others agree.

I head back to the stage and wait at the back of the crowd while Antonia reveals which boys have won a date with the girls on stage.

I'm just still shocked. Kamala and Zeke.

"So how come the new boy didn't offer to be a date then?" I glance to see Chloe Cassadentini there beside me. Her eyes still watching the stage. I check around to see if she meant me—we're alone. "I think many girls would be intrigued by that Georgia feel you got."

I smile out of politeness when she turns to me. She's just seen her ex-boyfriend be an available bachelor and receive a free limousine ride from her uncle's business to the Winter Snowdrop Ball.

"Ha, funnily enough, you're not the first to make that comment. But this sure is something we never did in Georgia."

She smirks.

"Well, we do like the entertainment here in Orlando," Chloe smiles. "I was nearly tempted myself to be up there." I watch as Antonia puts her hand in the covered bowl before the next girl. "I think my bio on the poster would have been something like *More than just cheerleading. Fun, family-orientated person who loves everything from the '80s and dreams of visiting Tokyo and seeing the cherry blossoms bloom.*"

My heart stops. The people around us clap—Antonia read out the boy's name. I look at the side. To Chloe Cassadentini.

"It's you."

Chloe's still facing the stage—then she turns. She frowns, confused.

"You're Tokyo?"

Her eyes widen. Shocked? Scared? Embarrassed?

"Brisbane?"

I'm lost for words.

There's a round of applause from everybody around us. Somebody's just won, or they've introduced the next girl—I've no clue because my mind is so bewildered by this.

I eventually nod.

There's a sudden smile that curls up on Chloe's lips—like she's suddenly been switched back on to function.

"I can't believe it. Wow," she says. I'm still a little overwhelmed by it all, but then the smile on her face disappears. "Oh—this isn't how I was meant to find out." She nervously pushes her hair back, keeping her hand against the side of her head. "I gotta go."

She abruptly walks off, heading away from the event. I watch—but I can't leave it like this.

I go after her.

"Chloe, wait!"

She stops by the end of the outside tables. We're away from everybody. She's a little upset.

"Hey, it's okay," I try to reassure her. She's got a hand up to her mouth. Biting nervously on a nail. I want to comfort her, but before I can, I must ask. "It's not me, is it? You're not asham—"

"What? No," Chloe answers, taking her hand away. "I'm pleased. That you're Brisbane, I am. It's just—" She briefly glances away and then back at me. "—I emailed it would be better to meet after the Christmas holidays. And now, I've—I've just gone and slipped up and ruined it. I didn't even think."

"Hey, hey." I place my hand carefully on her shoulder—to comfort her. "It's fine."

She notices my hand but doesn't push it away. She glances up into my eyes. With her big, blue eyes. I wonder what to say, where to begin with it all, but instead, I watch as she quietly sits down on the table bench beside us.

My brain becomes cloudy. I sit next to her, hoping it might help me think clearly because it's only now when the thousands of questions I want to ask her start to flood into my mind.

"Are you okay?" Chloe asks.

I nod. "I think I'm still processing this. I've been waiting ages to see who Tokyo is, and now we're here, I'm unsure what to say first."

She bites her lip.

Her blonde hair droops down over her face—drifting a rosy apple scent my way.

"You said you don't feel like your friends will like the real you. But you always seem so happy around them?"

There's a sight pause from her.

"A popular girl doesn't mean she's a happy girl," Chloe replies gently.

I begin to feel like a fool for asking that question. To just assume that if you're popular, then that means everything's fine for you. Perhaps she had to give up on things along the way when she became popular? Maybe she just naturally became somebody people look at and up to without a choice in the matter? Like Zeke. Or like how I pretend all is fine with my friends when it isn't.

"Sorry, I shouldn't have presumed like that."

She pushes her hair back, yet she now remains staring towards the ground. "It's okay. I suppose I should explain. With Jared—" I'm so caught up in this bizarre moment that I totally forgot she was with Jared. "—the intention was never to fall for somebody while I was with someone else. The emails started out as helping you, right?"

She momentarily looks at me, waiting almost for me to answer—I agree.

"And then things just became more personal and intimate. And—look, when me and Jared started going out, I thought it was serious. I mean, it *was* serious. Yet over time, though, we, I guess, just sort of fell in line together as if we had too, and not we wanted too—like because I became a cheerleader, and he joined the football team. Our statuses matched—but along the way, we ourselves didn't. We weren't in love like we used to be, haven't been in a long while—not since before summer. We've not been intimate for months. Been nothing more than friends since we returned to school as head cheerleader and quarterback."

Talking about Jared is still sore for Chloe—I can understand that—but it seems she needs to hear it more than I do. Like she's convincing herself to understand the truth of it all now everything's out.

"But we must have stayed out of fear, I think, scared to leave each other's comfort we've had for so long in our lives—because it's all we've ever had—like maybe nervous to accept to let go and move on, when really, it's been unfairly stopping ourselves from having something real. We simply stayed till one of us admitted the truth."

She stops—then lifts her head up, looking like her usual self, and now more alert, as if remembering where she is and her surroundings. She faces me. "And then me and you started chatting, and I realised later on that it wasn't right, with Jared and me—not fair on either me or him."

So, she ended it with Jared? Not him? That's why he was mad at Antonia's party, and not just from the football. I'd just assumed from rumours that he had.

Chloe repositions so her body is more directly to me. Part of me wants to glance away, but I don't. Her eyes are serious. Her cheeks are tucked in, like she's holding her breath.

"You've got to know, though, I think our relationship was always going to end, whether it was because I was messaging you or not," she says, almost assuring herself. "Jared likes to show off. I do that too at times, but our relationship recently was never anything more for him. Just comfort. Him volunteering himself to be in the Snow Date Raffle, just proves all this, right?" She pushes her hair to the side again. "But that's not what I wanted. I needed more. Something real. I can have feelings too, you know? And, I suppose, our emails made me understand that."

I desperately want to hold Chloe when she glances down—give her the comfort she needs. But at the same time, I don't. I don't want to push her.

"And that's why you wanted time to sort things out in your life?" I ask. "Because it wouldn't be right to move so soon after that."

Chloe smiles slightly timidly. "Right. Not even if Jared had moved on quickly. But I couldn't exactly tell you that."

"I get that."

My eyes avert to the KingsgateLeeConnect board opposite the cafeteria entrance. Strong. Bright. Colourful. There's a post with a selfie of Chloe and some of the dates standing behind her on stage. Posted from an account with Chloe's name on it.

A wave of unease hits me—realising something Kamala said.

"How did you get an account for Tokyo?"

Chloe's eyes stay on me. "What?"

"If you have your own account under your name, how did you get another for Tokyo? I thought it was just one per student."

Kamala said only if somebody was good at hacking the school system could they maybe do it.

"Oh right," she says, a little rocky. She repositions herself on the bench. "I just got one of the guys in our year who helped make it give me another account. Think it was for a student who enrolled this year but never came."

"Ah, clever." It's a smart idea.

In the distance, the Snow Date Raffle seems to be finishing. Antonia's speaking on stage, promoting the Winter Snowdrop Ball.

I turn to Chloe. "So, now that it's out, how do you want to deal with this?"

Part of me thinks I should be open with Chloe about my past—but this is already big enough as it is.

Chloe shuffles on the spot a little—she soon straightens her back. Suddenly, I'm in the presence of the confident girl I've always seen down the hallways.

"Well, we should take it slow…by you taking me to the Winter Snowdrop Ball?"

I whip my head to her.

"Really?"

She was so set last night on not even meeting there—let alone going together.

"Seeing as it's out who we are, we should take advantage of it. May as well make the most of the time we can if we're busy over the holidays."

The bell goes. People start dispersing from around the stage.

"Give me your phone."

"I don't have it. Grounded, remember?" I joke. "But I'm allowed it at the ball, though."

"Oh yeah, sorry, forgot." She pulls her phone out. She taps away quickly and then passes it to me. "Put your number in. And I'll message you the address and time. Meet me there tonight."

31.

The lights at the junction turn green. Colbey taps his hand on the top of the wheel and moves to take the car left. As I wait in the passenger seat, I'm still shocked with earlier. Zeke and Kamala going on a date—and then off to the Winter Snowdrop Ball—then the reveal of Tokyo, and now Dad's allowing me to meet with Chloe so we can go together.

Colbey joked earlier on the way that Dad agreed because of how embarrassed I seemed when I asked, and how excited he was that I wanted to go with someone to a ball—something I've never asked before.

My body begins to travel through the boat ride of emotions of tonight. Panic. Nerves. Excitement. Happiness.

I receive a text from Chloe—she's asking if I'm nearly there. We've messaged briefly since I got back home and was given my phone. They're short texts, but I think that's because we're both nervous. After many weeks, the masks are off, and it feels totally new. Different but exciting.

I never did receive a reply from her to my late email last night—I checked—but now, knowing Chloe is Tokyo, and, I guess, with how busy today has been, she probably didn't really have any time to read my email or reply—not that it's needed now we know who each other is.

Chloe's told me she's managed to arrange one of her uncle's limousines to take us from her place to the ball, which I think is sweet.

The fact Chloe was with somebody when we were first messaging did unnerve me at the beginning of our chat at lunch. But Chloe pointed out we were strangers back then, and she was only helping me then, and she explained that their split was about them already out of love. This isn't the huge, sweet and soppy romantic idea I had played out in my head for Tokyo, but it is what it is.

"You know you're never going to get to the ball, Cinderella, if you stay in here," Colbey jests.

I look up. We're here.

It's dark outside. The house we're parked by looks reasonably family-sized, with a long-grassed front lawn. A limousine with black-tinted windows is situated in front of Colbey's car.

My hands are already starting to sweat, and all I've seen is a house.

Colbey continues to make jokes as I get out of the car, but I'm so nervous I don't exactly pay attention until he stops. I lean down to look in the car at him.

"She's probably just as nervous as you. And you look the part. You're a nice guy, so just relax and enjoy it."

I blush a little. "Thanks, Colbey."

After we exchange smiles, I close the door and he pulls away from the curb. I glance over at the house I'm standing outside. Alone. It's silent.

It's just going to the ball. With Tokyo. This is what I've been waiting for. To be with Tokyo—with Chloe.

I brush my hands down against the trousers of my dark blue suit—blue for the ocean and my love for Marine Science—and walk up to the door. I press the bell.

My left shoe begins to tap the ground. A nervous twitch in trying to control my nerves from successfully escaping.

Through the frosted glass, I can see a figure moving. Quite slowly.

The door opens. I suck in some air.

It isn't Chloe. There's a man. An elderly man. Almost bald-headed. And in an untied yet closed dressing gown. It must be her grandad.

"Hi, I'm here to see Chloe," I say kindly.

The old man stares at me—eyes just managing to keep open. "You got my meal tonight?" He looks down at me. "Bit fancy dressed than the other delivery guys, but I'll take it—"

"No. I'm here to see Chloe. I'm her date for our school's dance. Is she in?"

A cold breeze drifts in by my left side. The man's gown moves ever so slightly. I stare back up to keep contact with his eyes. He's only in some pants. And he hasn't noticed I've seen.

There's a sudden group of noises. Giggling. I spin my head around—ignoring the front door being closed. The limousine's no longer empty. Or perhaps it never was. The sunroof's open—Chloe is poking out of it. I breathe out some relief—but then I see it.

There are a few bright lights below Chloe. The tinted side windows are now down—behind the lights, I make out the outlines of other heads. A mix of boys and girls laughing—holding their phones at me.

I look at Chloe but see she's got her phone in her hand. There's a smile on her face, but it's not kind.

"Oh my goodness, as if you actually thought I'd go with you? You, Hayden Mallard—the new kid! Nobody in their right mind would choose you," she leers and then laughs.

I watch in confusion. She sticks a finger into her mouth and pretends to be sick. Some of the others with her laugh.

How can she say this?

Something soars towards me from the window—it smacks into my chest. I wince. A wave of red covers my view. My eyes instantly close from whatever splashes onto my face.

I cough vigorously—there's a vile taste in my mouth. I hear a new roar of laughter. Slowly, I open my eyes—worried what's happening. There's red paint stained all over the floor, on the house, on my suit and all over me.

"See ya around, Mallard!"

The limousine moves, and I stand bewildered with everything.

Chloe spins. She shows off a devilish smirk—then blows a kiss with her hand stretched out to me.

As soon as the limousine has gone, the impact of what's happened kicks in. The hurt smacks me hard in the chest—I can't breathe. Every time I try to breathe in deeply, I think I have control—but when I exhale, my emotions escape, my voice quivers, and my body shakes. All I can hear is myself sniffing, tasting the paint stuck to my lips, and feel a shivering ache inside. I could break.

Because everything. All of it. Was a joke? The messages. The conversations. The connection. This was…just some fun?

I look back at the house—paint splattered on the closed front door. It's not even her house, I only now realise.

The red paint drips down my face, ruining the new suit. With the yard ruined already, I bend down to the ground and try to rub my face and body onto the long grass, hoping most of the paint will scrub off.

After some time, still upset, distraught and covered in red, I doubt any more paint will come off—so I begin to walk away. I should leave before any cops arrive if the owner has rung them.

I move, even though I'm unable to stop myself from blubbering—wanting to cave in. I have no idea where I'm going. But away. Anywhere from that humiliation.

Everything goes through my mind. I just relive the pain, the puzzlement, and the hurt again. *Why would she do this?*

This was a trick—*or maybe just tonight was?* My heart tries to justify. Maybe she was forced by her friends? They found out the truth, and she was forced to decide like some tragic *Romeo and Juliet* situation, but she didn't want to be disowned by them, so she did as they said to pretend she didn't care—she said she's scared to be truthful to her friends—that could be why!

Crap—I hate the optimism my heart tries to bring and give some reason so there could still be something between Chloe and me—with Tokyo. Because there is none. The reality is she isn't interested.

I soon enter the busier streets of Orlando. People are gawping at me in the now-smeared red clothing, with red splashed on my face and stuck in my hair. I try to ignore them all and walk on.

My phone vibrates—it might have been for a while, but I only check now. There are missed calls and then a tide of multiple texts from my friends.

Zeke
Hey man, answer your phone or call me!

Billie
Are you alright? Please let me know you are ok.
Message me when you're here.

Dacre
I've just seen, Hayden. Text or call me. Are you
with anybody?

Antonia
Chloe's vile. You didn't deserve that. Tell one of
us you're fine. We love you.

There's a horrid twist in my stomach. I want to throw up.

Fearing the worst, I open KingsgateLeeConnect on my phone and look at the main page—I freeze.

There's a post of a video. I don't need to press play because I can see the screenshot—it's me in my blue suit standing outside the house I thought was Chloe Cassadentini's.

My hands sweat. My body goes cold. My head spins.

This doesn't feel real—like it's not me. And yet it is.

I scroll through—the others have posted their videos, too. But I stop at Chloe's post—to my dismay, there are loads of comments. I click to view—only to sob when I read them. The jests and laughing remarks about me. The vile and mean insults for me thinking I had a chance.

I shove a hand through my hair—before locking it over my mouth, forcing myself not to choke up because this feels like a stab to the gut. Everybody's laughing at me.

I walk for who knows how long. I keep going—wanting to be home. I don't dare ring Dad or Colbey to pick me up. I hope they never find out about this or see the video.

I'm heading through a suburb when I hear a car pull up.

"Oh my—Hayden."

Car doors open, footsteps come up from behind, but I continue to walk.

"Hey!" Billie calls over.

"J-just leave me alone."

I hear Zeke somewhere behind speak to somebody. "Yeah, we found him. I'll let you know what we do." He's on a phone call.

Someone comes into my view and walks beside me. It's Billie. She's in a dark green dress. "What happened?"

I don't dare look at her. "I don't want to talk about it. Just leave."

Zeke comes around and stands beside Billie—in a maroon suit. "We can't leave you like this. You look like Patrick Bateman and Carrie's progeny gone rogue in Orlando." Billie smacks Zeke in the chest. "Sorry. I just mean you shouldn't be alone. What happened?"

I stare at them both—lips trembling.

"I thought she liked me. She asked me to go to the ball with her, and then—" I'm unable to continue because saying it out loud just makes the hurt boil into anger. I look down at the red mess that's sticking to my skin and clothes.

"Let us take you away from here."

"No," I reply irritably, feeling too ashamed, and then walk on. They soon catch up, walking before me, going backwards so they can face me.

"Yeah," Billie objects. She wants to reach her hands out onto my shoulders and stop me, but the paint's stopping her from trying. "We were planning to go to Andrew's after. Let's go there and clean you up while the others come over."

I shake my head from that name. "He's the last person I want to see."

Billie stops—I'm forced to halt. She tilts her head. Zeke realises we've stopped and walks back to us.

"What's that supposed to mean?" Billie's eyes latch onto mine.

I try to move ahead—but she doesn't budge.

"You can't say something like that, Hayden, and just walk away."

I tighten my lips together. Zeke looks confused but then nods in agreement with her.

The anger is brewing inside me. "Doesn't matter. Just drop it."

"No." Her eyes glaring at mine. "Why say that? Especially after Chloe's just done this to you. Andrew's a good guy."

I scoff—my anger's ready to explode.

Billie re-enacts my scoff. "What's that supposed to mean? He does nothing wrong—"

"Oh right, if he's such a good guy, then how come he's cheating on you?"

There's this beat of silence.

Billie and Zeke stare at me.

"He wouldn't." Her voice breaks—stunned. But the shock doesn't make me stop.

"I've seen it! At the football match."

The hurt etched on Billie's face vanishes—only for her features to emerge back to life, now with fury.

I realise what I've done.

"You've known since then?" Billie retorts.

My anger suddenly diminishes.

"Yeah," I stumble.

"What the heck, man?" Zeke interjects.

Shit! They think I was in on it with Andrew. Panic begins to pulse inside me. "But it's not like that. He said—"

Billie storms my way—I stumble to the side—she's heading for the car. "Yet you kept it from me!"

"But—"

"No!" She spins back around, pointing a finger aggressively at me. Zeke stands quietly by the side. "You knew what he was doing, and you let me live a lie. Led me to believe that everything was fine—and after you saying all that at Mt. Okesea, wanting to be honest with us because we're close to you. I thought we were friends."

"We are—"

Billie waves her hand at me. "As if! You better be thankful you've got that paint on you otherwise I'd smack you."

There's a moment when I think she might not care and hit me anyway—and I wouldn't object.

Her hard glare at me breaks for just a second, but it's enough to see the pain I've caused her.

"You wanted to be on your own, and now you can be. Don't bother talking to us again."

I want to object—beg her to listen—but she's already approaching the car.

"Not cool, man," Zeke says, following her.

I open my mouth—nothing comes out. I just gawp as they get in the car and then drive away.

I want to get my phone out. I want to message them, or even call them, just so I can explain—get them to understand that I was pushed into a corner—that Andrew was threatening me—and that I had no real choice.

Who am I kidding? I had a choice.

When I eventually make it home, Colbey's car is there—but I don't care. I go in through the front door of the house. The TV is on.

"Hayden? What the—"

I head up the stairs.

I hear Colbey getting off a chair to come after me, but I dart straight into the bathroom, locking the door shut behind me.

I look down at my ruined clothes.

I take my shoes off immediately and then move carefully out of my jacket and dump the items into the bath.

"Hayden?" I shudder. It's my brother. "Was that paint?" I sling my tie into the bath and start unbuttoning my shirt. "Let me in."

With every breath I take, I try to control my exhaling slowly so that I don't panic and become an unstable meltdown like I was earlier this year.

My head's stinging.

I throw my shirt, socks and then trousers into the bath to be with the rest of my clothes.

Colbey continues to try and reach me, speaking through the door—but I don't pay attention. I head over to the mirror.

The red paint is mixed into my hair, strands almost glued-like together from the texture. My entire face is red. From the paint stuck to my skin and the anger and the sadness of the night. There are tear marks against the bold redness that's splashed onto my face, and then irregular splotches on my neck and my hands.

"Please let me in," Colbey's voice re-emerges. "Let me know you're okay."

The last words reach me—I begin to cry. Soon, overwhelmed, water uncontrollably escapes my eyes. Everything drains me up so much—the pain, the aching, and the hatred at myself. I slip down to the floor. I fold my arms around my bare legs just to try and feel some comfort. I keel to the side. My bare shoulder rests on the cold tiled wall, but the coldness doesn't soothe me.

I just continue to cry.

And I can't do anything to stop.

I thought I couldn't feel any worse tonight after the prank. But I do. Everybody's seen a video of it. And then, worst of all, I've done the last thing I ever wanted to do—I've hurt my friends.

32.

There's a moment when I wake up in my bed, and everything feels fine. But then I remember—last night. And I feel terrible. Horrible. Disgusted. I don't want to leave the house today. I don't even want to walk out of this room.

My alarm goes off—I moan in protest.

I've got work today. I can't go.

I sigh. I can't. I can't do it.

Despite every bone in me disagreeing, I get out of my bed, sling on some clothes, shove my work stuff in my bag and leave my room.

There are voices down in the kitchen.

I turn around at the bottom of the stairs—Dad's in the kitchen looking back at me. Feeling like I have an obligation, I walk over—but when I enter, he isn't alone. Sat at the table, I see Colbey, Robin and Mr Gauran.

"Son," Dad begins—he only uses that to start *those* types of conversations. "Mr Gauran's come over because of last night. I know other kids at school have seen the video, and the comments can't be nice for you. And with your first therapy session not until the new year, I thought you might want to chat with Mr Gauran."

I glance over to Robin. She showed Colbey and Dad the video on KingsgateLeeConnect? I don't know why I find that so surprising—she's the only other person in this house who has access to it.

Robin's looking back at me. They all are.

Mr Gauran leans closer over the table. "What happened won't be tolerated at Kingsgate Lee High. Chloe Cassadentini—" I squirm inside from hearing her name come out of his lips, "—and those who took videos of the incident last night will be punished and—"

"Incident? That was a humiliation," I spit out.

Mr Gauran quietens and then merely nods. "You're right." I see through him—he's trying to be on my side. So I can open up to him. But I'm not having it. "Perhaps we could sit or go for a walk and chat."

"I can't do this now. I've got to go to work."

I charge out of the kitchen.

I hear Dad telling me to wait, but I walk out the door without looking back.

Aunt Sandra is very supportive when I hand my work clothes back and tell her I have to leave my job at Mt. Okesea.

I lie to say it's family commitments—when I actually just despise the thought of being around so many people over the break.

I feel worse when she informs me that I've been a great part of the team. I'm even humbled when she says I can come back when things are better—but I don't think that will somehow happen.

I head out of the office and head up to the gateway, unsure what to do next—but someone starts to call for me. It's Kamala. She's in her work outfit, standing in the hut.

"I've got to go," I murmur as I continue to leave—I can't face speaking to anybody. She'll have seen the video. "You were great in the talent show. Really looked like you were in your element."

I turn around and head out of Mt. Okesea before she thinks about coming after me. I grab my bike and leave.

I decide not to head back home; my family will still want to discuss last night—and they'll be wondering why I'm home early. I'd have to explain I quit my job, and they'd see it as a sign of me not doing well.

After some time, with no success in the ride calming me down, I take a few turns and soon find I'm not too far away from home.

Back where I must face my family—spending the Christmas holidays there, with their faces of pity staring at me.

A black car races by me, extremely close. It swerves and instantly stops before me—I collide with the side. I soar over my handlebars and slide across the hood.

I crash off the other side of the car—immediately wincing when I collapse hard onto the concrete, followed by my helmet smacking onto the edge of the curb.

I scowl at the pain and try to move. Something spins me around fast and slams me onto my back—my body and open skin graze against the concrete. The sun stops my eyes from seeing who's on top of me and holding me by my shirt. A punch launches into my stomach.

Some huge, wretched noise comes out of my mouth—no air comes back in. Desperately gasping for air, I try to grab the arm of whoever it is to regain my bearings and ignore the ache.

"You told her!" A punch hits me again—in the left cheek this time. My head bangs against the pavement—it stings tremendously. I'm still pinned to the ground. "One thing, I said one thing. To keep your trap shut. And you told her!"

My eyes open only slightly after the new burst of pain, but it's enough to see Andrew's furious look—right before a fist makes contact again with my stomach.

I gasp again—frantically inhaling, needing to breathe.

"She's ended it with me."

My back lifts off the ground. My shirt strains as I'm held up—closer to his face. His eyes, already dark, seem somehow blacker. Colder. And ferocious. I'm scared. But somehow, as Andrew continues to glare at me, I don't seem to care.

"Perhaps we deserve it."

Andrew furrows his eyebrows. He shoves me back down to the ground. Hard. A marathon of punches and kicks come my way—I whine and ache to each hit.

The hitting stops, but I don't move. I hear a car door open. The wheels of the car screech and then spin away.

When I think it's safe, I open my eyes—footsteps are coming closer. I try to lift myself up, but everywhere pricks and burns around my body.

"Hey, are you okay?"

I look to the side but almost stumble off balance. A hand grabs my arm and helps me up. I squint my eyes and blink a few times to see some stranger.

"Do you need to go to the hospital?"

I shake my head at the man.

"I think you should. And we should call the police. I live across the street and saw it all."

"No," I say hastily. I don't want anybody involved. "No. I'm fine."

I move away from the stranger and stagger over to my bike. The front tyre's bent to the side.

"You shouldn't head off. You could be hurt."

He's not wrong. I'm in agony. However, I pick my bike up. Parts crack and clink.

"I'm fine. Thank you."

Before the guy protests—or maybe he does and I'm too out of it to notice—I walk away from the scene, hurting emotionally and now also physically.

Thankfully, nobody's car is at home. I shove my bike down in between the garage side and the hedge next door so it's hidden in case anybody arrives. I go in, and I'm about to go upstairs when I see a phone on the cabinet by the side. It's mine. Somebody must have taken it off me last night. Part of me is hoping there are messages or even a missed call from one of my friends.

Nothing.

I fumble my thumbs over the screen for a second. I need to explain. I give Billie a call first. There's no answer.

I keep ringing, but it just goes to her answer message.

A text pops through.

Billie

Leave me alone Hayden. Don't talk
to me again.

My stomach hurls in pain. More than when Andrew was punching me. I want to keep ringing, but I realise now it will only make everything worse. I try the others. I expect none of them to answer, but to my surprise, Dacre does. His *hello* is off, but I ask if Billie is okay. He explains she told Antonia and him what happened and says she isn't fine.

"She needs to know I'm sorry. You all do. If I could meet up with you all, or you could help get Billie to see me, then I can explain—"

"I understand. But I can't. Billie's really upset. With you. And with Andrew. She's been hurt more times than anybody should from boys." He pauses. I want to argue and persuade him, but I don't. "Billie said she doesn't want to see you. It's not my place. Maybe it's best you stay away a little. Let her calm down. Wait till after Christmas and try then."

My heart sinks. I nod in agreement—and say it's okay. He says goodbye and ends the call.

I feel sick. Dacre was being nice, more than I deserved perhaps, but I need to take on his words. If I'm ever going to have a chance to amend what I've done, then I must give Billie and the others time. It makes sense—I can't fix it while they're angry at me.

I head upstairs and go into the bathroom. I stare into the mirror. There's a large cut on my left cheek from where Andrew punched me. It must have bled. I'm positive there will be a bruise. I try to clean up—hissing every time I dab a wet towel on my injuries.

My phone pings. There's an email.

FROM: TokyoCherryDustZ89@TokyoCherryDustZ89.com
TO: BlueC0ast1@bretteodmail.com
DATE: Sat 23rd December, 2:02 PM
SUBJECT: Hey

Hey, I haven't heard from you in a while.

Thought I'd pop an email and check everything was ok since we last spoke. I hope you read this soon. I hope you had a great time at the Winter Snowdrop Ball ;)

Love,
Tokyo

I just stand there. Staring at the email. The nerve of Chloe! Wasn't last night enough? To keep on with this torment? This torment where she made me fall for her. Because I did. I really fell hard for her.

And to put *Love, Tokyo* still.

I want to throw the message at the wall—but I don't.

Instead, I type quickly back, questioning how she dares to message me, and then tell her to leave me alone. With no *Love, Brisbane* back or any sign-off. I press send and then immediately block the email address—as well as her number.

I slam my phone onto the sink. My brain's throbbing, and my body's aching so much.

I storm into my room. I grab my headphones. Music can calm me down. I instantly throw them back onto my bed, though—it's what Tokyo showed me to do.

I rip a piece of paper out of my notebook. I sit down and begin to fold. Desperately, I try to remember anything Dr Oace told me back in hospital or—*dang it*, I'm making a flippin' origami parrot!

I return to the bathroom to get my phone. I begin to search through the few contacts I could ring. But there's nobody. Kamala's working. Jasmine is in Sweden. And all the others are my friends who won't have anything to do with me or are my family. I stare at the mirror. I lift my shirt. Faint brown and purple bruises are already beginning to form on my skin. On my weak, pathetic body.

I laugh—it breaks. And it soon turns into weeping.

All I wanted when I moved here was to feel better. To live a better life. I thought I had, yet now I've messed it up.

I despise how I handled the Andrew situation, but I'm also a fool for thinking that somebody could like me.

Last night, I hoped Chloe might have been forced by her friends to do that trick to me with the paint—and that she really did like me.

But as I recall the way that she was looking at me last night, I realise there's no way she was forced against her will to hurt me.

Those emails from her weren't a lie either, though—Tokyo wasn't part of a two-month prank.

Chloe would have posted the emails online or done something just as publicly if it was. And she posted music on KingsgateLeeConnect under Tokyo before I began messaging her.

Yes. Those emails were real. The honesty and openness about her life was genuine. So why did she hurt me?

I see the answer is staring at me in the mirror.

Because she doesn't like who Brisbane is. She found out I was Brisbane. Me, Hayden Mallard. She lied. And she ran. She didn't like me.

On email. Yes, she did. But in person…no.

The thought hits me hard—I have to hold onto the sink. I'm revolted and disgusted with my features.

I suddenly remember Dacre chatting to me at Antonia's party when we were changing, seeing his physique, and feeling rather uncomfortable about my flat stomach, minimal biceps, and non-striking face. I look again under my shirt. I'm repulsed with myself, with my behaviour and now with my body.

Mr Gauran said I should try and enjoy things not while I can but because I can, and yet, I can't think of anything that's good in my life right now. I'm back to being on my own—being nothing but a joke.

33.

I sit on the driveway, staring at the upside-down wreck of a bicycle I've just pulled out from by the hedge—staring in the hopes that with Dad's toolbox, I might be able to salvage it. I've been alone for a while, wondering what to do and wishing there was a friend here.

"Interesting place to store a bike." I turn. Cassio is coming up the driveway. "You know that building you hid it beside is normally where people store them in."

"Is this how you're always gonna meet me? You trying to correct me on how to do things?" I ask, recalling the first time he spoke to me was when the bike had a flat tyre.

"If I catch you doing silly things, then perhaps."

He flashes me a cheesy grin. I don't bother to reply. I tell him he shouldn't be here as I'm grounded—he doesn't seem fussed, though, but then teases with, "They won't know I'm here."

I stare down at the bicycle; I wanted somebody to talk to, but now there is somebody, I just want him to go.

"You ain't getting rid of me that easily," Cassio says. I look back. *What is he, some mind reader?* He walks over and sits down by the other side of the bike.

The metal framing inside the front wheel is bent, forcing the wheel more to be a right angle than a flat circle. I wonder how he knows where I live—then I think I know. "You helped Robin bring me back from the party, didn't you?"

Cassio looks at me. "You weren't in a good place."

So I wasn't imagining him being here. I was so out of it that I would have easily believed that I saw purple pandas or skyscraper-sized iguanas. I apologise.

He smiles. "Sometimes we need a way to cool off. Just don't think drinking should be yours."

I smile. "Don't worry, I've realised that."

I grab one item at a time from the toolbox and see which fits onto the part where I can take the front tyre off.

"So that thing with Chloe last night. It wasn't random."

Either I'm easy to read, or people are really good at deciphering others, and I'm just terrible at it.

I tighten the hold of the tool in my hand. He's seen the video. But I'm unnerved that he said it with such conviction that it was more a statement than a question to me.

"No." I try to go back to searching for the right tool as though the conversation is just nothing significant, even though it certainly is. "I was messaging somebody—didn't know who. Thought we were close. Turns out it was Chloe. She asked for us to go to the ball together. And, well, you know what happened next."

Cassio remains quiet.

I manage to find the right tool and begin unscrewing the wheel. "But she didn't like who her messenger was. Instead of just saying privately, she decided to do it so everybody could see." There's a sour taste in my mouth, but I press on with the wheel.

"That's cold."

There's a click. I take the front wheel off. "I didn't think it would matter because our bond was so strong—clearly looks matter."

"You shouldn't think like that," Cassio says. I argue it's hard not to when it's the truth. "Come off it, man, I'm sure your friends don't see you like that. You're tight with them. They don't judge you like that."

"No, but they have a right to judge if I betray them."

There's a quizzical expression on Cassio. I explain to him the dilemma I got myself into about Andrew and my friends.

"But that jerk was threatening you," Cassio disputes after.

"Still kept it from them. And I couldn't even defend myself from him when he did this." I point to my cut and show him my bruises. I glance away when I see the sadness on Cassio.

The front wheel rests on the side with one half bent and pointing up to the sky.

Cassio stares at the tyre. "You know that thing's flippin' done for, right?" I laugh at Cassio. He's right. "Pretty unfixable."

"Just like most of me."

Cassio leans over—a hand claps the back of my head before I can react. "What did I say? The merry-go-round. Don't let anything get to you, otherwise it already has a hold on you."

I don't reply—it's easier said than done.

"Let's make a pact." Cassio shuffles around to get nearer. On his knees before me, "To always be there for each other." This sounds like a dumb thing young and naïve kids do, not teenagers. But his eyes tell me he's serious. "And to never fixate on what's been done and help each other focus on what can be. No matter what."

I watch Cassio waiting for my response. "Why?"

"Because nobody should ever have to go through anything alone."

He puts out a hand. I look down at it. I wonder what's the point in this pact—but perhaps there doesn't need to be?

I put my hand out and shake.

"Okay." Cassio strongly shakes back, along with a grin. "So Dacre said to wait for the dust to settle before reaching out to Billie. Best take his advice on that. But as for your other issues—being bullied by Andrew and Chloe not liking how you look—you shouldn't judge so harshly on how you look."

"But it's true," I begin to argue—but stop. "If I want to stop being pushed over or be hurt, I—I need to get fit."

My hand brushes against my stomach. Sat down, I can feel the slight flabbiness and ease it is to wiggle and make it move. Then, I remember how badly bruised I am from Andrew. "I need to be strong." Strong. Good-looking. Built. All of it.

Colbey's changed himself around. He always had the looks, but I mean about his injury. After it happened, he didn't sit and crumble—he wanted to feel elite again. He forced himself to persevere and not give in till he got there.

"I need to work on it all, to be in shape, if I want to be better, if I want people to take me seriously and not push me around all the time."

Because I can't live another day with how I am. After all, they do say if you look good on the outside, you'll feel good on the inside.

Cassio looks at me. "If you want to get fit, then I'll help you. I want to help after what I did to you. And if there's one thing I know, it's how to get fit."

"I think the ice has done the job," I say in the kitchen, with my voice sounding slightly squished from the ice pack pushed against my face.

"Little bit more. I am the doctor of the house."

"You're a dentist."

"Close enough."

Dad smiles with his huge, beautifully clean white teeth. No whitening. No fillers. No fake teeth replacements. All completely natural and sparkling. I glance away from the sight.

"So, you say some car went by you, and you swerved?"

I then begin my web of lies. That a random car was too close, and I swerved onto the pavement and hit a lamppost. That until I buy a new tyre with my own money, Zeke will give me lifts to work. And that I've been asked to work nearly every day over the Christmas holidays.

When, in reality, I'm meeting with Cassio to train.

Not my best lie, but I don't want to tell him about Andrew—and if I say I've quit my job then I know he won't let me go out for runs and get fit when I'm supposed to be grounded.

"I'd prefer you home instead of going to work, but seeing as nobody will be here to watch you, I think you're right. At least I'll know where you are and know you're not moping around."

I keep my smile inside me and thank him.

He walks around and then pats me on my back. "I'm glad you're trying to be proactive."

The knife of guilt has somehow found its way back to me—making its way through my skin and touching my heart. Dad's not just talking about me being proactive while I'm grounded. He's referring to the red paint fiasco last night.

When Dad came back home today, he tried to convince me to see Mr Gauran—I told him I was fine and just wanted to move on.

I'm ashamed, though. Despite opening to Mr Gauran and then Dad the other day, which was great, I can't be honest with all of this—the truth behind last night, me being threatened by Andrew, the breakup with my friends, and quitting my job and using it to sneak out from being grounded.

I hope he genuinely believes I am proactive—because I suppose I am. I'm being proactive to make me better.

The next day, I walk down to meet Cassio at the end of the street as planned. We said here so he isn't seen coming up the driveway by my family, and so they don't question why Zeke's car isn't outside to pick me up when I walk out. I told them Zeke's getting me at the corner.

I'm still unhappy with everything, but I try to push it aside.

With everybody gone already today, I can leave the house in a grey hoody and some jogging shorts that I normally use for school.

I'm the first here and so wait for him at the corner…but I wait for a long time. I stare down the roads, unable to see him.

My foot begins to tap. The waiting starts to become too much—for what if he doesn't show?

Why would he? He has no obligation to do so.

I look again. Nobody is here but me.

This was a stupid idea. Why would he help me? It's just another person tricking me. Somebody else rejecting me…

"Hey."

I turn. There he is. I smile with relief, then try and play it off as though I hadn't been panicking. "Hi."

To no surprise, he's got his red hoody on, but what is shocking is his choice of trousers.

"Jeans?" I ask—he's always wearing those clothes.

"It traps the heat and makes me sweat more. Don't worry, I'm not suggesting you do that. But that doesn't mean I'm going easy on ya."

"Good. Bring it."

Cassio scoffs with a laugh. "Oh, you're so gonna wish you're the one wearing my lucky hoody now."

After a quick warm-up, we begin to jog. Cassio doesn't lead before me; he's running beside me. I quite like it because being ahead would just be a visual display of how out of shape I am.

We go down the streets, heading through the suburbs. It's nice. I like the gentle breeze briefly cooling us between each house. Peaceful. I wonder why I've never been keen on jogging before.

But then I remember. Sweat starts to form, thanks to the sun beaming down on us. My clothes stick to my skin. More so on my back, under where my rucksack is. Soon, my breathing gets harder with every move I make. My legs start to feel some ache.

"Hey, don't be slowing down," Cassio says, his breathing calm. I keep going on as Cassio gives out words of encouragement. But after so long, my body wants to collapse, and I stop. "What you doing?"

"I'm exhausted," I puff out. I bend over and rest my hands on my legs for support.

"That's no excuse." I glance up at Cassio but wish I didn't because my head begins to feel light. "Here, stand back up and put your arms behind your head. It's better for circulation and getting more air to you." I do as he says. "You can't just stop; when you begin to feel worn out, that's when you start making actual progress."

I dart my eyes over to him. "You mean none of that was progress?" I flick a flimsy arm back at where we've just come from.

"Seeing as you're starting out, yeah, a little, but not for long." I must still look dumbfounded because Cassio continues, yet I notice he doesn't even look like he's broken a sweat. "Getting into shape, it's not about doing some fitness and thinking that's it. Or being able to do the same each day. It's about the improvement you make each time—how quickly you do something, how much further you can go, or how much more strength you can hold."

I keep my arms behind my head as I think over what he says.

"It's like playing a level on a game, and you die. You don't start again exactly where you left off, do you? You must do the entire level again and get back to that point where you died. You might struggle sometimes, but eventually, you'll get to that point easily because you've been there so often before, but it's the next part that's the test, the part beyond your limit—that's the real progress. You must push on, do more each time. Feel the strain and work if you want to make that difference."

My body is aching, and my breath is a bit hasty, but I've managed to gain back some control of it.

I get what he's saying—but I wish it wasn't as hard. "Okay."

"Good—remember, no pain, no gain. No torment, no adjustment. No sting, no win." I look over at Cassio's abysmal rhyming attempts. "You get my point."

I fail miserably at trying to smile through my exhaustion—but I see the seriousness in Cassio's eyes. The determination to get through.

"When I'm training for football, I'm focused on why I'm training. Are you right now?"

"Well," I try to answer, taking a step forward. "I do think about everything that's happened. The hurt I got and gave on Friday night, and the beating up. I try and—"

Something swats the back of my head.

"What was our pact?" Cassio says when he puts his hand back down.

"To always be there for each other, and to never fixate on what's been done and—oh."

"Exactly! That stuff, with Tokyo, Chloe, betraying your friends and Andrew, that's negative. Negativity might be the engine rev that started this movement, but that'll get you only so far. You must think of the end result. The destination you want to reach. The aim of all this. The positive. Focus on how you'll look. How you'll feel inside when we get to that point. Remind yourself that the aim is to push yourself."

Cassio lifts his hand back. I squirm, expecting another playful yet hurtful smack on my head, but instead, I feel a gentle hold on my shoulder—almost like nothing is there.

It's hard to believe how we met a few weeks ago and to see where we are now. He's not trying to do this for himself—it's practically all for me. He's a good friend.

"Thanks, Cassio."

When it gets to five, I've lost count of how many houses we have jogged by or how many streets we've run down—or how many times I've had to stop for a break, but I know we're back near my street. My grey hoody has very vivid sweat marks on the back, under the armpits and also on the chest. I glance over at Cassio's. There's nothing. We must not have even scratched the surface of his fitness.

When I walk into my house alone, I've somehow planned it right because everybody is still out. I get undressed in the bathroom.

Before I hop into the shower, my eyes find the mirror. I see the nice reminders of Andrew on my body—but it's what the bruises are on that I'm looking at.

The frail form that my skin holds together. The bland, stretched chest. The not-cauldron-sized-potbelly but rather the vague curve that sticks out.

I straighten my back and broaden my shoulders out to improve my posture in the hopes it will make some difference. The tummy seems to disappear, and my chest flattens. But it still looks weak.

Today was only day one. It will change. I turn away and head for the shower. *It must.*

It's Monday. Christmas Day. I feel like how I imagine Father Christmas would be when he returns home after spending all night gallivanting around the globe and climbing up and down every chimney. Completely knackered!

And I'm comparing all that to me doing only one full day of jogging.

I force myself out of bed, ignoring the headache brewing, and get changed. My legs are very heavy with every move. I'm just glad it's Christmas Day so I can have some time for my body to heal.

"Merry Christmas," Colbey says to me in the front room. Dressed in his usual clothes as well.

I say the same back and sit on the other chair in the room. "Where's Dad?"

Colbey raises an eyebrow at me as if I'd asked the silliest question ever.

I stare at the ceiling when there are suddenly loud bangs from above—followed by a scream. There are muffled voices. A few seconds later, Dad comes down the stairs with a metal spoon and large wok in his hands and a huge grin on his face—then an unamused Robin follows. I'd laugh as it's always Robin who has to be woken up, but I don't bother this year.

I go first to get my presents under the tree and hand them to the family. Colbey and Dad say thanks when I hand over their present, but I'm almost terrified when I go to Robin; I expect her to throw it in my face. Instead, she smiles—a forced smile, I realise. If Dad or Colbey weren't in the room, it would probably be a different story. Today wouldn't be known as the day of the birth of Jesus Christ but as the death of Hayden Mallard. Probably still a day of celebration for most, though.

I don't get them much—with spending most of my money before on music from Tokyo's recommendations.

I give Colbey a collection of autobiographies from a range of football coaches. Some even signed. He seems pleased as he takes them out of the wrapping paper.

Dad receives a six-month subscription to a music streaming service. He doesn't exactly understand it all at first, so I explain what it means.

"You do realise what you've just done?" Colbey says. "Now we'll constantly hear nothing but his music all the time. Not just in the car, but everywhere he goes." I look over to see Dad's sparkling grin has made an appearance.

"It's a good present."

I look shocked over at Robin. Did she just compliment something that's associated with me?

"And thanks for mine."

I remove the surprise off my face before anybody can see it and try to give a normal smile towards her. Two compliments! She likes my present?

She's definitely being pleasant because Dad's here.

There's a company called Tovell's City Secrets, who create travel maps and guidebooks about the hidden gems of American cities, such as unique-themed bars, stores and festivals. As Robin is set on going to a college in Boston, Massachusetts next year, I got her one for there. I also got a copy of Miami and New York for her, too, because I know they're places she wants to visit.

By the end of the unveiling of the presents, I've received a personalised Atlanta Falcons football shirt from Dad, a high-quality aftershave box from Robin, which I assume is because she wasn't sure what else to get and not implying that I stink, and a book about the Great Barrier Reef from Colbey—the latest edition from a renowned environmentalist and world marine explorer. I thank them all.

We go for a walk—to which I try to ignore the pain in my legs. *No torment, no adjustment.*

After helping Colbey cook, we serve the food and sit down at the table with Dad and Robin. The food looks delicious—but I don't feel so hungry. I'm sure Cassio would encourage me to eat because meat's protein and that will help build muscle. I'd need a lot, though, for that to happen.

I eat as much as I can, but it's not a lot. I guess it's just so filling. However, nobody else questions the stuff I have left when I see there are bits left on their plates, too.

I want to head straight to my room and sleep, but I follow everybody to the front room for an evening of TV.

I don't want them to think anything's wrong, that any of last week got to me.

"You used to all love this," Dad says when Robin objects after he asks her to stop on a channel that's showing a film. *How The Grinch Stole Christmas.*

"This used to terrify me," Robin replies.

"Because of the Grinch?" Colbey asks.

"No, the Whos," she answers. They laugh. I pretend to smile like I am invested in the conversation and try to watch the film—but I start to feel as green as the Grinch because Chloe will not leave my head.

I can picture her with her family in her home. They're sitting watching Christmas films, too. All is well. She'll look over to her mom, knowing things are fine now between them after their chat about her dad. They're enjoying the last few days at their home before moving, all sitting together, with Chloe invested in the spirit of the day. And it makes me sick. Angry. Annoyed.

Don't fixate on the past, I hear Cassio say. I try to move away from the thoughts and use the notion of the result to calm myself down. The thought of me being better. Me not fazed by the whole Tokyo fiasco. Me no longer timid or shy. Me ending up as a stronger, more in-shape Hayden Mallard. The person nobody will walk over.

Dad finds out there's a Christmas special of a music quiz show he likes and wants to play along. *Another Tokyo reminder.* I unwillingly force myself to face the music because Dad wants to be paired with me. He and Robin get competitive as usual, and I just hold up a smile whenever he wants to hi-five because I get a question right—I get right because of Tokyo.

The night ends with Dad and me winning, and us then watching another Christmas film.

Everybody seems happy at the end. It has been a nice family day, but my mind has ruined it for me, for I've either been tired or been battling against my own thoughts. Thankfully, nobody mentioned Friday night and the ball.

When I lie in bed, finally, trying to soak up the softness of the duvet, I realise something—I never thought today about Mom not being here. Not once.

I turn over onto my other side as if that might give me some new perspective. My brain floats through the possibilities—I know from talking to Mr Gauran that I thought that I might have moved on from the horror of Mom leaving, but perhaps this is a sign that I have.

And that's a good thing, I decide. Sad but good.

It wasn't long ago when I was concerned with how I might be on Christmas Day without her here—so to be completely fine and not even bat an eyelid is unexpected. Strange perhaps?

But maybe I'm overthinking it. And I need to stop doing that with everything—even if that's what I desperately want to do after all that's happened recently.

I can't. I can't go into that web of concern, because that's kind of what messed things up for me before. I just need to understand that maybe I've nothing to worry about regarding my mom and life back in Georgia. Maybe I genuinely have now moved on from that part of my life…*yeah, you've moved on, Hayden, but now you must deal with another big ache in your life.*

Yourself.

34.

Cassio and I have been mainly jogging, but now some exercises have been added to the mix—I can't just have muscular legs and then a scrawny top half. I can feel the strain and the tightness in my muscles, beginning to stretch and having to work. Awaking ones I haven't used in a very long time. I'm tired, and my body is reeling, but it's fine, for if there's no torment, there's no adjustment.

"Glad you think so," I say to him, with my arms behind my head, after he compliments how well I'm doing. "But it's not enough. I need to do more if I want to see some progress."

Cassio looks over at me—once again, standing without a single drop of sweat on him. "These things take time. You don't just change after a day."

"I get that. And if this was the summer holidays, great, but there's less than two weeks left," I stop myself from continuing. Too late, though. Cassio has clocked on. I bend over to suck in more air so I purposely don't see him judge my remark.

"Are you scared of going back to school?"

I let my body catch a few breaths. My chest rising and dropping harshly.

"Wouldn't you be?" I reply when I think of how people won't have forgotten the video when I return to school.

"I'll be with you."

I'm expecting to see pity written across Cassio's face, but when I look—there isn't. I sigh and even wipe my forehead again.

"Thanks, but you won't be there every second of the day." I want to end this conversation, yet I'll have to give more because Cassio doesn't budge. "But if I feel like I've had some improvement on me, then I'll know there'll be less fear when I walk through those doors."

He doesn't say anything at first. It concerns me a little.

"I understand. We'll adapt the schedule we have today. A bit of jogging but more working on your core and muscles."

I smile. "Any chance we can work longer?"

Cassio pauses. "Possibly. It depends—aren't you grounded?"

"Not anymore." Dad let me have my phone back this morning, too.

I had no Merry Christmas texts from anybody. None.

"Okay then." Cassio begins to walk. I follow beside him. "If you want to really work on building muscle, we're gonna need to use equipment. A gym. The school's will be shut, and we're not exactly old enough to get membership anywhere. Maybe there's an outside gym in a park nearby?"

I stop.

Cassio tilts his head at me.

I smile again. "I know where."

"This is insane. Maybe I should look at going into dentistry?" Cassio says as he walks around the gym above the garage.

After a moment to take it in, we begin training, and Cassio gets me on the machines and tells me what to do.

Whenever I think about what I said earlier to Cassio or relive any part of the recent events, I snap back to the goal of why I'm doing this. Be it something funny in one of Tokyo's emails, a song I used to love from her recommendations, or the nights out with my friends at the drive-in or parties—I fight it back instantly.

By the time I'm on the rowing machine, my mind is in the zone, thinking of me, standing physically strong and in gorgeous perfection.

I row as if I can see the new me in the distance. Giving it my all and letting the sweat, that horrid unwanted waste, drip out of me. Allowing the aches in my body to keep growing because it means it's working.

"Since when did you start using this?"

I twist my head—snapped out of my work out. Colbey is walking away from the stairs. He's in his gym clothes. A baggy, black gym designer tank top, bold yellow shorts and his favourite electro-blue trainers.

I glance around—it's just us; I was so focused on my exercising that I don't even remember saying goodbye to Cassio. "I thought I'd give it a go."

Colbey perches himself against the treadmill. Now, in a more open view, I can see the long pale scar running over his knee. I look back up when he notices.

"It's not really a surprise that Sports is my lowest grade. Thought I could do some training over the break to get in shape. Well, some sort of shape."

As if my joke was bad enough, I pretend to give a short laugh to make it be funnier. It doesn't. And inside, I panic in case Colbey suspects something is up.

"Sounds like a good plan," he says with an adequate smile. I breathe slowly out. "I'd maybe go onto something else. Your hands look like they're going to get blisters."

Colbey pushes himself off from leaning on the treadmill and walks around to get on.

He's right. There are already small hard bulges on my palms.

"Forget the rowing machine. You look like you've been going at it all day."

I freeze. He's no longer looking at me, and I know he hasn't caught me out, but my body itches all over like he has.

I brush my hoody down and then push my hair to the side. It's drenched. I try to laugh it off. "I wish."

The days pass by. I work out as much as I can, and soon when I'm not working out, I'm thinking about working out.

I go to sleep and wake up always groggy and my body aching. However, I force myself to get out, do a little bit of lifting hand weights in the garage, and then meet up with Cassio. I'm no longer grounded, but I wait a few days before I pretend to Dad that Aunt Sandra's given me the week off from work.

I'm making the most difference when I'm working in the gym, where I'm testing and pushing myself to the maximum. And I'm sure I'm feeling a slight change. Like my stomach is starting to get tighter—but whenever I look at the mirror in the bathroom every night, I don't see much. Maybe some vague, minute difference in my cheeks, but not much on my arms or my stomach.

Under Cassio's rules, we still jog, although I'm pleased that he's getting me to do more drills in the park now, too.

"Hey, son."

I look across the gym and see Dad.

"Hi," I manage to say between working. I'm kind of dangling back on a piece of equipment to do sit-ups on. The bottom of my legs are locked under the top of the bar, and the flat seat is on a hundred and twenty-degree angle, so the real workout is when I have to lift myself and do sit-ups.

"Colbey's said he'll make his special tonight. Pizza." I feel some spit get lodged in my mouth. I swallow it down as I pull up. "Want to come with me to the store and get the ingredients? Get out for a bit?"

I lift my body up and hold the position, letting my legs take the pressure to keep me up. “I’m okay, thanks.”

He stands with what I realise is quite a good posture as I wait for him to go. My eyes catch the tightness on the sleeves of his shirt and then on his trousers. My dad’s more built than me! He’s older than me, doesn’t do much working out, whereas I’m going full throttle in exercising, yet he’s more in shape and attractive than me. What the heck!

Dad leaves me to be back in the gym alone, yet it feels like I’ve done almost nothing when Colbey comes and tells me food’s ready.

The food looks delicious. It’s my favourite pizza—ham, sausage, salami and some green peppers.

Water foams in my mouth just from the sight. The hot, fresh steam and the multitude of flavours swim their way up to my nose. And when they reach and it smells like it always does, there’s an unusual and unwanted twist in my stomach as everybody begins.

I look away from Dad because he even looks handsome when eating pizza. I try to block out Robin when she starts shoving her popularity and social life in my face. And as for Colbey, well, he’s just his usual self, but knowing I’m sat next to somebody who’s practically an athlete is irritating too—and I’ve seen the ripped figure under his gym shirt in the morning when I work in the garage—sure, Colbey’s an assistant coach, but he doesn’t play on the field and yet he’s still more jacked than me!

I pick a slice up and quietly eat. It tastes nice, but it feels bad. So much I can’t eat it all. Because I know it will just add to what I’m hopefully getting rid of.

A week to go until school begins—where I’ll have to endure whatever’s waiting for me. I can see it now—I won’t be able to sit with my friends for lunch and some other kids will have taken my old table for one, so I’ll end up either sitting on the grass slope by myself or in a locked cubicle.

The pressure of everything is for sure building. However, I continue to give my all when I go off with Cassio. I don’t think Cassio ever questions that. He’s there beside me, and he is encouraging me along. I use practically every chance I get to do some sort of fitness. And whenever I feel drained, I tell myself to do another, and I continue. If I reach the same number of miles as the day before or row yesterday’s distance in a quicker time, I keep going. My head might feel like it’s ready to break, but I push on. Until I can no more.

"Hey, are you okay?" Cassio asks as he comes back. I'm bent over, exhausted. Sweat is on my clothes and hair. Meanwhile, Cassio's hair looks completely dry. As does his clothes.

"Yeah. Probably shouldn't have skipped breakfast this morning. Do you mind if we have a break?" I don't want to, but my head's swirling.

"Sure."

We walk off the path in the park and sit on a patch of dry grass.

It doesn't matter what month it is in Orlando, there are always people in a park. There are a few families in the play area, a bunch of younger kids playing soccer on the right, and there's even a yoga class happening on the other side of the lake.

Despite all that's happening, I find my eyes watching Cassio, who is looking out across the park.

There's something—I've known it for a while, yet I suppose never acknowledged—Cassio's very considerate to others. He has his own family, with his own issues, like his dad leaving and then with how others treated him differently at school because of it—maybe still do, he's never said—and while he has had all this going on, he's out here trying to help me. Because of what? Some school humiliation? And he could be having so much more going on, yet I've never stopped to ask. I've never considered how he is. He's put his own stuff aside and been relentlessly there for me this break.

Cassio Socorro is a great friend. Even if he is the only one I have right now, he really is a genuine friend. One I've taken for granted.

"Excuse me!" I yell when I notice a young woman pushing a pram on the path near us. I get up.

Cassio watches with confusion and alarm, but I ignore it. I walk over to the woman and ask if she can take a photo for me. She kindly agrees.

I call Cassio over. He looks reluctant to come but slowly moves. As he stands beside me, I realise it will be a great shot. We've got the lake behind us. The trees next to us. And the weather is glorious.

"Okay, ready," I say after I've tried to brush my sweaty hair neatly.

The woman looks momentarily at us, somewhat puzzled, then moves down to the phone.

"Smile," I tell Cassio.

The woman looks back at us carefully, probably trying to get us in frame. I hear a few clicks, and I thank her.

She smiles, a little forced for my liking, but I shake it off as she grabs her pram and walks away. She's probably just weirded out that I want a photo of us, where one looks unfazed from the heat and running—and in his red hoody and jeans—and the other in gym clothes and completely drenched in sweat. I mean, it's not exactly the ideal look for a photo.

"Why'd you do that?" Cassio asks when I put my phone away.

"So I can send these to you later on, and you'll know I'll always be there for you. Like you have for me. So thank you."

And I mean it. Whether he is on his own or surrounded by his family and feels out of place, I don't want him to ever feel alone.

35.

When Cassio and I reach the park, I'm drained because it seems to be the hottest day we've trained on so far—within the hour, my hoody was drenched. I had already tired myself out in the gym this morning, but now my body is in complete exhaustion mode—more so when Cassio gets me to do press-ups and squats. But I don't let myself stop—not even when I feel a throbbing pain grow in my head or the dryness in my throat. Because no torment means no adjustment.

We start another jog, and I just keep fighting in my mind all the bad stuff that I'm dealing with and run over the image of why I'm putting myself through this to spur me on—the physique I should get. The strength I will have. The maturity I will have grown into.

The sun doesn't hide behind any clouds. My breathing soon gets tight, though. My head becomes worse than it was this morning. I hear Cassio at my side encouraging me to keep going, so I put one foot in front of the other.

Everything becomes distant, though.

The beeping traffic lights nearby sound muffled and deep. My feet feel extremely heavy and yet somehow sound like they're a mile behind me. I can't smell the roses on the bushes outside a house I go around. I wipe off any sweat that's caught in my eyes, hoping I can refocus, but the blurriness stays. The stinging, saltwater-like taste of sweat drips onto my lips and goes into my mouth.

It's extremely hot and clammy under my hoody, and I hiss from the burning pain in my head when it grows bigger.

The road swerves ahead—I abruptly see something green. A new burst of hurt rushes across the right side of my body. However, the new pain brings some sense back to me because my eyes begin to realign and see where I am; I've collapsed into a hedge.

I pick myself up, still breathing heavily. I look down at my leg. Some scratches, but nothing serious. My face itches a little; I'm sure there's some there too.

I hear footsteps; Cassio's probably just seen what's happened.

I brush any dirt off my hoody. I bend down to do my shorts, but there's an abrupt rush inside me. I spin back to the hedge and vomit.

"Hayden, are you alright?"

I wait a moment until I've finished to glance over. Completely terrible and disorientated, I expect to see Cassio coming to me.

But it isn't him—it's Colbey!

I look back so I can get my surroundings. I'm outside my own house. The chances!

"Yeah," I lie. However, I'm a bit shaken.

"No, you're not. Let me get you inside the house."

I want to object, yet my body willingly lets Colbey guide me inside. My head is too heavy and thumping madly to know what I'm doing.

He helps me down into the armchair in the living room. I remain silent throughout. I'm a little embarrassed and ashamed—he'll have seen me collapse and then be sick.

He disappears—momentarily I think, maybe longer, I don't know—leaving me alone. The ache in my head slowly pounds less.

Then he returns, with a glass of water.

I reluctantly take the glass and have a sip. The cold freshness relieves the taste in my mouth and down my throat.

"Do you want to tell me what that was all about?" Colbey asks.

I put the glass down before my nerves shake it for him to see.

"I—I was just dehydrated. I should have had more water," I lie. I hear the quiver in my own voice, though.

"Understatement of the Year right there. Wanna try that again?"

My body itches away at me inside because he has me trapped. I keep quiet, though. Yet I don't run either because my arms or body might tremble if I lift myself out of the chair.

But I just wish to be somewhere else—for this to end.

"Hayden, I work in this industry. Part of my job is caring for the team and noticing when something's off. And you're not okay. You're working out constantly. And it's more than for a grade improvement. I don't think I ever see you eat much, and you never really look at anybody now. You're either off in the gym or out jogging till you're exhausted—and just then, you trained so hard you collapsed and threw up. That isn't right. What's going on?"

I can tell his eyes are on me, but I don't dare look away from the table I'm staring at.

"Do you not like the way you look?"

My face almost begins to break. I scrunch it up to counteract it. My hand shakes. I close my fist to stop it. I glance up. It's a terrible mistake. Colbey's staring at me. The horrid tingle in my stomach tells me I'm caught out.

I press my lips together tightly a few times, but I can't hold it.

"Would you?" My voice cracks. "I thought I was doing okay here. But I can't do right because when I put my wall down and let people in, I've ended up either being threatened, humiliated, or I've become my own enemy and ruined what I had with friends who now don't want anything to do with me."

I lean to the side and place my head against my hand, with my elbow resting on the armchair. "I tried to trust in others, and I became an easy target to be walked over on. I want people to never see me like that and think they can hurt me."

"So you started doing this because if you're built, then they wouldn't?" Colbey asks.

I nod.

"I'm sorry you've felt like this. I knew you were down after the ball, but not like this," he says. I turn. He wants to ask more, but I just pray he doesn't. "I get it. I've been there in my own way. But you do know you're being excessive with it? And that isn't good."

I try and use some power to nod again, but I'm just so ashamed.

"Why haven't you said any of this to us? You told Mr Gauran about the other stuff."

"That's about my past, feeling like I was lying about myself to others. This is because…I feel…worthless—no, I do," I say before Colbey can stop me. "But when I work and push myself, it pushes everything bad out of my head. It takes me away from it all. Let's me think about the future. And it's like I can be myself again, even if just for a few minutes." I think about the recent times, though—how much I've been having to work. "But I think it's getting harder—to reach that point. To be fine."

"And that's why you keep doing it?"

When there's a bit of silence, my eyes instinctively check him. I feel like a fool—an idiot for letting myself become, I don't know, worse than before.

I think about his comment. I let all my thoughts rush around inside me as I think of an answer.

"Yeah—no—I mean," I pause. My body is starting to break, crumbling to pieces as I realise the harsh truth to his question. "I want to be built so I'm never like this again, but the truth is, it feels like the way in how I look is the only thing I can change in my life right now.

And I don't know how to stop that."

My lips become unsteady. I shove my closed fist against my mouth. Somewhere inside me, I want to scream in frustration. Instead, though, I close my eyes. I don't want my brother to see me like this. And I don't want to see the world either.

Colbey moves. I keep my eyelids shut. His arms then enclose themselves around to hug me.

And I break.

How long does he hold me for? I don't know, but I don't push the embrace away.

It's warm. Comforting. Reassuring. Something I don't think I've had in a long while.

Just when I decide I want to stay like this forever, though, closed and protected, Colbey does eventually pull away.

I open my eyes to find he's squatting before me; his eyes are in line with mine.

"Thank you for opening up to me," he says softly. "You know you'll have to talk about this to your therapist, right?" The thought is not pleasant, but I agree. "Okay. It's not until next week, so in the meantime, you can't be working as you are."

I realise how bad the relentless exercising has been on me—yet there's still a part of me wanting to be back outside and work out. And I'm ridiculous for thinking it.

I'm stupid.

"But I'll make a schedule. A toned-down routine that we'll do together. Nothing more. I understand we can't just cut you from it straightaway. And I'll make a menu of what you should eat and when."

He makes it sound like I'm on drugs or obsessed with alcohol, but I guess maybe it is. It's become a habit. An addiction.

"In fact, I'll make something now for us," Colbey says, standing up. "Dad's out tonight, and Robin's with friends."

The thought of food doesn't sit well with me, but I don't object. Restricting myself hasn't been good, and he does work with this sort of stuff, I guess.

When I dare to move my head, I see I'm in the room alone. I suddenly realise something.

"I need to head out," I yell over to the kitchen where Colbey's gone. I get out of the chair carefully and head out of the room. Cassio's probably been outside all this time.

He'll have no clue what's happened.

"Now? Where?"

"I've got to tell Cassio what happened. That I can't do this with him anymore," I reply, approaching the front door.

"Cassio? Cassio Socorro?"

I stop. I turn around.

Colbey's standing in the hallway. He's staring at me. And in a way that's way more intent than just a few minutes ago. Almost serious.

"Yeah," I answer, sceptically on why the curiosity. But then it clicks. "Oh, you've seen his name on the football team at school?"

"You're seeing him?" Colbey asks. There's a strange and puzzled expression on his face. A blank, pale look, like I'm a ghost he's just seen.

"Yeah. For a few weeks now." I spin around, ready to go out the door.

"So you remember him?"

I look back. "What do you mean?" *Remember him?* That doesn't make any sense.

A beat of silence occurs. Colbey shifts a little. "Nothing. It doesn't matter."

"No. What do you mean?" It's an extremely odd question to ask anybody. Clearly, something's up. And Colbey's keeping it from me. "Colbey, what aren't you telling me?"

"It's fine." He then walks away.

I follow him into the front room—not ready to end this. "Sounds like you don't like the guy. Look, if you've read about his dad being in prison, Cassio isn't like that. He's a good guy."

Colbey whips his head back at me. His eyes are wide. Shock is drawn over his face. He stares at me with bewilderment—it starts to freak me out. "It's happening again."

"What? What is? You're starting to panic me," I tell him. Because he is.

Colbey turns away. I think to compose himself. I don't really know; I'm just focused on receiving answers.

My breathing is getting hasty.

Then he looks over to me. Sorrow, and sadness, yet somehow there's also seriousness carved into his face.

"Cassio has gone."

I stare at him. "What? You mean as in gone home? Bit of an overreaction for that."

"No, listen," Colbey's voice is way sterner than before. Deep.

Desolate. Alone. He even holds his hands up to try and get me to lower my voice and stop. "I don't know how to say this, Hayden. But I need you to not get worked up when I say this. Please." He doesn't blink as he looks into my eyes.

I nod, trying to calm myself down—but really, I am completely confused.

"You can't have seen him. Not today or over these few weeks. Cassio's been dead for months."

There's a sting in my brain. I glare at Colbey.

"Dead? What do you mean dead? You're insane. I just saw him—"

"Let me explain—"

"No. Why are you saying this? I've chatted to him at school. At work. Everywhere. I've been hanging out with him every day for the last week."

His eyebrows decline in. "Really?"

"Yes. I even got photos with him." I pull my phone out of my pocket. Confidently yet also furiously. Why's Colbey saying this stuff?

I go into my photos and open the pics I got with Cassio in the park, ready to shove them in front of Colbey's face—but there's just me. I'm stood there. Drenched in sweat in my gym stuff. With the lake behind me. And nobody beside me.

My head stings. It hurts like a pain I've never felt before.

"I don't get it. He was right there, I swear."

I scroll through the other photos the woman in the park took. It's just me in every photo.

"He isn't there because you're imagining him," Colbey says.

The pain in my head stabs again.

I whip my head around the room, and begin pacing, unsure where to look.

"What? Don't be stupid. I know he's real," I hiss. *Maybe Cassio ducked out of being in shot*; he wasn't exactly keen on getting them. *That must be it.*

I go into my contacts and then my messages—nothing under Cassio Socorro. *Maybe I never got his number?*

"Hayden."

I glance at Colbey. "Why are you doing this?"

"Because I care. And you must be starting to remember. He isn't real," he repeats. "Look, we need to deal with this carefully. Tell me, if you're so sure, have you ever talked to him in a group or with somebody else? Have you seen anybody chat to Cassio besides yourself?"

I bite my lip as I try to think, but before I can get anywhere, Colbey continues, “Can you remember how you ever meet up with him?”

“Not exactly, but, well—it’s been by coincidence, or, since he started training me, we arrange the next time when we’re together,” I try to argue.

“And do you remember how things end when he leaves? Do you remember him ever actually leaving?”

Through the pain pulsing in my head, I try to think of whenever I’ve been with Cassio and how we’ve gone our separate ways. The night from Mt. Okesea. The night he walked back with me from the football game. Even all the times we’ve been working out.

There’s a disgusting churn in my stomach. We’ve met so many times, and I remember him arriving, but I can’t remember ever once seeing him leave. I mean, I said I had to return to work that time near Mt. Okesea’s gateway and he walked away—but I never physically saw him go around the corner or drive off in a car…to leave and go out of my sight.

The stinging won’t stop.

“No,” I quickly retort. “But what you’re saying is crazy.” The fact I have no proof is getting at me because Cassio is genuine.

There’s a hard tightness in my chest—it makes me feel sick. I can see Colbey saying stuff at me, but it’s like I can’t hear him over my own thoughts.

“I’ve got to get out.”

“No, Hayden, don’t!” I don’t give Colbey the chance—pushing his arms away when he tries to hold me. I dart for the door and run outside.

I welcome the air hitting my face, yet it doesn’t cool me down as much as I wished. And so I keep running. Down the street. Away from the house. Away from Colbey. Away from that horror. Hurting from Colbey doing this.

My head is in agony. I try to battle against it all, find some way to object to what he is saying. To find an end where I can make sense of it all. I have to. But somehow, through the chaos, I’m doing exactly what I shouldn’t be doing. Overthinking.

I stop and suddenly scream in anger. It’s just one problem after another. After another. After another.

I’ve known Cassio for months now.

I’d speak to my friends to ask, but they won’t answer. He was with Jared and his friends once when they beat me up, but there’s no way

I'm going to try and contact them. I race through my mind the times I've met up with Cassio because I know there's proof somewhere.

Then I know.

"So what are we looking for exactly?" Aunt Sandra asks by the doorway of the office at Mt. Okesea when I switch the computer screen on and begin flicking through the dates listed.

"Just need to see if somebody was here on a certain day," I answer vaguely while trying to give enough so she doesn't change her mind about letting me be here—she's even closed the small hut because she's working alone.

"Aaaah, like some CSI detecting? We're checking an alibi? Nice."

Aunt Sandra asks more humorous questions, such as what our detective names are, but my focus is on the screen.

The settings vanish, and then I'm shown on the full screen a view of the walkway leading up from the small hut to the gateway. It's the correct thing I want to see; I'm watching footage from the security cameras. In particular, the camera positioned behind the gateway and facing down. I check the date and the time on the screen just to make sure it's the right day I clicked. It is.

I skip through the footage for a while as it starts from the morning. If I want proof to show Colbey that Cassio is real, then this will be it. I wait impatiently for the footage to hurry up. Everything on the screen moves fast, but not fast enough. My foot taps rapidly against the floor.

Andrew comes out from under the gateway and goes down to the hut. I slow the recording down. He chats to me while I'm inside the small hut with Kamala.

"Is that the person we want?" I hear Aunt Sandra ask. With my eyes glued to the screen, I answer that he isn't. I watch myself leave the hut and walk with Andrew and then disappear under the gateway.

A chill slices my skin. This is footage from the evening Andrew came and threatened me outside Mt. Okesea.

I let the recording play as normal. I wait intently because I know what happens next—after Andrew threatens me, Cassio arrives to talk to me. And more importantly, we sit on the small wall beside the walkway. The small wall that's in view of the security camera.

I stare, leaning in closer to the screen and with such attention. I begin to think we're never going to arrive—when we do.

No—I do.

I appear at the bottom of the screen, walking a little along the walkway, and then I sit down on the small wall.

My eyes wait at the bottom, waiting to see Cassio. But he doesn't come into view. *He can't be out of shot in the photos at the park and this footage as well?* But I guess the camera may not have got Cassio because I can see myself talking away.

The group Kamala dealt with begin to head up the walkway. They go by, momentarily looking at me, but I continue to talk. Looking somewhat upset after what Andrew did before. It hurts to relive all this.

Feeling hopeless with the result, I move in to switch the computer screen off—when my eyes drift up and watch the centre of the screen.

There I am, sat on the wall. And I'm talking. My hands move as I speak. My head shaking.

My eyebrows furrow at the screen. Something's off. I thought Cassio was off camera, and if that were the case, then I'd be facing left to the gateway, near towards the camera.

But I'm not.

I'm looking to my right, down to the small hut, which is in shot. And there's nobody in between. There's just me.

The hairs on my arm prickle. My head bursts a new punch of tremendous agony. I watch in disbelief. I'm there on screen, talking to nobody beside me.

"Are you talking to Kamala? Why didn't you just go back to the hut?"

Pain ensues from Aunt Sandra's words—only confirming my horror. It's just me on the wall. No Cassio. Nobody. There's no one there where he should be—to where I'm talking to.

I glance to the small hut.

Kamala is in there. She's looking right at me—watching with confusion across her face—seeing me talk to myself.

I feel ill.

Everything around me feels off.

Somebody speaks behind me, but it all sounds muffled.

I get up, yet everything is almost moving. The computer. The desk. The walls. The floor. All of it is rocking, and it's throwing me off balance. Cassio isn't real.

How does any of this make sense?

"I gotta go," I mumble. I turn to make my way over to leave.

"Hey, you don't look so good."

Aunt Sandra isn't alone anymore by the door. Zeke's there, too.

"I'm fine." I need to leave.

"Hayden, is everything okay?" He asks. "Look, I've—"

I walk by Zeke and head out of the office.

It all feels tight. My legs. My arms. My stomach. My bones. The clothes I even have on seem to have shrunk and are strangling me.

I twist on alert—people are screaming. There's a loud eruption. I think it's my heart. But I hear water splashing down from somewhere behind. The mountain.

I'm so confused with everything—I just keep walking out of Mt. Okesea and then turn to go along the car park. Alone.

Have I been seeing Cassio this entire time? How? Why? It doesn't make sense. Nothing ever seems to make any sense.

A car beeps. I look vaguely to the side. The car pulls a little ahead of me. It's Colbey.

I intend to walk on. I can't deal with any of this.

"Hayden," I hear him say as he quickly gets out of the car.

Hearing his voice makes everything suddenly become real all at once. My breathing kicks in to become fast and in a panic. It's like I've done a marathon, yet it's only been a few steps.

I up my pace—hoping to get by him. But he reaches out and grabs my shoulder. I instantly try to smack his arm away.

"No. No. Get off!" I spit as I try to free myself from Colbey's hold. Everything inside me has escalated. "He's real. He was there!"

"Hayden, it's okay."

But it's not okay. None of it is!

I try to keep pushing Colbey off, but he doesn't budge. And I just panic and ramble on more.

"I was chatting to Cassio at work. But he wasn't on camera. He wasn't there!"

My legs cave, and I abruptly drop down to the ground. "I saw him, Colbey. I saw him."

Colbey kneels. He tries to reassure me as I quickly repeat the last words.

I lean back against the front wheel of the car behind me. He tells me to calm down, breathe and every other peaceful method under the sun, but I just can't stop. Because something's wrong. Something isn't right. Something's—I smack my hands over my mouth to force myself to stop.

My chest rises irregularly. I'm breathing through my nose. I impulsively want to listen to music or do some origami to calm my thoughts as they spin madly around. Despite all the reasons, though, I don't—because it makes me think of Tokyo.

I just pay attention to my breathing.

At some point, I notice Colbey is sitting opposite me on the ground. I don't look at him, though, not until I can eventually speak again.

"This has happened before, hasn't it?"

There are so many questions in my mind—but only one I have about Colbey.

He looks across at me, and I answer it myself, "Those questions you asked me at home sounded like you knew more than I did."

Colbey glances down at his feet. Ashamed or confused with how to respond, I'm not sure, but I take it as a yes.

"What's wrong with me?" I ask.

I ask because that's really what this is all about. Clearly something isn't right.

"This isn't the place—"

"Just tell me, please."

I wait, begging.

Colbey takes a moment.

"Back in Georgia, Cassio was your best friend. You met him at school last year, and you guys sort of really clicked. You'd hang out all the time. Kind of inseparable, really. You were quite different but somehow seemed to get on well."

Through the hurting in my head, I try to recall what Colbey is saying, but there's nothing. "Why don't I remember him then? I mean, the times I was with him."

"After the accident near Farm Bridge, your brain sort of—I can't remember the terminology of it, but you received selective amnesia. There's short-term and long-term amnesia, but there are other types where part of the brain can make people forget more specific aspects. Set periods. Occasions. And people. In this case, Cassio. It's rare, but it does happen."

"But why Cassio?"

I catch Colbey hesitating. But I must know.

"A few days after Mom left, you received a text from Cassio, and you suddenly left the house. You took Robin's car without us knowing and drove off."

As Colbey says this, the ache in my head returns and becomes extremely sore. It rapidly throbs. And getting worse each time. "I didn't take her car because I was upset about Mom?"

"No. You went off for Cassio. You headed to Farm Bridge on

purpose," Colbey pauses. His eyes seem to somehow get more serious. He thinks it's too much.

I hiss for him to tell me. The pain in my head is unbearable now but I need to know.

"You must understand none of this is on you. You went to the bridge, but when you got there, there was nothing you could do. You found Cassio in the river. He killed himself."

I scrunch my fists; there's a tremendous outbreak of pain in my brain. I hold a long blink with my eyes as if that might remove it. It doesn't.

"Why?" *Why would Cassio kill himself?*

Everything abruptly blurs. My breathing fast and short. In a matter of seconds, I find it hard to breathe.

"Hayden? Are you okay?"

I can see myself back in the toilets on the floor, with my old brown rucksack, and all the zips are working as I shove my belongings in, and Cassio is there helping me up—*that didn't happen at the toilets in Kingsgate Lee High.* And the toilet doors are red. I'm at the school toilets back in Georgia.

We're then eating together inside at the cafeteria. Cassio and me. Then we're in my old house, watching TV with my family. Then, at a field playing soccer. Then shaking hands while we're sat on the edge of a bridge.

The agony in my head erupts. The hiss I give out turns into a yell. I slump back against the car—my back aching from the impact on the tyre. My heart thumps madly. My breathing becomes irrational.

I place a hand on my forehead. I open my eyes. There's a frosty outline of Colbey. He's moving towards me.

Everything inside comes alive with hurt, yet everything around me gets further away. I try to fight the pain. But it gets too much.

36.

The first thing I sense is the stale smell of something. Then I hear the occasional beep. My eyes slowly open but then feel stung by the bright lights. There are white and partially grey tiles dotted around the lights above me, and when I tilt my head, I see I am on a hospital bed. I'm wearing the white hospital robe, which I reckon is what caught my nose. However, it's the room full of doctors staring directly at me that catches my attention.

I wonder if it's a memory from one of the times I was in the hospital in Georgia. But as I look closer, I realise these doctors look different. I don't see anybody I know.

They ask how I feel and the usual stuff you'd expect doctors to question, such as can I remember my name, when was I born, and do I know what year it is. They ask me what I can remember, to which I reply, "Which part?"

I give it some time to try and think. Slowly, I tell them what I can remember—from when Colbey brought me into our home after I was sick from running to sitting against a car in Mt. Okesea's car park and everything we talked about until it goes blank, and I remember no more. The doctors make notes on their clipboards. Clearly something I say is either really good or really bad. Even some of their eyebrows rise the first time I mention Cassio.

The main doctor, a young black-haired woman who tells me I can call her Jules, informs me I had a serious panic attack. Unsure how exactly to reply, I take her word for it.

She continues to ask the more pivotal questions. And every time I answer, she asks more in-depth questions. *How much do you remember before these events? Can you recall what happened the day you took your sister's car back in Georgia? Can you remember why you took it?* And so on…

And the truth is I do.

I know somebody might say I'm thinking I do because Colbey told me and that I must be just imagining and believing that that must be the truth, yet I honestly do remember. I can recall more than what Colbey said outside Mt. Okesea. There are more memories, and they're in more detail. Conversations I had with Cassio in Georgia. Eventful times I spent with him.

I remember everything.

It's strange. When I used to try and remember certain parts of my life—from after Mom left us to the second hospital visit—my head would push back, and everything up there would get fuzzy and hurt to the point where I couldn't function anymore, yet when Jules asks me all these questions related to those times and people and events, I feel nothing. Emptiness.

But then the emotions kick in—the happiness of the friendship with Cassio to then that night he died. It all comes back, so real and so raw, that I begin to overwhelmingly blub in dismay.

When I wake up again, it isn't smell or sight that's the first thing I sense. It's a sound. Colbey and Robin, to be precise. They're bickering. I watch them further down, sitting on chairs at either side of my bed. A TV remote clutched in their hands over my legs.

A short laugh comes out when the view becomes too much. They both turn to face me. I watch in silence when neither says anything. Smiles slowly appear on their faces, and that relaxes me.

The door opens, and Dad walks in. There's a slight startled look lodged on his face when he notices I'm awake. He puts down the tray of coffees on the table and comes over to me. And then he hugs me. I'm taken back a bit, but I accept the hug. It's weird. I'd normally be awkward about this, but as Dad holds me tightly, I feel comfort.

When he pulls back, there are tears down his cheeks.

"I'm so sorry, son," he says, looking down at me. I reply that it's okay. He doesn't seem to accept it, though. "It shouldn't have all come out like this. This isn't your fault. Or yours." Dad turns and places a hand on Colbey's shoulder. Nevertheless, Colbey lowers his head.

"I don't think anybody can really force their brain to become clear," I say. I then look on to Colbey. "And it isn't your fault. You had no choice but to tell me. It would have been worse if you let me continue to believe Cassio was real and that I was okay."

Colbey looks up and gives me a small nod. I know he knows that is the truth, but I can tell he's still beating himself up inside. I place a hand on his to show it's okay.

Dad wipes a tear away from under his eye. I want to tell him to stop it because it's making me upset. But I stop myself.

"Can I ask something?" I ask instead. Dad nods, and Colbey and

Robin continue to sit silently. "How come you never told me?"

I catch Robin glancing over at Colbey—they both look up to Dad. He shuffles on the spot.

"Hayden, you need to know we wanted to. But when the doctors discovered you had no recollection of Cassio or even the reason you took the car and had the accident, they said only your brain was the one who could let you know, for if the truth was pushed at you, your brain might not want to accept it, and it could affect you and you could—"

"—have something like a breakdown?" I finish.

"Or worse."

I try to take it in. I mean, if I were in their shoes, I wouldn't have known what to do, but if the doctors recommended that I had to remember myself, then I suppose I can't argue.

"But what about Mom?"

"None of us liked that you thought you took Robin's car and then crashed it because you were upset over Mom leaving," Colbey answers, leaning towards me just a fragment. Robin briefly turns away. "But the doctors said you could receive serious and permanent damage if you didn't take the truth well—and we were all out of our depth, and nobody knew what we could say to make you think it was something else without mentioning Cassio. The doctors believed it was better that way—till you remembered."

"Is that why I went back into hospital? The second time. I had the truth pushed at me?"

Dad tightens the grip he has on his wrist with his other hand. There's a sincere, humble glade of guilt across his face. It makes me feel guilty on my side.

"Nearly. You were fine at home with us. And, later on, you managed to return to school," Dad begins. "But then, one day in the kitchen, you told me you were heading to the movies with Cassio. And I tried to ask about it because I couldn't understand what you meant. But when I realised you thought he was alive still, I tried to carefully explain that he wasn't and—and you started to lose it. You stormed out to the garden, yelling at me when I tried to calm you down and explain. And when you freaked out, I had to call for help. I forced too much onto you, son, and you couldn't take it. But it caught me by surprise. I didn't know what to do. The doctors thought you might one day remember Cassio, but none of them thought that you would—you—you would imagine him."

"It's okay," I say as I look at Dad.

"No, I panicked. And I pushed you."

"That isn't on you."

"Perhaps," Dad contemplates. And now I do feel really guilty. Guilty over something that wasn't in my control. Wasn't in anybody's. But they're the ones who had to deal with it all.

"When you returned to the hospital, you still couldn't remember the accident and the truth—but then you also couldn't remember being at the hospital before and anything afterwards as well. All that time between. Gone. So, the doctors had no other suggestions but to not tell you," Colbey explains. "That we had to let your brain naturally remember. Except this time, we could look out for signs if you started imagining Cassio again."

"But I guess we failed on that too." Dad lowers his head.

"Don't say that."

"I thought a move would help start over. For us all. We never saw signs you were seeing him again, son. So we thought maybe we just needed to wait for you to just remember him. But it happened again."

I think it over, feeling terrible for how bad Dad feels. "But I remember everything about Cassio now. So why is this time different?"

"The doctors aren't sure. But they say it's a good sign," he answers.

I look around at my family. All staring quietly at me. Remorse. Almost shame. But I realise it's at themselves. Not me.

"I'm sorry you've had to go through this. You've had to put up with something when you shouldn't have had to. I'm sorry." Dad wants to object, but I don't break. "But this isn't on you. You all dealt with it the best you could, and that's all anybody can do."

Dad stares at me. So does Colbey. And Robin. There's nobody to blame. They need to know that. I need to know that.

Dad suddenly ruffles my hair. "You're right." I'm then embraced with another hug from him, and as he keeps me close, I hear him say, "I love you."

"I'm sorry, Hayden."

I turn away from the TV in my hospital room to look at Robin. Dad and Colbey have gone to get some food. "For what?"

Robin doesn't look away out of uncertainty. She doesn't move or give a nervous twitch like a shuffle in her seat. Robin just continues to keep her eyes on me. "For how I've been with you since we moved here. I know what you said earlier, but I need to apologise. With everything.

With how I was in the car the first day we went to school. How I was on the way to Jared Steele's party. Or when I found you drinking that night—although I did have a right to be annoyed with that last one."

"It's fine. I'm the reason we moved here, I know that. You had a life back home. A great life with lots of friends. And I took that away from you."

"No, that shouldn't be on you," Robin cuts in. "And it's no excuse, but I was so angry about moving that I let it cloud my judgment. You didn't even have a say in the matter of the move, but I pinned all the blame on you. That wasn't right. Even when I knew what was happening with you. I just found it hard moving here."

"But I've seen you with everybody at school. They all love you."

"Because I forced myself to. I had to work, like seriously work hard, to not make a mistake so I could be accepted," Robin explains. "You're supposed to celebrate your last year of high school with all those you grew up with. But I had that taken away. Last year *was* my last year with my best friends. Not now. I never got the time to appreciate it. Instead, mine was throwing me back in as the new girl. Senior year. Everybody in their groups already, wanting to revel with people they know and love—not with some new girl, somebody trying to fit in to get a glimpse of what it should be."

I feel for Robin. I never thought of it like that. I place my hand on her hand resting on the bed.

"But you managed to turn it around though. You have good friends here, too."

"Yeah. But even when I did, I used you as some punchbag to take my anger out on. And I shouldn't have. Family should be there for each other and always come first. We should know that more than most with Mom leaving us," Robin pauses, as if giving herself a moment to reflect on the last few months. "I don't like that it's taken this long to change me. But I'm sorry I wasn't there for you."

I find it hard and even confusing to see my sister like this. To be open. Well, she's always openly opinionated, but she's being honest to me without malice. And I know she means it. And I agree. I don't like that we've had to go through some rough times to be here, but it feels nice to be on the same page now.

"Thanks. And I know you say I shouldn't, but I'm sorry—not just for the move but for also not being there for you too." Because I am. Despite her moods towards me, I thought Robin had everything going for her in her life here.

"Thanks."

Robin smiles. She reclines back into the chair and pulls something out of the bag beside her. It's the Boston Hidden Gem book from Tovell's City Secrets I got her for Christmas. "How about you help me plan where I should visit when I'm at Boston before I throw the remote at the TV if I've got to watch another quiz show?"

I smile. "That would be nice."

It's late at night. Something wakes me up. I can't remember what I was dreaming about, whether it was good or bad, but the fact I managed to get some sleep on my own accord is pleasing.

I turn over, curious to see what might have disturbed my sleep.

Somebody is standing at the window. Looking out. I know who it is, though, before they turn around to me.

I had been wondering, no, more hoping, that I would get to see them again now that I can remember.

"I'm glad to see you're okay," Cassio says to me. He remains by the window. He looks like he always has every time I've seen him. Red hoody. Jeans. Trainers. It's what he wore the last time I saw him. But there's something a little different about him this time. I can't quite put a finger on what it is.

"Thanks," I reply. "I remember what happened now. Me. You. All of it. We met back in Georgia like we did here; you did belong to a group of guys that used to bully me. Yet you stopped them, and we became friends. We were close, right?"

"Very."

I wait to see if he'll say anymore, but he remains quiet.

"The other day, that pact we made outside mine when I was fixing the bike, that was a pact we actually did make back in Georgia?"

"Yes," Cassio answers. He stays on me. "After I apologised for being involved with those that hurt you and we started hanging out, you told me once when we were sat on Farm Bridge that I was your first real friend. So I decided we should make a pact—*to always be there for each other. And to never fixate on what's been done and help each other focus on what can be. No matter what*—it was so you'd know I'd be there for you, and you'd never have to be alone again."

I glance up at Cassio. "You left me, though."

"It wasn't an easy decision to make, Hayden."

"There shouldn't have been any decision to make but to keep living," I almost snap at Cassio from the hurt I'm remembering. He looks away for a second. I wait for him to speak. I have my memories now.

"You know that isn't fair. But once that thought was in my mind, it was hard to get it out."

"You should have talked to somebody, though. Someone at school. A therapist. Anybody, if not me," I say. I try hard to fight the irritation that's rising in me, but it's hard. So hard. Because he should be here. Alive.

"I know." Cassio steps towards the bed. I question if I want him to be any nearer to me right now because I feel like I could throw something at him. "But I was too scared. Too depressed. So hateful at myself."

"I knew things were difficult for you at home in the past, but you said it was all good with your mother and brothers. And you always seemed happy. To me, your family, and at school."

"Just because I showed it doesn't mean I was."

I think over his answer, and it makes me realise the times my friends and others have tried to keep quiet on their uncertainties. All those times I, myself, have tried to pretend to others here that I was okay. Lying that all was good to my friends when I knew the truth about Andrew. Trying to look okay before my family after the night of the Winter Snowdrop Ball and the video. Hiding my insecurities and that I felt like I had no control over anything in my life but my looks by focusing on exercising and saying to my family I was fine. All those times I was covering how I really felt.

"I get that," I then say to Cassio. "But you should have got help."

He nods—then he waits.

I do too. "Can I ask why?"

There's a beat of silence.

"Why did I kill myself?" Cassio says for me. "You already know, Hayden, I'm just an illusion of your imagination. A ghost from your mind."

I wait for his words to sink in. He basically means I'll only get from him whatever I already know.

"Yeah," I acknowledge. "I suppose I'm never going to find out, am I?"

I look up at Cassio.

He just continues to stare at me. There's a coat of sincerity spread over his face. Part of me wants to leap out of the hospital bed and punch it off him. Because I'm annoyed. I'm seriously angry that Cassio took his own life. We were close. And he didn't reach out and try to get help. He didn't give me or anybody the chance to save him from himself.

But instead, I feel ashamed of myself. This is about him. Not me.

"I'm sorry you never felt like you could reach out to me."

"I wanted too. But I was too scared to admit I wasn't okay," Cassio says. He takes a step forward. "It's not an easy thing to do, you know, break that pride to say you aren't, even though it's actually quite an ordinary thing a lot of people think. Just nobody likes to be honest when it's so personal. And to be honest, although I knew you and my family cared for me, that's the reason why it felt it would be the hardest to tell you guys. I'm sure you've seen it with yourself and others in your own dilemmas."

I nod. It's true. I have. "That doesn't mean I wished you'd have not gone for help, though."

Cassio nods.

"So the stuff you said about your family was true? I mean that I told myself," I correct because he is just my imagination right now. Cassio tells me that's true. "And the chat we had about the merry-go-round?"

"I mentioned that the day we made the pact. It was my way of warning you not to get stuck inside yourself. Because I was too far on the ride to get off."

I'm trying not to get emotional, because this is about him, but it's so hard that I can remember everything now and yet I still can't get any real answers. And there's nothing I can do to change his outcome.

"The night you did it. You sent a long text saying you're sorry and goodbye. And I knew where you were?"

My old phone broke in the accident, so Dad gave me a new phone after—I only remember the message now.

"We used to hang out at Farm Bridge a lot. Sit on the edge and watch the river come out from under the bridge and go into the distance. I said the last time we were there that it was a beautiful place to see the world end."

Short visions of what Cassio says come back to me.

It was a place where we could chat, from silly conversations to wondering where life might take us. We could sit on the edge and joke and laugh and watch the day go by.

We were there earlier that day with our rucksacks and food. I was perhaps too worried about my own concerns with Mom just leaving to notice if he was different—or realise what he meant. I don't know.

I feel awful.

But I remember that night—when it happened.

I drove madly in Robin's car to get there after I got the text. Then I pulled over on the bridge when I didn't see Cassio there. I leant over the ledge, searching desperately for him already in the water, hoping he was fine. Then I saw him. Stuck against some rocks in the middle of the river. Face down.

I drove down to a beck the road went beside, and I ran straight into the water. I swam as fast as I could to the rocks and carried Cassio back across. I dragged him up onto the beck. My body was tired and aching, but I didn't stop. I tried to resuscitate him. I cried through the hurt and fury as I tried to save my best friend. My only real friend. But it was too late. No amount of help could bring him back.

The ambulance arrived, and the paramedics told me what I already knew. I didn't save him. I was late. And I drove off, too upset and angry to pay attention to the roads—then I crashed into the tree.

"I know you wish you could have been quicker," Cassio says. I lift my head to listen. "That if you could have been that second faster getting there or taking me out of the river, then you might have saved me…but I was already gone."

My body hurts some more from his words. Hearing his voice say it. It makes me feel useless. Might be the truth, but it does. "That doesn't make me feel better."

"I know. But you need to know it."

I glance away, needing a moment to gather myself.

"And after it happened, after I left the hospital, I began to see you, even though I couldn't remember you? It's because of the pact, isn't it? I started imagining you at a time I felt low, and whenever I was lonely or hurt, and I didn't know where to go, I brought you to me," I say as it slowly begins to make sense—the notion had been there all along. The last piece of a jigsaw puzzle that had been missing finally found, having been in the open box the entire time staring at me.

Cassio nods. He's now beside me.

"But the real reason," I continue, "I was able to see you is that I felt guilty. We made a pact—to be there for each other, always. And you left—but it was me that let you down."

I breathe out, but I feel my hand shake. There's some sadness trying to escape from my eyes. Because what I'm saying is true.

"You never let me down. This was something out of anybody's control."

"But you needed me," I sob. "You made me promise we'll look out for each other, and I couldn't stop you from doing this."

"Because I never let you," Cassio answers. "I never wanted you to think me ending my life was your fault. And I didn't know you'd take those words so severely to then imagine me after I was gone. I hate what it's done to you. The entire reason I did it was because I didn't want anybody I cared about, including my family or you, to get hurt. To see me start to show my cracks. But I guess I never truly knew the consequences it might have." He keeps his eyes on me. "And I'm sorry. You imagined me because you needed me, and you were able to form me from a guilt that you felt you deserved—but it shouldn't be there. You've been holding onto me because you can't seem to accept that this isn't on you."

"Because you made me feel like I wasn't good enough. Enough to keep you alive," I cry. Argue almost. I rub my arm across my eyes, but the emotion doesn't want to stop coming out.

Cassio looks at me. "I know. And I hate that—but you have nothing to blame yourself for. Maybe your brain tried to block me and everything about that night out because it knew how much you were putting on yourself when you did. And yet, some part deep down must have known you had to remember me. 'Cause I'm here now, Hayden, so you can know that you didn't do anything wrong. It was me that broke the pact, and I let you take the fall."

Through the flow of tears, I find my head trying to agree with Cassio. My eyes have given in to the pain of it all.

Inside, my head wants to believe what Cassio is saying is the truth. I'm trying to believe his words, but part of my body still wants to fight that he's wrong and that it was my fault. I should have done more.

But my mind wins. I cry, accepting his words—but my heart aches even more from the truth.

I take a while to try and gain some control of my emotions, but, in the end, I let them pour out—long before I speak again.

"If I had a breakdown because I discovered the truth before and then forgot it all, how come I can remember everything this time?"

I watch as Cassio's lips curl into a smile. "Because the reason you need me is no longer required." I stare at him quizzically. "You're not alone."

"It feels like it."

"Hayden. You have a family who's always been there for you, and you've seen how much they care. But now you've also got what you've been longing for. Friends. Friends who love you."

I try to think it over. He means Zeke, Antonia, Dacre and Billie.

"They're not exactly speaking to me right now."

"Then change it," Cassio says. I almost scoff because he says it like it's that easy. "They still care for you."

"But I don't get it—I still saw you when I became friends with them."

"Because all this still needed to happen. You still had to remember the truth."

He puts his hand on top of mine. It's light. Soft. A feather almost. Because there's nothing there. "But now you know—you don't need me anymore."

The faint touch slips off my hand. I look down and see just my own. I glance back up and see Cassio heading to the door.

I'm confused. There's so much I want to ask. So much I need help with. Myself. My friends. Everything.

"Does this mean I won't see you again?" I ask, sobbing. Because although I know I must be ready, it still feels hard to think I won't see him again.

Cassio stops at the door. He turns around.

"You are ready. I'm glad you're good—and that you will be okay."

He gives me another smile of reassurance.

"Thanks," I say and then realise, "Doesn't it seem weird you're telling me that if you're supposed to be just my imagination?"

He chuckles a little. "You're looking at it the wrong way."

Before I know how to respond, Cassio pulls down on the handle. The door opens, and as the light from the hallway grows in, I watch in sadness as Cassio Socorro fades away.

I stare at the empty doorway for quite a while. For the entire time, I'm unsure what to do. However, the sadness inside begins to turn. There's still sadness there, but there's also something else.

Peace.

I stay rested up against my bed, watching the open door and listening to any noises down the hallway. But at some point, when I go through everything that has happened this last year, my eyes well up, and I begin to cry.

Only then do I realise, through the heartache, that last week was New Year's Day.

37.

Over the next few days, I stay in the hospital. Just so the doctors can keep an eye on me, so Jules reassures me. They give me more tests and brain scans and do regular checks with the usual *how are you feeling today* criteria. Mostly, though, I'm on my hospital bed in my own room.

Dad's relentless in being here all the time, but Colbey and Robin are able to convince him to see sense that it isn't fair on everybody who's got booked appointments at his dentistry. He comes straight to the hospital as soon as he finishes work, though. Every evening.

I think it's all sweet. The things that he does for me. I realise sometimes I don't give my dad as much credit as I should for being there for me. He's stood by me, Colbey and Robin throughout this entire time. And he's always tried to support us.

So I tell him this one night.

He says that although he never expects us to say it, he likes that he got to hear his child mention how much he means to them.

"It's nice to know I'm doing something okay," he explains, smiling through his tears.

Soon, Colbey goes back to work, and Robin returns to school. I may have been concerned when the day was looming, but it's kind of nice to have some alone time. The doctors and nurses see me occasionally, and there are also social times to go and chat with some of the other patients. However, I'm okay with being by myself. And I believe this is because, for the first time in a long while, I feel comfortable alone.

And he never visits me again.

I do get a surprise visit at the hospital one day after school has begun, though. On a Monday afternoon, Mr Gauran visits me.

"Well, this is nice," he begins as he sits down and lets his eyes check the place out. "And it's got a much sweeter view than my office."

"Yeah, I heard a nurse say it's got top marks on EmpireRoomRate," I jest from in bed.

Mr Gauran turns to me. There's a large grin on his face.

"I think that's top marks for you, too," he says. I understand what he means straightaway and smile back. My scale of humour. "Although I hope this will be the only time we have a meeting here."

"So this is official business?"

"Not exactly. But I'd be lying if I said your dad didn't want me to check on you as your family are going to be later than normal to get here," Mr Gauran admits. Of course, he did! But I'm not annoyed. "But I wanted to see you anyway. There are a few things to tell you."

He begins to explain that because of the online bullying and humiliation I received on the night of the Winter Snowdrop Ball, Chloe Cassadentini got suspended for her actions. I itch a little at the sound of her name. I think of that night and, in a flicker, all of the moments and messages I had with Tokyo, but I keep my hands by my sides. I refuse to scratch the itch.

Apparently, Chloe entered school the other day and was sent straight back out by Principal Shaw. The people who were with Chloe in the limousine that night also got into trouble and suspended, but not as severely.

I'm not entirely sure how Mr Gauran expects me to react. If I'm meant to stand on my bed and throw my fist into the air with glee or if I'm to make some smart remark that Chloe and the others deserved it. But I don't think any celebration is right. All I do is quietly stay in bed.

However, Chloe will be returning to school next Monday. The same day I'll be going back—if the doctors give me the all-clear later this week. The thought is a little overwhelming. I openly say that to Mr Gauran but add that I know we'll have to see each other at some point. I can't really hide away from it.

"I admire your bravery."

"Wouldn't say it was that. It's just she was in the wrong, and I shouldn't have anything to be ashamed of."

Mr Gauran nods. "That's very wise. I imagine it will be tough returning to school next week but remembering that should help."

I try to take in what he says, but he then continues to speak.

"Recently, I've been hassled day in and day out since term's started by a group of students. Asking the same thing every time—wanting to know if you are okay and if they can see you." I look over in surprise at Mr Gauran and ask who. "A Mr Dacre Ronsan. Miss Antonia Lu. Mr Zeke Palladino. And a Miss Billie Mendoza."

I find it hard to digest when I hear those names. I'm even more stumped when Mr Gauran adds they've apparently been asking Robin at school too and have even been ringing my dad's dentistry to ask if they can see me.

They've not been told anything except I'm fine and am in hospital.

I can't quite believe it. They want to see me? The last time I saw them, they wanted nothing to do with me. Because I had betrayed them. The thought becomes overwhelming. I thought I had lost them for good. And here I am, hearing that they're asking for me.

I begin to tell Mr Gauran that they can come when I abruptly stop—the excitement that was in me fades away.

"What's wrong?"

"Things weren't great between us before the Christmas break. Before all this." I feel a little vulnerable, but Mr Gauran's intentions are only ever good, I remind myself.

"Well, if they're reaching out to you, then that's a good sign."

"Yeah, but I was in the wrong," I explain and continue. "And, I don't want them to just want to see me and maybe be my friends again out of pity. Because I'm in here. Like it's some obligation or guilt."

In his chair, Mr Gauran lifts his leg and rests the foot on top of the other leg. "That's understandable. You know, trust and forgiveness, they both rely on each side to be open to work."

"I do."

If there's something I've learnt from this, it's that trust and forgiveness must come from either side. "I just don't think I deserve it. Not till I've proven to them to forgive me. A reason of sorts."

I look up to Mr Gauran. He nods carefully.

"Sounds like you know what you have to do."

Kind of. A little fear creeps over me at the prospect of it all.

I fold my arms against my stomach, hoping for some courage. Then I face Mr Gauran.

"How can we stop bad things from happening?" I ask—because I realise I'm scared. I'm terrified my friends don't want to accept me—that maybe their intention is only to find out they didn't play a part in landing me in hospital so they can then move on from me. Yet I'm also nervous that if they do allow me back into their lives that I might mess it up again somehow.

"Isn't that a question we wish we all knew the answer to…" Mr Gauran replies. "The truth is we can't. I think the world would be an entirely different place if we could stop every single bad thing. But just because you're scared doesn't mean you should try and hide from the world. Because if you constantly try to prevent the bad, and hide away in fear so you don't experience it, then you'll also prevent all the good. And that's no life. I can't give you the answers or reassurance you wish to have, Hayden. I can't tell you if things will work great with your friends because what you're asking for is impossible. Only you will know in time."

He puts his resting leg down to lean a little closer to me. "Some things, unfortunately, in life are out of our ability to divert. Sometimes, we must be brave with those hard-hitting truths. Sometimes, we must face the unexpected, the unknown or the unwanted. And that's okay—because it's how we deal with it that gives us control over it, that it cannot define us but can, in fact, also give us that incredible life we all wish to have. And I think you've already had a feel of what that's like. I think you're more aware of it than you know."

I'm given the all-clear on Friday by Jules. I'm nervous about returning home, but when Dad and I pull up outside the house, I somehow don't feel as scared. I've had so many tests that Jules and the other doctors must have some confidence to let me leave the hospital, so I should believe it, too.

It's the evening. Both Colbey and Robin are home to welcome me back, which I appreciate. And thank goodness they are because when Dad offers to cook tonight, it takes us all to convince him not to.

"He's just come out of hospital. The last thing he wants is to return the same night because you gave him food poisoning," Colbey says, pointing a thumb at me. I smirk at the joke, but Dad doesn't seem too impressed.

"Don't act so appalled by my offering," Dad says from the other side of the breakfast bar. "I'm like America's best chef."

Robin, Colbey and I stare at each other and then at Dad. He looks rather smug with his remark.

"Wow, it's only been a few days and I think we've already found ourselves the Understatement of the Year," Robin says.

Colbey nods.

Dad drops his jaw to look completely shocked. I know it's just put on, but I begin to laugh. The others join in, and Dad's jaw retracts as his lips turn into a smile.

Fortunately, we result in getting a Chinese takeout instead.

I tag along with Colbey to get the food. However, I ask if we can briefly visit Mt. Okesea on the way.

"I don't think you should be wanting to work so soon," he comments.

"I'm not. I just need to do something."

Colbey doesn't ask any more questions, yet he obliges and takes me to Mt. Okesea.

"Don't be long; you know what Dad's like if we're late back with the food," Colbey says when I get out of the car and see the big mountain.

I tell him I won't and then head towards the entrance.

My eyes are drawn to the side of the car park. Tension builds inside; the last time I was here, I was over there and having a panic attack beside a car after discovering the truth. I know my body wants to tighten. I can feel it slowly trying to close in.

I take a deep breath—a few in fact—of the warm night air. I relax and go under the gateway.

The rotas haven't changed since I left—I can see the person who I wanted to speak to is standing alone in the small hut.

"Hayden!" Kamala says. She doesn't hide any surprise. The excitement in the tone of her voice is what pleases me and forces me to grin. She leaves the hut and comes around to meet me. "Aunt Sandra and Zeke told me what happened. How are you?"

Colbey must have rung the ambulance that night and then shouted for help. And with the small hut being the first place to come to, it would have been Aunt Sandra and Zeke who heard. And if Colbey hadn't, they probably would have gone to inspect why an ambulance had suddenly pulled into the car park.

"I'm okay. Well, as can be expected."

"That's good. I'm pleased to see you are better." She pushes back her purple hair from her eyes. "I've been trying to find you at school to see how you are."

I never realised Kamala might be concerned for me. It's nice. "Yeah, I'm returning on Monday."

"Ah, that would explain it. But that's good you're coming back," she replies, still smiling for me.

"Not sure if I said it before, but you were amazing in the talent show."

"Yeah, I think you did when you left here," Kamala answers. "I nearly wasn't in the show—I bailed in applying for the auditions but then decided the week before to try. Had to do a lot of ass kissing to Chloe Cassadentini to let me enter."

I try to brush over Chloe's name. "Why the change?"

"I realised I was sick of not doing what I want."

I twist my body more to face Kamala. "Really? I thought you always did what you wanted. I mean, you pretty much got me to do whatever you wanted on our first shift together here."

"What do you mean got? I still could," Kamala grins. "No, even I have things I'm uncomfortable to share." I don't speak. I think there's part of her wishing I did, but she goes on. "Home's quite strict—my mother didn't speak to me for a month when I changed my hair to purple."

She repositions her stance a little. "But this dancing, which my parents weren't completely on board with either, is something that makes me feel better—and I just realised I shouldn't care what others think if I truly like it. Like I respect my family and my friends, but this is my life. And I knew if I could face my family when I told them, then I should be able to tell my friends and face people I don't ever speak to—and enter the show."

I stand in silence. Here's this tough girl, always opinionated and hard-going, and I just thought she's like that because that's who she is. But that isn't the case.

"Well, I'm glad you went for it. And for what it's worth, when me and the others saw you dance on stage, I could tell it was your thing. See it was something you love."

I expect Kamala to just give a mere nod or remain still when, to my surprise, she smiles. A genuine smile.

"Thanks. So, what brings you back to Mt. Okesea? Are you here to see Aunt Sandra? She's—"

"No," I answer, cutting her off. "I've actually come to see you."

Kamala tilts her head and then scratches her single blonde eyebrow.

I then explain why I wanted to see her, and I ask if she is free this weekend to help me with something.

"That's pretty cool," Kamala says after I've finished telling her my idea. I stand there waiting, hoping she will agree. What I've asked her to help with is a lot. Kamala doesn't owe me anything, and she doesn't have to waste her time for me. She has no reason to. "Luckily for you, I'm not working this weekend. And I love the idea. I'm in."

38.

Monday soon arrives. I was okay this morning, but as I get in the car and I'm on my way, I soon start to become horrendously nervous. At some point, Robin, who's driving, must notice because she keeps looking over and trying to talk. I don't know exactly what she's on about because all my mind can do is think that in a few minutes I will be arriving at school.

I had been so busy over the weekend meeting with Kamala that I had not let myself adjust to the fact that Monday was approaching and that I'd be seeing everybody. I mean, I knew it; I just didn't let it all sink in. Everybody will be there. Every student.

Robin takes a turn—in the opposite direction to school. I ask what she's doing.

"Let's go a little later," she answers. I thank her—normally, the thought of skiving school would make Robin's toenails curl.

She doesn't ask why I'm nervous, but I tell her. And when I explain, she never argues or interrupts. At the end, after I say it all, she simply says to me, "So tell them."

I wonder what she means. But I get my phone out when Robin finds somewhere to park, and I open KingsgateLeeConnect and start writing.

Hayden Mallard

Some of you will know me. Some will see this and wonder who I am. And some will simply know me as the boy in that prank video from the night of the Winter Snowdrop Ball.

I joined here in September, after moving from Georgia, and back there, I didn't have many friends. I was even bullied because of it. How ridiculous is that? And last year, I had a rough year in Georgia, so as you can imagine, when I moved to a new school in another state, I was beyond frightened. It seemed I had a right to be because I was bullied here too. Just for being the new guy. I hated it here.

But then there was a group of people. A small bunch who noticed me. They asked me if I wanted to join them, and they let me in. And I don't know why, but they kept having me around. And I loved it. The times we spent together. The random gatherings, the hilarious conversations, and the fun adventures. All of it.

However, because of other factors in my life, I was always so worried about my actions in case I might hurt somebody or destroy things. My friends. And my family. Or that I would be the one to be hurt. And so, because I had never had something like this before, I was really riding on a lot to not mess this up.

But I made a mistake. I discovered something that could hurt one of them. I was so scared that I let fear take over me, and yet I still ended up ruining the best thing I ever had. I was willing to let them be misguided and suffer, knowing how it would end, just so I was safe from danger.

They trusted me. And I broke that. And I need them to know that I'm sorry. For everything.

A great counsellor here told me that sometimes we must be brave with the truth and face the unexpected, the unknown or the unwanted. So this is me trying to be brave. I am owning up to my mistakes. And this is the beginning step, of many, to my friends in apologising to them for what I did.

But this post isn't just to make a public apology. This is also a statement. Fear has been controlling my life more than I actually knew until now. Got me overthinking. Panicking. It has stopped me from doing things. Made me self-doubt myself. Knocked my confidence to take that risk in life. And I know everybody has felt like this in one way or another. Fear has manipulated us all somehow in some part of our lives.

And I'm done with it. I don't want my fears to make me miss life. If I try to prevent any bad from ever happening, I'll also never be letting any good come into my life. And that isn't right. I don't want it to take control of me. I must take control.

I don't know why the person who did the prank on me before Christmas did it. I'm sure they had their own fears, but if you're wondering if I'm ever going to talk about that prank, expecting me to rant or pour my heart into how hurt I am for you to feed on, then all I have to say is this…

I don't care.

From,
Hayden

I see the big sign introducing us to Kingsgate Lee High as Robin drives the car in. I post the message, and when Robin pulls into a space, I hand her my phone.

As she reads, there are different changes in her face. She'll hate the bullying parts, upset she wasn't there to help, but that's because I made it oblivious to people.

The first thing she does when she pulls her eyes away from the phone is hug me. "I am proud of you. Aren't you concerned about what others might comment?"

"Did you not read the last part?" It was a joke, but there's still concern lingering in her eyes. "It's fine. I have a friend who's disabled comments on the post."

However, staring at the empty yard, knowing students will be on their lunch break soon, there's some apprehension in me.

"Do you want to walk in now? I can come with you if you—"

"Absolutely not," I say. "I mean, not till people are already out."

"Okay."

Writing the post probably didn't calm me down immediately like I wanted it to do—it probably brought me more to people's attention—yet it needed to be done. I had to say my peace with it. So I can move on.

"Hey." Robin shifts her body to face me more. "This is big, I get that. But those doctors wouldn't have given you the all-clear if they didn't think you were ready. You wouldn't have done that post if you didn't know you could do as you said. Have some faith in yourself."

There's a little tremor from me when I breathe out after Robin finishes. Those last words ring in line with what I heard at the hospital. Robin's right. I just have to believe in myself. And even Mr Gauran has said it to me. And now I must do it.

"Thank you."

Robin smiles. "It's fine. Besides, any issues, you call me, and I'll sort them out." I chuckle. "And that's no Understatement of the Year. It's the truth. I care about you."

I fold my lips in, just so they don't suddenly blub anything remotely embarrassing out at her. I return the smile back instead. "Me too."

There's a faint sound of the bell ringing. We look out the front window. Students begin to pour out of the doors. It's lunch.

"No time like the present."

Before I can ask what, Robin forces me to squish against my seat as in one swift move she quickly leans over, unbuckles my seatbelt and opens my car door. "You can do it."

I try to give my sister another smile as we get out of the car, but this time it's a little forced.

When Robin sees her friends in the distance, she asks if I want her to walk with me to the cafeteria. I tell her I'm fine. With my acceptance, she heads over to her friends—but I wonder whether it was the right call.

I look down at the time on my phone. I don't have long.

I make my way towards the school. It feels like I'm trying so hard not to think people might be watching me that the function of how to walk or look casual has been taken out of my brain.

When I reach the building and head down the hallways, that's when I notice that people are staring in my direction. They aren't so obvious as to point at me, but people go by with their eyes towards me. Then the flutter of whispers come from all corners.

Is that him? It's that boy from the video! Poor kid, as if he dared to come back, I wouldn't dream of it. He's the guy who did the post today.

I tighten the grip on my rucksack as I push on.

As I expected, the cafeteria is packed with students. Heads begin to turn. However, I go to the doors without glancing over and venture outside.

The courtyard is just as full. People already sat at tables or stood in their groups talking. I immediately look to the left at the end row of tables nearest to the field. There, to the side, I see them. My friends. All sat with their trays of food at the usual table. Zeke looking full swing in conversation, probably some deep film debate. And there's Billie. Still rocking the cool ponytail look. She looks happy.

Seeing them terrifies me, but my goodness I've missed them.

A loud shriek rings across the yard, which somehow develops into a giggle. My eyes dart to the source. Chloe Cassadentini.

She's laughing through her smile at something said to her. A crunching ache occurs in my heart as I watch her with some friends a few tables away.

It's just weird. And horrible. And wrong.

I check the time. There's enough time. I head over to Chloe's table.

"Look who it is," some guy on the table says as I approach. Chloe spins her body around so she can see me. My mouth is dry.

"Don't worry, I'm not stopping," I reply. The guy's face scrunches, and he slips back down in his place.

I look to Chloe. She's sat with her legs crossed and a face like she's sucking a lollipop of boredom.

"I'm not here to give some big speech to convince you to change your mind about me. You've made it pretty clear. I just find it hard to believe that after all of it, everything we've talked about, things you said you've never told others, and we opened to each other, that you'd do that. I get you might discover I'm Brisbane and decide for you that looks are more important than the connection—you could have just told me—but to do what you did…to attack me…I never thought the person I messaged could do that."

As I say this, there's no change in Chloe. If anything, there's more annoyance stretching across her face.

"You said as Tokyo that you were frightened to change and be more yourself because of how your friends might react, but I didn't think you'd succumb to that," I tell Chloe. "I just hope that prank you did, after all those emails between us, was worth it."

I don't dare give Chloe the satisfaction for anybody else to speak. I turn around and walk away.

I shove my hands in my pockets—they're trembling. I'm nervous, riled up, proud of myself…everything rolled into one.

I walk on, knowing I don't have long left.

"Hayden."

My eyes adjust to what's ahead of me. It's Jasmine.

"Hayden, are you okay? Did I just hear what you said to Chloe—"

"I can't right now," I say as I continue to walk by her. I look across the courtyard and see Kamala watching. I turn my head briefly around to Jasmine as I go, "I've got to do something."

If Jasmine heard, she probably doesn't like what I had to say to her friend—but I had to say something.

I take a deep breath. That's one thing I've confronted. And now the next. I look ahead, but it seems they've already noticed me. My friends.

"Hayden?"

They get up. It feels warm to see the delight on their faces when they look at me. It's like nothing had ever happened. But it has; I feel a bit of coldness and some more when I realise Billie is the last to get up.

"Are you okay?" Zeke asks first.

"I'm better," I quickly answer. "You don't have—"

"What happened?" Antonia asks. "Nobody would say anything."

"Yeah—Zeke even went to your dad's dentistry with a fake moustache, pretending to book an appointment, just so he could ask," Dacre comments. I look over and see Zeke nod with proudness.

"Look, I'll explain, but I have to apologise—"

"We saw your post today."

My body tenses. Billie.

But I don't have much time left.

"I know, and I know it isn't enough. And I'm not expecting you to forgive me for everything, but I will make it up to you. And I don't want you to forgive me just because I've been in hospital, and you might feel bad. I want to earn your trust and forgiveness again," I quickly say.

"Why don't we talk about it now?" Billie asks, pointing at the table.

"No," I say but then add, "I mean yes. But there's something I've got to do first."

Billie's eyebrows wrinkle. Everybody else looks just as puzzled.

"Something else? I thought you meant what you wrote in the post." She's annoyed. I pull my phone out. It's time. "What can be more important than this?"

"You're on your phone?" Dacre asks.

I put it away. I look over to the side. Kamala is there by the wall. In position. She nods.

"I'm sorry, but this is important. It's for you," I tell them. I begin to back away, going into the hustle of the courtyard. They're still confused, but I continue. "A while ago, you said, Zeke, and you all agreed, that if something ever happened, there was only one thing that would cheer you up. Something you wouldn't think I would ever do." Every one of them stares at me with no idea what I'm on about. Heads nearby turn to see what the commotion is. "Well, now that time has come."

I whip around without letting them ask and head towards the centre of the courtyard. When I get to the spot as planned, I stand legs apart. I take a deep breath. Every bone in me is shaking. I need to do this. I want to do this. For my friends.

I glance over to Kamala. I nod. She gives me a thumbs up.

The speakers around the courtyard come alive.

The solo choir voices serenade out across the yard. I lift my arms slowly up into the air—with my back to my friends.

"What is he doing?" I can hear Billie ask.

"I'm not sure," Dacre says.

"Oh shit, he isn't?" Zeke blurts.

"Language," Antonia snaps.

"Well call me fancy and cite me *Seven Brides for Seven Brothers*, he is!"

The music kicks in. I spin around to face them, and I begin to move on the spot.

There are so many heads facing me now. So many eyes glued in my direction with confusion, but I'm only focused on my friends. That's all that I care about.

I shimmy my shoulders. Sway my chest a little. And when the lyrics start, I leave my spot and move around. That's right. I'm dancing. Dancing in front of most of the school. I'm completely anxious and frightened as I cascade around the tables and through the people standing and watching.

However, I remember what my friends joked about after the talent show—that they would love to see nothing more than me dance my ass off if they were ever down—and I want to make them smile, so I just go through with it. I try my best as I move around and dance the routine Kamala taught me over the weekend.

Whether I'm any good at it or not, I have no clue. Probably not. But I stick to the routine. I run across and jump up onto a table just before the song hits the pre-chorus. Without any warning except my charge, the people sat there move their trays out of the way in time. But I don't care—I continue dancing and slowly move in line to the song.

When the pre-chorus finishes, I lean back and collapse off the table. There are a few yelps.

Kamala catches me. Just as planned. I leap back up to stand on my own and then begin to dance my hardest when the chorus jumps in.

People are bobbing to the song, even though they won't have heard this song before—but they know the artist. It's from Tokyo. It's the song she made for us. "From Brisbane To Tokyo While In Orlando, Florida."

It felt like the right choice.

I continue to pour my heart into the moves to the rest of the song.

At one moment, I notice Chloe's table is watching. There's not even a shred of gratitude on her face that I'm using her song. She doesn't even show a sign of regret or guilt for what she's done. But this isn't for her.

The song soon comes to an end. I collapse just as I rehearsed onto my knees.

My chest is bursting back and forth as I try to catch my breath. Sweat on my forehead. Hands clammy. My body completely aching. Everybody's watching me in silence. Nobody moves.

I stare at my friends.

They hated it. All of them. I've made a huge fool of myself for nothing but to receive more humiliation and teasing.

But then Zeke lifts his hands up. And he claps. Then Antonia does. And then Dacre follows.

My ears prick up—more claps come from all around me. There are even some whoops and cheers. My eyes move to Billie. The only person left to clap. I wait. Her face remaining blank. I begin to get up off the ground, but then I see it. A small smirk appears on her face.

My body jolts inside with excitement. The group head over to me—everybody else goes back to whatever they were doing before.

"Oh my goodness, that was…" Zeke then pauses. "The best damn thing I've ever seen." He slaps an arm around my shoulders, huddling me into him.

The others all shower me with compliments. I try to say thanks, but I'm still out of breath.

"You did good," Billie says. I'm curious if she's joking, but she isn't—the smile's still on her face. "I admit the chat was worth putting on hold for this, but perhaps we should have it now?"

I nod. "I just need to thank somebody first."

The group tell me they'll be back at the table when I'm ready. I thank them and go back to the cafeteria doors.

Standing by the wall is Kamala. I give her my thanks and say how grateful I am for the work she has done for me over the weekend.

"It's no problem," Kamala says. "A few more lessons and you might actually be some good."

The grin she holds up makes me laugh.

"Well, thank you." I know she won't like it, but I lean in and hug her. I don't get a push back or get thrown into the wall. Instead, there's a faint touch of her hands returning the hug.

I say goodbye to Kamala and head back through the courtyard. I notice Mr Gauran looking at me from across the other side. He lifts a thumb up and mouths the words *good job*. I reply with a *thanks*.

All my friends are at the usual table. I ask if we can sit somewhere else to chat. Somewhere away from everybody else. They agree, and we find a nice patch of grass on the slope to sit on.

Before anybody asks, I talk first. I don't exactly know how, but I find a way to open up about everything. The truth about why I went to the hospital when I had a panic attack outside Mt. Okesea. The fact I thought I had another friend here at school, but it turns out I had been seeing my friend from Georgia—my best friend who had killed himself. And that after my memory returned, I realised he was the real reason why I took Robin's car back in Georgia and had the accident.

And I tell them about Tokyo. How I had been messaging somebody here and falling for them. And that on the day of the Winter Snowdrop Ball, I discovered it was Chloe and then she…well, they already know.

"How could she do that?" Dacre begins.

"Why would she do that?" Zeke asks.

"I'd like to throw paint over her," Antonia remarks. They all look appalled.

"It's fine. I was just so upset when that happened. And then—" I look over to Zeke…and then Billie. I pause. "You were just trying to help me when you found me. But I snapped back at you in anger and told you about Andrew."

She looks away from me. I worry if I've hurt her by bringing that night back up.

"Billie, I should never have told you like that. But it never should have come to that anyway—I should have said as soon as I saw it."

I wait patiently, searching for the words to explain how Andrew was to me. But Billie faces me, silent but not crying—and then she opens up.

She was furious at me for what I did. It hurt her. Not just that Andrew cheated on her, but also because she thought we were close.

"True friends who would be there for one another."

I feel numb when she says all this.

She confronted Andrew about it, and he admitted he had been cheating on her, even when he knew she'd been cheated on before. He tried to apologise, but she ended it.

It wasn't until just after everybody knew I had gone to the hospital that Andrew visited her again and he told her everything. He admitted he tried to manipulate me and began threatening me to keep hush. He confessed he strangled me outside Mt. Okesea when giving me the ultimatum. And that when she told him I had said about his cheating, and she ended it with him, he came over and beat me up.

She feels somewhat to blame for the last part, with me getting hurt—but I tell her it's not her fault.

Apparently, Andrew was really upset and was crying at the end of his confession to her. He felt partly to blame for why I might have gone to the hospital when he heard the news and had put that together with the video of me from the night of the Winter Snowdrop Ball. He felt he had contributed to the cause of me being unwell.

And Andrew had, in a way. I'm more shocked that he opened up to

Billie and admitted everything. And from what she tells me, it sounds like he did tell her everything. They're not together, Billie tells me, not friends either, it's just…they've moved on.

At the end of her saying all this, I find myself teary-eyed. Sad.

"I'm sorry for everything—for even ruining the ball for you." It was her last year as a student to attend. "I just feel so ashamed with how I handled it all," I tell them. "You guys have been so good to me, and I hate what I did to you. To all of you."

"It's okay, Hayden," Billie says. She places a hand on my knee. Somehow, it only makes me feel worse.

"Do you think you'll ever be able to forgive me?"

"You think I don't ever want to see those moves you just pulled off again? I'm making sure you dance at every party we go to now I've seen that." Billie laughs. A big laugh at her own joke.

And I can't contain the glee erupting and overriding the sadness in me.

"Yay! We're all back together." Zeke launches himself into me and Billie to hug us, and when I hear the others cheer, they join in as well.

"But seriously, even before that *a-mazing* dance and before Andrew told me the truth, I had already forgiven you," Billie says when we pull away from the group hug.

The bell goes.

We get up off the grass and go to head inside, following the same direction as all the other students outside. They must see I'm nervous returning because Zeke reminds me that we've got Sports and offers to actually join this time—so somebody is with me. I appreciate the gesture.

I can't believe how things are. This is more than I had hoped. It feels like things are going back to before. No—not going back exactly, things are moving in a new direction. And it feels nice.

"Hayden."

I turn to the side. Jasmine is walking over to us. I say hi, yet realise it sounds a little forced. I'm not truly sure how to feel about Jasmine. She may not have been there at the night of the Winter Snowdrop Ball with those who humiliated me, and I don't know if she had any involvement with it or not, but if she's still friends with Chloe, then I'm unsure what to do. But we are friends.

"Can we chat?"

I look back to the others. No one objects. Billie says we'll all meet after school. I agree and watch them walk towards the main building.

"What's up?" I ask.

She pushes back her yellow hair, glancing briefly down, looking like she isn't sure what to say...*and yet she's the one who wanted to chat?*

"I'm Tokyo."

Something inside me must be broken. I stand, staring at her. Did I just hear her say she's Tokyo?

"No, Chloe was. Look, if this is some new way for you guys to humiliate me, I'm not getting sucked in." As I speak, I turn away, frustrated. "I thought you were—"

Jasmine grabs my arm. "I'm being serious. I am Tokyo."

Everybody's back inside. Chloe and that lot aren't here. We're alone.

Jasmine has a stern look at me. I want to object. She lets go of my arm. I watch in confusion when she pulls her phone out.

"If you need proof..." Jasmine says while staring down at the screen and typing away. When she finishes, she turns to look to the side.

The KingsgateLeeConnect board refreshes.

Tokyo

It's me, Hayden. Jasmine Keery.

My mind feels like it's about to explode. She lifts her phone to show me the screen. She scrolls with one finger. There are numerous rows of emails in her inbox. All from me.

"You?" My mouth stumbles when she puts her phone away.

Jasmine nods. "I only discovered you're Brisbane because I overheard you just mention you were him to Chloe...then the song you danced to only confirmed it more. The song I wrote about us—I had only sent it to Brisbane."

I try to take it in—she's right, but I find it all hard to digest. My body does not want to trip into another play of deceit.

"But—I'd have known. I've spent time with you. And—I've seen you with your dad at Mt. Okesea," I say, remembering about Tokyo's dad.

Jasmine's left nostril rises.

"Who, Greg? He's not my dad. He's my stepfather."

It's plausible, but I decide to sit down at the table beside us. This is all too much. "But, how? Why?"

"Everything I wrote as Tokyo was real," she says. I'm so confused that I don't stop her from sitting down next to me. "My life. My feelings. My passions. How I felt towards Brisbane. All true."

"But Chloe? Why would she pretend it was her? How?"

Jasmine briefly gazes down at her feet. There's shame carved into her face when she looks back up.

"Chloe asked me to help with preparations for the Winter Snowdrop Ball at her place the night before the event. I went to the bathroom, left my phone downstairs, and Chloe saw an email come through from Brisbane. She read it, realised I was Tokyo from KingsgateLeeConnect, then understood I was messaging a guy," she continues. "She deleted the last email you sent to me to make it look like I was still waiting for you."

"Which is why I got an email from Tokyo on Saturday after the ball?" I work out—because it was from Jasmine, unaware of the situation, and not, as I thought, from Chloe teasing me.

"Yes. I was so confused by your reply, though. I felt awful when you blocked me."

A wave of sorrow comes to me when I put myself in Jasmine's shoes. "I thought it was Chloe having more fun with me."

"I understand. It was just upsetting over Christmas break. I had no idea why you stopped messaging—and no idea what Chloe had discovered and done. And when I returned home, I was still clueless—until I just overheard your conversation with Chloe, and she confessed everything when I confronted her on why you thought she was Tokyo."

"But that doesn't explain why she'd do it."

"Because she was scared of losing me," Jasmine says. "That's what she's just told me, anyway." I apprehensively wait for her to continue. "Things aren't great with Chloe. Her parents told her they were getting a divorce. Her mom moved to Montana. And then Jared dumped her—and she then had to deal with all the trolls on KingsgateLeeConnect about it. And, because of this, she hasn't been doing well at school. She's even been told she could have her role as head cheerleader revoked, which is what she needs if she wants a scholarship in California."

So Chloe lied to me that she had dumped Jared. I try to collate all the things Jasmine has said, and I realise, from my own experiences, it seems that I'm not the only one who has had to deal with a lot too.

"That's tough," I comment.

"Yeah, and…well, she read enough emails to see I wasn't comfortable with my friends. And she panicked—that I was going too. Scared somebody else was leaving. She may be popular and appear to be loved, yet…well, I found it hard to hear just now when she told me, but she's quite alone," she explains. "She knew I might leave our group and be with Brisbane if I discovered who he was after the break—and we'd said online that we'd reveal who we were and meet after Christmas. Chloe didn't think she could cope if that happened because then everything in her life *would* have changed. Her parents had been together all her life. She'd been with Jared for years, and she's been friends with me for longer. So that's why she deleted your email. Then, the next day, she tried to discover who Brisbane was by going around and dropping hints about Tokyo to guys until she found you and then did the prank—so you'd forget about Tokyo. So we couldn't be together. And I'd just stay with her and our group."

"That's cold," I tell her. "I get how she might have felt, but that doesn't make what she did right."

"I agree. I only learnt about the prank on the first day of school after the break—'cause by the time I reached Sweden and then briefly got internet, the school had already taken down all the posts and comments. When we returned to school, and I found out, I snapped at her for doing it—because it was wrong. And because you are my friend."

The gentle breeze cools me down from the kindness and warmth I receive from Jasmine's words.

"So, I left them. That was the line. I didn't want to be with anybody who does that. I've been spending time with Zeke and the rest since. Chloe and the others never told me why they did the prank on you. All they said was that it was just for some fun."

She takes a long breath, looking as if she is replaying the conversation they had in her mind. It can't have been easy.

"I never connected that Brisbane blocking Tokyo and you being pranked by Chloe could be related—until today, now knowing the truth what she did," she says. "After admitting the real reason for the prank, and pretending to be Tokyo to you, I'm not sure how I feel about Chloe. I want to be there for her because she's not in a good place, but I think it's going to take time for us to heal before I can."

Even after what Chloe did to her and to me, Jasmine still has a kind heart and wants to help. It's quite admirable.

She pushes some loose strands of hair back behind her ear. She's nervous. I want to comfort her, but I find this a lot.

"So, the reason you didn't want to meet at the ball was because you weren't attending…or was it because you did need that time to sort things out?"

"Both, really. Couldn't really meet you there if I was heading to the other side of the world," she tries to joke. "And if I told you as Tokyo I wasn't going, you'd probably be able to narrow down who Tokyo was to only a few people."

"True. There have been times I was tempted to try and make a list, but I thought it was best not to force it," I comment. "Although this isn't exactly what I had pictured."

She laughs. It makes me smile. "Same. But I did need time."

I run my hand through my hair. "I can't believe it's you."

Jasmine turns to me. "You're not disappointed, are you?"

"No, no—I mean, I thought it was Chloe because she told me it was, so hearing this is some head spin, but at the same time, it makes sense," I try to somehow explain.

I wait, letting her take in my words—but then I realise I need to ask. "And you're not embarrassed that it's me?"

"What? No—why would you think that?" Jasmine answers. I don't reply—but then softly she adds, "I'm quite pleased it's you."

Her eyes briefly glance to the ground—then back to me. I look down at the hand she's just put on mine.

My heartbeat sounds so loud.

And then I relax, accepting the touch. Feeling nervous and yet excited by her words.

"Actually, I'd hoped near the beginning that it was you—until I saw you with who I thought was your dad. I thought I felt something between us. Maybe. I don't know—"

"At the Halloween party."

I look over at Jasmine. Her hand now back on her lap. "And the night we ate at Mt. Okesea."

Her cheeks slowly turn to a slight shade of rose. "I thought the same, but I didn't because—"

"You didn't know I was Brisbane," I finish. Jasmine mouths the word *no* to me in agreement. "And I didn't know you were Tokyo."

She looks up to the sky. "Wow, we might have saved so much trouble if we had considered there was something there then."

"True, but then all the good that came after might never have happened either."

A door in the distance bursts open. The boys in my class come out and head to the field.

"I think that message you did earlier was really brave—same with the dance to our song…even if you were done with Tokyo," Jasmine says.

I blush red instantly. "I'm pleased you're back, and out of the hospital. You weren't there because of Chloe and Tokyo, I mean me, were you?"

"No. Well, that probably didn't help—but no. It was a lot of personal stuff I hadn't dealt with. Some stuff I didn't even know I had to deal with, really. And the parts I did know, I wanted to tell you, to Tokyo, but I couldn't—because then you'd discover who I was. But I'm better now. I'm sure I will tell you soon. I'd like to tell you—after I've come to terms with all this."

"Okay. That's fair. I would like to be there for you," Jasmine says. "I'm glad you're doing well. And I think you've come a long way since you volunteered to tutor me, and how frightened you were with Jared at the Halloween Party."

I whip my head to Jasmine. Something clicks in my mind, something which I didn't realise I hadn't questioned since I discovered the truth about Cassio.

"It was you who spoke to Jared?"

I assumed when Jared had said friend, he meant Cassio. I'm embarrassed. She worked out I was being bullied.

Jasmine turns her head more in my direction. "I confronted him about it after, and when he told me they'd been mean to you, I told them all to leave you alone."

I exhale deeply out. Jasmine's been a good friend since I moved here. However, it's surreal to think that the girl beside me is not only Tokyo, who gave me a lot of courage, but she, as Jasmine, has helped me in more ways than I knew.

"Thank you."

Jasmine smiles back. "It's okay."

Some of the boys in the field begin to do some training.

I turn back to Jasmine. "So, we've both agreed this isn't exactly how either of us wanted to find out." She smirks at the comment. "So, how do you think we should go about this?"

"Well," Jasmine begins—then swirls around. Her body is facing mine. I look down—her bare knee is resting against mine. "Everything in those emails was true." I nod so she knows that it was for me, too. "And I don't think we ever finished our epic music adventure."

My lips turn into a small grin. "True."

Jasmine pauses. "But, I think we should get to know each other. As Hayden and Jasmine."

I look into her eyes. Her deep, big eyes. I get lost in them. I think of how much these last few weeks have changed.

It's been crazy.

I thought I had lost everything, yet somehow, through some miracle, things have turned around. No, not because of a miracle. Because of me. Because of my family. Because of my friends. We've been open and able to forgive each other. There may have been different causes and stories, and sometimes it was them or me who had to extend a hand out, but the reason we did was because of one thing: we care for each other. And I'd be a hypocrite if I didn't do the same right now. Jasmine is Tokyo. And what I had with Tokyo was genuine. It may have been all online, but it was real.

I hate what Chloe did and how she tainted the vision of Tokyo, but that wasn't in any way Jasmine's fault. And what matters is the person who was really behind the mask. And the connection we had. The strong connection we had. On and, now I realise, off-screen.

"I'd like that. I'd like that a lot."

Epilogue

"I'll be down in a sec!" I yell to Dad from upstairs.

I open my wardrobe and grab my hoody from inside. My old, broken rucksack drops out and topples onto the floor. Despite being surprised I never threw it away when I replaced it, I shove the brown rucksack back into the wardrobe. I am ready to close the door—but I notice something. The broken zipped pocket, which has been like that since Georgia, is no longer jammed. It's ripped open. And there's something white poking out of it. I reach in and pull it out.

It's a note. I read it.

I slowly drop myself down onto the end of the bed. I glance back at the note, hoping I didn't imagine what I had read. But I haven't. The note is real. The words are real. The signature is real.

Relief seeps into my veins. I smile back at the words. It's in his writing. I just can't believe—

"Hayden, hurry up!"

I grab my stuff and leave.

"Finally," Robin comments at the bottom of the stairs. Dad and Colbey are beside her.

"You've got everything?" Dad asks. I tell him I have. "And your phone's off silent? Fully charged? You got a charger with you, right?"

"Yes."

"And if—"

"I think he's sorted," Colbey interjects. He places a hand on Dad's shoulder.

"I know, I know," Dad tries to brush off his worry.

"It's just the weekend," I say. Dad tries to remove his concern, but I know he cares. I used to hate that he did so much, yet now I appreciate it.

"They're still waiting," Robin says. I give Dad a quick hug, say my goodbyes and head outside.

Two cars are parked outside waiting for me. With their heads poking out, I see it's my friends.

"Hayden, you're with us," Kamala says in the front passenger seat of

Zeke's pickup. I nod and head over.

Zeke pokes his head out from behind Kamala and smacks his hand on the steering wheel in excitement. "Come on! We could have served Sirius Black's sentence in Azkaban by now!"

"You mean we could have taken Doc Brown's letter from 1885 and delivered it to Marty in 1955 by now," Kamala follows on.

Zeke turns to her. "Ooo, nice."

Despite not knowing their references, I get the gist. I smirk at their film talk.

As I shut the trunk, I look back at the second car. Dacre's in the driving seat. There's Dean—the No Armadillos Allowed guy, who is now Dacre's boyfriend—sat next to him, and I can see Antonia and Billie in the back. Both smiling and waving at me. I return the gesture.

"Okay. Let's go!" Antonia cheers.

I give a quick look back at the house. Colbey, Robin and my dad are watching at the door. I wave and then jog around the car to the other side.

I open the door, and there she is. Sat in the back. Jasmine Keery.

"Hi," she says. My lips curl in glee. I lean over into the car and kiss her lips. Soft. Cute. Desirable. I find it hard to believe, even weeks later, that Jasmine is my girlfriend.

"Okay, okay, you can do that with your entire body in. We! Gotta! Go!" Zeke yells.

I eventually pull my lips away from Jasmine's cherry-flavoured ones and slide into the pickup.

"Alrighty then! Miami, here we come!" Zeke gives a loud cowboy cry, to which we all laugh, and he begins to drive.

I feel something slide elegantly between the fingers of my hand on my lap. I look down. It's Jasmine's fingers.

Soon after that day we discovered who was Brisbane and Tokyo—the real person behind Tokyo—I opened to Jasmine about what happened in Georgia with my mom and Cassio. I explained the truth of what happened and the real reason I went to the hospital.

She's been nothing but understanding, kind and supportive to me. And she's opened to me too. And I'd like to think I've been just as compassionate to her too. We really respect and care for each other.

"Did you bring all your stuff?"

She nods. "All my equipment. All my tracks."

We're heading to Miami because Jasmine is performing tomorrow night. And not just for anything. Jasmine's the warm-up act for none other than a Star Dirt Lagoon concert. I know, it's insane!

Star Dirt Lagoon's manager heard Jasmine's latest remix online and got in touch—uploading them under her own name, not Tokyo.

Jasmine's been so elated, and I don't blame her. It's a big thing! And Zeke's Aunt Sandra has a place in Miami where we can all stay for the weekend.

"Even got our song."

I return the smile—I genuinely love the song she made about us. "Good. But is it bad that's not what I'm most excited about this weekend?"

Jasmine's eyebrows furrow. "What is?"

"I'm excited we're off to see Tokyo."

Jasmine laughs. Before Christmas and before the Chloe ordeal, I had already gotten Tokyo a gift. I saw online there was a competition for people to name some new animals that had arrived at a zoo in Miami. I entered and won. There were some new llamas.

The name I chose was Tokyo.

After we decided to go on a date, I told Jasmine I had won our little animal challenge and gave Jasmine her late Christmas gift. Well, it may not be Orlando, but it's in Florida, so I count it.

"I think I can accept that," Jasmine plays along. She knows I'm most excited about her show. I'm just thrilled that I'm spending time with her, to be truthful.

As we head down the International Drive, we see the towering mountain above the palm trees that is Mt. Okesea. I've not gone back to work there yet, although Aunt Sandra told me I could. Maybe one day. But at this moment, I just want to live in the now.

Water suddenly bursts from the mountain and up into the sky. My eyes blink in amazement—*Zeke wasn't lying.*

He'll be gutted I didn't see the display by winning the last hole myself, but sometimes you need help. Sometimes, it's okay to lean on others. And I'm fine with that.

We're soon out of Orlando and on the way to Miami. I press the window to go down a little. The breeze ruffles the top of my light, sun-caught fair hair as we drive on.

The DJ on the radio talks about something I don't quite tune into, but then a song begins.

"I love this song," Kamala says. She leans in and turns the radio up before placing her hand back on Zeke's free hand in between them.

Everybody sings along to the lyrics. I do, too. But, at some point, I fall silent and watch everybody around me.

They've all got beams of joy across their faces. And it makes me happy. It makes me more than happy. To think what was beginning to unfold nearly a year ago back in Georgia to where I am now, a lot has happened.

There are parts I don't like. Parts along the tough road I wish didn't happen. But I realise that's okay. It's fine if you aren't sometimes actually fine. Because I know that if those things didn't happen as they did, then I wouldn't be where I am right now. I had to face it. I had to be open to the ones I cared for. For I wouldn't be here feeling like I'm the closest to my family than I have ever been. I wouldn't have the friends who are around me today. I wouldn't have the girl sitting beside me as my girlfriend. I wouldn't be the person I am today. And I'm in a good place.

I pull the piece of paper I found in my old rucksack out of my pocket. I give it another read. I smile once again at the words. I put my hand out of the open window. I watch the note flap frantically in my hand. And then I let go.

As the cars make their way down the road, going into the warm and vivid distance, the small note floats up into the air. Swirling and twirling, the note lets the wind take it wherever it needs to go, with only the writer and the recipient having ever read it.

Dear Hayden,
We created a pact—for which I'm sorry I broke.
But you can continue on, and are enough to still make good.
Always,
Cassio

The End

This book explores aspects of psychology and mental health, and contains themes of alcohol abuse, amnesia, body dysmorphic disorder, exercise addiction, online bullying, physical abuse and suicide. Please read with care.

If any of these elements cause any distress when reading, then please seek professional help, support and advice.

Acknowledgements

I would like to say a warm thank you to all those who have given support while I have been writing this book, from close connections to editors that read early drafts.

To my mum, who has been there for me from the day I told her I was writing this story to the very end and seeing the finished piece. For being relentless yet also compassionate and encouraging when proofreading this and for also keeping me in line whenever I would step on my own merry-go-round and overthink.

To Ellie, this idea and novel was written before we had even met and yet you were one of the first to read an early completed version of this book. Thank you for your support, for listening to my forever spiralling conversations late at night so I had someone to relay my thoughts to and I could make sense of them all, and for also reminding me I had a story to tell and that this was something special.

Also, to the rest of my family and my friends who knew I was doing this and were patient with me. It's been a forever dream to write a story and for it to be turned into a book for others to read, to laugh, to cry and, hopefully, to connect with. I guess what I am saying is, without any of you, I would not be here, finally writing this part.

About the Author

This is the first published novel from J. J. Tallahay. He is an English author, who grew up on a farm, surrounded by the wonderful settings of the countryside and the coast. He has always been creative – designing theme parks and rides on pieces of paper when he was a child to later on organising fundraisers and events – and somehow that creativity over the years has always returned him to writing. He earned a first in BA (Hons) Radio Production at university, and it was during this time he decided to take the dive and go deeper in writing stories, dreaming one day he could write a novel for others to read. He loves to write contemporary fiction, prominently YA, as well as whodunnits and fantasy.

When J. J. Tallahay is not writing, he tries to enjoy the free time by being with his family and friends. Spending days out, travelling or seeing what the world has to offer…which has included the likes of a bierkeller in a barn, skydiving for a friend's bucks party in Sydney, a few too many competitive games of rounders on the beach and also nearly getting thrown out of a club in the Alps for simply starting a game of limbo. But that's for another story.

Visit
www.jjtallahaybooks.co.uk

From BRISBANE *to* TOKYO *while in* ORLANDO, FLORIDA

www.ingramcontent.com/pod-product-compliance
Lightning Source LLC
LaVergne TN
LVHW041149150826
845673LV00001B/113

* 9 7 8 1 0 6 8 6 5 1 9 0 8 *